DEALING WITH THE DEMON

ALYCE CASWELL

For Darren

before I met you, my world was tilted on its axis

If I didn't get off the train, everyone was going to die.

Part of me hoped that the man sitting opposite me in my section of the carriage would be the first to go, because he'd spent the entire trip from Town Hall station ranting on and on about how Magic Corp was actually the Illuminati and out to take over the world. He probably wouldn't have said that if he'd known that I worked at Magic Corp's headquarters on Castlereagh Street in the Sydney CBD. But who'd have thought we magic-users had nine-to-five jobs just like everyone else?

Magic has been around for millennia, but we'd only been 'out' for six months when this went down, so naturally people were still a bit suspicious of us. Even though the government stopped freaking out when the Australian branch of Magic Corp offered to become affiliated with them, that meant very little to the normals. To them, it looked like a secret society of extremists had started appearing all over the world.

By my count, there were five other people in that three-level train carriage. With me on the 'ground level' was Conspiracy Nut (still ranting), as well as a grey-haired granny (she had one of those two-wheeled trolleys with her—in a floral print, no less). The lower level was occupied by two snogging teens and upstairs seemed to be the domain of someone coughing up a hairball (couldn't see them to be sure, but that's what it sounded like).

I suppose I probably looked like any other office worker, given the black pants and the (mostly) uncreased blouse. My shoes were casual by comparison, a pair of new purple-and-white New Balance sneakers. I'd hoped to nab myself some glory at work with those kicks, but Dennis Chan had turned up with his fancy velvet Adidas slides. Naturally, everyone had wanted to see them, not my ordinary and boring footwear.

I had no idea how to make friends with my colleagues despite the fact that we'd grown up together at the only school in the country for our kind. I could, however, buy into the sneaker culture craze that had infected those who were doomed to remain in the admin department or slide their way into other paper-pushing jobs. Anyone with a lick of talent got to ride the lift up to the more fun levels instead of whiling away their hours on the first floor. I'd spent three years there already and despite other graduating classes coming through in that time, I was still on the bottom rung. To add insult to injury, I was now getting coffee for teenagers with (only slightly) better jobs than mine.

I nodded along with Conspiracy Nut's continuing tirade but kept my eyes on the other ground level section, the one divided from us by the upper and lower seating areas. I wasn't doing this because the train's interior was more interesting than my companions (even if it was!). No—the doors connecting us to the next carriage at that end had just whooshed open. By themselves.

The teens downstairs were still making a go of mixing truancy with PDA, so they didn't notice the stench that wafted past them to slap me in the face.

Wet dog. Wet dog that's been in sewage.

Unfortunately, Hellhounds prefer to go after magic-users first.

We're apparently quite tasty. Even more unfortunate? I completely and utterly lacked Perception.

In magic, there are two Ps: Physical and Perception. While I could create solid balls and projectiles and whatever else using my mind's eye, I had missed out on the less tangible ability that allowed my colleagues to read minds and see Hellcreatures (technically they're called demons, but the more colloquial label seems to have stuck).

Look, throwing magic around is great and all, but if you can't actually get eyeballs on the thing you're supposed to be hitting?

I'd survived twenty-one years of my life without Perception and the only job I would ever have saw me confined to a desk. But earlier that day I'd lost mobile reception and, with it, access to the app that helped 'see' for me. This just had to happen right when I was taking the annual test that was supposed to prove that I could locate demons. Oh yeah, and no one from the first floor had access to the wi-fi. Which was fantastic.

Yep, I'd been found out. And promptly suspended.

For being utterly useless without Perception? Or for hiding the fact that I didn't have it? I wasn't entirely sure. Either way, I was on the 1:43 PM train from Town Hall on the North Shore line, bound for Hornsby and beyond.

I had no idea why the Hellhound was on the train.

And I seriously doubted that he'd tapped on with his Opal card.

I stood up, one hand sliding into my handbag while the other groped for the bright yellow pole that should keep me from falling over if the train suddenly braked. Maybe I was imagining things. I couldn't sense or see Hellhounds, after all. A random power fluctuation could have opened the carriage doors, right? Maybe the smell was actually the fault of Conspiracy Nut. Or the granny. Talk about your toxic emissions.

But then I saw the claw marks being gouged into the vinyl floor beside the teens. And one of them broke away from the other, demanding, 'Do you *smell* that?'

My breath caught.

Hellcreatures—look, I'm not calling them *demons*—are one-hundred-percent invisible to the naked unmagical eye (and apparently mine too), but I'd been near the secure Hellhound pen enough times that I knew what to look for. What to smell.

The normals on this train?

They didn't even have that going for them.

'Oh shit,' I said, earning myself a reproving look from the granny.

Conspiracy Nut nodded emphatically, as though I'd just agreed with something he'd said.

'The next stop. Is. Artarmon!' announced the eternally cheerful woman who had given the train its voice.

I looked outside. We were on the bridge that guided northbound trains safely from St Leonards to Artarmon. Artarmon station, from memory, had an island platform with no gates, few cameras, and a hell of a lot less people than the next stop along. If I really wanted to move from suspended to fired, I could bail at Chatswood station instead and get myself killed at the busiest nexus north of the Sydney CBD. Worse still, the Hellhound might decide that I wasn't a satisfying meal. Creatures from the demonic realm aren't all that fussy about what they eat when they're desperate—after it had finished crunching on my bones, normals would be next. Lots of them.

It would be a PR disaster for Magic Corp, and not just the

Australian branch. All across the world we were tethering ourselves to the relevant governments so we didn't look like a threat to humanity. But those governments and the media had begun demanding transparency. They wanted to know how we operated, what we actually did, and if we let any innocents die on our watch.

Hell, I wasn't going to last long enough to reach Chatswood anyway.

I snatched my phone out of my handbag and tried to keep my hand still, but my thumb trembled and skidded past the app I needed. I swore. The granny must have decided I was a lost cause, since no lecture was forthcoming.

When my thumb finally behaved, I slammed it down onto PercApption. Within seconds, I was looking at the carriage through the camera on my phone. My fellow passengers probably thought I was trying to take a photo, but what I was really doing was using the magical app to scan for my unwelcome stalker.

The phone buzzed angrily in my hand when I aimed it at the empty stairs in front of me. I needed to get off the train *now*.

The train coasted into Artarmon.

The doors opened.

I threw myself out into an undignified sprawl on the concrete, my handbag sailing several paces away. I was at the southern end of the platform, which tapered off into a narrow strip, so I didn't have a lot of room to manoeuvre. And just my luck, there was a whole gaggle of students nearby. Don't they ever go to school?

Oh wait. This happened during the Year Twelve exams, didn't it? The normals sit a bunch of tests, get a bunch of results, and then get to choose their path in life, not have one forced on them just because they were born with magic. Lucky bastards.

The carriage doors in front of me beeped innocently while they popped back into place. As the train began gliding away, its windows gave me a glimpse of the wild expression my reflection was sporting. My brown eyes were wide with fear and my cheeks were bleached of colour. No wonder the students were giving me nervous glances. I looked like the start of one of those zombie apocalypses.

My chest heaved as I swung the phone around. It continued to mirror the scene, silent and still in my hand, indicating nothing out of place. A gust of wind chose that moment to hit my nostrils, snatching away any telltale scents.

Shit, I hadn't just condemned everyone on that train to death by bailing, had I? What if the Hellhound hadn't followed me? Look, even though I was suspended and all I'd really done was boring old data entry (the government definitely appreciated our keeping so many records, especially since everyone wanted proof that we were relying on private investments instead of drawing on public funds), it was our duty to protect normals from demons and any other magical threat.

Six months before a Hellhound followed me onto a train, the American branch of Magic Corp had openly resisted an attempted demonic invasion in New York City, thus revealing our existence to everyone with Internet access—frankly, I think they did it because they'd wanted to prove that the US really did save the world on a regular basis, and not just in the movies.

According to my teachers back at school, you *never* took on a Hellcreature unless you were a qualified field agent with a sufficient amount of power and/or backup behind you. Hellcreatures were nasty and could rip you to pieces. Or just roast you, if you happened to come up against a Helldragon. I wasn't sure that particular demon was real, but I'd overheard Dennis Chan at the water cooler insisting that he'd walked in on our superiors discussing one.

I blew out a breath, my phone slack in my hand. Then the camera hit a different patch of the platform.

And the damn thing buzzed.

I shot to my feet and started screaming at the students to run. They stared at me. To them, I was a crazy adult who didn't deserve their attention or their respect—pretty much how I viewed my new boss. I shut my mouth and backed up until I hit the small fence that stoppered the end of the platform, supposedly to keep you from falling off. That was the least of my worries.

I let one hand drop to my side and started twirling my fingers. I could conjure grey wispy stuff, maybe even make said wispy stuff solid if I put my mind to it. So there I was, frantically preparing the heaviest and spikiest ball I could—which, given my embarrassingly weak magic, wasn't very heavy or spiky. I wasn't as powerful as my colleagues who could make longer-lasting and enviably solid black shapes, and I might not even manage to hit the Hellhound before my power reserves ran dry, but there was no way I wasn't even going to *try* to save my life.

My phone was shaking violently in my hand when the Hellhound decided to stop stalking me and go in for the kill.

Yeah. I definitely thought I was about to bite the big one.

Or have the big one bite *me*.

2

Good news? I didn't die.

Bad news? A foul-smelling Hellhound landed on top of me.

I went down hard, my head clipping the fence, and the phone skittered out of my hand, narrowly avoiding the edge of the platform. But my other hand wasn't empty. I threw my prepared ball of Physical upwards and it collided with—hopefully teeth.

I wheezed. The damn thing was heavy and it had me pinned.

Claws whispered down my arm, drawing parallel lines across my skin. I started bleeding. The kids started screaming. Normals might be scraping up against adulthood in Year Twelve, but they're still not prepared for bloodshed.

We'd been shown photos of Hellhound massacres at our decidedly not-normal school when I was thirteen. Pretty sickening stuff.

So it was super weird that I wasn't taking much damage. I cast a flinching look down at my arm, then peered up into the yawning maw that was presumably above me. Was the creature toying with its prey? Well then, I was definitely going to take advantage of that. I had lives to save, including my own.

'OFF!' I shouted and punched the Hellhound, my fist encased inside a shimmering glove. I envisioned the glove to be harder than steel, but at that point I was willing to take anything more resilient than flesh.

The Hellhound yelped. And then I heard more screams. Just my luck—when it had fallen away from me, the demon had knocked over three or four of the students. The ones that weren't flat on the platform were now whipping out their phones. Yep, this was going to be all over the news by nightfall. I knew how it'd look—a magic-user turned rogue, attacking people with invisible creatures and extremely visible projectiles!

I was *so* fired.

I snatched up my own phone and froze when I felt a sudden blast of hot air beside me. A harmless, normal train? I wish!

Despite the imminent danger I was in, I let my eyes drift to the side—only to stare into what looked like the mouth of a volcano. It hovered over the train tracks, a perverse magma puddle hanging in midair. I'd never seen anything like it, but it appeared appropriately hellish *and* sent a prickle of unease cascading down my spine. I figured it was demonic in nature. I knew Hellhounds were born in an entirely different realm, so it made sense that they'd need *some* way of coming into our world. A fiery doorway, for example...

The shallow slashes on my arm stung. But I had a feeling this was nothing compared to what would happen to me if I fell into the mini-volcano thing.

The Hellhound kept on coming.

I jumped off the platform, onto the side that didn't have a Scary Pool of Fire—and looked back just in time to see the fence crater beneath the impact of something invisible and clearly out for my blood.

I huffed and swore as I ran down the tracks. I might have lost thirty kilograms and my enviable DD cup size, but I hadn't gone jogging since my weight had stabilised—and that'd been several months ago. I guess I'd let myself get away with not exercising since then because thin's supposed to be healthy, right? Damn it, when I was bigger I could've put on a bit more speed. And speed was something I desperately needed right then.

I rounded the northern end of the platform and came back down the opposite side, this time towards the Doorway to Hell. I hoped the Hellhound was following me instead of going after the easier targets who were dressed in uniforms and carrying bags filled with way too many books.

I had to think. Fast. I could keep throwing objects at the Hellhound, but its hide—according to my teachers at school—was thick and impervious to most magical constructs. My own constructs were pretty laughable to begin with, because my power reserves were abysmal and dripped reluctantly whenever I called on them. Things were looking dire.

I was alone. Outmatched. And every other Australian magic-user was either back at HQ in the CBD, manning far-flung outposts near demonic hotspots in the outback, helping out ASIO in Canberra with their Perception, or wielding Physical overseas. We were meant to be making sure that 'the enemy' wasn't using magic against our armed forces, but lately there had been rumours that we'd diversified away from slaying our brand of demons to government-sanctioned ones. Although it made us look good in our local media, this had caused no small amount of tension with other branches of Magic Corp, especially in countries where we were deployed.

So basically, there were a lot fewer of us in Sydney than usual. I could request backup but there was a good chance it wouldn't get there in time.

This situation called for WatchDog.

Unfortunately, that meant sacrificing my artificial Perception. Only one of the damn magical apps would open at a time.

Pity I wasn't near a police station. The cops had been given a handful of apps created by Magic Corp's tech department, to assist us in the field. According to the higher-ups, we needed all available eyes scanning for demons, even if said eyes belonged to normals. Most of us office juniors figured it was a political thing, some way of making the government trust us. I could have used the help, if not the accompanying suspicion the cops always brought with them when a magic-user requested their presence.

I clambered back onto the platform, trying to catch my breath. PercApption, when I managed to get the camera pointed the right way, informed me that the Hellhound was currently pelting down the tracks after my scent. It too skidded around the northern end of the platform, intent on catching up to its unlucky prey. And the screens above me were announcing that another train was due in under five minutes.

Shit, shit, *shit.*

I rose unsteadily to my feet and looked over at my audience. The kids still had their phones out (recording the crazy woman with the messy brown hair, of course), a station-based train employee was asking if I needed assistance (he was a portly man in his fifties, hardly the backup I needed), and a wide-eyed mother had just come up the stairs that led to the tunnel underneath the platforms (she was wrestling a squalling three year old).

It was my duty to protect them. No matter what.

So if I was already fired for engaging a Hellhound in public, then Magic Corp couldn't penalise me any further for using illicit copies of magical apps in public, right? Right? I mean, they gave them to the police. Why shouldn't a Perception-blind employee like me get to use them?

I fumbled beneath the collar of my blouse and pulled out the keypass attached to a white lanyard that had gone grey over the past three years. I cleared my throat. 'I'm with Magic Corp. You're...you'll be safe in a moment. Please stay where you are.'

There was a script for this, but our PR department was ridiculously new and not everyone had bothered to read the email they'd painstakingly compiled for just such an occasion. We'd never had to worry about the normals before. And as someone who sat at a desk, I rarely needed to interact with them outside of buying my groceries.

I didn't blame the mother for running back down the stairs with her kid.

I exited PercApption. This time my thumb stabbed WatchDog.

My palm collided with the screen and my skin instantly began to burn. I think I might have cried out—I'm not sure. I was out of it for a second. Blood rushed down from my head and I swayed, nearly falling flat on my face. I shook my hand, but the phone was stuck fast.

Something was attacking my very core, where my minimal power reserves were stored—if I hadn't bled them dry already. That wasn't supposed to happen. A dog capable of taking on a Hellhound was meant to appear, fuelled by Magic Corp's servers, not the person who had summoned it. The whole point of WatchDog was that the phone's owner could still use their Physical in conjunction with app.

Somehow the app had found something to eat. Was it eating *me?*

Shit, maybe there'd been an update that I'd missed?

My knees hit the platform and my hand lunged forward, trying to yank me along with it, but I managed to brace myself on the concrete. I had to grit my teeth pretty hard.

Because using this app? It fucking hurt.

3

Just when I thought the phone would overheat or burst into flames, a dog-shaped blur exploded out of the tiny camera lens. The charcoal silhouette of a shaggy—but definitely solid—Border Collie barked at me, circled my almost-prone form once, then took off after the Hellhound.

My wrist ached fiercely when the phone began to jerk violently around in my grip and my elbow wasn't far behind. Gasping, I waved everyone away with my other hand.

'Get out of here!' I shouted at them. 'Jesus Christ, don't you get it? You'll die!'

The students stayed where they were, their phones now aimed over my head. The train employee, looking dapper in his jumper vest even though he had been to be sweating in the heat, held out a hand to help me up. I took it. And then I looked over at what everyone else was seeing.

My magical dog, controlled by the app and clearly better than anything I could make with my own Physical, was going at it with thin air. But that wasn't all. Very obvious and very black ichor was spewing out of the Hellhound, running across the platform and over the yellow line that was supposed to warn people about getting too close to the tracks.

My WatchDog wasn't impervious either. Great big chunks were being ripped out of it and while the construct didn't bleed, it was losing its solid qualities. It would soon disintegrate. I had to help the poor thing, manifestation of magic or not. It needed me.

I wound my phone-free hand around, reaching into my core and hoping my reserves had regenerated enough to form a spear—hell, any object would be great at this point—and found nothing. Zip. No power. I stared at my hand and swore, mostly angry at myself. My magic needed time to recover and I freaking knew that. Was danger eroding all of my common sense?

Or maybe it was the pain messing with me. My phone was searing my skin, seemingly anchored onto my palm. I couldn't shake it off.

'Are you alright?' Train Guy asked me. 'I've called the police.'

Oh. Good. They'd have WatchDogs of their own to unleash. But I seriously doubted they'd get there in time. And it'd take at least an hour for my pitiful reserves to fill up again.

People's lives were at stake. I couldn't wait an hour. I had to do something *now*.

'I need more power, damn it!' I cried.

To my surprise, that's exactly what I got.

My spine jolted and I fell sideways into the surprisingly sturdy Train Guy as a great tide of power ripped through me. Screaming, I forced my Physical to surge out of my spare hand. I didn't have time to shape the magic, I just sent it.

'*Die*, motherfucker!' I shouted, dropping to my knees.

The Hellhound emitted a broken whine that would haunt my nightmares. I must have got it, and pretty solidly too. To my relief, the fiery doorway at the end of the platform abruptly sealed up with a great suctioning noise, just in time for the train that had been whirring down the southbound tracks to pull in unhindered.

Straightening up and panting heavily, I hoped to hell the creature was actually dead (or had departed through the now non-existent pool of lava) and wasn't going after the students. They seemed okay—well, giddy and thrilled to be more precise.

I pitched forward suddenly but my forehead grazed the platform instead of slamming into it, thanks to Train Guy's hold on me. Then, finally safe and in no danger of losing any normals, I released everything. Not just the breath I'd been holding, but the tension in my shoulders and limbs as well. I must have let the adrenaline go too because the claw marks were stinging again.

'Ow,' I muttered. At least they were shallow and thin enough that I could get away with using the bandaids in my handbag.

Something touched the back of my head. I looked up to see my WatchDog hovering in front of me, as though waiting for a command. My trembling fingers reached out and scratched the fur behind its one remaining ear.

'Thank you,' I whispered.

I know, the dog wasn't living or breathing. It was a magical construct generated by fancy tech. But it had saved my butt—well, several butts actually—by giving me those extra few seconds I'd needed to get my shit together.

The construct lowered its muzzle and sniffed me, then made a small, interrogative sound. I nodded in response, letting the creature know I was done with it, and held up the phone. My WatchDog whuffed, as though amused by the gesture, then started shrinking into a tiny speck. I wasn't sure how it was meant to vanish, but that seemed legit enough for me. The phone clattered out of my fingers and I just knelt there on the platform, stunned and exhausted.

I could already hear the sirens.

Train Guy helped me up again (passing me my handbag in the process—what a legend) and when I could finally stand on my own, I noticed that one of the students was now rewatching the whole adventure on his phone. I was too tired to try and take it from him—and to be honest, I didn't want to. If that kid could use the video to finally grab some popularity in the playground and not be invisible for once, then more power to him. It was something I'd never managed to achieve.

I couldn't see any marks or blemishes on my palm. There might not be any evidence on my body to indicate that I'd used WatchDog, but there was enough footage to condemn me. This was going to be awkward to explain. Look, I'd failed my Perception test. That was bad enough. But at least my boss hadn't inspected my phone and found my unauthorised copies of the magical apps. Now he'd know I had them installed.

I'd got away with sneaking my phone into my tests for nearly three years, but it hadn't helped me during that morning's loss of reception (a brief service outage—at the worst possible moment). Unsurprisingly, I hadn't been able to identify the location of the Hellhounds in the pen on the roof of Magic Corp HQ. I'd just randomly coloured in squares on the grid paper they'd given me and hoped for the best. But I'd failed. Big time.

My boss of six months, Tom Chapman, had sure as hell noticed.

Don't know how he hadn't noticed my lack of mind-reading abilities, considering he'd yelled at me enough times about not doing the daily tasks he was supposedly thinking at me. Something else was bothering me, actually. How were the Hellhounds not getting out of the pen on a daily basis if they could create their own personal Eyes of Sauron to transport themselves?

Tom had told me that I was lucky I was only being suspended while Magic Corp figured out what to do with me.

If I had a choice? Getting fired was a better deal than quitting. There was a clause in our contracts that said we'd be put on the Kill Register if we chose to leave of our own accord—something about us becoming crazy lone wolves and forgetting we shouldn't kill people.

Obviously this wasn't something that had been made public, because I'm pretty sure there'd be an outcry (or not—a lot of people wanted us dead, if the comments on the Internet were any indication). I didn't *think* anyone had told the Minister for Magical Australians and Related Affairs that we had a squad of magic-users whose sole purpose was to hunt down absconders and kill them for breaking their contracts. See, this was the main reason I doubted that magic-users were among those we were fighting overseas—their own kind would kill them before they even had a chance to join up.

Yeah, so it sounds unfair, but when they plonked my employment contract in front of me at the ripe old age of eighteen, I'd had no other offers. And let's face it, no sane employer would ever accept a candidate who claimed to have graduated from some secret magical school.

I'd been doomed to a lifetime of having my career chosen for me, ever since my mother had practically thrown me at Magic Corp when I was eight—they'd shown up after some scouts had Perceived my magical self. I didn't remember my mother or the incident, but good riddance. I bet my colleagues' families had actually put up a fight when Magic Corp had come knocking at their doors.

What had Magic Corp said to convince people to give up their kids—especially before we went public? I didn't know. I didn't *want* to know. I did know that everyone signed the lifelong contracts when they turned eighteen. I'd never asked those who could have gone back to their families why they hadn't. I didn't want to pry and besides, it's not like they'd tell me. It's kind of personal.

If you were really lucky, one or more of your parents was already *in* Magic Corp and you got to spend time with them at nights instead of whiling away your hours at boarding school with nothing better to do than sneak into the gymnasium and bang Dennis Chan.

Anyway, I'd been assured that the Kill Clause didn't apply to being suspended or fired. So why did I feel like I'd just avoided a much more permanent method of termination?

Magic Corp had Hellhounds locked up in a pen. All they had to do was herd one onto a train (never mind how much Physical power that would take), make sure I was the only tasty magical morsel on board, and wait to see what happened.

But they wouldn't do that, right?

The Kill Squad was quieter and a lot more discreet than a Hellhound. And they wouldn't have to endanger any normals in the process. I shivered, shrugging off the hand that Train Guy had clamped onto my shoulder—he'd been trying to comfort me, I guess.

No, the Hellhound had been a rogue creature, randomly popping in from the demonic realm. That's all.

Yeah. I'd soon figure out how very wrong I was.

I knew I had to get out of there when one of the kids tried to get me to say something to their Weibo followers. Dodging past them, I sprinted down the stairs and through the tunnel, then kept running until I hit the Pacific Highway, where I managed to flag down a taxi. I couldn't stop wincing as I watched the digits on the meter jumping up and up and up. We were coasting towards humble Mount Kuring-gai, which lay much closer to the Central Coast than the actual city.

I'd picked the taxi for a couple of reasons. First of all, I didn't want the police—or worse, the media—somehow tracking me down on public transportation. Secondly, my local station only got a train every thirty minutes during off-peak times, so I'd have been waiting forever just to get home. Ah, the joys of only being able to afford rent on the outskirts.

I leaned against the taxi window and tried not to cry.

I knew I was going to end up on the evening news, undoing months of work by our PR department who'd wanted to assure the normals that magic wouldn't affect their daily lives—and, knowing my luck, I'd also derailed the government's painstaking attempts to sanitise our very young and very tenuous connection.

I'd been alive for twenty-one years, spent over a decade of that attending Magic Corp's version of school and preparing myself for a lifetime of comfortable servitude—and in just three years I'd managed to get myself suspended, possibly even fired.

Great work, Jen Cooke.

4

Okay. Flashback time.

I got the magical apps at a party three years before a Hellhound boarded my train.

Parties for our kind involve the usual excessive drinking, sex in a back room, poor karaoke singing—but when it gets closer to midnight, people start using magic. Showing off. Making beer kegs out of Physical and then being comically surprised when the magical construct loses its shape and spills booze everywhere.

Anyway, I was eighteen at the time and legally allowed to drink. And I sure as hell was taking advantage of this, because in two days I'd have to sit the placement tests so Magic Corp could suggest a job for me based on my skill set. There was no way they weren't going to discover my dirty little secret.

'Jen, you don't look so good,' my best friend, Merindah, said to me. 'Might want to stop after this drink, okay?'

Merindah never looked green around the gills. She wasn't pale and prone to obvious tells like I was—her complexion hovered somewhere between beige and tawny. And her burnt-brown hair had an amazing amount of volume that I totally hadn't been coveting since we were kids.

Merindah had no idea that I had a perfectly good reason to get drunk. Mine was an embarrassing problem to have, especially when your best friend was so good at Physical that she had already been offered a position on the Kill Squad without even *taking* the tests.

'But it would be rude not to fully enjoy this rager the MC guys threw for us!' I shouted over the music. No need to say 'Magic Corp' when all the cool kids were using an acronym. 'Them welcoming our graduating class into adulthood and all. You needn't hang around worrying about me. Go have fun.'

Merindah's severe expression didn't alter. 'I'm not leaving your side, Jen, you know that.'

'Fine, you can babysit me, but only if you go get me another drink,' I said, trying not to slur my words too much.

Shaking her head, Merindah stalked off towards the unstaffed bar. Magic Corp had hired out the entire place to make sure no one witnessed our magical shenanigans. That meant we could drink the bar dry if we wanted to. And we probably would.

Something started squirming in my gut. Something pretty urgent. Merindah was taking ages and I could already taste the bile, so I staggered towards the bathroom. Thankfully, by the time I was sliding along the much cooler passageway outside the main area, I felt a lot better. Enough to prop myself against the wall and take deep, steadying breaths.

And that's where Simon Bradley found me.

He had that hot-tall-guy thing going on and a cute tuft of grey hair at the front of his otherwise jet-black mop, despite only being five years older than me. And those eyes! Sapphire. Hypnotic. Almost swirling. It was enough to make me want to hurl again, but after a few moments of us staring at each other, bass throbbing beneath our feet, my head cleared.

'You okay?' Simon asked in a strange lilting accent that I couldn't quite place.

He was Tech's finest software developer, so the rumours went. A veritable genius, he could fix any problem magic- or code-related. And he was always wearing black—black jeans, black shirts, and that amazing slick leather jacket.

I figured I would never see him again because there was no way I was going to be allowed into Magic Corp, so to hell with it—shy, meek Jen Cooke was about to stop playing it safe. I hadn't shifted all those kilos yet, but at least I was making headway with growing out the dorky fringe.

Dennis Chan was ancient history. He was a boy. *This* was a man.

'I'll be okay once you give me mouth-to-mouth,' I managed to say.

My straight face didn't last long. I burst out laughing. To my relief, so did Simon.

We were in the deserted men's bathroom in under a minute, making out in the grossest place imaginable, but it didn't smell as bad as some I'd walked past in my life. I'm not sure I would have cared much if it did—I hadn't had any action since Dennis. Totally TMI, but I'd learned how to make some useful shapes out of Physical to keep me from climbing the walls. It really wasn't the same though, mostly because my power reserves were never good enough to give me the right amount of *oomph*, so to speak.

Anyway, when Simon and I finally came up for air, I found myself blurting out my shameful secret. I'm still not sure why. Maybe because he seemed nice. He had a reputation for being patient, harmless, good-natured—he even played Dungeons & Dragons with some of the other Tech guys.

'Give me your phone,' Simon said.

I stared at him, trying not to focus on the fact that the background to this strange encounter was comprised of urinals and cubicles. 'What, yours is out of battery so you're going to use my own phone to dob me into MC?'

He pursed his lips. 'Absolutely not. I just...I can help you.'

'How?' I demanded, shooting an angry look at the door. It seemed terribly far away all of a sudden and it should have been coming to rescue me. 'By giving me Perception with a wave of your hands?'

Simon chuckled. 'No, I can't do that. But these hands are responsible for making most of the apps that Tech releases. I can give you PercApption right now.'

'You mean...' I probably gawked at him. I can't remember everything about that night with clarity. 'PercApption is real?'

It'd been a rumour, talked about in hushed whispers after the teachers left us alone in the dormitories for the night. I hadn't believed it existed, because I hadn't wanted to get my hopes up.

'Yes,' Simon answered with a firm nod. 'And I'm going to give it to you.'

'But—they'll search me for a phone and take it off me before they let me near the Hellhound pen,' I fretted.

Those blue eyes trapped me again. I couldn't look away. I didn't want to.

'They won't,' Simon promised. 'I won't let them.'

I gave him a suspicious frown. 'Are you going to make me sleep with you for it?'

'What? No!' he exclaimed, looking scandalised—or as much as he could while leaning against a graffiti-smothered wall in a men's bathroom. 'It's a gift, Jen. Freely given.'

He knows my name! I inwardly crowed.

When I was sober I could clear my mind so that no one heard me freaking out about things, such as my lack of Perception.

Surface thoughts were the extent of what the others could snatch from me—sometimes that was bad enough! Unsurprisingly, my ability to shield my thoughts had already been flushed down one of the nearby loos. But I didn't care that Simon had to have heard what I was thinking. He was seriously hot. And he was giving me way more than the time of day.

So I stood there, grinning stupidly while he loaded two different apps onto the second-hand phone I'd barely managed to afford on my Magic Corp allowance.

I forced myself to nod along and pretend I was listening carefully to Simon's instructions on how to use the apps. And then I decided he really did deserve something for his services, so we started making out again, but the damn alcohol monster dwelling in my stomach leapt up my throat and had me staggering for the nearest cubicle.

By the time I emerged, vomit staining my face, he was gone.

Merindah found me sobbing over a basin some time later. She held me for a bit, listened to my tale of woe about yet another guy abandoning me, then took me back to the dormitories. Even though we'd been given separate rooms in our senior year, she camped out on the threadbare carpet beside my bed.

I've never found the words to thank her for that.

***

Three years after The Bathroom Incident

The advertisements for my studio apartment in Mount Kuring-gai had boasted that it was 'ideally located for transportation'. That meant it was near both the train station and the Pacific Highway. It was also, unfortunately, beside the Pacific Motorway. If the freight trains groaning past didn't keep me up, then it was the non-stop traffic, all night long, somehow always worse at 3 AM. Summer was a nightmare. Couldn't keep the windows open—and my landlord hadn't bothered to install any air conditioning. Fantastic.

Burying myself in the dusty green bushland behind my apartment complex usually calmed me down after a crappy day, but I decided against hitting the nearby fire trails. Mostly because I was afraid of how I'd react if I came across some normal walking their dog, no matter how non-threatening their pet appeared to be.

I went to check my letterbox instead and found Frew Publications' latest issue of *The Phantom* waiting there for me. Hell yeah! Once I and my prize were safely ensconced inside my apartment, I smeared Savlon onto my Hellhound-inflicted scratches (they'd stopped bleeding, thank God), changed into a soft lilac T-shirt that said 'I simply walk into Mordor', and then slipped on my old outdoor-friendly TOMS slippers—they were fluffy and white, kind of looked like tiny sheep if you squinted.

I had just curled up on the lounge to read my comic (yeah, I know, *The Phantom* is old school, but I really liked the idea of a smouldering Kit Walker coming to my rescue—better yet, the Billy Zane incarnation) when someone buzzed my apartment.

I scowled and kept on reading.

The buzzer went off again.

Sighing, I stood up to slap the relevant button on the intercom.

'Yellow,' I muttered. Usually I sang it, even when couriers buzzed me, but I just wasn't feeling it.

'Grey,' Merindah Angus replied. She'd used various colours to answer me before, usually referring to her mood, so this was a very bad sign.

She was obviously there to kill me.

5

'Go away, Merindah!' I said. 'I haven't finished the latest *Phantom* and I am so not dying until I've done that!'

Silence, then—'What the hell are you on about, Jen?'

'They sent you to kill me!'

'Jen, calm down. I'm not here to kill you. Can't I check up on a friend while I'm off on sick leave?'

Merindah, who had no idea about my Perception blindness, could have told me to peer into her mind and find the truth there, but she had never pulled that one on me the way my colleagues so often did. She herself had told me to be suspicious of surface thoughts because they might not actually be someone's true feelings, and she had always respected my preference for verbal communication. She'd never even asked why, just accepted it as a quirk of mine.

Merindah had been nothing but honest with me. I think. I was pretty good at reading her body language, but I couldn't exactly see her right then.

Her voice did sound a little raspier than usual, actually.

I frowned. 'What've you got? I'm not catching it, whatever it is.'

Her sigh caused static to bounce through the intercom. 'I'm on the tail end, you're fine, and you already had glandular fever, Jen. Back at school. You caught it off Dennis Chan, remember? We were both glad he hadn't given you something else.'

I winced. Yeah, I did remember. But... 'I also remember that you're on the Kill Squad!'

'If they wanted you dead they'd have called me and I've got nothing on my phone about it.' Merindah dropped a lengthy pause. 'You didn't quit, did you?'

I forced myself to breathe deeply. She was right. Her boss would have let her know if I was slated for execution. And for fuck's sake, this was Merindah. She wouldn't kill me. Right?

I buzzed her in. She began clomping her way up the stairs and I made sure I opened the door before she got to the level my apartment was on. My eyes tracked her feet when she entered—she was wearing generic K-Mart joggers. Merindah had never been into the sneaker culture thing like us admin folk were (we had to get our jollies somehow on the first floor) but I couldn't help it. Merindah was a jeans and button-up shirt kind of woman. Practical and uncomplicated.

I looked at her hands, which I should have been doing from the start, but they were bare of any magical constructs. If I was lucky, I could catch her off guard with my own Physical—only for her to overpower me the moment my power reserves ran dry.

'I'm here for you, Jen,' she said and hugged me. Didn't even ask for an explanation.

Thank God for Merindah. Honestly.

I was relieved to see that she didn't look that sick, because otherwise I might have been a bit ungrateful about the hug.

When she was sitting on my battered couch, a cup of coffee in one hand and the other stroking a nearby box of tissues, she said, 'You seen the news?'

I sank onto the cushion beside her. 'I have a feeling I *am* the news.'

'You got that right, but don't worry, the PR people are all over it,' Merindah said, then quickly excused herself and caught a cough in a fistful of tissues. Once this was dealt with, she grinned at me. 'They're making it sound like you were there on official business. And now the whole country thinks you're a field agent! Ha! MC could at least give you a nice Christmas bonus—that's if they're not gonna promote you for real. What were you doing on the train at that time anyhow?'

'I got suspended,' I mumbled.

'Why?'

I gripped my knees, keeping my gaze on them instead of my best friend. 'I can't do Perception. Like, I literally do not have it. At all. I never have. They finally caught on when I failed my test today. I've been cheating this whole time.'

Merindah set her mug down on my Marketplace-sourced coffee table. Her expression went grim for a moment, then she attempted a smile, but it was small, uncertain. 'Don't be silly, Jen. Everyone has the two Ps.'

'I'm not joking. I can't read your mind or see demons.'

'But we grew up together and I never noticed,' she said.

'I've learned how to guess what people are thinking.' I grimaced. 'I don't always get it right. Anyway, I didn't need Perception to know that everyone at school thought I was a freak. Well, except for you. You just thought I was shy. You even said so. Haven't you noticed how I never respond directly to people's thoughts and say off-topic things all the time?'

'Yeah, but you must've seen the Hellhound at the station, you knew where to throw your Physical,' Merindah argued and leaned forward to study me closely, as though she could find some proof of my freakishness if she looked hard enough.

'I was using PercApption,' I said, holding up my phone.

Merindah didn't even ask me how I'd got the app, just frowned and said, 'I see.'

'I don't,' I joked, then laughed weakly. 'So how useless am I?'

'You work in Admin, Jen,' Merindah pointed out. 'You don't need any magic to do your job.'

'Do you think my boss will accept that excuse? I bet Tom is getting permission to fire me right now.' I dropped my phone into my lap, frustrated. 'Could be I inherited too much normal or something.'

Magic seemed to appear willy-nilly in a lot of people, but it was known to amplify if magic-users bred together. Probably the main reason we were encouraged to date our colleagues. I'd heard that someone based at HQ was married to a normal, but I didn't know the specifics.

Speaking of which...

'Do you know much about your family?' I asked.

Something came over Merindah's face then, dark and indescribable. I was usually pretty good at reading her expressions—I'd had to be, being Perception-blind as I was—but this one was beyond me.

Her eyes met mine. 'You mean the family the government took my mother from, or the one Magic Corp took *me* from?'

Shit. Merindah had never been shy about her Aboriginal heritage, but I hadn't given it the thought I should have. Her mother was from a Stolen Generation by the sounds of things. And for Merindah to be taken away in the same fashion? Just...shit.

There's not a lot you can say in response to that. But I tried anyway. 'I'm sorry.'

We drank coffee in silence for a couple of minutes, until I finally mustered up the courage to ask, 'Merindah...what is it MC does to keep people from going back to their families after they finish school? Like, how do they get everyone to sign the contracts?' I swallowed. 'I mean, I signed because I had nowhere else to go. But nearly everyone else had to make a choice, right?'

Merindah viewed me over the rim of her mug. 'It's different for each person. But for most of us, they give our families a house and some money, even send our brothers and sisters to uni for free. If we leave when we're eighteen, then all that stuff has to be paid back in full. I did it for my mum. Do you think anyone would give a Blak woman who never finished high school a job good enough to pay for a house on her own?' Merindah shook her head. 'No. I signed for her. I hope she understands that.'

'That's....that makes sense,' I said, wondering if my mother had received any compensation when I'd been taken. Probably not. Her reward must have been a life free of having to look after me. I was kind of glad I didn't remember her.

The Australian branch of Magic Corp had always defended this practice of removing kids, but several branches across the world were in favour of offering voluntary training and employment to magic-users who were old enough to make their own decisions. Other branches argued that the current system kept magic-users from going rogue and killing everyone they came across. Normals could not be entrusted to instil the proper values in their magical children, after all.

It was tabled for discussion at the next big international Magic Corp meeting, but I didn't expect much to change for us Down Under. The United States, the major players, were more in line with us—or should I say we were more in line with them?

We took our friendship with the US a lot more seriously than the Kiwis did. We actually had our own secret version of the ANZUS Treaty, stipulating how our three branches should work together. Collectively, we'd managed to stop three demonic incursions in the Pacific Ocean in the past fifty years—a roaring success, even if New Zealand hadn't helped with the last one. See, I do pay attention in Magical History.

Anyway, I might not have my mother (not that I'd want her anyway), but I got paid enough to rent an apartment (okay, it was a studio all the way up in Mount Kuring-gai, but still) and I could occasionally save up enough to buy some cool shoes (I was eyeing up a pair of second-hand Nike wedge sneakers on eBay—they were *purple*, ooh). My life wasn't so bad. Then again, I didn't really know what I was missing.

'But none of that matters right now,' I said abruptly, kicking away my *Phantom* comic. 'Jesus Christ, a freaking Hellhound tried to kill me. I thought we had people who could sense where these things were? So we could, you know, keep the normals from being torn up?'

Merindah's lip twisted. 'Our scouts can't see everywhere at once, Jen.'

She was referring to those lucky few whose Perception had a quirk that allowed them to pick up magic, demonic or otherwise, up to two or three hours' drive away from their location. Their career path was assured from the moment they displayed their long-range abilities. And they could even ask for transfers to outposts in regional Australia, where they weren't stuck on the same floor as Dennis Freaking Chan.

'Doesn't help that our really strong Perception people are down in Canberra right now,' Merindah continued with a disgusted shake of her head. 'And the cops might have PercApption but it only shows what's in front of them, not what's lurking around the corner. Tech needs to get a move on and come up with something better.'

I didn't doubt that Tech would get a move on. They seemed to spit out new apps every week: stuff that mimicked magic, stuff that made it easier to reap rewards on the stock market, or sometimes just stuff. The tech department was up on the second floor, which suited me just fine. I'd been trying to avoid their senior developer for years.

I couldn't remember if I'd ever properly thanked Simon for giving me those apps. Shit. I hoped he wasn't in any trouble because of me.

'Don't know if we should have gone public,' I said after a while, mostly to distract myself from falling into the past and moping, something I did way too often. 'Having to deal with the cops isn't the worst of it.'

Merindah chuckled. 'Didn't choose to go public, did we. World-ending demon incursion in New York's gonna get some attention, isn't it?'

We'd received a lot of *negative* attention, even after the government had accepted us into the fold. The radio shock jocks had bayed for blood. Clickbait sites had written their catchiest headlines ever. The public had demanded oversight and accountability and we'd had to give it. After all, we now operated like ASIO—our activities were not made public, but we were watched. Monitored. Made to liaise with the Minister for Magical Australians and Related Affairs. All so the government could make sure we were operating in the best interests of our country and its people.

But we hadn't been forthcoming about the Kill Register, that big thing that goes against the interests of Australian magic-users. The government was bound to start noticing the executions at some point. I hoped the PR department had something in place to deal with that. Or maybe I should have wished the bad press on them, because right then it was *my* life on the line.

Merindah's mouth shrank. So too did her eyes. I knew what that intense look of concentration meant; she was using her powers. I strained my ears, my nose, every hair on my arms—and got zip.

'You sense something?' I asked.

Merindah's eyes popped open again. 'You really don't have Perception, do you?'

You know, it's a wonder I hadn't managed to get myself killed before that day.

It's a good thing my best friend showed up, huh?

6

I grabbed my phone and switched back over to mobile data. My wi-fi wasn't going to be much use if I had to run. And running seemed pretty likely.

I cleared my throat. 'Uh. So. What do you need me to do?'

'You're not going to do anything, Jen,' Merindah told me, sounding ridiculously unconcerned. 'I don't need your help with this.'

Well, there *was* a reason she'd been headhunted for the Kill Squad. She was bloody good at wielding her Physical.

'Yeah, but even hotshots like you need backup, right?' I attempted a grin. I'm not sure it managed to hide just how freaking terrified I was.

'Hellcreature nearby,' Merindah said, standing and moving to the window.

From there she'd have a pretty good view of the national park, nice leafy stuff, but she wouldn't be able to see all the way down into the valley, where Cowan Creek threaded its way north towards Brooklyn.

I shivered. 'Did it come out of a Flaming Ring of Fire?'

Merindah tensed and leaned forward, her gaze raking over the lawn outside. 'Only big ones, like Helldragons, can tunnel through to our realm.'

Okay, so the biggest, baddest demons had a way to enter our

world. Yeah, I'd never earned a spot in those advanced classes back at school. Merindah, on the other hand, had. She knew way more about Hellcreatures than I did.

'Can Hellhounds jump through one of those tunnels if a Helldragon makes it...?' I wondered.

Merindah didn't answer. Her eyebrows were scrunched together in concentration.

'Two Hellcreatures,' she amended.

I swallowed.

'Three...four...' Merindah shot me an apologetic look. 'Five. Sorry, Jen, looks like I will need some help.'

'Hellhounds? *Helldragons?*' I squeaked.

She grimaced. 'Nah, these ones didn't pop in from the other realm. They're hybrids. Probably sloshers.'

So in Australia we have our own special native Hellcreatures—hybrids, to be precise. It happens when demons cross over from their realm and, er, make merry with the local mammals. Ours are some of the oldest hybrids in the world. Still invisible to normals though—and me, unfortunately. The first magic-users to set foot on this land, tens of thousands of years ago, must have noticed these hybrids and their more destructive relatives, even if no one had found any evidence of demonic incursions prior to colonisation (AKA invasion).

Merindah had a theory that there wasn't any fighting, that demons and First Nations Australians got along and lived in harmony. I guess we'll never know, because while the British branch of Magic Corp was pre-emptively wiping out a good chunk of the native hybrids (none of the creatures had attacked them on arrival, but it was a given that they would eventually), their normal government was busy taking out a good chunk of people.

It took until Federation in 1901 for Australia to get its own flavour of Magic Corp. Our fledgling branch didn't really do anything new, just continued the traditions they'd inherited from the motherland (we'd deviated a little since then—not by much, but enough to annoy the British branch). This system had always worked, right?

Sometimes I wondered.

Anyway, yes, sloshers. It's a catch-all label for the type of hybrids that like to slosh around in creeks and rivers—I'd read about them in one of the few demon-related books the school library had stocked. That book had also assured me that no hybrids had lived in Sydney for over a century.

Right. Since when did Hellcreatures care about lines on a map?

They were here. And they. Were going. To kill me.

Well, *us*. Because there were now two yummy magic-users in the building.

'Aren't sloshers supposed to be water-based creatures?' I asked timidly.

'Yep,' Merindah replied, waving a hand at the window. 'There's a creek just down there. Feeds into the Hawkesbury, doesn't it? They've got a nest on the other side of the river, in Mooney Mooney.'

Ah. Mooney Mooney. The first suburb *outside* Greater Sydney on the Pacific Motorway. I guess that book wasn't so wrong after all.

A loud bang reverberated from downstairs. Then another.

'Throwing themselves at the outside door now,' Merindah said.

More banging. The sound of splintering wood.

'Merindah,' I began, my voice rasping as though I'd tried to swallow fire, 'are you sure I'm not on the Kill Register? I feel like I've really pissed someone off. First the train, now this...it's not a coincidence, is it?'

I didn't think anyone could politely tell Hellhounds or sloshers to attack just *one* target in particular...but I had a nagging feeling. A bad one.

'They said you were only suspended, yeah?' Merindah asked, her eyes boring into mine.

'Why? What happens if I'm fired?'

'Don't ask me that,' she said—way too seriously.

My ribs started crushing my heart.

'I don't want you to get into trouble because of me,' I whispered.

Merindah snorted. 'If I'm already in trouble for just being here, can't do much worse, can I? And I don't know if you're fired or not. No one's told me anything. So I'm protecting a fellow MCer from demons.'

I really needed to start thanking people more often.

There was a loud crash as the door downstairs was smashed to smithereens. Then a chorus of clacking came up the stairs, as if our assailants had talons—I had no idea what type of sloshers we were dealing with. There were so many different variants. But they all had this in common: they liked water, but they liked the flesh of magic-users a *lot* more.

I stabbed the WatchDog app.

And nothing happened.

I checked the signal on my phone. All good. The app just wasn't working.

'Shit,' I said.

'Two of 'em stayed outside,' Merindah said, peering out the

window. 'Can't jump out without facing them. Better get that app working, Jen.'

Yeah, I didn't see that happening any time soon. So I used the phone to ring my former boss instead. I still had her number because it had only been six months since Mackenzie Roberts had become our liaison to the government. She was the public face of our branch and worked with the Minister for Magical Australians and Related Affairs these days, but she couldn't have forgotten me that quickly. And she'd always been a lot nicer to me than Tom ever was.

I got Mack's voicemail. It'd have to do. 'Um, Mackenzie, hey, it's Jennifer Cooke—there's a group of sloshers attacking my apartment complex and I've got Merindah with me, but we're totally screwed. Send help.'

'You rang *her?*' Merindah gritted out.

I might have been a little snippy. 'I don't trust a lot of people, okay? Just be glad you're one of them!'

I shoved the phone into my pocket and readied my hands. There was no point using PercApption. It would only tell me the obvious—that we were completely and utterly surrounded. There was a good chance I'd manage to hit something, blind as I was. And I wanted to have two hands free so I could do as much damage as possible.

My door was now shaking and groaning under the sloshers' assault.

Merindah bit her lip. 'Just tried reading their minds. They've got tiny brains but sometimes you can get stuff out of them.'

I felt a stab of envy. If I had Perception, it would speed up conversations like this, when there wasn't time to stand around talking. Back at HQ, the whole admin department gossiped away in their heads at lightning-fast speeds and I was cut off from it all. Try pretending you get the inside joke when someone says it out loud for the first time.

I'd just been lucky that mind-reading was considered one of those abilities that was the same strength for everyone, so it wasn't something they tested or judged your future on. They probably should have, though. I hadn't heard of an app that simulated telepathy.

'So what are they, uh, thinking?' I asked Merindah.

She turned to me, her face paler than usual. 'They're after you, not me. And this is way more serious than what happened earlier. That Hellhound on the train wasn't out for your blood. Not like these sloshers. They want you dead now.'

'Demons don't play favourites!' I argued, though I couldn't disagree that the Hellhound hadn't done its best to kill me. 'They are Crazy Indiscriminate Creatures of Doom!'

I don't know, maybe it was my frustration at being so useless all the time, maybe it was the fact that I'd never properly thanked my best friend for helping me over the years, but suddenly I knew what I had to do.

'Okay, I'm going to make a run for it,' I declared.

'What?' Merindah stared at me.

'I can't let them kill you,' I said—rather calmly, I thought. 'These fuckers'll leave you alone if you're right about them being after me. So...bye, I guess.'

With shaking hands, I tore a giant hole in the flyscreen that was stretched across my window, pulled myself through—and jumped.

7

You ready for another flashback? Tough. You're getting it.

Seven years before I hurtled out into certain death, I was stuck inside a stuffy office at school while the screams and laughter of the kids playing outside wafted in through the window.

'Jennifer, if you won't cooperate with me and be honest about your powers, how can I recommend a career path for you?' My careers advisor pinched the bridge of her glasses and set them down on the desk between us. 'Don't you want to be guaranteed a good position at Magic Corp when your schooling is complete?'

That gesture with the glasses, and the minute lines sketched between her two eyebrows, were the main indicators that she was frustrated with me. She had been doing this a lot lately during our sessions together.

I kicked the bottom of my chair. It was one of those low plastic seats, with rough texture on both sides. Clearly, I didn't deserve the cushy wheely chair that my interrogator was allowed. Every time the heels of my scuffed black shoes collided with my seat, it sent a jolt shuddering through me. This was somehow satisfying, a punishment for a shortcoming I couldn't quite explain.

I was fourteen. And I'd passed loads of written tests, some of them identical to what normals had to do (essays for English, multiple choice for Maths, whatever) and some of them checking to see what I'd learned about demons. As for more practical

Physical lessons, that wasn't something I'd ever get to enjoy. It would be a waste of time and resources to teach everyone, since those of us who got stiffed with admin positions would never actually *use* our powers. We were allowed to experiment with Physical for fun and games, so that our teachers could assess who had an aptitude for it, but they didn't want all of us knowing how to really hurt people.

Around me, puberty was accelerating everyone's abilities. I was getting left behind and packing on weight from the stress of it. I'd had Physical for years longer than most of my peers, but I was nothing special—not like Merindah, who got to take an advanced Physical class with a handful of others. This made them the envy of the school.

'Well, let's not worry about that for now,' my careers advisor said. Her expression morphed briefly, revealing the truth beneath her pleasant smile. I'd disappointed her. 'Let's talk about your social skills. Your teachers tell me that, apart from Merindah, you're not making any friends. Do you have trouble talking to the others? Are they excluding you?'

My cheeks grew steadily hotter. Eventually, I couldn't stand the silence.

'They don't mean to,' I said.

'Oh?'

It was now or never. Ms Cleary, my Maths teacher, often said that you would never learn how to solve a problem if you didn't ask for help when you needed it. Teachers were always right, weren't they? And I was now desperate enough to mention my little problem.

My legs stilled. 'I can't read their minds. They're always talking in their heads and I can't hear anything. It's not fair. And they don't believe me.'

The careers advisor shook her head slightly, as though I was a kindergarten kid who'd said something stupid about how the world worked.

'You don't believe me either!' I accused her.

'Oh, I believe you,' she assured me. 'You just need to be patient. You already have Physical, don't you? Your Perception will manifest eventually. It always does.'

'But everyone else has it now!' I wailed.

'Someone has to be the last one to get it, now, don't they?' she said gently.

So I waited. And it never came.

Sick of people not believing me, I instead got really good at pretending. I knew how to tell if someone was cracking a joke, if someone was making fun of me, or if someone was being kind. I knew when to smile and nod, and when to throw a Physical ball in response to an unheard insult. Not that I could ever do much damage.

I gained a reputation for being quiet. Not just in mental conversations, but in verbal ones as well. Merindah thought I was shy and wanted to avoid saying something inappropriate and off topic (which I did a lot, because I had no idea what the topic even *was*). She actually seemed to like me! No matter what I said or how weird I was, Merindah never stood up and left.

That's why adulthood really sucked when it happened.

Once we signed our contracts, she was sent away to a different department. And I was stuck on the lowest rung possible, running around and getting coffee for everyone.

No one ever looked up to thank me when I delivered their

drinks. No one except Merindah noticed when I lost the weight. And no one cared when I bought and wore the shoes they thought were so damn special.

I was as invisible to my first-floor colleagues as the Hellhounds were to me.

***

Seven years after that delightful chat with my careers advisor

'Your left!' Merindah screamed from the window.

Luckily, my apartment was only one floor up and I'd been able to use the downstairs neighbour's lattice fence to get to the ground, or I'd have seriously injured myself. Not that it mattered. The sloshers would be more than happy to injure me instead.

I tossed a cricket ball-esque wad of magic in the direction that Merindah had indicated. I'd always been hopeless at cricket, but at least I could do an overarm throw—those lunchtimes in the school playground hadn't been entirely wasted. Ha!

Something howled. The ball must have struck its mark. How much damage it inflicted I had no idea, but knowing me I'd probably just pissed the slosher off. I could tell it was still gunning for me when the stench of rotting mud intensified—and I couldn't help noticing those large clumps of grass and soil being torn out of the ground.

Merindah shouted a warning, but I already knew I was in trouble.

I formed a spear out of magic and hefted it. This pointy object had served me well in my Physical tests—sure, my spear barely nicked the outermost ring of the styrofoam targets, but I'd always hit it.

I did my best, okay? And I must have nailed the slosher, because its red—definitely red, since it's a hybrid—blood sprayed all over the grass. I was stunned. I didn't think I'd actually be able to hit it! But I guess at that close range it was impossible not to.

I stabbed repeatedly before realising that my weapon was stuck and the creature was spitting blood instead of writhing in death throes. The spear, unfortunately, chose that moment to start misting away in my hands.

'Your construct's done for—drop it!' Merindah barked from nearby.

I obeyed, hit the ground, and rolled away. There really wasn't time to have a go at her for clambering down from the window to join in the fun.

A chunk of bricks from the knee-high fence next to the footpath hit the ground beside me. I kept on rolling, rotating my body even faster. And then I barrelled into something solid, big, and slobbering. It raked thick gashes into the grass with its talons as I frantically spun away from it. I wasn't hurt, but that was enough to make me scream in panic. When I'd tapered off into a whimper, I balled up some magic and tossed it where the hybrid's maw might be, trying to smash those teeth—

So I'm guessing I missed. Because fangs tore right through the shoulder of my shirt. Thank God it was a shirt from Before Weight Loss, because it was baggy all over and the slosher hadn't managed to get a mouthful of flesh along with the fabric it ripped off me.

But it was my favourite fucking shirt! Stained with crimson

blood and suddenly a lot more revealing. I nearly forgot to roll again because I was so angry.

I know, I know—that was stupid.

Once I was about two metres away from my previous position, I threw up a shield, something I'd had to do a lot back at school to defend myself against my classmates when the teachers weren't looking. The shield wavered ominously as soon as it formed. Luckily, the hybrids now had something else to focus their attention on.

Merindah swung wide in a circle around me, wickedly long Physical hooks in her hands. Her whole body was encased in midnight-black magic, like a suit of armour except far more flexible. I saw teeth marks spreading over her construct, but none of the sloshers managed to puncture it. They made echoing booms of rage as Merindah went to work, saving my worthless hide while I simply lay there, mouth hanging open. Her power—and her control over it—was frankly amazing.

I really didn't want to end up on the Kill Register if she was the one they sent after me.

I realised I was gasping for air. Shit, shit, *shit*. So not the time to hyperventilate. Yeah, I thought that's how I was going to die. Either from panic or from opportunistic sloshers once my weak shield gave out. I figured it had ten seconds left, tops.

'Freeze!' ordered a voice that definitely didn't come from me or Merindah.

Strangely enough, the sloshers-trying-to-eat-us sounds dropped away, but Merindah was quick to fill the silence. 'What are you doing here!?'

'Go to sleep!' the newcomer snapped in response.

I heard a body hit the ground. It sounded a lot smaller than a slosher.

My shield whimpered out of existence and I forced oxygen into my lungs, hoping I hadn't started to hallucinate. It just didn't make sense. But there he was, Simon Bradley, leaning over and offering me his hand. His grin was mischievous, as though he knew something I didn't, but most people in the tech department had that look about them. And he was wearing his usual leather jacket, even though it was over thirty degrees Celsius.

Beside Simon, wagging its tail and looking up at him adoringly, was the shadowy WatchDog that had emerged from my phone earlier—I could tell by its missing ear. It came up to me and blew hot air into my face.

Startled, I jumped off the ground and looked around wildly. 'The sloshers...!'

Simon nodded. 'They're probably still there—I can't see them either. But they won't do anything, not while I have control over them. You're lucky your dog ran and got me.'

'Merindah...' I spotted her crumpled form on the ground. She looked so vulnerable, robbed of her Physical shielding as she was.

'She's sleeping, and it's not her they're after,' Simon said. 'Come on. We've got to go before more arrive to finish the job.'

I remained where I was, still extremely confused, as he walked not towards the road but over to the small pedestrian walkway that had its own bridge over the Pacific Motorway. It was the easiest way to cross the six lanes of traffic dividing my apartment complex from the train station and the Pacific Highway (yeah, I know, we're not that creative when it comes to choosing names Down Under—Megalong Valley, anyone?).

The WatchDog, now at my side, whined. Simon stopped and turned around.

'What's wrong?' he asked.

It took me a few attempts, but I managed to get the words out. 'Hellhound. Merindah. Sloshers. Now you. What the hell is going on?'

Simon watched me for a moment, lines growing across his forehead. 'I don't have time to explain. You're in danger, Jen. Merindah isn't. So you're coming with me.'

'No, I think I'll wait for MC,' I said, trying not to sound as unsteady as I felt.

Simon laughed darkly. 'Magic Corp? They're the ones trying to kill you. Or hadn't you figured that out by now, contract-breaker?'

'I didn't quit, I was suspended!' I exclaimed.

I could hear sirens now. Not unusual, given how close we were to the motorway. Simon jerked his head towards the sound. 'You think they're coming to help? You're the enemy now. And Magic Corp will make sure everybody knows it.'

I stepped back, shaking my head. But I didn't make it very far. The WatchDog growled and latched onto my pants, tearing into the fabric.

'Hey!' I cried.

Simon smirked. 'At least he didn't take a chunk out of your TOMS. And don't blame me, you're the one who made him. That's some impressive power you have.'

He was spouting nonsense, I decided, to confuse me. For most magic-users, Physical creations lasted a few minutes, tops. Some people, like my boss Tom Chapman, could sustain their constructs for longer, but they were few and far between.

'I'm not going with you,' I said. *Even if you do know what brand of shoes I'm wearing!*

Simon's feet were boasting a pair of New Balance sneakers, but they were the typical black ones you could get anywhere, not just at speciality stores. Still, it was something.

'I can keep you safe—you saw how I dealt with the sloshers,' Simon said calmly.

I hesitated. Well, actually, I hadn't *seen* what he'd done, but they weren't ripping into me so...

Simon grimaced. 'I didn't want to have to do this, considering you're one of ours. Sorry.' A shadow fell across his face and his eyes seemed to swirl. 'You will come with me to my car. No questions. Just follow.'

My mind turned to mush. I felt instantly drunk and wavered, but I wavered towards *him*, and within seconds I was running and tripping along behind him. The WatchDog stayed at my heels, growling whenever I slowed, but I wasn't going to stop. My feet kept slapping the concrete on the pedestrian bridge. Below me, trucks and cars whooshed on by.

I wanted to turn back. I couldn't.

I'd been through a lot of scary stuff that afternoon. But none of it—*none of it*—compared to losing control over my own damn body.

I was terrified.

8

It wasn't until I'd run past the station and was buckled into the front seat of Simon's ancient Hyundai Excel (sporty green, twin cam, spoiler at the back, white tyre rims—it looked like a typical hoon mobile) that I was able to shake my head and clear the cobwebs. I watched Simon tilt the driver's seat forward so that the WatchDog could clamber into the back of the car.

'But...Perception doesn't do that...' The words escaped me reluctantly, slurred and thick.

'Open the door if you're going to throw up,' Simon told me.

'It was...one time...' I protested as he clunked his seat back into place and fired up the engine.

Simon grinned. 'I saw you at all the other office parties.'

'Oh yes! All those times you avoided me after The Bathroom Incident!' I snapped, jerking against the seatbelt when I tried to reach over and swat him. I missed. 'Look, you could have fobbed me off with some lame excuse instead of outright bailing like that. Beer goggles fell off in the bathroom, did they?'

Actually, ew, I'd probably have regretted that sleazy scenario later if I'd gone through with it. Maybe Simon had done me a favour.

'I haven't stopped thinking about you since that night,' he said.

My fingers started searching for the buckle on my seatbelt, but they were shaking too badly to do anything useful. So I stalled.

'Yeah, whatever. I've no idea why every woman on the first floor—and Jason in Accounts—moons over you. Maybe I should tell them all what a dick you are.'

'I had my reasons for not taking things any further, Jen. I don't have time to get into it.'

Five seconds later, we were speeding down the Pacific Highway, headed south and—presumably—bound for the CBD. Simon seemed to be avoiding the motorway (and those sirens).

I grabbed the seatbelt in another attempt to get it off me, glaring at my captor as I struggled with the damn thing. 'What the hell was that? Perception lets you read minds, it doesn't let you manipulate them!'

'I don't have Perception,' Simon said. 'None of my people do.'

'What!?'

Simon flicked his eyes at me. 'Magic Corp has done their best to hide this from everyone, but there are *four* Ps in magic. There's Perception and Physical, which you know about, but there's also Portal and Persuasion.'

The WatchDog whuffed his agreement from the back seat. The absurdity of my situation made me laugh hysterically. I'd just been kidnapped by Tech's hotshot software developer in a car that was even older than me—right after said software developer had saved me from demons simply by telling them to *freeze*. And he'd somehow made Merindah fall asleep! Not to mention his magical canine sidekick.

'Okay, what do these extra Ps do?' I snorted. 'Do they have colours, like provisional licence plates?'

Simon shot me an aggravated look. We were now sailing past Asquith Boys High School, where hundreds of green-clad boys were being ejected from the gate. The school zone sign was

56

flashing, but Simon clearly wasn't in the mood to obey traffic laws and/or protect normals from the front bumper of his car.

'Portal,' he began. 'The ability to create and travel through Portals connecting the two realms.'

My gut gave an uncomfortable squirm.

Persuasion,' Simon went on. 'The ability to dig into someone's head and make them obey you. That's if they can't fight back with their own Persuasion.'

'So that's what you have,' I said.

'That and Portal,' he agreed. 'I Persuaded all the humans at Magic Corp to think I was an employee there. And I made sure they never checked my pockets for my phone so I could use the apps during my tests. I don't have Perception or Physical because we only get two out of four Ps. That's how it works.'

I sighed. 'Nope. There's people who only have one P.' Then I frowned. 'You said *humans*. What's that make you?'

That grin made him look ten times sexier. I wanted to smack it off him.

'Demon,' Simon answered.

I decided not to bother saying that demons were supposed to be creatures, not hot tall guys with questionable taste in second-hand cars. It was becoming pretty fucking obvious that I knew next to nothing about anything, because Magic Corp had deemed it unnecessary to enlighten someone as unimportant as me.

Thanks to them, I had no idea how to deal with a demon kidnapping me.

So I grabbed the door handle.

Simon lunged over and locked the door. He contorted himself back into the driver's seat just in time to brake at a red light.

'You could at least have kidnapped me in something with central locking,' I said.

The WatchDog whuffed again. Simon growled, sounding a lot like a magical creature himself. 'Shut up, Fido.'

Fido obeyed.

'Good boy,' I ventured.

Fido's tail started thumping the seat.

'I could make you stay in the car.' Simon's voice was low, throbbing with—power? Danger? I hated to admit it, but it sounded good coming from him.

I considered my options. There weren't many. I was hesitant to give him a reason to dig into my head again and I really didn't like the idea of getting busted up on the road—which was what would happen if I hurtled to freedom. 'Okay. If you're saving my life, I guess it's a stupid idea to try and leave. Are you really a demon?'

He nodded. 'Yes.'

'But you can't see other demons?' I bit back the laugh.

Simon lifted a hand off the steering wheel and waved it casually, as though the answer should have been obvious. 'The smaller creatures evolved to avoid being found by us—they're our main food source in the demonic realm.'

Well, that made sense.

But I really didn't need to envision him eating a Hellhound. Ew.

I frowned. 'Just how many of you are there?'

'Here, in this realm?' Simon pursed his lips. 'Quite a few. You didn't see them on the news when New York happened because they were Persuading the creatures to attack from the safety of nearby buildings.'

Which meant...shit. All those thwarted demonic incursions I'd heard about—we were just nixing expendable Hellcreatures? We weren't even getting the people responsible?

'Like them, I've made it my mission to destroy Magic Corp,' Simon finished.

I shook my head. 'And take over this world in the process, I'm guessing. Jesus Christ, you sound like a Saturday cartoon villain. Hate to break it to you, but working for MC and helping them make fancy apps isn't really the way to go about it.'

Simon's lips quirked into a small smile. 'The tech department taught me what I needed to know to make PercApption for my people—except we have a version that works without mobile reception or wi-fi, since we don't exactly have that back home. And just so you know, we're not after this world; we have our own. We only want to rid yours of Magic Corp.'

'Oh, is that all,' I muttered.

Fido leaned forward and licked the arm I'd foolishly left in range. I jerked against the side of the car, trying not to freak out because that raspy tongue had felt ridiculously *real*. Sure, I'd seen those teeth in action, but magical constructs weren't supposed to be this detailed.

Simon's hand moved on the gear stick as he prepared to overtake someone. He waited a few moments more, then dropped the car into second gear and gunned it. 'I'll point out that those fancy apps I made saved your butt. Since it's a nice shapely butt, I consider my work well done.'

Fido turned to Simon and growled.

Simon nodded over his shoulder at the dog-like creature. 'Sorry. I only helped you "see" your attacker, Jen. You were the one who actually made Fido and saved yourself.'

'But I didn't—' I tried.

59

Simon flipped a grin at me. 'The WatchDog app isn't what you think it is. Basically, it creates a flexible Portal inside your camera lens. When someone's phone sends a request, my people send a hound—Hellhound—through it, which should be invisible to normals and any cameras. But here's the thing. Though a Portal opened up in your phone, my friends never got the chance to send you anything.'

I shook my head. He had to be wrong. I'd never excelled at any of the Physical tests. And if I really was that powerful, then MC would have told me, they wouldn't have had me running errands.

Terror slithered into my guts. 'Wait. You're sending *actual* Hellhounds into everyone's phones? How has no one noticed this yet?'

'My friends Persuade the creatures to defend whoever has the phone,' Simon explained. 'It helps that I told my superiors at MC that I deliberately made the app's creation resemble a Hellhound.'

It took me a moment to snap my jaw back into place. Oh man, we were so screwed.

Simon smirked. 'PercApption actually does what it's meant to, if that makes you feel any better.'

I snorted. 'No. It doesn't. So what happens when you decide that the Hellhounds should start killing the people holding the phones?'

'It'll be their fault for relying on the app, won't it?' he mused. 'Don't worry. I'll make sure the hounds don't kill any innocent bystanders.'

So *that* was his plan. And it wasn't a terrible one, unfortunately. It'd be a lot easier to catch a magic-user unaware if you gave them software they're supposed to trust—and it would be more effective than sending Hellcreatures to lay siege on a Magic Corp building. In this case, they'd already be inside the building.

Shit. I really had to start warning people.

'I got a shock when Fido here turned up at work.' Simon was talking again, his gaze focused on the traffic. 'Had to Persuade everyone to look away from him. At first I thought he was a glitch so I shut down the WatchDog servers, but he stuck around. Then one of my friends popped in to tell me about your phone's strange behaviour. I didn't get to talk to them for long—Fido was quite insistent on dragging me out to save you.'

Fido got a bit of side-eyeing from me. If the dog thought my safety involved a demon, it was clearly malfunctioning. Let's not forget that it had tricked me into thinking it had disappeared, when what it had really done was shrink and run off for Simon.

I cleared my throat. 'But I'm with Magic Corp. You're supposed to kill me.'

'I would never,' Simon said, his mouth firm. 'It's Magic Corp that's trying to kill you.'

'But why?' I demanded, kneeing the dashboard and shifting back in my seat.

Simon sighed. Fido echoed him.

'Because, Jen, when you failed your Perception test, they realised you had to have another P instead,' Simon answered. 'Which means they now know you're part demon.'

'That's insane! I'm not a demon!'

'Hybrids like you go missing at Magic Corp all the time, and someone's already tried twice to make you disappear,' Simon said, then paused to glower ominously out the window when someone cut him off. 'You have two out of four Ps. That's how it works. So your second P is either Portal or Persuasion, but given that I can get into your head so easily, I'm thinking Portal.'

I choked back bile, but what he was saying was a lot harder to swallow. 'A hybrid? What's next—are you going to tell me I'm a slosher? I've never seen one of those Portal things before today!'

Simon just shook his head, apparently unwilling to argue any further—that or he was concentrating on driving. After navigating some pretty shocking school traffic, we were actually starting to make some headway. We even passed Artarmon station again, though I couldn't see it from the highway, and then turned off towards the city.

When we hit the Sydney Harbour Bridge, I took a moment to admire the CBD. I saw the city every day on the way to and from work, but it always impressed me. And sometimes the view changed—that afternoon, for example, a giant white cruise ship was docked at Circular Quay.

'Where are we headed?' I asked my captor.

'Demon HQ,' Simon replied. 'Don't worry, we've got wi-fi and Netflix.'

'Why would I be worried?' I muttered, looking at Fido.

I had no idea how I'd made the damn thing, why it hadn't disappeared yet, or why it had gone running to Simon, but its presence soothed me. And I was going to need every friend I could get if I was about to enter The Den of Demonic Doom.

'You'll look after me, boy, won't you?' I asked quietly.

Fido barked once.

I took that as a yes.

9

Yeah, yeah, I know. Another flashback. Deal with it.

Four years before a demon kidnapped me in his clunky old Hyundai Excel, and two days after my seventeenth birthday, I used Physical to throw a spiked ball, narrowly missing Dennis Chan's head. I hadn't realised what he'd been saying at first, because he'd been thinking it at everyone and of course I couldn't hear him. But I knew it was bad because Merindah had gone as still as a statue beside me.

'What's going on?' I demanded. 'Just tell me!'

Merindah caved, probably because she figured I'd read it in Dennis' surface thoughts anyway and figured it would sound better coming from her.

I kind of wished she hadn't told me.

He was boasting about what we'd done last night—we had sneaked into the storage room in the gymnasium with condoms from the bathroom dispensers crammed into our pockets. And everyone sitting with him was laughing, telling him he'd have to pick a harder target next time, because 'fat chicks' always give it up way too easily.

He'd seemed like the only decent guy in the entire school. He had been so *nice* to me, so patient. But I should have noticed he was only like that when it was just the two of us, mooching about in the shadows. When he was surrounded by his dickhead friends, he was someone else entirely.

I started crying. Dennis' friends asked me if I was on my period, as if my feelings didn't count, as if they were somehow less authentic because they could have been caused by PMS.

So I got angry. And I threw that ball.

'What'd you do that for?' Dennis shouted. 'You could have killed me!'

'As if,' one of his friends chortled. 'She doesn't have the power to give you anything worse than a nosebleed.'

They were right. And they all showed me how weak I was by pelting me with far more solid projectiles. My shield went up in an instant, but it was almost transparent, barely even there. When it broke apart, Merindah got in the way and repelled their constructs, using what they'd taught her in that advanced class.

But that just made things worse.

Because everyone knew I needed her to protect me.

Dennis threw rocks at my window every night for a week. He told me that he hadn't meant it, that what I'd heard had just been his surface thoughts, that I should know how he really felt.

I ignored him and threw a sheet of Physical across the window, pretending it blocked the sounds he made on the other side of the glass. He never stayed long enough for the shield to disintegrate. If he'd really cared, he would have waited that extra thirty seconds. And he definitely wouldn't have given up after only one week.

'I'm told you don't agree with your PE teacher's assessment of your Physical,' my careers advisor observed the next day. I swear I was the only one my age still forced to see her. 'Why is that?'

'I feel like I have greater power reserves somewhere, but I...I can't find them!' I finished, frustrated.

'It's good to know your limits,' she said. Her glasses were on the desk again. 'And just as someone is the most powerful, someone has to be the least powerful.'

I hadn't told her that my Perception hadn't arrived yet, like she'd said it would. I didn't see a point, to be honest.

'That's bullshit!' I shouted at her and landed in detention.

I stopped dreaming about the power that surely existed somewhere inside me, and started dreaming about everyone accepting me.

But the office was yet another playground, one where a childish taunt became a cheerful request for supplies, or some other demeaning task. *Oh, you were on your way out? Sorry, Jen, but I need that coffee so I can do some real work.*

Hey, Jen, can you go send this by registered post in your break? Needs to be at the British branch by the end of the week. I want to get my full hour of lunch.

Need you to step up this time, Jen.

They didn't sit in groups and laugh at me anymore. They probably thought of themselves as decent people, incapable of doing what they had done.

I hated them sometimes.

***

Four years after The Dennis Chan Incident

Demon HQ ended up being at The Rocks, of all places.

Simon ditched the car in a public parking structure and the

moment my feet touched the concrete I was overwhelmed with the urge to run. Before I could give in to that urge, Fido barked crossly and leapt at me. I threw my hands over my face, shielding myself, only for the creature to shrink and tumble into the pocket of my mangled pants. I felt him wriggling about and heard him snuffling, no doubt passing judgement on the used tissues that were still crumpled up in there.

'I'm glad you've got him with you,' Simon said as we walked side by side down George Street (named for King George III, which isn't surprising considering that our country is part of the Commonwealth, but I seriously doubted Simon wanted to hear that right then). 'You'll need some protection if we get separated.'

I shot a furtive look around the street, spotting a police car crawling by—but that wasn't the kind of protection I needed, especially if the cops were using WatchDog. I really didn't want more Hellhounds showing up, even if Simon could control them.

I slid a hand into my pocket and curled it around Fido. The ensuing warmth in my fingers didn't quite reach my chest.

No one was bothering to give us a second—or even a first—glance, which might have been because of Simon's mind powers or because these normals were used to seeing women wandering around with torn shirts, chewed pants, and frazzled expressions.

Pretty sure it was the Persuasion.

We passed several restaurants, bars, jewellery shops, and other tourist traps (filled with cruise passengers who never had enough time to work their way further into the city) before we stopped at the door of a gentrified building. I wondered if the demons set up a stall at the weekend markets that drew so many people to the area. This thought almost made me laugh. In fact, the whole situation was pretty damn laughable. I leaned against the exterior sandstone wall, shaking with silent mirth as Simon unlocked the door and shoved it inside. He waved impatiently at me.

'No way am I going in there with you.' I shook my head when he opened his mouth. 'And don't tell me I should go with you if I want to live. I haven't figured out if that's what you have in mind.'

Shadows grew beneath his eyes. 'If I need to Persuade you, in order to save your life...'

I lifted my chin, trying to look just as intimidating. But he had it down to an art.

'Since you took me by surprise when you first mind-whammied me,' I said, sounding about as confident as I felt (which was, admittedly, not very), 'I'm sure I'll be able to fight you off a second time.'

'That's not how it works,' Simon said, smirking.

'Are you going to test my theory then? Because I'm not moving.'

Simon's expression soured so quickly I wondered if he'd sneaked a Warhead into his mouth. You know, those tart lollies that come in some of the showbags at the Sydney Royal Easter Show and give you the most peculiar expression for about five seconds?

Clearly, his Warhead was lasting a lot longer than that.

Impressive.

'I try not to Persuade people if I can help it,' he said lowly. 'It's not right.'

'So the demon has morals after all!' I exclaimed. 'We're saved!'

Simon scowled and grabbed my arm, not too tightly but enough that I could have made a deal out of it by screaming at the nearest souvenir hunters. That's if they could actually see or hear me. Simon's eyes locked onto mine and immediately I felt like I was drowning in twin blue whirlpools. I held my breath and waited for him to bend my will.

Fido made a tinny, disgruntled bark and my pocket abruptly bulged as he started growing in size. If he kept this up he'd split my pants open. Simon could convince people not to see a magical dog appearing out of a woman's nether regions, though I hoped it might distract him. Long enough for me to make a break for it? I wasn't sure.

Simon released his hold on me.

Fido swiftly shrank.

'Yeah, you help me *now*,' I grumbled at the dog. 'What about when he was Persuading me earlier?'

Fido was mysteriously silent.

'What will make you step inside?' Simon asked me. 'I've already told you your life is in danger.'

'Doesn't mean it's any safer in there,' I retorted. 'I only have your word that Magic Corp is gunning for me. I seriously doubt anyone at MC would risk innocent lives or the ensuing bad press—*especially* the bad press—by chucking a Hellhound on the train. And none of us can use Portal or Persuasion. We're human. The way I see it, only one of your kind could have made a Portal and sent that Hellhound after me.'

'You're not usually this chatty outside of men's bathrooms,' he remarked.

'You know, at work I tend to do this thing called *work*,' I sniped back, then nearly smacked my palm against my forehead. I had been kidnapped by this guy and yet there I was, engaging in what could only be classed as banter. 'Jesus Christ, Simon, can't you see how bad this looks?'

He frowned. 'Jen, if I wanted you dead, I wouldn't have

bothered helping you with those sloshers. I want to protect you. And this is the safest place in Sydney.'

'But they might still find me, even here,' I said. I wasn't sure who 'they' were, but I knew he'd understand what I meant.

Simon was already shaking his head. 'I used my time at Magic Corp to develop a device that erects a nullifying field—it blocks magic-sensing scouts from finding us. Not to toot my own horn, but it hasn't failed us yet. MC doesn't know we're here.'

'What about Hellcreatures?' I prompted.

'They can't sniff us out, I made sure of that,' Simon said, smiling now. He could probably sense that victory was imminent. 'But you're right to be careful, Jen. Not all demons are the same. Some disagree with what I'm trying to do.'

I snorted. 'Right, so some of you *are* hell-bent on killing every single human instead of just Magic Corp and everyone I grew up with. Any other big defining differences I should know about?'

So apparently it's a lot easier to engage in banter than escape a situation like the one I'd landed in. I started shaking again, which meant I was experiencing my second adrenaline crash in as many hours. I was exhausted and seriously couldn't take any more of this weirdness. I had no idea who to trust, who to turn to...

'Well, yes, there are important differences, but I'd rather we didn't get into that right now.' Simon shrugged. 'There's a lot more to us than you realise.'

'Yeah, I'm getting that,' I said, stepping past him and into the room beyond. 'There's a lot more to *you* than any of us ever realised. I bet you've been Persuading everyone to like you. It's a bit disturbing, to be honest, knowing I've locked lips with a...'

I trailed off, taking in the scene. The naked bulbs hanging from the ceiling were dim, all the chairs were upside down on the tables, and the bar lacked any bottles or glasses. The place didn't exactly look open for business and I wondered what people passing by thought, if they even suspected that in here were demons capable of Persuading them to drop all their cash.

I braced a hand against the wall when Fido burst out of my pocket and grew to his normal size again. He immediately started sniffing around. Watching him case out the place for me, I felt a dizzy whoop of relief. I wasn't alone. Sure, Fido was a magical construct, but his teeth were real enough. He could bite anyone who came after me.

The door behind me shut and locked with a decisive *thunk-clunk* sound.

I turned to look at Simon. 'You lot were responsible for the attack in the US, then?'

He pursed his lips for a moment, his gaze tracking Fido. 'Not exactly. My people disagree with the methods our brethren use elsewhere. The group in New York attempted to destroy that branch of Magic Corp by drawing them into open conflict. There were casualties among the American hybrids. And innocent bystanders got hurt.'

'Careful, you're starting to sound concerned about us humans,' I warned.

Simon's brow dipped low over his eyes. 'I do care about the people in this realm, Jen.'

'Not just those who share your powers? Can I get that in writing?' I asked, snickering. 'Hate to break it to you, but I've never exhibited any Portal-esque ability. I'm not a hybrid and I'm definitely no demon.'

'So you don't feel any connection when I do this...?'

Simon flicked his hand towards one corner of the bar. A large molten puddle blasted into being, his own Personal Portal to Hell. It roared at us, hungry for fuel and destruction, furious that we supplied it with neither.

My gut gave a savage, fearful twist.

I really didn't want to throw up in front of Simon again, so I swallowed the chunks back down, but I didn't quite manage to banish the acrid taste of them.

Fido bounded over and headbutted Simon's knees.

Simon dropped his hand. The Portal vanished.

'So that fiery hell imagery in films and stuff,' I said. 'Not a complete stab in the dark, huh. But seriously. Will you turf me out the moment you realise I'm an ordinary old human?'

'Never,' he vowed, leaning into my personal space.

I couldn't help it. I sucked on my bottom lip slightly, unsure how to respond to the dark desire I saw in his eyes. I'd seen it before, when we'd made out at that party three years ago, but I'd been incredibly tipsy and had figured it was my own beer goggles giving him that fascinating smoulder.

'Never?' I repeated. 'Why?'

'If you have to ask...' Simon murmured.

Nope, forget asking questions. I wanted to do something far more pleasant with my mouth.

Oh. Hello.

I needed to remind myself that this was a *demon* in front of me.

10

Before I could do something really stupid, like kiss a demon, Simon swiftly withdrew and went behind the bar, to a set of stairs that led up to the next floor. Fido and I followed after giving each other wary looks.

Part of me wanted to keep near Simon and the aura of confidence that he projected, and it was slightly larger than the sceptical part. I wouldn't stand a chance against a horde of sloshers or Hellhounds, even with Fido at my side. He was missing an ear and several bite-shaped chunks. That kind of damage would have killed a real dog. It had to have made Fido vulnerable.

Like it or not, I needed Simon's help.

When he reached the top of the stairs, Simon stepped aside to give me space on the landing. I peered past him into what seemed to be a large living room, its ceiling kept up by wooden support beams. The open plan was definitely needed for the twenty or so demons hanging out in there. At least, I thought they were demons. They looked deceptively normal.

Any lighting the muted lamps managed to provide was washed out by the decor. Everything was black, from the carpet to the curtains to the battered leather couches. The dark cushions arrayed around the demons on the furniture were almost too well camouflaged to notice. I found myself scanning for coffins, master vampires, and simpering servants.

'Wow, this place is a little stereotypical, don't you think?' I said, a good deal louder than I intended. My heart spasmed uncomfortably when every pair of eyes swivelled in my direction.

Fido didn't make a sound, just leaned against my leg. My hand fell to his head.

A woman rose from one of the couches and gave me a once-over. She was shorter than me and carried some extra weight that added emphasis to her curves. Sigh. My body had never filled out that evenly when I'd been heavier.

She seemed unimpressed by what she saw—that was until her eyes alighted on my feet. Either the TOMS passed muster or they amused her (yay for my grass- and blood-stained slippers), because she smiled and spoke to me in the same peculiar accent as Simon. 'So you're the one plastered all over TV and social media at the moment. Your little dog doesn't look so fierce in person.'

Fido bared teeth that grew and grew until they stopped well past his chin. He added a growl for effect. I tried not to stare at him, or think about the fact that everyone in the country probably knew what I looked like, thanks to those damn kids at the station.

I forced myself to meet my opponent's eyes. 'Hello. I'm Jen, your captive or your guest. Your preference.'

'Dot,' she answered, blowing some hair out of her face. I noticed that despite her breezy tone she kept watching Fido warily. 'What have you got, Jen? Persuasion or Portal?'

'Neither, I'm no demon,' I responded testily.

Dot clucked her tongue. 'Sorry, but you totally are. There's no other reason Magic Corp would be going after you.'

'How would you know?' I demanded. 'Look, Simon gave me the same story, but I'm not going to suddenly believe it. Unless you *make* me believe it. But I'm hoping the rest of you have morals like my colleague here apparently does.'

Dot raised her eyebrows at Simon. 'She's the one you met at that party? I approve.'

I flushed. 'If I'd known what he was...'

'You'd have gone running to the higher-ups at MC and got my brother killed,' Dot said with an impatient shake of her head.

It really shouldn't have surprised me that demons could have siblings. Next they'd probably reveal that they had parents and even used toilets like regular people. I knew they could definitely kiss, thanks to the handy (and handsy) demonstration Simon had given me three years ago.

I scowled. 'No offence, but demons are the ones who go around destroying things. Not us. We're the good guys. And there's no reason for MC to come after me.'

'Weren't you cheating on your tests?' Dot asked dryly.

Beside me, Fido grumbled but did little more. I tilted my chin down at him; I could have sworn he nodded in return. We'd both decided that Dot wasn't a threat. For now, anyway.

Simon released a hiss of air. 'Dot. That's enough.'

'Clearly you haven't bothered to tell her why you're so sure she's got demonic blood,' Dot remarked.

I transferred my glare to Simon. 'Oh? Go on. This should be interesting. Have I been accidentally Persuading everyone at the office to be massive dicks to me? Pretty sure I wouldn't have had to do the tea and coffee run if I could tweak their minds.'

Simon cleared his throat and indicated towards a couch with his hand. 'You should probably sit down.'

'No way.'

'Too good for the likes of us?' a man jeered from the couch.

I eyed him. 'Maybe. Not sure yet. But I'll give you the benefit of the doubt while there aren't any Hellhounds or sloshers trying to rip my face off.'

His ensuing chuckle lacked any warmth. 'You better hope none of them show up then.'

'Saul,' Simon said warningly.

I shot a pleading look at Simon. This amount of attention, after being ignored for so long on the bottom rung at Magic Corp, was not easy to deal with. My tongue felt slimy and my skull was starting to ache.

I planted my hand on Fido's head again, focusing on the strangely real sensation of fur against my skin. I couldn't discern individual strands of hair when I looked at Fido—he was a silhouette of a dog, for goodness' sake, not a real one—but I didn't see a point in questioning this when other, weirder stuff was going on.

Simon moved closer, conveniently placing himself between me and that Saul guy. 'You were taken from your family. Can't you see how wrong that is? We'd never do that. Family and community are very important in our realm. Ripping you away from that...'

I wanted to retort with 'I turned out okay, we all did', but Merindah's face during our earlier conversation filled my vision. I could still see the shadow of pain flitting through her eyes, never settling, always lurking. I wondered what went on behind those other smiling faces at work. I didn't like how my colleagues treated me, but many of them were just as motherless, just as fatherless.

Fido rubbed his nose against my thigh. I blinked the tears away. 'I have no memory of my family, so I guess I'm one of the lucky ones.'

'But you clearly knew a demon at some point,' Simon said.

I stared at him. 'What?'

'Your mind'—he pointed at my forehead—'has a substantial Persuasion block on it. And it's very old. I first noticed it when we met at that party.' His hand dropped back to his side, probably because I'd started flinching the moment he'd aimed it at me. 'Anyway, this means you've encountered demons before.'

Saul barked out another mirthless laugh. 'Oh really, Simon? That's all you have to go on? Who did it to her then?'

Dot tapped her chin, eyes unfocused. 'Well, this mysterious demon might've blocked her memories to protect her, so Magic Corp wouldn't know what they had.'

'How can you tell who's a hybrid?' I demanded. 'None of us magic-users look any different from anyone else and thank fuck for that—the media would swarm us if we could be recognised on sight.'

I swallowed nervously as I remembered that my face had been splashed all over the news. The decision to hole up in this Den of Iniquity didn't seem quite so bad now.

'We've been casing out Magic Corp for a while,' Simon said. 'Even before I infiltrated them. And let me tell you, Jen, when hybrids don't think they're being watched, they will do things they know they shouldn't, things they know they *shouldn't* be able to do. I'm good at figuring out who needs me to slip them the apps. This is how I've been protecting them. I don't know what happened to the hybrids that came before my time, but it can't have been good.'

I frowned. So I wasn't the only one with the apps? Who else had been on the receiving end of his special attention?

'Do they know what they are?' I asked.

'Nope, they're completely in the dark, like you were,' Dot said cheerfully. 'But they'll know soon enough, when we ask them to help us take out MC's leadership. They'll probably agree to do it, if they're sick of having to hide their gifts.'

'So you're treating us like...' I bit my lip. '...sleeper agents?'

Dot considered this, head tipped to the side, then she nodded enthusiastically. 'Yes! We'll need inside help to liberate our hybrid brethren from the grip of Magic Corp. No one should have to live under the threat of death, just because of what powers they got born with.'

I shook my head. 'I still don't think MC are the ones behind this. Maybe they're not as good as they should be, and I guess that's why they don't want the media knowing about everything they get up to, but killing...'

'Don't they have that Kill Clause in their contracts, but?' another demon asked.

My cheeks flamed. Magic Corp was sounding worse by the minute and Merindah kept springing to mind—Merindah! Guilt churning up the bile inside me, I turned to Simon. 'Wait, is Merindah safe? Those sloshers...'

'Were after you, not the Kill Squad agent,' Simon interrupted.

'Her name is Merindah,' I snapped.

The demons were watching me avidly now and all that was missing from their impromptu show were the buckets of popcorn. I wondered just how many humans or hybrids they'd seen close up. I felt like an exhibit instead of a living, breathing being. And they were expecting me to jump ship and join them.

So I didn't remember my parents. I didn't miss them. Magic Corp had given me everything I'd ever needed: an education, a hand-picked job, a salary, an assured place in the world. Sure, I spent most of my days hiding out amongst the filing cabinets and desperately trying not to cry. I was stuck getting tea and coffee for people who didn't care what else I could offer them. Not that I had much to offer, but still. If I could have just gone to university, or applied for another position inside Magic Corp, I might have found something I actually liked doing...

I cleared my throat. 'Why bother trying to save any of us? You're happy in your own realm, with your families and your questionable food sources. You don't need us. We're nothing. You could just blow up our HQ.'

'But that might take out the building next door, the one with that pie place you like so much,' Simon said, grinning.

I wanted to smack that look off his face. I didn't get to enjoy my full lunchbreak (I spent most of it running all those frustrating errands for everyone), so the pie place was more convenient than it was palatable. Huh. Not that I'd actually need to go there for lunch if the Australian branch of Magic Corp didn't exist anymore.

Wait, how did he know where I went for lunch? Had he followed me? Creepy. Also annoying, because I could have used the company.

Dot swept up to me and slung an arm over my shoulders. I was too stunned to evade her. 'You're one of us, Jen. We look after our own people—and we consider all the hybrids ours.'

'But what about the others at MC, those who don't have demonic powers?' I insisted, trying not to squirm under Dot's arm. 'Not everyone was happy to sign those contracts, you know? It'd have been great to have another option! Christ, my best friend signed so her mother could have a house of her own.' I paused, taking in the lines writing their way across Simon's face. 'You *are* thinking about helping everyone in Magic Corp, not just the hybrids, aren't you?'

'Simon?' Dot questioned.

'Sure you don't have Perception, Jen?' He wasn't smiling.

The room suddenly got very chilly. And I don't think it was because the air conditioning had been cranked up. Demons from all over the room were pinning Simon with sceptical, even angry, looks. So they might be willing to go along with his plan to help hybrids, but they weren't in it to save innocent humans from indentured servitude. Interesting. And also not good, because they weren't likely to spare our lives just because Simon told them to. I had a feeling they weren't as easy to Persuade as I was.

Fido's head was flinging between me and the rest of the room. His hackles were up. Yeah, I really didn't want to be standing out there in the open if the demons were about to start fighting each other.

I looked frantically around for something more substantial than a couch to hide behind. Nope. Maybe there was another room? With a lockable door?

'Um, is there some place I can just...nap?' I blurted.

Evidently such a place existed, because Fido and I were shown to it.

11

So I'm about to hit you with another flashback. My bad.

'Incompetent piece of shit,' Merindah muttered six months before I bedded down at Demon HQ. 'Might as well call him Mike "I'm Not Racist But" Jones.'

I looked up, startled, my fingers skidding across the keyboard. I had to quickly backspace some gibberish. This email to Tom, my new boss, wouldn't carry the same weight if it was filled with errors. Still, no matter how perfect my syntax was, he was probably going to refuse my request to email or fax the required documents to the Darwin outpost. Tom was *all* about security and confidentiality.

Emails could be hacked so I wasn't supposed to add sensitive material as attachments—and as for the dusty fax machine in the corner, we weren't allowed to use it. At all. I suspected this had something to do with the fact that someone had faxed an image of their backside to the Minister for Magical Australians and Related Affairs.

Basically, snail mail was now my only option. But Tom was such a stinge he wouldn't even spring for registered post. That kind of rendered the whole 'security and confidentiality' thing moot.

'Merindah?' I blinked at her. 'What are you doing here?'

I hadn't seen her inside work hours since...well, since that first day we'd walked into the lobby together, her with her kick-arse position in the Kill Squad and me with my decidedly boring admin role. Sure, I liked hanging out with her, but I was coming to appreciate not seeing her every hour of every day like I had at school. It meant we had far more to talk about when we did meet up.

'Needed to see a friendly face,' Merindah said, then jerked her head up at the ceiling, indicating our colleagues on the levels above us. 'One of the scouts has located a contract-breaker in the Northern Territory and my stupid boss thinks I should go after her. Brian's the one who actually worked with her at the Darwin outpost—and the one she'd be more likely to trust. She told Brian a lot of stories about her childhood in Arnhem Land when they went drinking.'

'Why aren't they sending Brian then?' I asked, frowning.

'Mike, my boss, said I'd be better at tracking her down, since we have *so much* in common. I guess because we both happen to be Blackfullas.' Merindah gripped the edge of my desk, shadowy Physical icicles spreading across the laminate surface, threatening to crack it apart. 'Never mind that I'm a Worimi woman, which makes me Koori—not that Mike ever bothered to ask. I've never been to the Northern Territory. Not even once!'

I opened my mouth, then closed it. I could tell she didn't really want a response, just needed to get it off her chest, just needed someone to *listen*.

'Never mind, I'll still be able to get the job done,' Merindah finished and performed a shrug that looked more than a little forced. 'What are you up to?'

'Trying to send the personnel file of your target to Darwin by tomorrow,' I answered, outlining a task that was nowhere near as cool as what she got to do. 'Tom thinks I should mail it.'

Merindah snorted, shaking her head. 'Stupid. Give me a look. If I'm gonna have to deal with it, I may as well know what she looks like.'

I double-clicked on the PDF file. An employee headshot filled the top-right corner—she was only a few years older than us and her smile was warm and friendly. I couldn't stop scrolling. I shouldn't have read it, I know that, but Merindah kept making a sound in her throat when she wanted to see the next page.

'She was taken from her family when she was nine,' Merindah noted. 'Old enough to have her address and any important phone numbers memorised. And it says here she asked repeatedly to be transferred to Darwin, our closest outpost to Arnhem Land.'

I bit my lip. 'You think she was trying to reconnect her family.'

'Yeah, reckon so.'

'You can't...' I tapered off.

'Can't what?' she demanded. 'Can't kill someone who's done what we've all thought about doing, at least once?'

I said nothing.

'You have access to all the personnel files,' Merindah said, lowering her voice as her eyes darted around the empty office. Lucky for us, there was a food truck down on Pitt Street giving away free doughnuts so everyone else had buggered off. 'You ever looked at your own? It might have something about your parents in it.'

I squirmed in my chair. 'The files are in a password-protected folder. Dennis is the one in charge of retrieving them for me.'

'Bet you could just bat your eyelashes at him though, he still has the hots for you.'

'He's a dick!' I exclaimed.

I'm not proud of it, but I managed to shift the conversation onto the topic of my non-existent love life. Merindah duly played along, but I noticed her gaze remained furtive for the rest of her visit.

I never told her that I had done exactly as she'd suggested. I'd asked Dennis to give me my own file. And I'd read the words. Seen the painful truth.

My mother hadn't wanted to keep me.

***

Six months after I missed out on a free doughnut

Allowing myself to sink into the soft, plush mattress and trying not to imagine the demons who'd slept on it before me, I finally checked my phone. The battery was completely drained, thanks to PercApption and WatchDog, but someone had handily left out several chargers, one of which matched my model. I stabbed the cable into my phone while I cased out the rest of the room. There was a second door (presumably leading to an ensuite), a bedside table, one lamp in the corner, and a small, filthy window.

Outside, lights were winking on and people were pouring into The Rocks, seeking some after-hours entertainment. I've never been the type to wine and dine, but I envied the normals for being able to sit down without worrying about motherfucking demons turning up to add them to the dinner menu.

With Fido curled into a ball beside me and my phone now lit up beneath my fingers, I started flicking through my messages. Most of them were from Merindah, though I quickly deleted the 'u ok?!' text from one Dennis Chan who had no doubt gleaned my contact details from my personnel file. Dick. Why couldn't MC have given him a job upstairs, away from me? I didn't think his powers were bad enough to warrant a position on the first floor.

There was nothing from Mackenzie Roberts, my former (and much preferred) boss. She might have changed her phone number or maybe she'd been too busy to check her voicemail. I allowed myself to hope that there was mayhem going on at Magic Corp. If Hellhounds were attacking all human magic-users instead of one Jen Cooke, that would mean MC *wasn't* after me, that we were all in danger, and I was staying with the demons for no good reason...

Or maybe she hadn't returned my call because Magic Corp wanted me dead.

I quickly shoved that disturbing thought away and selected Merindah's name in my contact list. It only took one ring for her to pick up. Except she didn't say anything at first, so I had no idea if she was actually listening.

'Yellow?' I tried.

'I think we're beyond "yellow", Jen,' Merindah said. 'Today's colour is no longer grey. It's shit brown.'

I closed my eyes and flopped down onto Fido, who gave a world-weary sigh before rearranging himself to make sure we were both comfortable. He was even softer than the bed.

'Merindah,' I breathed. 'I'm alive.'

'Oh good, I can kill you myself then,' Merindah said.

My eyes snapped open. 'I'm fired for real?'

'No! And anyway, I wouldn't go through with it. You know that.' She made an aggravated sound. 'Where are you? What the hell happened? One second we're fighting sloshers, the next I'm

85

waking up to Mackenzie Roberts standing over me. She got there pretty fast. Guess she does check her voicemail sometimes.'

I groaned and pressed my palm to my forehead. I didn't have a temperature, unfortunately—God, it'd be a lot easier if the past few hours had been a harmless, fever-induced dream. 'I was rescued. I think.'

'You think.'

'I'm okay, aren't I?' I fired back. 'Did Mack say anything?'

'She wants you to get into contact with her,' Merindah said slowly, cautiously.

'You don't think I should.'

There was a tickle in my auditory canal: *laughter*. 'For someone who reckons they don't have Perception, you're pretty good at reading minds.'

'Merindah!'

My exasperation stirred Fido who lifted his head and gave a loud bark.

'What was that?' Merindah asked.

'My WatchDog. He hasn't disappeared yet.'

'*What?* That's not how it—'

'No time to explain,' I interrupted. 'Just tell me what's going on at your end.'

'Jen, I haven't been able to get a look at the Kill Register,' Merindah told me. 'And I tried calling my boss, but Mike won't tell me anything. Maybe because I'm on sick leave. Or maybe it's because he knows I'd rather kill the whole squad than kill you. Good thing he doesn't know the half of it.'

'The half of what?'

Her voice dropped to a whisper. 'I can protect you, Jen. Just like I've done for the others.'

'The others?' I was starting to sound like a parrot.

'You know how I get sent out? By myself?' Merindah paused. 'I haven't killed anyone for Magic Corp since before I got sent to the Darwin outpost.'

I sat up, the edges of the phone digging into my palm. 'But...'

The words exploded out of her, as though she'd kept them locked up tight for far too long (which she had, really). 'I've been hiding them, the contract-breakers. It's MC's own stupid fault they took my word for it when I said I'd disposed of my targets.'

Jesus Christ, she was in even worse trouble than me.

'Shit,' I said. 'Shit. Merindah, what the *hell?*'

She kept talking over me, going on about how she'd formed a rural sanctuary somewhere, so that the people she'd saved could live in peace, without Magic Corp dictating their lives. And I should get there, somehow, and live with them.

But how long would I be safe if I did go? Up until the moment MC decided to send their scouts to a place near where Merindah was keeping everyone? Those scouts could pick up a single adolescent magic-user if they looked in the right spot—a whole group of trained adults would be far easier to locate.

'You gonna dob me in?' Merindah asked, an edge to her voice.

'Of course not!' I exclaimed, wounded. 'It's just that getting out of Sydney is a little impossible for me right now. I'm safe where I am. I think.'

'Where are you, Jen? I can come get you.'

Something very heavy and very solid hit the door to the living room.

Fido flew off the bed and put himself between me and danger, growling. My chest tightened. I croaked in fear.

'Jen? Jen!' Merindah kept calling my name. But what could she

87

do? If she was at her apartment, she'd be all the way over in Epping.

Yeah, I was on my own again. Unless you count the magical dog.

Oh God.

12

I shouted a hasty goodbye to Merindah and ended the call.

Time to adult!

I debated using WatchDog, but then I remembered who had actually made it. Guessing that the app wouldn't be much use against anyone with Persuasion, I dropped my phone onto the bedside table, where it continued to charge. I'd have to rely on Fido. His teeth had started growing out of his jaw again and he wasn't acting like any dog or Hellhound I'd ever seen, but I'd take what I could get.

When I reefed open the door, I saw a woman lying on the carpet and wearing a dazed expression. I looked up quickly, preparing to dodge if I had to, but then I saw the victor with his hands raised above his head. He was the beefy demon who hadn't been terribly welcoming earlier—Saul was his name, I remembered. He had such a large neck that his small face didn't seem quite right. He could have been a rugby player in his spare time, when he wasn't doing demonic stuff.

Saul's next challenger stepped forward. It was Simon, barefoot, his arms loose by his sides.

A chill started creeping its way up my spine.

Since it wasn't likely that they were using Portal to spar against each other, the weapon of choice would have to be Persuasion. Simon had inferred that people with Persuasion could fight back against someone using that power on them, but I hadn't given much thought to how it would work. I suspected the winner would be whoever managed to invade the mind of their opponent first.

Simon didn't twitch or stir, just kept staring straight ahead. Saul eclipsed him in both size and height—and it occurred to me that the crowd swelling behind Saul was backing him in more ways than one.

There was tension in Dot's face when she caught my gaze from across the room.

I got the message. This was more than a friendly match. This was about what had happened earlier, when Simon had revealed that he wanted to protect humans as well. Now he was going to have to prove that he was still worthy of his people's leadership.

I really hoped he won.

Fido nipped my thigh, trying to force me back through the doorway. I shooed him, entranced by the scene in front of me.

'BEGIN!' Dot shouted.

Simon's blue eyes deepened, becoming so glacial and beautiful that I made myself look away in case I fell victim to his powers. Saul's eyes were dull silver, as though they were expensive spoons that definitely should not have ended up in the dishwasher. He was smiling and showing teeth, apparently unworried.

But barely a handful of seconds later, that confidence was gone, and beads of sweat started to slide down Saul's cheeks. He cursed. His supporters shouted frantic encouragement, egging him on, demanding that Saul end it. I glanced at Simon. He wasn't smiling or grimacing—his face was entirely blank.

Then his eyebrows snapped together and the man opposite him crumpled to the ground.

I expected something more violent. Evidently so did the demons, because they called out, telling Simon to Persuade Saul to throw himself against the wall, the way the larger demon had done to the previous challenger. I winced and looked aside at the woman in question, who was slowly rousing. I held out my hand; she took it.

Once she was steady on her feet, she said with a frown, 'You didn't have to help me up. I wasn't Persuading you.'

I tried not to roll my eyes. 'I did it because I wanted to—and because it was the right thing to do. Something you demons know nothing about.' I could see I was losing her attention so I quickly asked, 'Did that hurt?'

'Yes. Saul is very powerful.' She smiled at Simon, who was now instructing everyone to direct their anger towards Magic Corp instead of their own brethren. 'And though no one's beaten Simon yet, that's not the only reason I follow him.'

She licked her lips appreciatively. Anxiety twisted inside my stomach. I'd hoped for a better reason than lust for her to be supporting Simon. If I could choose who took down Magic Corp (some choice!), it was the demon who seemed to have a soft spot for humans. Not that Saul guy, obviously.

When a new challenger stood opposite Simon, boldly claiming they'd buy drinks for everyone if they lost, I decided I'd had enough and let Fido lead me back into the bedroom.

Simon's laughter followed me. 'You can try, Queran! There's a reason no one's yet to supplant me!'

'Your own arrogance will supplant you!' his opponent retorted.

I shut the door and kept my back to it, breathing slowly. Fido trotted over to the bed and whuffed impatiently when I didn't immediately follow him. Sighing, I trailed after my magical pet.

Persuasion definitely looked demonic to me. It made people throw themselves against walls. And it could make someone *willingly* get into a car with their kidnapper.

I could understand why Magic Corp would want to execute someone if they started exhibiting that kind of power. But wouldn't they prefer to keep that person alive so they could study Persuasion? Understand it? Know how to defend against demonic attacks of that nature?

Someone needed to convince Magic Corp that it might be in their best interests to keep their hybrids alive.

I snorted. 'And who'll that be? You, Jen Cooke?'

I found a set of pyjamas—shorts and a button-up top—folded neatly inside the top drawer of the bedside table. The silky fabric featured tiny yellow stars set on a black background. Not really my style, but my pants, apart from missing as many chunks as Fido, were uncomfortable to sleep in. My favourite shirt, also a casualty of the day's events, was bordering on indecent so that had to go as well.

Once I was clad in the pyjamas, I buried my face in a pillow while Fido stretched out beside me. Drowsiness started creeping in, but I jerked my head back up, frowning.

How did I know I was there of my own free will? I couldn't even trust Fido; he had run off to bring a damn demon to my very doorstep. Swallowing nervously, I sidled away from my magical dog until I was poised on the edge of the bed. From there I could reach my phone; I used it to leave yet another voicemail for Mackenzie Roberts.

Later, I would wish that I hadn't rung her, but at the time I didn't feel like I had a lot of options. There was no way I was staying at Demon HQ, among killers who were barely kept in check by their leader, and nor was I going to risk my hide by trying to stumble my way to Merindah's secret commune. Merindah was good, but even she couldn't hold her own against the entire Kill Squad.

I wasn't fired yet. I could still make Magic Corp see that I only had one P, not two of them, and definitely not the wrong P either. And since human magic-users couldn't form Portals or Persuade creatures to jump through them, I figured I knew which camp was more likely to have sent that Hellhound after me.

So I told Mack where I was.

13

I dreamed of whirling vortexes, edged with charcoal and filled in with fire. A man stood in front of the Portals, their creator and my tormentor. He was a shadow, a faceless figure, but the voice that shouted my name was so familiar, even though I'd never heard it before in my life. His fingers came towards me, intent on clawing into my forehead and cracking my skull apart.

'No, no!' I cried.

But how do you fight a demon whose greatest weapon is his ability to rob you of your will?

The growling woke me before the splitting headache could.

Blinking against the gloom, I could just make out Fido on the floor beside me, his silent snarl aimed at the window. He wasn't the one making the noise. The Hellhounds outside, however...

Fear surged from head to toe and back again. I imagined the creatures circling the building, lunging at weak spots, barging their way in through the door before tearing into my flesh. But I couldn't fight, I couldn't run—my skin was burning and my insides were frozen solid. I gripped the sheets inside my fists, mouth bobbing open and shut, unable to scream.

Then I felt something on my hands; Fido's hot breath, slowly unsticking my fingers and parting them, helping me let go of the sheets. Suddenly able to move, I jumped out of bed, grabbed my phone off the charger, and headed for the grimy window. I couldn't see the Hellhounds, but I could hear them.

Hell, I could even smell them.

A heavy body smacked hard against the outside wall. I held my breath, waiting, tensing. Then it happened again and I figured there wasn't any point in asphyxiating myself. I sucked in and spat out several short, shallow breaths.

Simon had boasted about having some sort of device that kept Hellcreatures and magic-users from locating him and his people, but he clearly wasn't as good as everyone in Tech thought he was.

The Hellhounds had found me. But I wasn't going to stand by and let them gut me. At least, I'd *try* not to let them gut me. Um.

I set the phone against the windowsill, PercApption activated. It buzzed continuously so I knew the beasts were converging in one area—beneath the window, of course. I wondered when they'd figure out how to make a literal dogpile and reach my eye level, not that I'd be able to see them.

I lifted one hand and pressed it against the glass, summoning what power I could from the core inside me. The window darkened slightly, as though someone had given it a light tinting job, and then my Physical surged away from the building, forming criss-crossing lines as it went. I dropped my net-shaped construct, hoped I'd managed to catch something, and cinched the cords tight. I wanted the net to draw blood.

'Die, motherfucker,' I whispered.

Of course it didn't.

My pathetic net had probably just pissed it off.

There was a brief silence, as if the Hellhounds were clustered together, trying to decide how best to get at me. Then the growling started up again. I tried not to panic, even though I had already used up most of my power reserves.

Fido leapt past me and headbutted the wall until my phone fell off the windowsill. Cursing, I knelt down to rescue it from the carpet and saw that WatchDog was now activated instead of PercApption. My strange pet didn't exactly have fingers, but I wouldn't put it past him to have some weird ability to mess with my phone.

I stared at Fido, who seemed to be waiting for me to praise him. 'What? This is useless to me. It just makes a Portal. And I really don't want a demon-controlled Hellhound in here right now.'

Fido latched onto my arm, his teeth firm but not tearing, and yanked me down. My palm collided with the screen of my phone.

And then an almighty blast of power rocketed through me.

'Holy *shit!*' I reared back, slamming into the bedside table behind me.

I saw billions of stars, those tiny pinpricks of light swiftly growing into one solid white mass that blinded me for precious seconds. When my vision finally cleared, I knew I could smash the Hellhounds, all of them, and leave their broken corpses littered across the footpath. I swayed, confused and disoriented.

Sense smacked into me when the next beast threw itself at the wall. I hurtled over to the window, somewhat unbothered by the searing heat in my left hand as the phone again took root. I didn't care about this insignificant discomfort because my veins were on *fire* and if I didn't channel this power into magic immediately, I was going to explode.

My right hand formed a fist and I drove my knuckles into the windowsill, sharp shocks shooting up into my wrist. Swearing loudly, I smashed the windowsill again and again, knowing that a giant replica of my fist was copying the exact same motion outside. I could easily picture bones snapping, pelts splitting, skulls shattering.

And then—silence. This time it lasted.

Uncontrollable shivers took hold of my body, forcing me to lean against the wall.

Fido flopped down onto the floor and released a heavy whuff of relief. I couldn't manage one of my own because it felt like my limbs were being dragged down into the harbour and my heart was still frantically spasming inside my chest. I wobbled over to the bedside table and managed to plug my phone in, then clapped a hand over my mouth, trying not to retch.

The door banged open and Simon charged in, flinging questions at me.

I pointed at the window. 'Look.'

He did, then turned quizzical eyes back onto me. I belatedly remembered that he couldn't Perceive Hellcreatures either. So I told him everything—okay, except the part about the app somehow boosting my Physical, because I didn't want the demons knowing I was defenceless the moment they took my phone off me. No, thank you.

Simon's expression darkened. I wasn't sure if this made him look scary or sexy—or both.

'The nullifying field should have stopped the normals noticing the fight,' he said. 'But it's supposed to stop the Hellhounds from finding us in the first place...' His voice roughened. 'Are you alright?'

It was then I realised he was only wearing baggy trackpants—black, of course. I don't think I'd ever seen him wear a different colour. His feet were bare and likewise was the hair-dusted torso that revealed he still found time, in between working for *and* plotting against Magic Corp, to hit the gym.

'Oh well, I didn't see anything so it wasn't that bad,' I said, attempting a shrug. Then, to my horror, I began to cry.

Simon left swiftly after that. I couldn't really blame him—I wouldn't have wanted to stay with a mess like me either. I sought sanctuary in the ensuite and splashed water onto my face, but the puffy eyes and splotchy cheeks decided to stick around.

Massaging my temples, I re-entered the bedroom. I could hear some people chatting on the footpath outside, probably heading home from one pub or another. I was pretty sure that if they'd seen something concerning, they would have screamed and called the police.

I drew up short when I saw that Simon was back and sitting on the bed. He'd turned the lamp on at some point so it was throwing soft light over his features.

'I checked on the nullifying devices,' he said, his cheeks so tight they barely moved. 'They're still working. No one should be able to sense any magic here—I don't know what tipped Magic Corp off. I'm sorry, Jen. I promised you'd be safe. And I failed you.'

Fido planted himself in front of the window. Clearly, he had decided that the danger lay outside rather than in the room with me. I eyed Simon, not quite agreeing with my pet, but the demon didn't seem to be doing anything untoward. Or at least I hoped he wasn't. He could have been using his powers.

Shit. How could I tell?

I held back the hiccup but it escaped me anyway, making my shoulders jump. 'Damn it. I'm wrung out. No wonder Magic Corp stuck on me on the first floor. I'm utterly useless if I can't last more than a couple of minutes in a fight.'

'You dealt with at least nine of the creatures with relatively little effort,' Simon pointed out, tipping his chin towards the window. 'We can't be sure of the exact number, but that's our best estimate. The bodies will disintegrate in a few hours so all we'll have to deal with is the blood. The pavement will reek of bleach for a while, but I don't think the non-magical humans will find that too suspicious, even if the nullifying field fails.'

Nine? I thought in shock. I was having a hard time focusing on anything but that.

Simon must have opened the window because a gust of fresh air blasted across my face. Grateful, I gulped in some oxygen and sank onto the bed beside him. I could already feel strength slowly dribbling back into my core.

'Apparently I'm recovering,' I said, then winced. 'Apart from the headache, anyway. But slinging around so much power took a lot out of me. And I don't have the proper training. Magic Corp never bothered to teach me.'

'I don't know how they overlooked your talent,' Simon said, frowning. 'People in the Kill Squad can't even do that. I've seen them.'

I'd never seen Merindah manage it either—but shit, I'd never seen any signs of her little side venture either. If I didn't know the true extent of her powers, then how the hell was I supposed to know what else she had going on her life?

I narrowed my eyes at Fido. The dog had made me use my phone, which had provided a massive wellspring of power—not for the first time that day, I might add. But I wasn't so sure I wanted to keep tapping into WatchDog to amp up my Physical if it made me feel like *that*. Not just exhausted, but physically ill, knowing I'd caused the destruction outside. I could just as easily do that to people. And I'd have to, if Magic Corp came after me. I didn't want to paint the pavement with my own blood.

Fido nuzzled up alongside me. I ran my fingers through his fur, plucking at loose strands. It looked like I was pulling yarn off a seamless blob.

'It gets easier,' Simon said.

I snorted in disbelief. 'What? Using my powers? Or killing living things?'

He sighed deeply. 'Having to kill, having to lie to everyone at MC, having to Persuade all of you to think you know me is...necessary. I do it because I want to help you and people like you. I want to make sure that Magic Corp doesn't hurt anyone else.'

'Ends and the means and all that,' I said sourly, thinking of all the hilarious anecdotes I'd heard about Simon at that party three years ago. How many of those had been real?

'Exactly,' Simon replied. 'You'll need to accept that if you choose to stay here. And I hope you do. You belong with us, Jen.'

I howled with laughter. Apparently this offended Fido because he jerked away from me, gave a baleful yip, and leapt towards the window. He shrank in midair and landed lightly on the windowsill. A short whuff later, he started marching along it like an oversized bull ant.

I shook my head, annoyed. 'Simon. I don't fit in at Magic Corp and I sure as hell don't fit in here with you lot. I don't *belong* anywhere.'

'Yes, you do,' Simon said quietly, his hands hovering between us.

I watched his fingers warily, not sure what he meant to do with them, but then he wrapped them around my trembling ones. The gentle pressure of his touch sent a calming wave through me, until my body gave one last shudder and went still.

I leaned against him, muttering, 'Seems like you need to keep me around to deal with all the demonic creatures you can't fool into looking away from you.'

'We do lack Physical abilities,' Simon agreed. 'If Persuasion fails, we retreat by Portalling out. It's not a particularly offensive strategy, so I can understand why some of us have resorted to more violent means overseas.'

I hesitated, then decided to get it over with. 'I think I've seen Portals before.'

Simon nodded. 'Yes, I watched the videos of what happened at the train station, though how Magic Corp got a Portal working worries me...'

'Yeah no, I'm still not convinced it's MC behind all this. And that's not what I was referring to, anyway. Listen, I had a dream and I want to be sure it's just that, and not—not—'

'A memory?' Simon suggested.

It was hard to be afraid of him when he was giving me such a gentle, understanding look. He seemed much less like a demon now—and a lot more like an eternally patient IT professional who had to deal with people who couldn't find the power button on their computer towers.

I blew out a breath. 'Okay. In my dream, I saw those Fiery Vortex Things. Portals. Whatever. And there was someone standing in front of them. He was saying my name.'

'Fiery Vortex Thing is as good a description as any,' Simon remarked.

I made a face at him and would have said something sarcastic, except that I was suddenly awash with deja vu. Fiery Vortex

Things. I'd called the Portals that a lot, hadn't I? Long ago. Long before a Hellhound had tracked me down on the train. Somehow, I *knew* this.

'Ah,' I said, resting my palm against my forehead. 'Damn it, that hurts.'

Simon pursed his lips thoughtfully. 'It could be that today's events have stimulated the memories behind the block on your mind. You might not agree with me about Magic Corp being involved in these attempts on your life, but you can trust me on this. I can remove the block.'

'And if there's no block or anything behind it?' I challenged.

He shrugged. 'Then I'll drop the matter and go get you some Panadol for that headache.'

I looked down into my lap, then at the carpet that lay beyond it. 'I wish I wasn't stupid enough to consider this.'

'Why?' Simon asked, a smile tainting his words. 'Afraid you'll find out you really do have demonic blood? Afraid that if I'm right about this, it will prove that Magic Corp really is after you?'

'It wouldn't mean you're right about everything,' I groused. 'And how do I know that what I'm seeing is real? You could just Persuade me to see whatever you want me to.'

'I wouldn't. I'm not like that.'

'None of us MCers really know what you're like, do we?'

The smile slipped from Simon's face. It was a wonder I didn't hear it splatter on the floor. 'I guess I deserved that. But please, Jen. Let me help you.'

Him being bare-chested had absolutely no bearing on what I said next. 'Okay. I'll let you into my head, but you're not going to find anything.'

'Are you trying to convince me, Jen,' he said softly, 'or yourself?'

I turned to the dog-shaped figure on the windowsill. 'If he tries something he shouldn't, you tear off one of his legs, okay?'

A minute bark of confirmation. Simon raised his eyebrows.

'Simon!' I snapped. 'Give me a fucking break. I'm in enemy territory here and all I have for protection is the equivalent of a rabid Border Collie.'

Simon dutifully gave me an apology before he went silent, his eyes whirling as he began to concentrate. When I felt the first touch of Something So Not Right in my head, I jerked backwards. I couldn't go through with this. Not when he could damage my mind beyond repair, the way I'd seen it done to...someone. Someone I couldn't remember.

'No,' I said with more vehemence than I had ever used or felt before.

Fido made a small growl that sounded closer to a squeak.

Simon's gaze softened. 'I won't proceed unless you want me to.'

It felt like tentacles were writhing around inside my gut. I wanted answers. But I also wanted to run far, far away.

'Fido, it's okay, everything's fine,' I lied. 'Simon? Do it.'

He did nothing at first. Just watched me carefully, giving me one last chance to back out. I gave him an emphatic nod.

And then a demon slid into my mind.

14

Last flashback, I swear. This one's important so pay attention.

Thirteen years before Simon removed the block on my mind, Magic Corp took me from my family. I can't believe I went so long without remembering it.

'There's ten of them!' That was my father; I'd know his voice anywhere. He was never angry, never scared. But today he was both. 'I can't use Persuasion on that many—and even if I try, they'll know what I am! What *she* is!'

Tears poured down my cheeks. We could have tried to run, but anywhere we went they'd soon find us. Once a scout latched onto our magic, they could track us endlessly across the country.

He turned to Mum first. Her brown eyes, so much like the ones I saw in the mirror, narrowed and grew hard. I shared most of my features with her, a blessing considering my fate, though my nose was a little less hook-shaped. But I hadn't inherited anyone's courage or strength.

Mum hesitated, a small spiked ball shivering in the palm of her hand. Her Physical wasn't strong enough to defend us, and wielding it against her former colleagues would only endanger me.

I knew it was all my fault.

I existed and therefore I made it impossible for them to be happy. I was the reason they had to stay up late, talking in hushed voices about what they could do to protect me. Even though I was only eight years old, I wanted to protect *them*. It wasn't fair, what I was putting them through. I'd never said this out loud, but Mum had seen it in my mind enough times. She'd kept trying to talk to me about it.

I would just run away from her, my feet tossing up sand on the nearby beach. I was gone for so long when I did this that it must have worried my parents. They never chased me. I guess their guilt was as bad as mine, because when I came home there would be apologies and my favourite dinosaur-shaped chicken nuggets for dinner.

I didn't need Perception to know how much of a burden I was.

'We have to make sure they take her in instead of killing her outright,' Dad said. 'We can't present them with any kind of threat.'

Mum closed her fist, relinquishing her hold on her powers. She gave a small nod. 'I understand.'

They kissed. It wasn't the sweet peck I was used to seeing. It was a deep, passionate kiss that spoke of longing and farewell. Dad pulled away and Mum crumpled to the ground, her eyes glassy. She kept murmuring my name, but then her lips stilled and when she refocused on me there was only confusion in her gaze.

I knew, I *knew*, I was lost to her. Dad had erased her memories.

She couldn't go through Portals. She had two Ps, the right kind, but her husband had the wrong kind, the kind that had made her hide her marriage and rip up her contract.

'I don't wanna go with them!' I shouted as Dad's Fiery Vortex Thing burst into being. 'I wanna go with you!'

Along with colourful children's books featuring magical puddings and possums, the tales of Magic Corp's cruelty had formed my bedtime stories. They were the bogeymen that lived beneath my bed with their hands stretched out, always trying to grab my ankles and pull me down into darkness. I had only just managed to stop leaping onto the bed the week before. I liked to think I had conquered my fear, but my heart still quivered every time I walked into my bedroom.

Agony was etched into my father's face. He didn't look like a demon, the word that branded him. He was blond and fair, one of God's angels, but to Magic Corp he was closer to the Devil. I was angry, angry that he couldn't reassure me, angry that he couldn't make it go away. He wasn't even *trying* to pretend that things would be alright.

'I don't know if you can survive a Portal,' he said, moving steadily towards me. 'You'll be safer with them, but only if they don't know what you are. We can't let them read it from you.'

I backed away and hit the kitchen counter, but he kept advancing, determination overwriting his desperation. Even my tears couldn't stop him.

I'd manifested my Physical abilities really early, way before the usual age, and Mum had been so proud. But even though she knew who her husband was, what he was, she'd still had that sad look on her face when I'd failed to see the Hellhound that she could.

I remembered my father sitting me down one night for a Persuasion lesson. He'd found his way into my head within seconds and then he'd just as quickly withdrawn, disappointment clouding his eyes. But there had still been hope, that I would have that other ability, the one that would help me run away and hide with him in the other realm while Mum stayed behind. It would be easier and safer for us all, if I'd inherited Portal.

Dad had tried to teach me to create Portals, but he'd had even less success with that than he'd had trying to get me to stop calling them Fiery Vortex Things. And he couldn't bring himself to throw me into one. I'd be torn to pieces if I didn't have the ability to protect myself. It was a risk that my parents had refused to take. I was too special, too precious, and I hated that I was the cause of so much misery and uncertainty.

Dad grabbed my shoulders, pinning me in place. I tried to squirm out of his grasp, but he was too strong.

His eyes, a mixture of blue and green like Earth seen from space, swirled and became so beautiful, so irresistible. I couldn't look away. He was inside my head, sweeping my memories into a shadowy corner, hiding everything that made me *me*.

'No, Daddy, no!' I screamed.

I knew what was happening. I'd seen him do it to one of Mum's colleagues who had accidentally stumbled across us while they'd been on holiday. They'd trotted back to Magic Corp, convinced they hadn't found anything but sunshine and surf. I'd once seen Dad do it to a supermarket manager so we could get a whole trolley load of groceries for free. I'd just seen him do it to my own mother.

And now he was doing it to me.

***

'Jen? Jen!'

A demon's fingers were on my tear-stained face, so close, so terribly close to the skull encasing my vulnerable mind. He was going to erase my memories!

I slammed sideways onto the bed, away from the threat, and fell onto the floor.

'Ouch,' I said.

My hip was a little bruised—but on the plus side, my headache was completely gone. I pulled my knees up to my chin, my shoulders and arms aching from the effort of suppressing my shivers. Fido hadn't come to my rescue, but I suppose he figured I could handle it. That made me feel better somehow.

'Jen?' Simon repeated, kneeling beside me.

He looked so adorably worried and the heat radiating off him was safe and comforting. But he was a demon. I should have been shoving him away or trying to kill him, but how could I justify doing that when I was my father's daughter?

'Do you want to know...?' I asked, snuffling. Attractive. Very attractive.

'Only if you're comfortable with me hearing it,' he said.

It took a shockingly short amount of time to fill him in on the life I'd had before Magic Corp. Simon didn't interrupt. He nodded a few times, made soft exclamations in the appropriate places, but that was it.

Finally, when I was done, I mustered a wobbly smile. 'I *told* you I only have one P. I told you.'

He laughed. It was a good sound, one that drove away the shadows that had been threatening to eat the lamp in the corner. 'That's what you're leading with? Not the fact that you're half demon and your father wiped your memories so Magic Corp would take you in instead of killing you?'

My fingers kept trembling so I squashed them beneath my backside. 'He couldn't take me with him. I wouldn't have survived the trip through the Fiery—Portal. Better for MC to think they'd found a defenceless contract-breaker and a kid to replace her.' I swallowed. 'Mum wasn't in her right mind. That's how they got her to sign me over. And then they...oh Christ, they would have killed her. She died not even knowing who I was.'

Yeah, my personnel file was definitely missing more than a few details. It hadn't even listed her name. But I could remember it now. Lucy? Lucinda? Lucinda Cooke. That was it. That was the name I could put on a gravestone or a park bench one day. I had no idea what the Kill Squad did with the bodies of its victims.

'She died to protect you,' Simon reminded me.

I dissolved into tears again. Not something I'd ever wanted to do in front of Simon Bradley, much less this often—and that was before I'd found out what he was. But it was so hard to remember that he was my enemy, especially when he picked me up like I weighed nothing and cradled me against him.

If this was a nightmare, it was a damn good one.

Simon was still shirtless. His warmth seeped right through my pyjamas and I held in the sigh. He smelled so male. So enticing. And it had been a really long time since I'd been with someone and that 'someone' had been Dennis.

Okay, Dennis hadn't been completely awful—he'd been the only guy at school who'd bothered to talk to the shy girl who couldn't remember her parents, who didn't collect anime trading cards, and who didn't give a shit about cricket or footy. But Dennis had never smelled like this.

Oh, I was in so much trouble.

15

'Do all demons smell as good as you?' I blurted.

Simon's grin deepened as he set me down on the bed. His hand slid to my cheek and his lips parted slightly as they came for mine. I should have stopped him. But I needed...I needed company, and it was a lot easier (and less embarrassing) to let this happen than to ask him to stay simply because I was scared of being alone.

His kisses were tentative and promised a lot more, so I grabbed his shoulders and tried to pull him onto the bed. Simon resisted and reared back, his eyes sparkling as he took me in. I realised I was still wearing the cutesy cloud pyjamas—but not for long, if I had my way. I started unbuttoning my top.

His hands closed over mine, halting my progress. 'Are you sure you're in the right headspace for this?'

I scowled and sat up. 'I want to hump your brains out and you're getting torn up over whether or not I'm in the right *headspace*?'

Frowning, Simon scrubbed the heel of his palm over the bristles on his chin.

Was he...brooding? Sure looked like it.

'I was just inside your mind,' he said, the words reluctantly grating their way out of him. 'Breaking that block could have left bruises on your psyche—and you were crying in my arms not two minutes ago.'

Ignoring the urge to descend into a fresh wave of tears, I studied him closely. He was looking at me like I was the sexiest thing since—well, not sliced bread but you get my meaning. I could also see chagrin and regret lurking in his beautiful blue eyes.

'What are you not saying?' I demanded. 'Because I don't buy that this is just about me.'

I mean, three years ago I might have thought it was—it had to be the extra weight, the timidness, the inappropriate comments, *something*. But I wasn't reading this wrong. He had the hots for me.

'I don't want to put you in a position where...where you can't consent.' Simon pressed his lips together for a moment. 'It's not unheard of for demons to lose control of their powers. We can end up using Persuasion without meaning to.'

Disbelief moulded the glare I gave him. 'Not to be judgemental or anything, but at your age you should probably have better control over your powers.'

Simon scoffed. 'Of course I have control. I can control myself *now*.' His expression darkened. 'But I'm afraid of what I'll do when...when I'm distracted.'

Yikes. It was like being surrounded by the boys at school again. They'd used lust as an excuse for practically everything, from pulling on my hair in class to hurling sexist insults as I crossed the playground. They'd never done it when Merindah was around. She'd have punched them until they said sorry. I could never do what she did. Too afraid of the consequences, of drawing attention—especially from our teachers. Because they might have discovered my secret.

Something on my face must have shown my scepticism because Simon's gaze hardened. 'I've been with women before, but how can I be sure I did right by them? I'm a lot stronger than most demons; I might have overpowered my partners without realising it. In the end, I couldn't stand the thought that some of them might be questioning what they'd done. This is part of why I didn't take it any further in the men's bathroom that time.'

He swallowed lengthily. I watched his throat, somewhat hypnotised by the movement of his Adam's apple. When he spoke again, there was a playful note running through his words. 'What about you? Any regrets of your own? Dennis Chan, for instance?'

He was changing the topic with the grace of a bull rampaging through Victoria's Basement, but I couldn't help it. I laughed. 'Of course you heard about that. Who hasn't? Dennis told practically everyone about it afterwards.'

'So it's true, you and Dennis'—Simon shook his head, as though he couldn't quite believe it—'the human who has six pairs of limited-edition Nikes lined up on his desk at work?'

The memory of those shoes neatly stacked around Dennis' workspace made me laugh even harder. 'Yeah, what a loser. I'm surprised MC hasn't tossed *him* out.'

'He has both Perception and Physical, a combination that guarantees him a permanent position at Magic Corp,' Simon said as he stood and put some distance between us. Well, if anyone would know what powers my colleagues had, it was the demon who was sneaking around and giving magical apps to anyone who looked nervous. 'But they might get rid of him when they realise he never shuts up about his access to the personnel files. Made it easy to know who to Persuade to put mine in there. And no one's ever questioned my false details.'

I caught my startled cough in my hand. 'Shit, we're in trouble if it's that easy to get into our files.'

'Magic Corp—or whoever your attacker is—will come after you again, now that they know where you are,' Simon told me, politely ignoring the fact that I'd said 'our' and meant Magic Corp instead of his Band of Merry Demons. He drew the doona over me. 'You should get some rest before that happens.'

'I'll get right on that, Boss,' I said. 'Totally easy, now that I know you demons are *so good* at protecting me.'

He shook his head and left without another word. He didn't turn the lamp off, which was a little aggravating because it meant I had to leave the safety and warmth of the bed to do it myself. I contemplated the lamp from afar, wishing it had one of those dim energy-saving bulbs. Unfortunately, it had one that was round and bright, a menace to society.

I tried whispering my request to Fido, who immediately stopped pacing on the windowsill and performed a judgemental head tilt. Then he shook his head, whuffing for good measure. He stayed put.

'Some help you are,' I snapped.

Rugging myself up in the doona, I hopped across the floor, cursing everyone in the entire universe for making this the worst day of my life. I'd just touched the switch on the lamp when I looked back at the bedside table and caught sight of my phone. I quickly shed the doona and grabbed the device.

I'd received three messages from my former boss, Mackenzie Roberts.

We should meet.

Royal Botanic Garden.

One hour.

Before I'd let Simon dig around inside my head, I would have said yes immediately. Now, though? Suspicion made me pause. Magic Corp didn't have anyone who could make Portals of Doom, but they did have Hellhounds in a pen on the roof of HQ—and it seemed awfully convenient that a bunch of Hellhounds had turned up right after I'd told Mack where I was. I hadn't mentioned any of this to Simon. For obvious reasons.

I shook my head and texted back three messages of my own.

Nope!

Don't want to get mauled by Hellhounds on my way there.

Thanks for the visitors, by the way. Not.

I grimaced when I realised that I'd fallen back into using proper sentences with full stops (Mack had insisted that all of her inferiors do this when contacting her—and shortening her name was banned, as were emojis).

Aren't the gardens shut this late anyway? I added.

Mack's response was lightning fast. *You're in danger no matter where you are. No more excuses.*

She hadn't denied that the Hellhounds had been sent by Magic Corp, which wasn't reassuring. At all. I bit my lip. Was I in danger because of my demonic parentage? Shit, I hoped no one knew. If I could just keep the Big Bad Secret to myself...uh oh, what if she *did* know? Had she heard about my failure during the annual Perception test?

My thumb hovered over the keys displayed on the screen. I debated blocking her or even smashing my phone to pieces, so that no one else could contact me and trick me into revealing where I was.

But then more lines of text appeared. *Jennifer, I could have gone to the front lines with my Physical if I'd wanted to. My magic is that strong.*

I can keep you safe.

Just get your arse down here.

And like the idiot I was, I obeyed her.

16

My hatred of the Royal Botanic Garden goes back to a Christmas work party that was held down near Mrs Macquarie's Chair (a nice bit of convict masonry erected for Governor Macquarie's wife back in the day—okay, I forget I'm the only one who finds this stuff interesting).

The gardens had been open when I'd ambled through there before sunset and since it was the quickest route from Circular Quay station, I'd decided to reuse it for the return journey. Unfortunately, when I'd left the party the gardens had been closed, blocking the shore-hugging route that bent towards the Sydney Opera House. I'd had to fumble my way along a much longer path in The Domain instead.

Not the worst outcome, but The Royal Botanic Garden Incident had left me with a lingering dislike of the area.

Anyway, on the night I went to meet Mackenzie Roberts, I used my Physical to get inside the gardens—because this time there *was* a worst outcome. I shook out my hands and envisioned the steel ladder we had in the storage closet on the first floor back at Magic Corp. So that's what I got, along with a sickening rocking motion as I climbed my construct—it's not like I had someone to hold it steady for me.

I managed to leap off the top of the barred gate barely a second before my ladder misted away behind me. Whew. Once I'd started breathing normally again, I jogged around a bit (the gardens are freaking huge) and kept low to avoid the gazes of any security guards hunting for drunks who'd fallen asleep before the gates had shut.

I wasn't alone—I'm not that stupid! Travel-size Fido was stashed in my pocket and I had my phone out, thumb poised over WatchDog. I couldn't figure out why the app gave me so much power, but I sure as hell was going to take advantage of it.

The gardens were an eerie place at night. Weird shadows aside, the gentle rustling of leaves was punctuated by the ghostly honks of ferries coasting past Fort Denison in the harbour. I slowed to a walk as I neared the water. I had no idea where Mack wanted to meet, but I could lead her straight to me by focusing on my surroundings and letting her Perception pick up on these images. So I did this, staying hidden among some orchids. They had a very pungent smell and I was close to sneezing—alerting who knows what to my presence—when I heard Mack's prim faux-English accent.

'Stop skulking over there and come sit down,' she ordered.

I obeyed without hesitation. The grass was wet and I couldn't help but shudder when my worse-for-wear work pants met the ground. Even though the starry pyjamas had fewer holes in them, I couldn't exactly have turned up in those. Mack had always insisted on her admin underlings presenting themselves to her in a professional manner, but her saving grace had been her adherence to a paper trail. Everything we were expected to do was broadcast in blessed emails, not in her mind. She always wanted to make sure we knew who to blame if something went wrong.

I guess that's why she'd been chosen as our liaison to the government.

The filthy TOMS slippers I couldn't do much about. I had dainty size fives (forget the price tags—this was the real reason it was difficult for me to get the cool shoes that everyone else on the first floor squeaked around in) and I'd only been able to find men's size eights back at Demon HQ. I assumed those shoes were Simon's, because they were Adidas—the typical black-and-white kind, but still stylish—and the other demons I'd seen didn't wear anything remotely branded. Clearly, Simon could make fun of Dennis' love of sneaker culture while dabbling a bit himself.

At least I'd located a fresh shirt. It had a unisex cut so it was long and loose, but I figured the extra room wouldn't hurt if I had to fight off a bunch of Hellcreatures. Naturally, the shirt was black. I was starting to wonder if colour could actually harm demons.

Mack wasn't the type to sit straight on the grass. She threw down an old towel covered in a fine dusting of dog hair. She only had two dogs, both of them cute poodles that weren't supposed to shed as much, but even someone as meticulous Mack couldn't completely erase the evidence of their existence.

She lowered herself gracefully onto the towel, looking as though she was seated on an inclinator, and kept her knees perfectly in line with the heels of her calf-length leather boots. I couldn't see any obvious logos, but I suspected they were from Diana Ferrari; she bought most of her workday dresses there. That night she was wearing a stylish khaki jumpsuit, something I'd never seen on her before.

I suppose this was her version of slumming it.

'Why didn't you tell me you don't have Perception, Jennifer?' she demanded.

I realised I was sitting cross-legged, like a child at school, and immediately adjusted my position. I made sure my grip on my phone didn't slacken, though. 'And risk getting suspended? Or worse—*fired*, with Hellhounds trying to use me as a chew toy?'

Moonlit shadows stretched over Mack's face. 'Magic Corp does not send Hellhounds after contract-breakers.'

'Well, someone's trying to kill me!' I cried. 'What about my new boss—Tom Chapman. He's never liked me.' Mack raised her eyebrows. I hesitated, momentarily thrown by her obvious disapproval that this was my only evidence against Tom. Then I crossed my fingers behind my back and decided to take a gamble. 'But I'm guessing he's not important enough to know all of MC's secrets. He doesn't know there's four Ps, does he?'

There was a careful pause. 'You have demonic heritage.'

It was stated coolly, a fact instead of a wild guess. Mack knew *exactly* what my lack of Perception meant.

I focused on Fido's warmth seeping through the lining of my pocket instead of immediately responding. Somehow, I managed to make my voice sound normal. 'So you're confirming that there are more than two Ps and you suspect I might have Persuasion or Portal. Right? Is that what you're saying?'

Again, a lengthy pause, one that allowed me to clearly hear the crowd exiting the Opera House. It was approaching midnight, so their event must have had a decent runtime. I had no idea what was showing there. I felt horribly uncultured.

'Just what have the demons been telling you?' Mack asked, each word as long as an exhale. 'You can't believe anything they say.'

'And I'm supposed to believe *you*?' I demanded, too furious to care that I might be blowing my last chance to get my job back. 'Don't think I didn't notice that those Hellhounds only showed up after I told you where I was. So far the demons have been a whole lot more truthful about all this. I didn't even know they could look like us until today.'

Mack cleared her throat, but in a gentle sort of way that lacked any phlegm. It was a signal for me to shut up and listen.

But I clenched my phone even harder and held it up in front of me, brandishing it like a weapon (which it kind of was). 'Don't try anything. You know how powerful I am now. I took out nine Hellhounds. *By myself.*'

'Very well,' Mack said and started fumbling through the pockets of her jumpsuit. She withdrew a cigarette and popped it into her mouth, but didn't light it. 'Humans and demons have been interbreeding since time immemorial, even before the wingers and sloshers appeared. It was never this rampant, however. Given that we consistently defeat them in battle, the demons decided they'd weaken us by spreading their filth through our bloodlines instead of trying to kill us outright. They're still at it.'

'So you chuck all hybrids onto the Kill Register.' I shook my head. 'Nice.'

Mack gave me a hard stare, impossible to miss even in the dim lighting. 'Better that than risk one killing us all.'

'You could at least give us a chance,' I muttered.

'Hybrids such as you'—Mack jabbed the cigarette towards me—'are abnormal. You do not fit in. It breeds resentment which can be exploited by our enemies. I've read your school reports, Jennifer. You were a security risk even before your true nature was revealed.' Mack frowned heavily, accentuating the lines she'd earned over three decades of dealing with screw-ups like me. 'I have always questioned the higher-ups' decision not to inform the school's careers advisor about the existence of hybrids. She would have picked it up much, much earlier. Before anyone liked you enough to miss you.'

I gritted my teeth. 'I know you want to kill me. I even know why. But you haven't tried for a couple of hours. What gives?'

Mack didn't answer, instead drawing a deep, nicotine-deprived breath. She had been trying patches when she'd still been my boss, but I wondered if she'd fallen off the wagon because of her new job. She'd been dealing with the Minister for Magical Australians and Related Affairs for six months. Usually I wouldn't have dared to challenge her, because she was my superior and should therefore be right about everything (as opposed to the woman who ran around getting coffee and tea for everyone).

But things had changed. And my life was at stake.

I strengthened my voice. 'Don't you think that everyone would be a hell of a lot safer if we knew what powers our enemies had at their disposal? What they actually looked like?'

'Indeed, I have raised this issue with some of the higher-ups,' Mack noted. 'But they are too slow to take my suggestions on board, no matter how sensible.'

Oh man, we were all so screwed. The demons didn't need their elaborate plan of making Magic Corp rely on the apps that would eventually result in their deaths. Simon's people could just walk in and take HQ any time they wanted to. Most people wouldn't even know what they were until too late.

'I can forget the attempted-murder thing,' I said, gnawing on my lip. 'What I really care about is going back to work. I didn't mean for any of this to happen.'

Please take me back, I thought. *I need to renew my* Phantom *subscription.*

I was almost embarrassed that this was one of the first things that had occurred to me.

Almost.

'You would risk your life for something as trivial as a comic book,' Mack mused. 'You can block most of your surface thoughts, Jennifer, but not all of them.'

The trees around us shook and swayed. Wind ghosted over my face. I suddenly felt very nervous. My lack of Perception was bad enough on its own, but if you combined that with a lack of backup...well, shit.

I activated PercApption and my phone's screen lit up my face, turning me into a beacon. I winced, but I figured I'd rather be booted out of the gardens by a security guard than have someone—*something*—sneak up on me. I started roaming the camera over the nearby flora. I did spot one piece of fauna (a rogue feral rabbit), but that was it.

The phone stayed still in my hand. But that didn't fill me with confidence.

There might be a demon lurking nearby, using their powers to Persuade Mack to ignore an approaching Hellhound. They could even make me think my phone wasn't reacting when it was.

I allowed myself to hope that Simon was hiding in the bushes, that he'd seen me sneaking out and had come to my rescue. But he didn't appear.

And I was alone with someone who clearly wanted me dead.

Yeah. This wasn't the best idea I'd ever had.

17

Mack seized my wrist, her gaze locked onto my phone as I scanned the grass. 'How did you get this? The apps are not meant for people like you.'

Admin staff or hybrids? I wondered, wincing as Mac dropped my arm.

I didn't dare think *his* name just then, in case she caught it in my surface thoughts. She'd easily nab him at work and I kind of wanted to give him a head start. I mean, he had saved my life. It seemed only fair.

'I can't say,' I said flatly.

Mackenzie Roberts: Queen of Dramatic Pauses.

I wanted to start screaming at her to get some kind of reaction, but I'd waste precious time doing it, she'd get angry, and then we'd fight. Even with my improved Physical, I was hesitant to take her on. She was good. *Really* good. And she'd had decades of practice. I had wondered, sometimes, why she wasn't a field agent or on the Kill Squad, with magic that strong. Being the Head of Admin had been such a waste of her skills.

I focused on the distant lights on the opposite side of the harbour. I wished that I was on a train headed north across the Harbour Bridge, bound for my humble studio apartment in Mount Kuring-gai and its neighbouring sloshers. No such luck.

'Mack—Mackenzie,' I said, breaking the silence because she

clearly wasn't going to. 'How does Magic Corp control the Hellhounds they're sending out? You can't just show them a photo of someone and hope that's the only person they kill, right?'

'That's none of your business.'

'It is if you guys are still trying to kill me!' I cut myself off, grimacing. 'Please. I don't want to die. I'm on your side—I'll be on your side if you'll just let me.'

'Very well.' Mack straightened and smoothed her hands over her lap, though I didn't see how she could have possibly wrinkled her jumpsuit in the past few minutes. 'I've been authorised to give you an offer.'

My heart started playing my ribs like a xylophone. She was about to wipe away all of the problems I'd been having for the past twelve hours. And I would never have to think about the demons ever again—well, aside from their upcoming hostile takeover, which I'd obviously have to mention to someone...

'Magic Corp is prepared to promote you to field agent, given your sudden prowess with Physical,' Mack began. I perked up—this was even better than I'd hoped. 'And you will be given a new contract to sign, thereby taking you off the Kill Register—'

'How long is it?' I asked before I could stop myself. 'The Kill Register, I mean. And how many of the people on it didn't even realise they had demonic abilities?'

Mack's voice was like a blade of ice, one that cut right into my chest. 'No name stays there for very long, regardless of the infraction.'

Infraction. Yep, being born was my infraction.

'Okay,' I murmured rather than bring this up. I really didn't want Mack to rescind her offer and I doubted she had any sympathy for me.

'As I was *trying* to say, before I was so rudely interrupted...' Mack's tone took on a bite—not quite crocodile-sized, but large enough that I winced. 'These are privileges, not rights, and they must be earned. Especially since we are willing to overlook any demonic qualities you might display in the future.'

'So what's the catch?' I asked. Maybe I'd have to renounce all demonhood, which wasn't hard given that I'd never displayed Portal or Persuasion, even when...

Even when I'd been with my father.

That struck something inside me, like a loud clanging bell. I hadn't inherited anything from my father. I didn't have his facial features, his strength, or his powers. I had *nothing*. This caused a great spasm of pain in my chest, one that briefly overwhelmed the fear I was feeling. But I knew I could do it. I could give up on finding my father because I had to fend for myself, like I'd been doing ever since he'd abandoned me for the safety of the demonic realm.

'Of course there's a catch, but it is quite minor,' Mack assured me. 'You'll visit your friend, the Kill Squad agent, and you will convince her to take you to that sanctuary of hers. We know she has been shirking her duties, but what we don't know is where she's keeping the fugitives.'

Oh God. Magic Corp wanted me to betray the only person who'd ever been there for me. I didn't need Fido's tiny nip through the fabric of my pants to tell me that I couldn't do it.

Shit, I'd have given up my parents in a heartbeat. But not Merindah. Not ever.

'Hell no,' I said.

Mackenzie stared at me for what felt like an aeon. Then she nodded. 'Very well. There's another way, but it will not be quite so easy. You might prefer to betray Merindah's confidence.'

'I doubt it. Spill.' That deafening silence again. I swallowed, but my mouth stayed stubbornly dry. 'Mackenzie. What do I have to do?'

One of her pockets produced a lighter. She clicked it a few times until a small flame emerged, engulfing the end of her cigarette. She visibly shuddered as she began puffing away. 'New York City was just the start. There's a war coming. I'm trying to keep the government and the press from getting wind of it.'

'I seem to recall us promising the government we'd tell them about these sorts of things, it being part of national security and all,' I said, thinking of the angry and sceptical posts that had popped up on social media since magic had gone public. 'We have to let them know what's coming. To protect people.'

'Not much they can do if shit does hit the fan,' Mackenzie stated, taking a long draw from her cigarette. 'We can give them Tech's fancy apps, but what happens if those fail? They'd only have pitiful guns for backup. Better to keep it quiet.'

Since the Australian branch had gained a reputation for doing its own thing, I suspected this wasn't an internationally sanctioned action. We'd had problems with our global cousins in the past—most notably the British branch, due to their disapproval of us getting involved in various non-magical conflicts.

Our century-long feud had been exacerbated by them not lifting a finger to help Australian magic-users trapped in Singapore during WWII—our people, of course, had been unable to use their powers in any obvious way because of A) the risk of revealing magic and B) the chance we'd alert the Japanese branch to our interference. Anyway, we were now openly getting involved for PR reasons, which was making us unpopular with just about everyone.

Since when did any of the branches agree with each other anyway? I'd never heard of the Russian branch paying much heed to anyone else (they even had a different name, for God's sake) and the Americans were also chipping in with their government's overseas actions. We only pretended to be a united front to the world so that no one would realise just how fractured and vulnerable we really were.

'Okay, but where do I fit in with all this?' I asked Mack. My stomach was churning in a way that made me sure I was about to hurl, even though I hadn't eaten anything for hours.

'You're in with the demons, they think you're one of them,' Mack said. 'We need someone on the inside, someone who can report on their every move, someone who can give us an accurate headcount, someone who can lead us right to their base of operations—when the time comes, of course.'

'I won't do it,' I told her.

'You will if you want Merindah to live. She's good, but once I put her on the Kill Register she'll have no chance.'

My thumb drifted back over to the WatchDog app. Part of me wanted to know if I could take her on—I'd heard she'd sparred with the head of the American branch and had broken both of his legs before he'd managed to say uncle. Was it possible to defeat her? Could brute force triumph over skill? I wasn't confident enough to find out.

Simon was nice enough, hot enough, had been a decent enough snog. He'd even saved my life. But what could I look forward to if I chose his side? Hiding out in demon-filled dens, always afraid that a Hellsomething would manage to kill me? And what would happen to the human magic-users at Magic Corp when Simon lost control of his people? With someone like that Saul guy in charge, the demons would kill everyone at MC. All of them. Even Dennis Freaking Chan didn't deserve that.

'Fine.' I lowered the phone, ignoring another of Fido's nips. 'I'll spy for you. How long are we talking? A week? A month? Am I getting paid?'

Mack released an uncharacteristic snort. It could have sprung from amusement, but I suspected derision instead. 'I can arrange back pay, once we are satisfied with what you have given us.'

'So I *can* ask for conditions.'

'Jennifer,' she said warningly.

'Just a few,' I insisted. 'I'll need incentive, right?'

'I'll pass them on to *my* boss, but don't bank on it. You're getting your life, which is more than anyone else on the Register has ever been given.'

Fair enough. But I had to at least try or I'd never forgive myself. 'I want to talk to people who worked with my mother, people who knew her. And I want to know where she's buried.'

'Goodness, Jennifer, is it really that important?' Mack removed her cigarette from her mouth, apparently just so she could cluck her tongue at me. 'You shouldn't wallow in the past.'

'Those are my conditions, along with the back pay,' I said firmly. 'Oh, and don't touch Merindah. Or try to find her sanctuary. Those people have suffered enough, don't you think?'

Mack stubbed her cigarette out on the ground and left the butt there, hidden among the blades of grass, where any child or hapless dog could find it. I resisted the urge to call her a tosser—it didn't seem a particularly wise move, given the circumstances.

'It doesn't help,' Mack said abruptly, her voice raspy. I figured this was because of the smoke until I saw her pained expression. 'Knowing who your parents are, that is. They didn't make you who you are. We did. Trust me, Jennifer, it's not worth forging or maintaining connections like that.' Her eyes drifted to the ground for a moment, then snapped back up again. 'But if you insist, I'll see that it's done. Now go be a good little spy or you won't live to waste my time ever again.'

I stood up as fast as I could, sweeping my phone's camera around the immediate area and trying not to look too nervous. 'Mackenzie...the Hellhounds have been called off, haven't they?'

She grinned. Even in the poor lighting, I could see how far her lips stretched up the sides of her face. 'Don't want the demons to start suspecting you now, do we?'

There was a chorus of growls, sounding far too close for comfort.

'You bitch,' I said. 'The higher-ups wouldn't have authorised this.'

'Are you *sure*, Jennifer?'

Nope, nope, nope. I was not.

So I turned and ran.

18

'Surely you can run faster than that, Jennifer!' Mack called after me with what could only be described as malignant glee.

If you'd asked me what her biggest character flaw was a day or so before this, I would never have picked 'enjoys the thought of dismemberment a little too much'. But there I was, sprinting for my life because of her.

I crammed my hand into my pocket, scooped up Fido, and tossed him over my shoulder. A huge thud followed, letting me know that he'd expanded to his full height. Then came the yelping, the snarling, the unearthly cries. I looked back and bit my lip. Fido wasn't doing so well. I couldn't see his assailants, but I could definitely see his growing number of injuries.

And I'd slowed down, all because I was worried about a damn dog that wasn't even real.

'Shit, Jen, that was stupid,' I gasped and put on more speed, knowing that I was only delaying inevitable. I couldn't outrun Hellhounds.

I was going to have to fight.

I quit PercApption and swiftly activated WatchDog. I expected the savage surge of power but cried out anyway, needing to vent the pain somehow. Shaking with a potent mix of fear and excitement, I whirled around and threw out both hands, one still clutching the phone—

—and an enormous Physical shockwave blasted out of me, snapping branches, flower stems, and (hopefully) necks.

I staggered backwards and hit the sandstone wall that ran the length of the shore, nearly toppling into the water in the process. After a worrying couple of moments, I managed to pitch forward onto my knees. My ripped pants didn't do much to cushion the impact. That fucking *hurt*.

I'd apparently only nixed the first wave of creatures, because it sounded like there was an entire stampede of Hellsomethings headed my way. I frantically shook the hand that was attached to my phone. Instead of another boost of power, I got nastily throbbing temples and an upset stomach for my trouble. Ouch. Definitely not a good sign.

So I turned and ran. Again.

The exit closest to Mrs Macquarie's Chair was my chosen destination. Strangely, a Physical ladder appeared on the gate before I was in range. I didn't have time question it, just threw myself onto the rungs and started climbing. Look, I'm not particularly strong, but I made it up and out of Hellhound range in two seconds flat.

'Jen!' someone screamed. 'Jump! That's not a Hellhound!'

'*Dennis?*' I exclaimed.

Dennis Freaking Chan was on the other side of the gate, taking pot shots at thin air. I couldn't exactly hang there gawping. The gate shook beneath me and flames were starting to lick their way up from the bottom, buckling the metal, peeling the paint—and heading straight for me. Fido was nowhere to be seen, but evidently Dennis was just as capable of inflicting damage because a fountain of black blood suddenly erupted.

Wow, I really didn't want to know what kind of Hellcreature *that* had been.

I threw myself onto the ground, wobbled ominously before I finally stuck the landing, and then resumed staring at Dennis. He was wearing a dark hoodie with lime-green jeans—of the skinny variety because, damn him, he could pull that look off.

His mouth opened, but I got in first. 'What the *fuck* are you doing here?'

'Saving your life!' Dennis replied.

He swung me behind him and kept on hurling spiked Physical balls through the bars of the gate. Blind to the creatures as always, I had to hope he was actually hitting them. I wrestled my way out of his grip and shoved my phone back into my pocket. WatchDog had failed me. And PercApption wasn't going to be much help—I didn't need it or Dennis' panicked expression to know that there were multiple targets converging on the gate.

I reached for the core inside me and nearly wept when I felt my intact power reserves. Perpetually weak and so much less than I needed, but still there. No magical app required.

'Um, should we run or something?' I ventured when the gate dented inwards.

Dennis' face didn't even twitch.

'Dennis!' I whacked him to get his attention. When his eyes flitted to mine, I said, 'We can't take on this many. Let's *go.*'

Please have a car, I thought in his general direction.

Dennis grimaced.

Shit. I took that as a no.

He turned towards me, hand outstretched. I took a big step backwards, because there was no way I was going to let him slow down our retreat by making me run hand in hand with him.

Happily, I didn't need to come up with a polite way to refuse, because the next thing I heard was, 'GET AWAY FROM HER!'

Dennis immediately backed off.

I flung myself around, preparing to run again—and smacked into something very solid, very male, and very pissed off. The leather jacket was a big hint.

'Where's Fido?' Simon demanded.

'Probably dead,' I said, my eyes watering.

Simon pushed me away, visibly steeled himself, then bellowed at the oncoming Hellcreatures, ordering them to freeze. Whatever was attacking the gate took a breather. But then the ground shook under much heavier footsteps, a one-creature advance that sounded a lot like vengeful thunder.

'That's not good!' Dennis threw a wild finger at the gate. 'Are you seeing this?'

'No! I fucking can't!' I snapped. 'And I'm not going to hang around long enough to feel it.' I spun to Simon. 'Helltroll?'

He nodded. 'Sounds like it.'

'I was joking!' I cried. 'There's always Hellthis and Hellthat—'

'Dennis, cover our retreat!' Simon said.

No human could refuse a command like that.

I watched Dennis Chan turn to face the Helltroll all by himself. He might very well have been standing at the gates of hell, not a set that opened to the usually serene Royal Botanic Garden. He was a doomed one-man army.

A wisp of Physical curled out of my palm. My power reserves were laughable, but there was no way I could let someone die for me. Not again. *Never* again.

I threw a pleading look at Simon. 'We can't just leave him!'

'Yes, we can!' Simon insisted. 'They're not after him.'

His face was like stone—stubborn, uncompromising. There was no point arguing with him. But I knew one way to make sure he stuck around.

I ran to assist Dennis.

'Almost—got—it!' he wheezed. 'I've weakened a spot on its chest, I just need...'

I formed a spear and lengthened it into a medieval pike, just like the one I'd seen on a history program (you know, those docos with the long-haired Scotsman who might actually explode the TV with his enthusiasm?). I caught Dennis' nod of approval at the full Five Metres of Death I was holding, grinned back at him—and then rammed it up with as much force as I could manage.

Dennis had done most of the work. And I was damn lucky. Just as the gate crumpled and my Physical was about to give out, my weapon hit home.

A shower of ichor drenched us. Thick gooey strands of it slid down my borrowed shirt and onto my pants, ruining them for good (not to mention my poor TOMS). The experience was a lot like being dipped in tar.

'Fucking *gross!*' I shouted and got a mouthful of the stuff for my trouble.

And then, naturally, the closest thing to me got hit with a stream of black vomit. Poor Dennis.

'Sorry,' I mumbled.

Dennis had other things he wanted to spew out. 'Simon Bradley? What are you doing here? And you just—'

'I'd rather know what *you're* doing here,' Simon said.

Dennis held up his hands. 'Whoa, no, it's not what you think.'

'Did you follow Jen?' Simon demanded, lunging forward to

seize the collar of Dennis' jumper. 'How long have you been stalking her?'

The hood flopped back off Dennis' face and he gasped, 'What? No! I followed Mack!'

Oh shit. Simon must have thought that Dennis had found Demon HQ and given away its position.

'Simon!' I spat out some bile-flavoured chunks of Helltroll soup. 'I told Mack where I was. It's my fault.'

His blue eyes pinned me in place. And they weren't dark with desire this time; Simon looked downright demonic. 'You told her. No wonder. Just as you were done sneaking out, we were attacked again. I had to scatter my people before I went after you.'

Well, I had left them without a Physical defender, hadn't I?

I didn't think that scrounging up an apology would do me any favours. I settled for focusing on another, much friendlier face. Huh. Dennis was looking way too interested and not scared enough, in my opinion.

Before I could ask him about it, Simon snapped, 'I can't hold the creatures forever. Someone has to keep them occupied while we escape and I *will* make him do it.'

'Uh.' Dennis coughed. 'I'd rather you didn't get inside my head again. I'd have covered your butts anyway.'

Simon and I both stared at him.

'Hey, hey!' Dennis' hands went back up. 'I'll hold them off for you. I swear. And if they're not after me, then I'll be fine. Won't I?'

Simon chuckled. That didn't sound very comforting.

'Dennis...' I trailed off.

What could I say? He'd been such a dick to me, but now he was offering up his life in exchange for mine. Of course he just had to perform this big romantic gesture in front of Simon, who I'd been making out with not an hour ago.

This was...super awkward.

'If I survive, I'll be at work tomorrow,' Dennis said quickly. 'Find me there. I'll explain everything. Now go!'

Simon started running. I stayed put for a few seconds, torn, but only until the ground started shaking again. I left Dennis behind. My mother had died to protect me and I'd just abandoned someone else to that same fate.

Maybe I really did deserve to be hunted down and killed.

19

I chased Simon and caught up to him when he hit the road. I saw his Hyundai Excel parked across two spaces, gestured my disapproval, got some foul words out of him, and then threw myself inside the car. I tried not to think about the Helltroll blood that I was smearing all over the seat.

Simon jabbed his key into the ignition and shoved the gear stick into second, accelerating until we hit a speed more appropriate for a motorway than city streets. I tried not to freak out.

We shot past the castle-shaped oddity housing the Sydney Conservatorium of Music, but had to quickly slide to a stop at a red light. Simon scanned the road for a heartbeat, then took off without waiting for the light to go green, fanging it towards the Sydney Harbour Tunnel.

'Holy shit, this car can move!' I said.

The throbbing *John Wick* soundtrack being ejected from the speakers seemed appropriate, but the volume was down too low for me to miss any of Simon's words.

'I didn't buy a third-hand Hyundai just because it was cheap,' he said, a small smile tweaking his lips; it faded within seconds. 'Are you hurt, Jen?'

'No,' I replied.

We must have passed a speed camera because the car lit up brilliantly. I saw Simon wince, then he turned his blade-thin eyes onto me and let them linger, long enough for me to worry about us hitting the buildings on the side of the road.

'What did she offer you that was good enough for you to betray us?' he asked.

'Apart from my life?' I muttered. My face was burning.

'You're one of us,' Simon went on, shaking his head in disbelief. 'And you went back to *them*.'

'I don't know who's more dangerous at this point!' I snapped. I was already feeling bad about Fido and Dennis sacrificing themselves for me. I so did not need this extra guilt. 'I just want to sit back down at my shitty entry-level job and forget any of this ever happened.'

'You can't change what you are,' Simon told me. 'MC will never forget your demonic nature. And they won't let you forget it either.'

Damn him, he was right. Magic Corp would always think of me as a weak link that could be exploited by the enemy. Because of my father's contribution to my genetic makeup, I was a threat. A ticking time bomb.

'You still saved me, despite me going to Mack,' I said quietly.

'I saved a potential double agent,' Simon returned. 'If you're a spy, then you might as well be mine.'

With my hand on the door handle, just in case I needed a quick getaway (never mind how much it would hurt), I told him, 'No. I already made the mistake of thinking I could be someone's spy tonight. I won't do it. You'll just have to kill me.'

'You're not my enemy, Jen.'

'I'm not your ally either.'

We dived into the tunnel beneath the harbour, Simon continuing to accelerate. This time I gave the speed camera that flashed us a thumbs up. Then my hands flew down to grip both sides of my seat as we came up behind two cars blocking both lanes, neither of them budging even though Simon blasted his horn and flashed his high beams. The white Toyota Camry was the one that finally gave way. Its driver wound down her window and risked bad tunnel air just to yell 'slow down, you maniac!' at Simon.

Well, his driving *was* a tad scary. There probably weren't that many cars or roads to practice on in the demonic realm, mind.

'You weren't happy working for Magic Corp,' Simon said tersely as we left the bright tunnel behind us, the road outside sparsely lit and empty. 'Any fool could see that. And they're only trying to placate you now because they suddenly realised you exist and can give them something they want.'

'At least they aren't like you—notice I exist for two seconds, then drop me the moment you lose interest,' I said and blew a snort out through my nostrils, managing to noisily shift a chunk of snot in the process. Ugh. So attractive.

Simon sent a frown in my direction, one that morphed strangely beneath the streetlights. 'Jen. I wanted to take things further that night. You know why I didn't. And at the time I had other, more important things going on.'

'Yeah, the Big Bad Plan to take down Magic Corp,' I said tiredly. 'I can see how unimportant I am in the grand demonic scheme of things.'

'You can do so much more, be so much more,' he insisted. 'I've seen how powerful you are when you're not being held back.'

Nope. He needed to know the truth. Needed to know how useless I was. I couldn't be the great Physical defender he wanted for his people. I pulled out my phone and dropped it into my lap. 'It's not me. It's the app.'

'What?'

'WatchDog, it gives me all this power. Every time...' I swallowed. Well, the worst he could do was laugh at me. I could take it. So I charged on. 'Every time I need a boost, I fire up the app and it amps my Physical. It's...amazing. I've never been able to source this much power before. But it hurts. A *lot*.'

Simon didn't fob me off or try to tell me I was imagining things. He actually seemed to take my words seriously, even if he did look bewildered.

'But all it does is make a...' He pursed his lips. 'Hmm. I'm glad I had the servers turned back on.'

He said nothing more for a while, apparently lost in thought, so I cleared my throat. 'I'm worried you'll lose one of your Persuasion duels to Saul and then your people will slaughter everyone inside Magic Corp at his say-so.'

Simon's lips peeled open, revealing gritted teeth. 'I'll do everything in my power to make sure that doesn't happen.'

'Your people would be a lot happier if you launched a full-on attack,' I pointed out.

'No,' Simon growled. 'I won't let them do it. I'll fight them all if I have to.'

Jesus Christ, he sounded like he meant it.

I guess that's why I said the next thing that popped into my head.

'Okay, maybe I can be a double agent. Maybe. I'd be risking a lot, but I'll do it. Because...' I stilled my trembling lips. 'Because Merindah's risking shitloads to help people who break their contracts. And I...I've done nothing.'

I coughed up the hard lump forming in my throat. My life was forfeit the moment Mack found out what I was doing.

Simon may have lacked Perception, but he seemed to know what I was thinking. His voice took on a hard edge, each syllable striking me low in the abdomen. 'I'll kill anyone who threatens your life. Mackenzie Roberts is already at the top of my list.'

His expression grim, Simon took the exit towards St Leonards and headed for a surprisingly small apartment complex for the area. The gate of the basement car park clacked shut behind us and we sat there in silence until the lights on the ceiling (presumably activated by motion sensors) dimmed, leaving us in semidarkness.

'Are we safe here?' I asked.

Simon nodded. 'For now, sure. Until someone decides to tell Magic Corp where we are.' I grimaced; I definitely deserved that. He continued, 'Some of my people also live here, in other apartments, so we have backup on hand. The building's rigged with my nullifying tech, so the magic-sensing scouts can't find us, and I've also got PercApption loaded on the nearby traffic cameras—we'll have some warning if Hellcreatures are headed our way.'

'Okay, that's great,' I said. 'But—Dennis. We just left him there.'

Simon's expression twisted. 'We can check on him tomorrow, if it will make you feel better.'

'It will,' I told him firmly. 'And we should ask him a few questions. He didn't seem all that surprised by what was going on. But I don't think he's involved. He's an admin stooge, same as me.'

Simon said nothing.

'You need all the allies you can get,' I argued into the silence.

'Not just people who can help you take down Magic Corp from the inside—people who can replace it with something better. Something that protects all of us from Hellcreatures and other magical threats, without taking children from their families.'

'Do you realise how impossible that is?'

I tried to shrug my shoulders, but they ended up slumping. 'We can't leave this country and its people undefended, normal or otherwise.'

'Jen, it's not that I don't want to,' Simon said cautiously. 'But I'm not sure I'll be able to get my people on board. I won't Persuade them.'

'So *convince* them!' I pressed.

'To help you protect demons, humans, and everything in between?'

'Yes!'

'Even Dennis?' He sounded incredulous.

'Even Dennis!' I said.

Simon's stern expression melted into a laugh and I felt some of the tension in the car disperse. Maybe everything would be alright. Maybe I wasn't as screwed as I thought I was. There had to be some way out of this. Not just for me...for *everyone*.

Something ticked underneath the car bonnet as the engine cooled.

I hesitated. 'Simon, do you and Dot have parents?'

He smiled in a way that could only be described as fond. I envied him even before he spoke. 'Of course we do. They live in the demonic realm. I haven't seen them since...well, it's been a while.'

'Do they approve of you infiltrating and working for Magic Corp?' I asked.

146

'No, but they know that this is important to me,' Simon answered. 'They support my decision. They even made Dot come back with me last time I visited them, so I'd have someone to watch out for me.'

The whole concept of having a family to support me was so alien and strange, though I'd seen it enough times in movies to know that I craved it for myself. But now, remembering my parents, I wasn't sure I wanted the pain and loss that came it.

My next words escaped me in a whisper. 'And how would your mother react if you threw away your only chance of knowing who she really was?'

'My parents would want me to do what I think is right.' Simon rested a hand over mine; I hadn't realised I'd been clenching the gear stick until he did this. 'Yours would want that too.'

'They're the ones who made me forget them in the first place,' I muttered, but the hatred lacing my words was missing from the empty cavity inside my chest. 'I don't owe them anything. I don't. I have to look after myself. Like I always do.'

'I'm here for you,' Simon said, his grip on my hand tightening.

I met his eyes. 'So you'll do it, you'll help me create something to replace Magic Corp? And hire people no matter what Ps they happen to have?'

Simon's voice was curt and clipped. 'I'll consider it. But human magic-users can't be trusted. We'd need to control how they use their powers and monitor them activities closely.'

'I see, you'll protect them but you won't let them have any say in how their lives are run,' I snapped, groping for the door handle. I ripped my other hand away from his.

'We're not the bad guys, Jen,' Simon called after me as I bailed from the car. 'Demons don't rob families of their children—that's something humans like to do. You should ask Merindah's ancestors.'

I bent back down into the car to sneer at him. 'Oh, you don't kidnap kids? Do you want a medal? Just because someone else did it doesn't mean you get to ignore the consequences! Can you imagine how hard it's going to be for my colleagues to reconnect with their families? How hard it'll be for them to get jobs in the outside world?'

'That's not our problem, Jen.'

'I'm half human, Simon! Or had you forgotten that?'

I slammed the door in his face before he could apologise (if that's what he was going to do) and stormed through the car-lined basement.

Ugh, why did I still want to kiss him!?

20

I drew up short in front of the lift's silver doors, suddenly feeling very foolish. My righteous march away from the most aggravating demon in the Southern Hemisphere would have been a lot more satisfying if I'd actually had somewhere to go.

Simon caught up to me pretty fast. 'Jen. I'm sorry. I didn't think. It sounds bad.'

'That's because it *is*,' I countered. 'If you want humans and hybrids to help you take down Magic Corp, you're going to need to offer them something worthwhile.'

'Which is why I need you.' Simon cleared his throat and shoved his hands into his pockets. 'Why *we* need you. You can help us do this the right way.'

'Jesus Christ, can't you find someone a bit more qualified?' I chortled. 'Oh well. You're stuck with me, I guess, since I have nowhere else to go. And I'm pretty sure you're going to regret choosing me, but I figure that's your problem. Not mine.'

He grinned. 'I'm beginning to see why Dennis said you were exhausting.'

'He said that!?' Okay, I wasn't feeling quite so torn up about leaving the dick behind now. 'I see he's found other shit to say about me since school.'

Simon leaned in, unsheathing one of his hands to brace himself against the wall. He said lowly, 'Personally, I don't think he has the stamina to deal with you, but I'm sure you would know this better than me.'

'Fuck you,' I said.

And then I started giggling, because he was totally right about Dennis. But how can a teenager be any good at sex, especially if it's his first time? I'd not done any better. Since The Gym Crash Mat Incident, I'd figured out my own body and thought I might actually know what I was doing the next time someone's bed become available.

Simon's other hand slid around to the small of my back and he hovered his lips close to my ear. He whispered, 'Fuck me, huh? That can be arranged.'

Shivering, I closed my eyes and tilted my head back. His open-mouthed kisses devoured my throat, awakening those vampire fantasies I kept out of my head whenever Merindah was around.

I didn't care that Simon might be Persuading me. It felt so damn good.

I gave an encouraging moan and his lips slid the collar of my borrowed shirt—along with my bra strap—down to my shoulder. Not content to sit on the sidelines, his fingers drifted to the bottom of my shirt and crept their way up beneath the fabric.

Okay, I might have stiffened, imagining what he'd think of the loose skin I'd got saddled with After Weight Loss. But he didn't make a comment and I suddenly couldn't remember why I'd been so worried. His expert kisses and caresses might have had something to do with that.

God, he knew exactly where to touch me.

Simon abruptly shoved me away, against the lift doors, and I thought, *Okay, I can work with this*—but then he said, 'I'm sorry. I didn't mean to.'

'Uh, you didn't mean to kiss me and set my skin on fire?' I chanced.

He ran his fingers through his mop of hair, which somehow managed to gain an extra couple of centimetres of height from the gesture. The grey tuft at the front bounced back down over his forehead.

'I can't do this,' Simon told me. 'I don't want to accidentally Persuade you to...'

He gestured crudely with his hands and looked almost as embarrassed as Dennis did whenever he walked over to my desk to ask me a question. Usually something to do with office supplies. Just last week Dennis had wanted to know if he could borrow my stapler. He still hadn't returned it.

'I'd know if you were doing that, right?' I asked Simon.

He shrugged helplessly. 'I don't know.'

I considered this. 'Well, what if I said I didn't mind if you slipped up? That I was game for things to go all the way regardless?'

'How do I know that *you* made that decision?' he agonised.

I scowled. 'Are you trying to tell me I can't make any decisions without you forcing me to do it? I'm not some robot, damn it. And who told Mack where your headquarters were, huh? You definitely didn't make me do that!'

Well, that killed the mood. We stood side by side in the cramped lift, very carefully not looking at each other and not discussing A) the fact that I'd endangered his people after they'd taken me in, and B) the fact that we were both growing steadily more aroused and frustrated in each other's presence. My need wasn't so obvious (and I was hoping demons didn't have a particularly keen sense of smell) but his was, straining at the front of his black jeans.

And then I realised we were both covered in Helltroll blood, some of it now smeared over his lips from our little, uh, indiscretion downstairs. Clearly, it didn't bother him as much as it did me. Must be a demon thing.

'Not bad, pretty roomy,' I said when we entered Simon's generous two-bedroom apartment.

'You won't be saying that when everyone gets here tomorrow,' he said with a grim smile. 'It'll have to do until I can find a new location for our headquarters.'

I coughed into my hand. 'Yeah, sorry about that.'

Simon directed me into the master bedroom's ensuite where I found fluffy towels, a face washer, and a bathmat (all black, of course). His toothbrush and electric razor were lined up neatly beside the hand soap on the vanity.

I rolled my eyes at the obsidian tiles and the matching tap in the shower, but I wasn't going to complain about Simon's preferred aesthetics when I had a chance to make myself halfway decent. I washed the crap out of my hair and my pores, using the nice spicy-scented body wash that was perched on a shelf in the corner of the shower.

When I emerged into the living room, a long towel tight around my armpits, I found Simon hunched over his laptop on one of the comfy leather couches. He was muttering, 'But how are they controlling the hounds without a demon on staff?'

I figured it wasn't safe to sit down, in case I dislodged the towel, so I settled for standing on the dark tassel-edged rug in front of him. I waited until he looked up before I answered, 'Maybe someone in Tech found a way to do it? You can't be the only genius in the department.'

'They don't have anyone better than me,' Simon argued, tilting his laptop screen forward so that he could see me better.

'Maybe Dennis knows something about it,' I said.

Simon made a noncommittal grunt.

And then something really horrible occurred to me.

'Oh God, what if there *is* a demon on staff, someone apart from you...' I hesitated. 'Do you think Magic Corp knows about this demon and doesn't care? Maybe even uses their powers? Because a demon could easily Persuade the Hellhounds in the rooftop pen to hunt down hybrids.'

Simon and I stared at each other, I think in mutual horror at first, but then the simmering hunger in his eyes grew even more potent, causing something to unfurl in my abdomen.

I crossed my arms. 'Damn it, Simon. Stop looking at me like that—unless you want to do something about it.'

He lowered his gaze. 'No, I think I would have encountered them if there was another demon at work. And I doubt anyone at Magic Corp could stand to work with my kind.'

'But it's possible that someone at MC has Persuasion,' I pointed out. 'It wouldn't even have to be a full-blooded demon, right? I'm not the only hybrid in existence.'

Simon's teeth dug into his bottom lip. 'Perhaps Mackenzie has made offers to other hybrids before. One might have been given a stay of execution in return for, say, Persuading families to give up their children.' My heart clenched. He continued, 'The personnel files might give us some indication of who has demonic powers. If they've marked you as a hybrid, then this other person will be as well.'

'We need to have a look at those files,' I decided.

Simon nodded. 'Yes. So you're going to Magic Corp in the morning. With me. Just a normal day at the office.'

I rolled my eyes. 'Except for the Hellhounds trying to rip me apart in front of everyone.'

'I'll Persuade the hounds to stand down.'

'And if there's a Helltroll?' I demanded.

Simon smirked. 'I'd like to see them fit one of those inside the lift.'

He had both arms resting on the back of the couch now. He had no right to look that relaxed—or that smug. I felt like I should remind him of a fairly important detail. 'Dennis is the one with access to the locked personnel files.'

'Then it's a good thing we'll be talking to him tomorrow,' Simon said calmly.

I gingerly perched on the couch. 'But he might be dead. It could be a wasted trip.'

Simon indicated the phone beside him—*my* phone. There was a text message from Dennis displayed on it, informing me that he was alive and waiting to hear back from me.

'Can't you go in by yourself?' I tried not to whine.

'Dennis might not want to tell me anything,' Simon said with a shake of his head. 'He'll talk to you.'

'Why? Because I have boobs?' I chortled, shimmying the towel as far down my thighs as I could without exposing the aforementioned assets. 'Hate to break it to you, but he liked my old DD cup size. I'm barely a C these days.'

'But he has a photo of you set as his lock screen.'

I scowled. 'Really? Creepy. And anyway, what if this hybrid at

Magic Corp is only pretending to play nice so they can destroy MC themselves?'

Simon's lip twisted. 'Whoever it is, if they're in control of the Hellcreatures that Magic Corp has at their disposal, then they clearly don't have a problem with endangering non-magical humans. I need to put a stop to that.' He paused, his forehead creasing. 'If I didn't know any better, I'd say that Mackenzie Roberts is the one we're after. She's definitely mean enough.'

'Yeah, but she's got Physical and Perception,' I reminded him. 'You said we can only ever have two out of the four Ps, right?'

Simon nodded briefly. 'Right. Jen, you should get some rest. Hounds will quite happily devour prey that is yawning instead of fighting back.'

Okay, the demon had a point. Sleeping would also help kill time until I could see Merindah at MC (hopefully she'd be back from sick leave) so that A) she could help me with any Helltrolls that may or may not come out of the lift, and B) we could have a private chat about certain things. I couldn't exactly tell her that her secret was out over the phone. Call me paranoid, but that's not how I wanted to find out that Magic Corp had my number tapped.

'Sure, Simon, a good night's sleep is all I need to go to work tomorrow.' I held a finger to my lips. 'Oh wait, I have no decent clothes or shoes to wear. My boss, Tom, might have a problem with me going in naked. You'll have to Persuade him not to notice me anyway, given the suspension thing.'

Simon raked his eyes over me. 'I have shirts you can wear; it wouldn't kill you to go casual like everyone else does. And I think Dot left some jeans behind.'

'I'll also need a belt, I'm a smaller size than her,' I pointed out.

'Noted,' Simon said. 'What time does that trendy shoe shop near Magic Corp's HQ open?'

'Half past eight. Why?'

'We won't be late if we stop by there first. Then we'll go into work together. I'll protect you, Jen, I promise,' he added, his voice softening.

I burst out laughing. 'Oh sure, my wiles will definitely work on Dennis if he sees me turn up with you—*and* in one of your shirts.'

Simon smirked. 'He can handle a bit of jealousy. I've bailed bucket-loads so far.'

And that's what pushed me off the precarious cliff of common sense.

I stood up from the couch and dropped the towel. It didn't gracefully puddle to the floor like they seem to do in romance novels; instead it whomped onto the rug in one big pile.

'We've got a problem,' I declared.

Simon's eyebrows shot into his hairline. 'We do?'

'Yeah, I'm probably going to die tomorrow,' I said with a sorrowful sigh. 'And I really don't want Dennis to be the last one I jumped in the sack with.'

Simon nodded solemnly. 'Yes, I can see how that would be a problem.'

'Just so you know, there's no need to be jealous.' I turned around and headed for the master bedroom. 'I'll be in your bed, naked, in case you want to come find out if I can make my own decisions.'

A strangled sound emerged from his throat, but the demon did not follow.

It took me ages to fall asleep—I actually missed having Fido stretched out beside me. The loss of that damn dog seemed to hurt more than the loss of my parents. They were fuzzy memories seemingly transplanted into my head; Fido had stayed with me long past his Physical expiry date, protecting me and helping me feel brave enough to defend myself.

Given my current situation, I'd rather have Fido back than see my parents again.

They would probably be disappointed in me anyway.

21

At 8:53 AM (according to my phone), I followed Simon into Magic Corp's headquarters. My ruined slippers had been tossed into a bin and my feet were currently encased inside the most awesome pair of sneakers that I would never have bought with my own money (they cost as much as a grocery shop that was meant to last for two weeks!). Nubuck leather, dark soles, an incredible shade of purple—the new Nikes went very well with the black jeans and muscle shirt that Simon had given me.

So basically, I was bedecked like some sort of demonic groupie.

I definitely hadn't imagined Simon's smirk when he'd checked me out back at his apartment.

The building that housed Magic Corp wasn't a particularly tall one for Castlereagh Street; it was seven storeys high and had the tired concrete look that had been popular before someone somewhere decided that all high-rise buildings had to be made almost entirely out of glass. Our headquarters were unremarkable to anyone who didn't know its purpose and the Minister for Magical Australians and Related Affairs was never spotted in the vicinity—mostly because of the time he'd been shown the apparently empty Hellhound pen and one of the creatures had thrown up the remains of its roommate all over his suit.

The receptionist in the foyer (notably sitting on a better salary than me, but she also had sufficient Physical to subdue any intruders) perked up when she saw us—well, Simon. It was pleasant to be on the receiving end of that sexy smile, but playing second fiddle to it was incredibly irritating.

I mimed retching when the receptionist coyly ducked her head and flicked her hair behind an ear, totally unnecessary steps in the process of verifying that Simon was allowed to approach the keypass-activated lift. She lifted her eyes from the desk and I froze, caught in the act. But she was looking right through me, at the automatic doors dividing the foyer from the street. She started greeting the next batch of people—all of whom said hi to Simon when they saw him.

Not one of them seemed to notice me.

At first I wasn't sure if Simon's Persuasion was responsible—I never did get a cordial morning greeting from anyone—but then the receptionist went back to marking off names on her tablet and completely failed to press a finger to the box next to mine. I know because I leaned over the top of her desk and darted my eyes across the list displayed on the screen.

Tom Chapman, with his surname right before mine in the alphabet, was easy to find. He wasn't in yet. I blew out a sigh of relief.

One of the newcomers swiped their keypass against the sensor on the wall, opening the lift doors, so we all bustled inside and my colleagues just *had* to start discussing the latest NRL salary cap scandal. Ugh. No thanks.

Simon's fingertips pressed against my back, a little lower than was polite, as he guided me out of the lift and onto the first floor. Some people followed us out; others stayed on for the other levels. It was pretty obvious why we referred to them as 'higher-ups'—that and their extended lunchbreaks.

The moment Simon's hand fell away from me, I started catching looks from people. Dennis' head popped over the top of his desk and his cheerful expression instantly segued into something more stony. The stylish semi-rimless glasses he now used to read up close really suited him, but I didn't feel a hot dizzy whoop when I saw him, not like the one I got from simply standing in Simon's presence.

Impulsively, I turned to Simon and kissed his cheek. He stared at me.

'Thanks for last night,' I said with a wink.

Simon raised his eyebrows, then slowly smirked.

Unable to kill my grin, I sidled over to my desk while he remained by the lift doors, just as we'd planned. If Tom came in while I was there, Simon would Persuade him to roll right past me without noticing that his most recently suspended employee had shown up for work.

While I waited for Dennis to take the bait, I checked my phone. There were no more messages from Merindah. Maybe she was being extra careful. Or maybe she was deathly ill and couldn't reach her phone.

Oh God. Maybe it wasn't glandular fever. Maybe it was another variant of The Plague.

Dennis, predictably, wasted no time in throwing his shadow across my desk. His deep scowl was getting deeper by the second. 'Him? Really?'

I set my phone down with a decisive clunk. 'Yes. Him. So what?'

'You're not going to make a habit of it, right?' Dennis demanded.

'Are you fucking serious?'

Dennis blinked.

'For God's sake!' I said, slinging a leg over my opposite knee and showing off my new pair of Nikes in the process. Dennis definitely saw them, because one of his eyebrows did The Dance of Approval. But I wasn't going to let him get distracted. 'Last night you saved my life and I helped you skewer a Helltroll, but now you want to talk about *Simon Bradley?*'

Dennis took a step back, looking as though I'd smacked him with my K-Mart frying pan. 'No, but—'

I sagged in my chair. 'Dennis, please. I don't have time to revisit our ancient history. I need to see the personnel files. I have to know if anyone's ever managed to get off the Kill Register. And if so, *how.*'

Dennis' eyes narrowed. I'd seen him do that enough times to know he was using Perception. My scalp tickled, but I wasn't sure if this was because I knew what he was doing or because I could actually feel it. I wondered if he was annoyed that he couldn't get much out of me. Finally, he said, 'You're not on the Kill Register.'

'What?'

Dennis knelt beside my desk and started pummelling my keyboard, his tongue poking out of the corner of his mouth. 'The Kill Squad's not after you. They haven't been given your name or your file.'

'Yeah, well, forgive me if rogue Hellhounds and slosher attacks have made a little sceptical,' I muttered, crossing my arms and forcing myself to stay seated when the lift dinged. 'Merindah might not be after me, but she plays pretty fast and loose with her orders. Jesus Christ, she picked a bad time to get sick. I could have used the backup today.'

'She's not on sick leave,' Dennis corrected me. 'She's

suspended, pending investigation. The higher-ups think she's been falsifying her reports.'

An icy, jagged boulder embedded itself in my stomach. Merindah had sounded hoarse the day before and she'd managed some pretty convincing coughs, but it could have been a performance. So yeah, I was a bit hurt that she hadn't told me the truth earlier. She'd only told me about the fugitives when I became one myself.

What sort of person did she think I was? A pushover who'd do anything and sell out anyone in order to keep my job?

Oh wait. Never mind.

I swallowed. 'How many people know about this?'

'Uh, well, no one on this floor. I shouldn't even know, but...I've seen the classified files.' Dennis' chest seemed to swell, but it got nowhere near as big as his ego clearly was. 'My Perception is pretty weird—it works on computers, so I can read files just like I can read thoughts. Neat, huh?'

I stared at him. With that kind of ability...

'Shouldn't you be helping out ASIO or be chilling upstairs with the Tech folks, if your Perception's this good?' I asked.

Dennis shook his head vigorously. 'MC doesn't know. No one does. They'd transfer me.'

'Uh, Dennis, you wouldn't be stuck down here,' I said, watching as he pulled up several folders that I knew no admin stooge should ever have access to. 'Better pay and perks and all that.'

His head swivelled on his shoulders until his smile was aimed right at me. 'But I wouldn't be near you, like I am now.'

Christ. Oh Christ. He did not just say that.

'Are you telling me...' I paused, because it was just so *stupid*.

'...that you've spent this entire time trying to get back with me? When you could have been advancing your career?'

'It was a sacrifice I was willing to make, Jen.'

Luckily, he'd turned back to the screen so he didn't see the horror I was no doubt wearing on my face. He double-clicked on a file that was so obviously named it couldn't possibly be what I thought it was. But yep, it was.

The Kill Register was a perversely innocuous Excel spreadsheet that had three columns: employee name, infraction, and status. Fifty people were listed in Times New Roman as 'terminated' or 'missing'. I recognised some of the names, but my own definitely wasn't there. Neither was my mother's—it seemed the list only went back five years.

'I checked after you were attacked at Artarmon station,' Dennis said, swinging around to fix his gaze back on me. His glasses remained perfectly in place, probably because his brow was scrunched up in concentration. 'It seemed weird that they'd send a creature instead of the Kill Squad, but it's not like we don't have Hellhounds in a pen on the roof, huh.'

Hot pinpricks swarmed over the back of my neck. 'A lot of people have access to the Hellhounds, Dennis.'

Dennis' forehead crinkled ever further, if that was possible. 'Yeah. True. There are enough hybrids upstairs that any of them could have sent it.'

'They...what?' My temples started to throb. 'Hybrids? Dennis, what the hell are you talking about?'

'Well, duh, people like you and Simon,' Dennis answered.

A Physical knife shot out of my hand and I seized his shirt, pulling his throat down in line with my distressingly translucent weapon.

Our colleagues didn't react to my sudden display of violence. I assumed I had Simon to thank for that.

Dennis had a grimace on this face, one that was part chagrin, part oops. 'Hey, it's fine, I don't have a problem with it. And it's obvious Simon's got Persuasion, though I didn't see it in his file. It's also weird that his address has him living somewhere that doesn't exist. Someone must have entered the wrong details.'

The knife misted away before I could withdraw it. I sat back down.

Dennis' fingers resumed their dance over the keyboard as he pulled up my personnel file. I'd seen it before, but it had been updated since then.

Powers: Physical, possibly Persuasion or Portal

Status: suspended, pending transfer to field work or the PR department (see attached video—Cooke is proving popular online)

I rested my hand over Dennis' on the mouse, to keep him from scrolling any further. I didn't want him looking at the lies MC had written about my mother, even though he probably had already.

'I don't understand,' I muttered.

Dennis piled another hand on top of mine, warming it between both of his. It wasn't an entirely unwelcome gesture.

'There's heaps of hybrids,' he said. 'They usually get picked up during the tests, when they fail to show Perception or Physical. They have their other Ps trained up. You know. For whatever job their skills are needed for.'

I stared unseeingly towards the lift, where Simon was waiting. Simon, the demon, who thought he needed to protect hybrids by giving them magical apps that masked their lack of Perception and Physical. I thought about my parents, panicked to the point of blocking my memories, because they feared I would meet my death at Magic Corp's hands. And all they would have done was assign me to a better job.

Shit. Had it all been for nothing?

22

'How many...' I struggled to work moisture into my mouth. 'How many people know about this? About the hybrids? The four Ps?'

'Not many,' Dennis replied. 'They're keeping it hushed up.'

'Okay...' I withdrew my fingers from his. The hand pile was starting to get a little too sweaty and intimate for me. 'But if hybrids aren't being hunted down...that doesn't explain Mack's offer, or why she sent those Hellcreatures after me last night, or what the hell you were doing there.'

Dennis tapped out a staccato rhythm on my desk, caught my frown, and quickly desisted. 'When I started poking around and finding out about all this stuff, I noticed that hybrids were disappearing a lot. No mention of broken contracts though.'

Okay. So we *were* going missing. Not comforting.

'The higher-ups have been worried about this for years,' Dennis went on. 'I saw it in some top-secret meeting minutes. But Mack said they must have been contract-breakers that had gone on the run and were still out there somewhere because the Kill Squad hadn't managed to deal with them. Mike, the Head of Containment, didn't like the fact that she was practically accusing his lot of not doing their jobs properly.'

'Mack pissing someone off is not a good enough reason to start following her around,' I pointed out.

'Yeah, true,' Dennis agreed. He didn't seem to want to look me in the eye. 'So, funny thing, my Perception works on other tech like phones—I can read messages at a distance. And like, I knew if you ever got into trouble you'd contact Mack instead of Tom. So I kept near her. She stayed back pretty late last night.'

'And she didn't notice you skulking around?' I asked.

'My Perception also picks things up through several floors...'

'Holy shit, Dennis.' I couldn't believe it. 'You really shouldn't be trapped down here with me and the others. Seriously. And I don't know how you can possibly put up with—'

'I did it for you,' he interrupted.

'I dumped you! And I didn't ask you do this!' I said, belatedly remembering to lower my voice. I didn't want to make it any harder for Simon to obscure my presence. 'You think I appreciate you stalking me?' I finished in a hiss.

'Yes! Because me stalking you saved your life!'

Before I could form a rational response to that, the lift dinged again.

Dennis peered over my desk. 'Oh hey, Tom's in. You can ask him about your suspension, if you don't believe me. He's the one who initiated your transfer.'

I made a wild grab for Dennis' arm and missed entirely. He was already standing up and waving.

But our boss wheeled himself right past us, making a beeline for his office with Simon trailing in his wake. I noticed the slightly vacant expression in Tom's eyes and was glad that he still had the mental capacity to steer straight.

Having been born without legs, he used a wheelchair to get around and had done so for most of his life. So it'd look a little suspicious if he suddenly crashed.

Tom Chapman had a unique magical quirk that allowed him to

maintain a construct for two to three hours at a time. I'd heard people wonder out loud why he didn't use his powers to give himself legs—presumably they'd said (and thought) it too often, because Tom had once come out of his office and berated them for assuming that he'd waste his power reserves on something so unnecessary when there could be a demonic incursion in Sydney at any moment.

I'd hated to agree with him at the time, since I was no fan of his, but he'd had a damn good point. Happily, Tom spent most of his time comfortably ensconced in his office, supposedly thinking tasks at me and anyone else in range.

'Simon,' I explained when Dennis shot me a confused look.

He frowned. 'Does he make a habit of reaching into people's heads?'

I snorted, thinking of all the people in MC who were convinced that Simon had been with us for years. 'You have no idea.'

I don't know who stood first, but Dennis and I both followed Tom into his office. Simon was pacing wall to wall when we entered, clearly impatient.

'Drop it,' I said, jerking my hand at Tom. He'd parked himself behind his desk. 'I need to talk to him.'

Simon gave one sharp nod and Tom immediately blinked, dazed. 'You're suspended, Ms Cooke. What are you doing here?'

'Wondering if it's true,' I snapped. 'That you really do know what I am, that it's actually no big deal, but you made me freak out about being suspended instead of, you know, explaining what was going on.'

'I wasn't the one cheating on the annual tests now, was I?' Tom mused. He tugged at the cuffs of his shirt, ensuring that they were perfectly parallel with each other.

I slammed my palms onto his desk. 'Fuck you, Tom. You made me feel like shit every time you had a go at me for not reading your mind. You could have figured it out yourself—I don't have Perception!'

Tom jerked backwards, hands gripping his wheels.

'Jen!' Dennis objected.

'She needs to do this, Dennis, so shut up,' Simon said flatly.

Tom was now *squirming*. 'Ms Cooke, you must know I was unaware that you were unable to read my surface thoughts until you failed the Perception test.'

'You made me hate this job so much I almost quit and took my chances with the Kill Squad,' I said.

Tom's eyes widened in apparent horror. 'Heavens, no. Don't do that. Don't waste your skill set, dear. You'll be invaluable in Intelligence if you have Persuasion—even Portal has its uses there. Although, I think PR might claim you.' Tom tsked disapprovingly. 'They probably want to make you the poster child for Magic Corp, since you saved all those people yesterday. The hits on those Internet videos got you noticed far more than your actions did.'

'Why would Jen be so good in the intelligence department?' Simon asked quietly.

Tom blinked at him. 'Oh, Mr Bradley. Hello.' He paused, frowning slightly, but either Simon got into his head again or he decided that Simon's random appearance didn't matter. 'It's common sense to send someone with a demonic ability into the den of the enemy—the demons can look just like us, how terrifying—since they can spy without arousing too much suspicion. I believe Magic Corp is planning to deploy as many as ten Portal-gifted spies in the demonic realm in the next twelve months.'

Simon's jaw worked from side to side, but he said nothing. He was probably thinking about his parents back home. How many demons would know to look for a threat in a place where they were supposed to be safe from humans?

'So, in summary, hybrids aren't killed for being hybrids,' I piped up, trying to distract Simon from his no doubt turbulent frame of mind.

'But they are still stolen from their families,' Simon said, his voice rough and his expression darker than a Hellhound's blood.

Okay, I failed, but he totally had a point.

'Our families signed us over,' Dennis interjected. 'No one stole us.'

'Dennis, think about it.' I held his gaze. 'If Magic Corp has people with Persuasion, don't you think they could make our parents do anything?'

'It's for the best,' Tom said.

We all stared at him.

Tom shrugged. 'There are more difficult families, those who are harder to convince that this is the best path for their children. I wasn't always in Admin, you know. This hellhole is a punishment for people like me.'

'Shit,' Dennis said. His face was quickly losing colour.

But I had a feeling he wasn't reacting to Tom's pronouncement, because our boss was also staring at the door, his mouth slightly ajar.

'What's up?' I asked Dennis.

'There's a lot of Hellhounds heading our way; they must have escaped the pen upstairs,' he deduced. 'You really can't Perceive, can you?'

I sighed. 'No, and I can't do Persuasion or Portal either. How many is "a lot"?'

Dennis refused to answer. Tom seemed to be afflicted by an equal amount of mute horror. Leaving them to their stupor, Simon and I moved to the door of Tom's office and took in the chaotic scene before us.

People who usually carried coffee cups and paper were frantically brandishing Physical swords, lances, balls, and even cricket bats. Someone leapt behind the fax machine and curled up into the foetal position. Someone else went screaming for the bathroom. My colleagues, usually calm and in control of most (if not all) of their faculties, were losing their shit.

And yeah, since most of us didn't have Physical good enough to get us a promotion off this Floor of Hell, we were all so freaking screwed.

'Tom!' I hurled over my shoulder. 'You need to help us. Your magic's the strongest here!'

My boss coughed awkwardly. 'I am no longer capable of fighting demons.'

'It's true,' Dennis added. 'I saw his file. His power reserves were huge, but they didn't replenish. They had to last a lifetime and he burned through them.'

Tom looked down at the floor and said nothing.

There was no time to digest this piece of information—or to feel sorry for my boss—because the lift dinged, cheerfully announcing its arrival. I assumed it was carrying the newly escaped Hellhounds from upstairs.

They were the least of my concerns.

Because two large Portals of Demonic Doom had just appeared on either side of the lift doors. And they definitely lived up to my new name for them. Whatever they started spewing was heavy enough to make the floor shake beneath me and tall enough to punch craters into the ceiling, spilling wiring and chunks of plasterboard everywhere.

I think we had about a second to just gawp.

And then all hell broke loose.

23

If there's one thing Hellsomethings are good at, it's inflicting damage. These creatures seemed eager to show off their deadly skills: crushing desks, smashing chairs, and ripping into limbs and skulls.

'*Freeze!*' Simon roared. I had noticed that he used words to bolster his Persuasion when faced with multiple threats.

There wasn't time to worry about the pain. I whipped out my phone, hit WatchDog, and rocked back against Simon as power flooded through me. Gasping, I formed a semi-spherical shield in front of us and *pushed* (making sure it avoided my colleagues, of course). My construct connected with several Hellthings and I assume they died on impact because small explosions of ichor painted the carpet.

Heavy masses began slamming into my Physical barrier. I raced along the shield in my mind, shoring up its weakest points and hoping my quick fixes would survive the onslaught. It occurred to me that it might be helpful if we could fire stuff out *through* the shield, so I allowed it.

Using my magic was just so easy. Too damn easy.

My head throbbed. My palm stung. My ribs were needling my lungs. And each blast of my colleagues' Physical through the shield was like a tiny slice in my skin, barely there and bleeding sluggishly—but those cuts would become deadly if they kept mounting. Regardless, I continued to let every single ball or spear through. Not all of the projectiles struck their targets—I could tell by the lack of blood splatters—but some did.

It wasn't enough. Nowhere near enough.

'Simon, you should Portal out of here,' I rasped. 'We need you to keep your people in line.'

'I'm not leaving you!' his voice insisted from somewhere nearby.

More power. I needed more power. I yanked hard and something twisted inside my navel. Oh yes. That's what I needed—*and* I managed not to hurl. Score.

My hand wasn't hurting anymore. My magical core, though...ouch.

Water exploded over my face and I spluttered. Someone had destroyed the water cooler instead of one of the Hellthings, but that didn't bother me. No way. Because now I knew my shield would hold even without my full concentration.

I darted a frantic look around for Dennis—and found him standing beside me, shooting balls across the room. I swayed on my feet, unable to look away from his face. I knew that frown, knew how it felt. I'd run my fingers over those lips more than once.

Suddenly I was eating carpet. Not very tasty.

Simon's hands snapped over my wrists and pulled me up from the floor. I sagged against him as he towed me back into Tom's empty office, away from the chaos, away from any accusing eyes. Once we were safely inside, he slammed the door shut. I didn't hear any more human screams, which meant that no one had been stupid enough to venture past my shield yet.

'Is Mack *insane*?' I exclaimed.

If I didn't know any better, I'd think the Hellcreatures were under her control. But Mack had two Ps—the human kind. She couldn't have Persuasion. Which meant she had to have a hybrid on her side, doing her bidding.

'Mack knew I'd find out the truth!' I realised. 'She knew if I came here I'd figure out that MC wasn't after me and now she's busting up HQ just to keep me quiet.'

'Then we need to get you out of here before she hurts any more people,' Simon said.

I managed a grin, but it felt very wobbly and I imagine it looked even worse. 'My shield can hold the creatures off. It totally can.'

Simon caught me when my body attempted to do a repeat of my earlier swan dive.

My relief at avoiding another close encounter with the floor vanished when I looked down at my hand. Holy shit, the phone was gone. I don't know where or how, but I'd dropped it. So why hadn't the shield collapsed yet? The power reserves I carried around inside me would totally have been exhausted by now.

'Jen!' Simon said, urgency thrumming through his voice. 'Jen, you'll burn yourself out. And then everyone will die, us included. We need to get you out of here.'

My head was banging something fierce. I wanted to bang Simon something fierce too, but it wasn't like that was ever going to happen.

Okay. I was sure there was a much more pressing matter I should be focusing on...

I wasn't so far gone that I didn't notice the small Portal that Simon had opened up underneath Tom's desk, or the fact that he was clearly dragging me towards it.

I started thrashing. 'No! Are you insane? I don't have Portal—it'll kill me!' Another thought swiftly occurred to me and

I slapped Simon's shoulders, furious. 'And no way am I letting anyone else get killed because of me! How do we know the Hellcreatures will leave once I'm gone? They'll devour anyone with a drop of magic!'

Simon swore and the Portal sealed up with a pop.

The door he kicked open. The view he took in with a twist to his lips. And then he used that booming voice again, one so full of magic and power I'd have done anything for him had he asked—'*FREEZE!*'

I saw his jaw bunch up, saw the tendons in his neck slither around, and knew he was going to have to use a lot more of his power than he usually did.

Then he threw his hands out in front of him.

The Fiery Vortex Things either side of the lift seemed tame by comparison when his Portal exploded into being, a loud, hungry monster that tossed unsecured stationery between desks and blasted stunned expressions onto my colleagues' faces.

'*Get into my Portal!*' Simon snarled.

I braced myself against the doorframe, the floor vibrating violently beneath me, and watched Simon's Portal shake and shimmer as he forced as many Hellcreatures as he could into the tunnel he'd connected to the demonic realm. I hoped there was a really unpleasant destination at the other end. Maybe a cave with a hungry Helldragon that didn't care what it ate.

Suddenly remembering my part in all this, I checked on my shield and found it beginning to waver. Which definitely wasn't good, even if that wasn't a surprise. My construct was weakening with each spasm of agony inside my head.

'Demon!' someone shouted, pointing at Simon. And it wasn't

Tom Chapman—he had already booked it over to the fire exit. Not that I could blame him.

Clearly, Magic Corp wasn't doing a fabulous job of keeping the truth about demons and their abilities under wraps.

I wondered just how many people *did* know.

Simon's expression became thunderous. 'If you don't want this demon to butcher your mind, you will kindly use the stairwell. And will someone please pull the fire alarm so our friends upstairs don't get eaten in our place?'

'Simon, man, what the hell?' someone else exclaimed. Yep, you could definitely spot the people who hadn't figured out that demons could come in human form.

'Jen is killing herself keeping this shield up,' Simon growled. 'And I'm killing *myself* to make our visitors go through that exit I created. Yes, I'm a demon. But know this: despite our historical enmity, I will do everything I can to save you. Got it?'

More indecisive looks. More muttering. Then one of our colleagues took a shot at him—only for their Physical ball to smack into a second, much smaller shield that I definitely didn't have the presence of mind to create.

I was surprised to see Dennis step forward, hands extended as he kept his construct in place. 'We need to go! We don't have long.'

'Head to the fire exit!' Tom added, wheeling his way back over. 'If you want to keep your useless jobs, leave now!' His voice dropped to a mutter. 'Before someone else tries to block our escape route. They already locked the door, but they didn't count on me copying a key for myself.'

I stared at him.

'Please, Ms Cooke,' he said with a sigh. 'I may be a mean old bastard, but I really don't want any of you to die. I've long suspected that Magic Corp would sacrifice this level if it had to. Hence the key. Now stop gawping and cover our retreat—no excuses!'

People started fleeing. Distantly, I heard Tom continue to shout at them, even ordering some of them to carry him and his wheelchair. He seemed to have it handled, so I went back to watching the strain on Simon's face instead. I didn't know how much longer his power reserves would last.

I hissed in surprise and grabbed his arm. 'Simon, something big just hit my shield.'

'I can't Persuade trolls without help,' Simon snapped.

Dennis pitched his voice low. 'Come with me, Jen. I'll get you to safety.'

'I can't leave yet!' I said. 'There's still heaps of people in the stairwell.'

'You'll die if you don't go now!' Dennis cried.

Simon snarled. 'Shut up! Both of you!'

He had a phone to his ear and a hand thrown up in our direction, clearly asking for some silence. He wasn't using Persuasion on us; he had nothing to spare because of what he was expending on the Hellcreatures. But Dennis and I shut up anyway. I mean, it was only polite. He was on a call.

Little Portals started popping up all over the place. Demons leapt out of them, wearing their usual black clothes and smug expressions. But when they saw where Simon had summoned them, they looked more than a little pissed off.

'Run, Dennis,' I said hoarsely.

He was a dick, but he had saved my life. He didn't deserve to get taken out by some cranky demon.

Dennis stubbornly shook his head.

'You brought us to MC!?' a demon roared. 'Why? They are our enemies!'

Simon gestured tiredly at my shield. 'These creatures. They were sent by someone in Magic Corp to kill Jen.'

The demons exchanged glances.

'But how did a human get control of them?' Dot asked.

'This really isn't the time to discuss it,' Simon said through gritted teeth.

Big and beefy Saul stepped closer to my barrier, eyes narrow. 'There's no need for this, Simon. Drop the Persuasion. Give them the hybrid. She's the one they want.'

'No—' Simon started to say, but then Saul surged forward and struck him in the face.

Simon stumbled, dazed, his concentration broken. My shield abruptly took on the brunt of the Hellcreature attack and I screamed. My Physical construct was at breaking point. And so was I.

I wasn't surprised when my shield shuddered and gave a metre, exposing one of the demons to the Hellcreatures on the other side. Barely a second later, dark ribbons of blood were torn into his throat and he went down hard.

The demons stared at his mutilated corpse.

I suspect they weren't thinking 'oh, so they do bleed black' like I was.

'Are you going to let them kill us all?' Simon demanded. 'And there are other hybrids here, not just Jen. We need to cover their escape. We should be *saving* people, otherwise that makes us no better than Magic Corp.'

This caused a rash of angry muttering. Simon turned his gaze onto each and every dissenter and they quietened, probably nervous about the smackdown he would give them in Persuasion duels later, when his powers weren't tied up in defending the entire first floor of Magic Corp's HQ.

Dot stepped forward, her eyes blazing. 'We can argue about this later, folks! Let's do this.' She nodded at me. 'Jen, keep your shield up for as long as possible.'

I think I may have croaked a response.

The demons spread out until they stood in a line, Simon at their crux, their expressions hard and focused. I wasn't sure what they were doing at first.

'They're turning the creatures against each other,' Dennis whispered in awe. 'It's like they're combining their powers.'

Unified, the demons were unstoppable. Tar-like ichor splattered the walls, the floor, the ceiling, and rained steadily down my shield. The sounds that filled the air were plainly animal in origin, causing the hairs on my arms to stand to attention.

Dennis got back in on the action, shooting balls of magic towards Hellcreatures already entangled with each other. My shield was creeping steadily inwards, swallowing up every safe space and cutting us off from the fire exit. I gasped for air, trying so hard to let the damn construct shrink instead of shatter.

To my knowledge, no besieged shield had ever lasted this long in the history of Magic Corp's Australian branch. Okay, we'd only existed for a little over a century, but that's still a long time, right?

My temples gave one last vicious squeeze and darkness poured over my eyes, blinding me, drowning me until—

I could resist no longer. I tumbled into the abyss.

24

I woke up in bed. Not an unusual way to regain consciousness, but there was someone lying beside me, a flimsy sheet shielding their body from mine. Momentarily panicked, I struggled against the cocoon of bedding, trying to get a good look at my companion—only to exhale in relief when I finally managed to see who it was.

Propped up against the barred headboard and wearing yet another pair of black trackpants, Simon dozed with his lips slightly parted. We were in his apartment's master bedroom and, judging by the murmuring on the other side of the door, his living room was now the base of operations for his demonic takeover. I guess I felt bad about that, because I was the reason Demon HQ had been abandoned.

But I didn't feel bad about Simon cordoning off this prime bit of real estate just for us.

Determined light snaked its way in through the dark grey blinds shuttered over the window. I wouldn't have minded if they'd been open, actually. My head didn't hurt anymore and I felt ready to start slinging Physical again. I searched for my phone for a couple of seconds before remembering that I'd lost the damn thing—not to mention the power surge that had come with it. Fear exploded inside my chest, but I tamped down on it. I didn't want to wake Simon.

I carefully lifted the sheet and confirmed that I was indeed missing pants. However, I still had the shirt on and everything else that really mattered—and besides which, Simon was with me. I knew he'd protect me from anything, including himself.

I found myself taken in by his slack features. He seemed so much younger when he was like this, lost to oblivion and not worried about the fate of hybrids and demons and whatever else. His trackpants were loose, I noticed, and lacked a drawstring, though there were gaps in the waistband that suggested it had once been there. The pants skirted his abdomen, revealing a trail of dusky hair that led down and out of sight.

God, he was amazing to look at. And here, ensconced in our own private lair, I wanted to do more than just look.

I leaned in and whispered, 'Hey. Do you realise I'm lying half naked in your bed?'

He jolted awake, smiled blearily down at me, then swiftly rolled over and pinned me underneath him. I barely had time to see the darkness in his eyes before he started ravishing my mouth with an intensity I did not expect. He grabbed a fistful of his pants and yanked them down his legs. His kiss became a growl as he surged against me, now unencumbered, his hardness pressing into my abdomen.

Oh God. I was so close to coming apart already and I wanted him inside me when that happened.

I tugged desperately at my uncooperative underwear. Simon solved the issue by tearing them right off me, my shirt receiving the same treatment barely a second later. There was no barrier left between us. I was his for the taking.

But then he detached his lips from mine, gasping, 'We can't.'

'If you're about to tell me you don't have any condoms...' I laughed nervously.

Simon groaned. It was a primal sound, one born of epic frustration. 'I don't have any. But even if I did...you'll soon fall prey to my powers and I'd rather...rather not...'

I held his gaze. 'Simon. You're not forcing me to feel hot for you, because I liked what I saw the moment I opened my eyes. Um, unless you can use your powers while you're asleep. You can't do that, can you?'

Oh shit, I really hoped not.

Simon clambered back onto his side of the bed, his breathing ragged but slowly evening out with each draw. Quietly, he admitted, 'No. I can't.' He held up a hand when I opened my mouth. 'Jen, this is too dangerous. I'm awake now, if you hadn't noticed.'

I cast an eye down at his straining member, still on full display. 'Yeah, I can see that. But I'm calling bullshit on you not being able to control yourself.'

'Really?' Simon snorted. 'You think you know more about me and my powers than I do?'

Okay, he might have had me there, but I was on a roll. 'Well, I'm pretty sure I know when you're doing the Jedi mind trick thing. Your eyes start whirling and my head gets all fuzzy. And that's not happening right now. So I'm going to take this opportunity to touch you. Of my own free will. If that's okay?'

'Fuck,' Simon muttered. 'Yes. Yes please, yesss...' He trailed off, somewhat distracted by me ducking forward and licking the sensitive patch of skin beside one of his nipples.

'My parents obviously didn't have this hang-up about sex,' I went on, kissing my way down Simon's ribcage. He squirmed.

'Because I exist—and I don't remember Mum ever being unhappy about that, even when Dad wasn't around to Persuade her. Or are you going to insult me and say that my mother only stayed with my father because he made her do it? Just so you know, they were very much in love.'

'I wouldn't dare say such a thing...' Simon rasped.

'So clearly it's possible for you demons to stay out of other people's heads,' I said, sliding one teasing finger down that delectable trail of hair on his abdomen.

Simon grabbed my finger before it could reach its destination. Smiling, he bent forward and gently kissed the tip of the digit. 'You make a compelling argument.'

'I sure do,' I said, trying not to feel too disappointed when he withdrew from me. 'Maybe I can distract you enough that you can't form a coherent thought in your own head, much less plant one in mine.'

A short laugh escaped him.

My gaze roamed towards the headboard. 'Or maybe I should tie you up. That might work. I'll have all the control then and I seriously doubt you'll want any of it back once things get started. And it goes without saying that I'll stop if you want me to; you won't need to Persuade me.'

'Jen, I...' Simon bit his lip. 'You're very stubborn.'

'Which is exactly what I need to be if I'm going to convince your Band of Demonic Demons that my idea about replacing Magic Corp with something better is any good.'

'Demonic demons?' he repeated, grinning.

I grimaced. 'Damn it. That sounded better in my head.'

Simon anchored his hand on my hip, a firm, possessive gesture that flushed heat through me, from navel to neck and back again. I parted my lips as he leaned in, ready to accept his kiss—

'Don't you want to know if Dennis is safe?' he asked suddenly. 'We brought him back with us.'

'Why are we talking about Dennis?' When Simon's mouth stayed resolutely shut, I rolled my eyes and said, 'I trust you. And I trust that Dennis hasn't been dismembered or mind-whammied. So about that me-tying-you-up thing...'

Simon's fingers crept up from my hip and I dared to hope for a moment—until they skipped over my chest to cup my cheek instead. 'Jen, there's nothing more I want right now than for you to tie me to the bed and make me forget about everything outside of this room. Because you are tempting me to the point of insanity and I'm not sure I can resist for much longer.'

Definite improvement.

'*But*,' he continued, 'there's a lot more going on here than just us.'

He pinned me with a look that demanded I take him seriously. I released the breath that I'd trapped behind my teeth. He was right. And, admittedly, I'd wanted to chase all thoughts of Magic Corp, Mack, and Merindah out of my head with a badly timed boink session. Simon would have made a convenient distraction.

It wasn't until Simon chuckled that I realised I must have said at least part of my internal monologue out loud.

He smirked. 'Boink session?'

'Yes, *boink session*,' I said testily.

And then we were both laughing, the bed shaking beneath us. When our mirth finally petered out, Simon pinched the sheet between two of his fingers and drew it up over my shoulder, concealing both of our bodies, which was probably a wise move.

'How screwed are we?' I asked. 'I mean, your demonic demons didn't seem terribly pleased about you calling them to MC to save a whole bunch of humans.'

Lines spiralled out from the corners of his lips. 'They will obey me. For now. But they won't be so quick to follow any orders like that again.'

'That's reassuring.'

He sighed. 'Jen, what can I tell them? Magic Corp pursues them every time they set foot inside this realm. They want every branch of it gone. They don't care if full-blooded humans get hurt in the process, normal or otherwise.'

'Well, *I* care,' I grumbled. 'And holy shit, I am totally going out there to give them a piece of my mind.'

I surged out of bed, but Simon snagged my wrists and pulled me back down. I bit back my protests when I belatedly felt the chill on my chest and my thighs.

His smirk was back with a vengeance. 'I'd rather no one else got this view. Especially the human house guest.'

'What, you're more concerned about Dennis getting an eyeful than you are about your people shredding me?' I demanded.

'You're one of us.' Simon's eyes narrowed. 'They won't touch you.'

'Look, Simon,' I began, yanking my arms away from him, 'I don't have any demonic abilities. And I lost my phone, which was the only thing boosting my powers to a decent level, so I'm pretty fucking useless right now.'

I hammered my fists against my hips and winced, realising how childish that must have looked, but I was too scared to step out there with nothing but my usual weak Physical to defend myself.

'You don't need the phone,' Simon said.

I stared at him. 'What?'

'I've been thinking about that, Jen.' He swung out of bed and made his way over to the tallboy in the corner. He started rifling through one of the drawers. I wasn't surprised to see that he had a vast array of black shirts stashed in there.

'It makes a Portal, that's what the app does,' Simon said, turning back to me after he'd pulled a shirt over his head. 'And that's *all* it's doing right now, since I've stopped my friends sending the hounds through for the moment. You could be sourcing your extra power from the demonic realm via the Portal inside your phone. The reason Fido appeared the first time was because you used your Physical to create what you expected to see—a WatchDog.'

'And that's why you tried to throw me into a Portal earlier? Because of this crazy theory?' I demanded. 'I could have died! And do Portals even work like that?'

Simon shrugged. 'If Portals can transport matter, such as creatures, into this realm, then pulling energy through them is not too big a stretch, is it?'

I suddenly missed my phone for another reason. I needed to talk to Merindah. She'd say something to make me feel better, like how Simon was clearly off his rocker for even suggesting that I had some mutated version of Portal, and then she'd tell me that my taste in men had significantly improved—a demon with scary mind powers was a far better choice than Dennis Freaking Chan. We'd both laugh and conveniently forget that we'd been keeping secrets from each other.

'Whatever,' I muttered in Simon's general direction. 'I need clothes.' He held up one of his shirts and I rolled my eyes. 'Clothes in my size would be nice. And some clean underwear. Oh God, just the clean underwear if that's all you've got.'

'I'll send my sister in with something,' Simon promised.

He came over to me and wrapped me up in his arms, his soft cotton shirt grazing my nipples in a way that made me shiver pleasantly. He gave me a soft peck on my lips, his smile covering my own as I melted into him.

I'd kind of forgotten what I'd been angry about. Damn him.

25

Shortly after Simon left, Dot entered the room bearing gifts—AKA clothes that actually fit me. She offered me size-ten jeans (black, of course), a fitted Acca Dacca shirt (also black), a matching bra-and-underwear set (black and black), and socks (you guessed it—black). At least my new Nikes were intact and didn't need replacing. They sported some slime on the heels, but were otherwise unharmed.

Dot wouldn't stop grinning at me. Yeah, she wasn't going to believe I slept naked all the time. I'd had to hop my blanket cocoon over to the pile of clothes she'd left for me on a chair. There was also the matter of the shirt and underwear that Simon had torn off me and hurled halfway across the room.

'Nothing happened,' I blurted.

Dot's eyebrows, a much darker shade than her asymmetrical blonde hairdo, shot upwards. 'That's a shame. Thought my brother had finally got his groove back.'

I yanked my shirt down as far as it would go, conscious that its tighter cut didn't hide quite so many ills. I hadn't planned on saying anything else—but Christ, if I couldn't talk to Merindah, then Dot would have to do. Not to mention that Dot would get the whole demon angle a hell of a lot more than my human BFF ever could. If there was a risk that Simon might accidentally

Persuade me into having sex, then I had to know. Even if it did mean awkwardly asking his sister.

I wrung my hands. 'Dot, he says we can't do anything, because he couldn't be sure if he was Persuading me to, you know...'

My turn to make crude gestures.

'Oh,' Dot said.

'Oh?' I repeated, my heart sinking.

Dot plonked herself onto the bed and patted the space beside her. Belting the jeans up around my waist, I nearly toppled over in my attempt to reach the bed. When I was no longer in any danger of becoming intimate with the floor, Dot said, 'Easy enough to figure out when you're in someone's head or not.'

'So I gathered,' I said.

'Yeah. Lately Simon's been doubting himself—and doubting that he can do any good with his powers.' Dot wrinkled her nose. 'He broods too much. Has to make everything his responsibility, his fault. But he's nothing like our brother.'

'You have another brother?'

'*Had*,' she corrected grimly.

That didn't sound good.

Shadows flickered through Dot's pale eyes. 'Jon was the oldest of us three. Older, more popular, very powerful, incredibly dangerous—he was the one everyone liked. But no one could defend themselves against him. And he knew that. He *revelled* in it. I always hated him, even before he...'

Dot fell silent, looking uneasy.

'He Persuaded someone to sleep with him,' I guessed.

Dot nodded. 'Violent Persuasion leaves scars.' She pointed at my temple. 'Like what Simon saw in you. He saw it in the woman our brother attacked. Her Persuasion wasn't as strong as Jon's so she couldn't fight back and he blocked her memory of the assault when it was over. Simon was the only who was powerful enough to identify and remove that block. He knew exactly who'd done it...and it was his duty to inform our clan's rulers. Even with Simon's help, it took ten of our clan's best to overpower Jon and get him to confess. Jon was executed the next day. They beheaded him.'

Yikes. But I really didn't feel sorry for the guy.

'Now, the Persuasion duels you've seen recently,' Dot went on. 'Everyone involved in them agrees to the intrusion. Interfering with your fellow demon's mind without permission is not only against the law, it's reprehensible.'

I snorted. 'I see, Persuading is bad, unless it's being used on humans or Hellcreatures. Wait—Simon made me follow him to his car yesterday. Isn't that, er, illegal?'

Dot shook her head. 'There's a loophole that allows it to be done in a situation where it will save the person's life.'

My chest tightened. 'So what my father did, forcing me to forget...'

'If it saved your life, then he had every right to do it,' Dot answered.

Yeah, well, the jury was still out on that one.

'Okay,' I said slowly. 'But what if someone is using Persuasion to force people to keep away from their families? Not to save them, but to control every aspect of their lives?'

Dot frowned. 'Persuasion is one of our abilities, so anyone using it that way should be punished by our laws. Family is important to us.'

'But, say, if it's being done to human magic-users and not just hybrids?'

'Depends,' Dot said.

'On what?'

Her lips curved into a sardonic grin. 'On how badly you can get us to feel about it.'

***

I crept out into the living room, using Dot as a shield for as long as possible. When she left my side, I noticed that Dennis was squeezed onto a couch between two demons. I was glad to see him in one piece, but I wasn't exactly happy about being in the same room as him after finding out that he'd deliberately hobbled his career for me. The whole situation made me nervous. Because he was definitely going to bring it up again.

Simon caught my eyes and jerked his head at the other couch. I ignored his non-verbal command and chose to stand beside him, arching an eyebrow when he stared at me.

'Go on, do it,' I challenged him. 'Make me sit down. Or prove to us both that you can control yourself.'

I didn't expect him to laugh—and apparently neither did the demons because they side-eyed us both. I quickly diverted my gaze to Dot. She was standing behind Dennis, a hand hovering over the top of his head while she checked for a block on his mind. I wasn't sure why she'd agreed to do it and I was kind of hoping she wouldn't find anything...

Her intense frown quickly morphed into outright disgust. Then she nodded at me, her hand dropping back to her side. Dennis continued to glare at Simon, none the wiser.

Oh shit. I was right?

Simon took centrestage, or rather centre room, and his combined audience of demons, hybrids, and whatever else (oh alright, Dennis) fell under his spell. And not because Simon was abusing his magic. I could tell—my head felt as clear as the Pacific Motorway when it was shut down during a bushfire. Simon didn't need to draw on his powers to command our attention.

'There's a third party involved that we weren't aware of,' he began. 'Someone with Persuasion. They could be a demon or a hybrid.'

'Are they the one who sicced the Hellcreatures on the humans at MC?' one of the demons bordering Dennis piped up. 'Should have left 'em to it!'

Dennis shot him a filthy look. 'You demons don't care about anyone or anything, do you.'

The demon laughed and elbowed Dennis, hard enough to elicit a pained wince. 'We care about plenty—we just don't care about you MCers getting what you deserve. I'm all good to sit back and let someone else destroy you. Makes my job a lot easier.'

The rest of the demons began adding their opinions to the conversation. And most of them agreed: it wasn't their problem. I gritted my teeth.

Simon raised a hand. Silence fell, allowing him to speak uninterrupted. 'Mackenzie Roberts, MC's liaison to the government, appears to be operating independently of Magic Corp and she has someone on her side who is strong enough to control multiple creatures simultaneously, including trolls.'

'Mack also seems to like sending Hellhounds after demons,' I added. 'Or did you forget about the attack on your own headquarters?'

I wasn't going to mention who was responsible for Mack *finding* the aforementioned headquarters and I really hoped Simon wasn't about to out me.

Simon flashed me an appreciative smile. 'This means, for the moment, that Mackenzie Roberts is our priority, not Magic Corp.'

The demons weren't wholly convinced, judging by the sceptical frowns. Saul, who was rapidly becoming my least favourite demon, emerged from a darkened corner. I had a feeling another Persuasion match was imminent, so I cleared my throat and stepped forward to address the room. My hands were shaking but that's what pockets are for, right? Never mind that since I was back in jeans marketed towards women, I couldn't fit more than four fingers into the damn pockets.

'Let's put the Mack issue aside for a sec,' I said, wondering why I was saying anything, and why the demons weren't looking away from me. It was pretty freaking uncomfortable. 'You need to know what's going on at Magic Corp. About what's being done to both humans and hybrids.'

'And we should listen to you why?' Saul demanded. 'You don't have any of our powers. Imposter!'

I blinked furiously, somehow remaining steady on my feet and not giving in to a tide of angry tears. 'Because Magic Corp knows about the hybrids and their powers and *they use them*. MC gets someone with Persuasion to force families to hand over their children. It's not consensual. Don't you guys behead people who do that sort of shit?'

'Prove it,' Saul sneered.

Without any prompting on my part, Dot swiftly planted her hand on Dennis' scalp. I'd never seen him jump quite like that before.

'This one has a block on his mind,' Dot announced, as if it had just occurred to her.

More silence, the type that someone needs to fill before things get awkward. I looked at Simon for support, but he simply smiled and spread his arms instead of coming to my rescue. Fucking fantastic. Hunching my shoulders as if preparing for a rugby tackle, I went over to Dennis and knelt before him.

'What does she mean?' Dennis asked, his voice wavering.

'Someone Persuaded you,' I said.

'Yeah, Simon did, he did it last night,' he growled.

'No, I mean, someone blocked your memories—they made you forget something long ago,' I explained. 'Tom practically admitted it, that some families need Persuading to hand over their kids. What if it's more than some?' I gave his knees a gentle squeeze. 'Do you trust me?'

Dennis visibly swallowed. 'What are they going to do to me?'

'I'm going to ask them to remove the block,' I said. 'I don't like putting you in this position, but if we can't get them to care...we have no hope of them ever helping us.'

'I'm never helping humans!' the demon to Dennis' left snarled.

I spitted the offender with a glare, dredging up all the resentment I'd been hoarding every single day for three years. The resentment caused by being stuck in my own personal hell on the first floor, always forgotten while the rest of my colleagues went out and bonded over Oporto or free doughnuts, never once asking if I wanted to join them.

'Shut up,' I told the demon. And he did, suddenly unable to meet my gaze. When I turned back to Dennis, my glare morphed into something hopefully more sympathetic. 'If you don't agree to this, I swear I won't ask again. Dennis, do you want them to...'

Dennis laid his hands over mine. 'Fine. I'll do it. But if they make my brain explode, I want you to avenge me.'

'I will,' I promised.

Dennis closed his eyes. 'I'm ready. Do your worst, demons.'

26

Dot volunteered to remove the block by herself, but several of the demons wanted in on the action—presumably to make sure she wasn't lying about its existence. One by one, they focused on Dennis, their eyes whirling.

I shivered and tightened my grip on Dennis' knees. He didn't seem to react at first—his face remained as still as stone, weathering the onslaught, but then the cracks started to appear. A tear stole its way out of the corner of his eyelids. His lips moved soundlessly. His hands began to tremble on top of mine.

And for the first time in forever, I felt really bad for him. No matter what he'd done to me, what he *still* expected from me, this...this was far worse.

'Dot?' I whispered.

'Not long now,' she said softly.

Dennis broke. He sagged, limp and lifeless, and when his eyes finally opened they wandered vaguely across the ceiling. I'd destroyed him. I might not have been the one who'd got inside his head, but I wasn't blameless. I'd forced him to go through with this intense invasion.

'Oh, Dennis,' I said.

He shook his head in disbelief. 'Someone at Magic Corp with Persuasion got my family to give me up. And I just...walked away, thinking that's what I wanted. I was nine! How could I want that?

That's not even the last time they Persuaded me. I didn't...' Dennis drew a shuddering breath. 'I didn't want to sign the contract when I turned eighteen. I wanted to see my family. But someone *made me* do it.'

'I'm so, so sorry,' I whispered.

'Not as sorry as MC's gonna be when I get my hands on them,' he vowed.

A demon slammed their fist against the wall, fury tightening their expression. 'Magic Corp's evil knows no bounds!'

'Arseholes!' another demon added.

'Do you see now?' I asked, standing so that I could glower around at our audience. 'Do you see what Magic Corp does? My best friend, a human, just got suspended—possibly even *fired*, which mean she's in serious danger—because she was helping contract-breakers who'd left to find their families. And can you imagine the guilt that some of my colleagues must be feeling, thinking they signed themselves over *willingly?*'

'Wait a minute,' someone interjected—rather politely, I thought. I realised it was Dennis. He was biting his lip thoughtfully.

'What?' I asked.

'I'm remembering something, something more recent...' Dennis sat up straight. 'Mack. Mack saw me at the office last night. And she had a bunch of Hellhounds with her! She was obviously controlling them and I confronted her and—she made me forget I'd seen them.' He looked stricken. 'I'm lucky she didn't kill me!'

Holy shit. This was serious.

'But you still followed her afterwards,' I told him. 'Why didn't she stop you?'

Dennis rubbed away the sweat that had gathered on his

forehead. 'I guess she didn't know I'd planned to do that, so she didn't Persuade me otherwise. I was so surprised to see the Hellhounds that it wasn't anywhere near my surface thoughts.'

'And you saw no one else with her?' Simon pressed.

Dennis shook his head.

I glanced at Simon. His eyebrows were knitting together into one firm row and I figured I knew what he was thinking. Mackenzie Roberts. Controlling Hellhounds. By herself. She wasn't using a hybrid or a demon to do her dirty work. She could do it all on her own. But how?

'It's our duty to punish those misusing Persuasion,' Dot declared. She tipped her chin in my direction, letting me know she was backing me up.

I nodded repeatedly. 'This is why we have to go after Mack first.'

'She's not one of ours!' Saul argued.

Simon stepped forward until he was standing beside me. 'No, but Mackenzie has Persuasion and has used her powers to Persuade creatures to attack hybrids—and she got them to attack us.'

'But how is she doing it?' I asked. 'Mack's bested plenty of people with her Physical. She always knows when there's a Hellhound around and she's never had any trouble reading minds...how can she have three Ps?'

Simon's grimace lasted for several seconds. 'It's possible the interbreeding in previous generations has led to this.'

'So what?' Saul interjected, cracking his knuckles. 'We should be taking out all of Magic Corp, not just one woman!'

'Mackenzie is killing hybrids while Magic Corp currently isn't,' Simon responded. His eyes remained still instead of whirling, so I knew he'd restrained himself instead of using any mental pressure on his main rival. 'Destroying MC might not stop her, if she's acting independently of them. And we cannot allow her to continue to slaughter our brethren.'

This time there were murmurs of approval. Some of it seemed to be directed at me. I propped my hand up on my hip, though I'm sure the pose looked awkward. I didn't know what to say or do. I'd never received this much attention while at MC.

Simon drew a breath and I instinctively held mine as he spoke. 'If we do not help them and earn their trust, we have no hope of convincing the humans and hybrids to help us replace Magic Corp with our own group, one that can protect *everyone* in this country from magical creatures and those who use their powers to harm others.' His eyes flicked to me and I felt warmth swell inside my chest. 'We need people with Physical on our side. We cannot keep Portalling away when we are threatened. It's not sustainable.'

'Replacing...!' The murmurs swiftly segued into indignant mutters.

'You're mad, absolutely mad,' Saul said, then jerked a hand at me. 'That hybrid has found a way to mess with your mind!'

Simon lifted his chin. 'If my mind is constrained, then so are my powers. I won't be able to fight you off in a Persuasion duel—and you're welcome to give it a try. Right here and right now. But I warn you, I won't show you any mercy this time.'

'Saul, don't do it,' came a hushed whisper from the other side of the room. 'Remember how powerful Jon was.'

Judging by the shudder that passed through him, Simon had heard them.

'Simon's making sense,' Dot declared. 'What do you think'll happen when this branch of MC goes down? The other, more powerful branches will band together and come after us. We'll

202

have giant targets on our backs! Best to get some people on our side who'll help defend us.'

Dennis cleared his throat. 'Hey, um, can we have this argument later? I think we've got more important things to worry about just now.'

'The human is correct,' Simon said calmly. 'Our current problem is Mackenzie Roberts. We will discuss this at a more convenient time.'

These words had a rather predictable effect on both demons and Dennis the Human. The room filled with noise again, but it quickly dissipated when Simon held up his hands. 'Dennis, you've got access to the personnel files on your work computer. I need you to go in and get Mackenzie's home address.'

Dennis flushed. 'So, funny story, but um...' He dug into his pocket and retrieved a USB stick. 'I keep the personnel files on me.'

'Dennis!' I exclaimed. 'That's incredibly dangerous. What if...'

'Demons got a hold of it?' Dennis laughed darkly. 'What can they do with this information that's worse than what MC did to so many of us?'

I watched the surrounding demons with interest. Not all of them had cloned the hostile scowl that Saul was blatantly wearing; some looked at Dennis with sympathy and concern. Maybe if we could all work together to deal with this Mack problem, then they'd see what we could do as a united front in the long term.

'How are we going to defeat her if she's that strong, Simon?' a demon demanded. 'We had enough trouble with the creatures she sent into MC.'

Simon rubbed his jaw, looking weary. 'Queran, we have all four

Ps represented in this room. If we combine our powers, then it should be possible to overcome her.'

Dennis leaned forward on the couch, his eyes hard. 'And we'll catch her by surprise, when she's alone in bed. Her file doesn't list a significant other.'

'I'll confront her, by myself,' I said, then rushed on before anyone could object, 'Mack will be expecting me. I'm supposed to be her spy. She'll let me approach her, but only if she doesn't see a pack of demons behind me.'

'You're going to kill her, aren't you?' Queran asked. He was grinning with excitement.

I'm pretty sure I blanched.

Were they really expecting me to do that?

'No,' Simon said flatly. 'We need all the information we can get out of Mackenzie. We can't kill her until we she's answered our questions.'

Relief sang through my veins, but it did nothing to quell the rising tide of panic inside me. I'd volunteered to face Mack. Alone. And she was pretty damn powerful.

I patted my empty pockets. 'I'll need a phone, with WatchDog.'

'Done,' Simon said.

'I'm going in with you,' Dennis insisted. 'You can't do this alone, Jen.'

'The hell I can't,' I said, gripping my belt until my knuckles ached. 'You have no idea what I'm capable of, Dennis. And besides, Mack's already Persuaded you once. What if she does it again and orders you to attack me?'

'I wouldn't!' Dennis said, but he didn't sound sure.

Simon flew into action. Some of his people he sent straight out the door and others he grouped together, discussing with them how best to support my crazy plan to confront Mack. He gestured for me to join in, but my gaze slid back to Dennis. My first-floor colleague was wilting into the cushions on the couch, his eyes hollow. Now that he had nothing to distract himself with, he had to face the realisation of what had been done to him. It seemed kind of crappy to leave him dealing with it alone.

Simon closed the distance between us in three quick strides. He was practically simmering, but I wasn't about to let him intimidate me.

'I need to talk to Dennis,' I said quietly.

'Fine.' Simon waved a dismissive hand. 'You can waste time coddling the human.'

'Don't be a dick! You know how badly shaken up I was after you got into my head. Dennis deserves compassion right now. And someone has to get that USB stick off him.' I snapped my fingers at him. 'Simon, would you just look at me?'

'Why?' he said to the floor. 'I know what I'll see on your face.'

'You sure about that? You're not your brother, Simon.'

He glared at a certain someone who was busily looking anywhere but at her older sibling.

'*Dot*,' he growled.

'Doesn't matter who told me,' I said. 'Because I don't regret anything we did in your bedroom. In fact, I regret what we *didn't* do.'

'But you seem to prefer the human's company to mine and I can't be sure if...'

His gaze dropped down to his chest, where I'd anchored my hand against his shirt. I hastily retracted my touch. 'Simon. How tempted were you to Persuade everyone to agree with you just now?'

'Very,' he admitted.

'Could you Persuade a whole room of demons?'

'Most of them, yes. There's a few exceptions, like Saul.'

'Then why did you have to work so hard to convince them? If you really don't have any control over your powers, some of them should have just capitulated, right?'

'No, I—' Simon cut himself off, his expression slightly dazed.

I grinned mercilessly at him. 'You didn't want to force them to agree with you. So you didn't. I rest my case.'

'But you—'

I tipped my head towards Dennis, who was staring at an invisible spot on the wall. 'He's pretty destroyed. He needs me. As for you...looks like I need to stick around so I can keep knocking some sense into you. I'm done with Magic Corp. I'm all yours now.'

Wetting his lips, Simon said in a very hoarse voice, 'Jen...if there was no one else in this room...'

I tried to stifle the shiver.

Didn't really succeed. Didn't really care.

'But there are a lot of someone elses, so you'll just have to wait.' I cast a quick, furtive look around. 'And make sure you get some damn condoms, Simon.'

That sexy smirk of his really did things to me. Whew.

I sat down beside Dennis. He didn't respond to my presence at first, but he did start violently when I put my arm over his shoulder. When he'd calmed down, though he was still kind of twitchy, I told him the usual stuff, that everything was going to be alright, that we definitely weren't going to get chewed up by Hellhounds—well, not ones controlled by our friendly demons anyway. Dennis chuckled at that comment.

But it was going to take a lot more than a few laughs and a handful of minutes for him to heal. I'd had—still had—Simon to help me through it. No matter what Dennis had done to me, he needed someone to help *him*.

Suddenly all that shit from school didn't seem so important.

Oh God, did this mean I was going to forgive him or something?

I hoped not.

27

I wasn't sure it was a bright idea for four identical black vans to park along the street outside Mack's charming two-storey house—which was slap-bang in the middle of leafy, suburban Turramurra—because it looked suspicious as hell.

We hadn't been able to spot anything untoward on the property itself (certainly nothing as untoward as us) and Dennis had even used a pair of binoculars to check for any Hellcreatures. PercApption didn't quite have the same range as human eyes, apparently. He'd said there was nothing snarly and vicious in my way, but I couldn't shake my Very Bad Feeling.

In a matter of minutes I would have to face Mackenzie Roberts, who could wield three Ps to my one. Totally safe.

Simon and I sat in the front of one of the vans, rain beating down on the windscreen with increasing ferocity while we waited for Mack to bed down for the night. Finally, just when I was wondering if she had turned into a vampire at some point in the past six months, the light in the upstairs window winked out.

I stiffened.

Simon's fingers squeezed mine. 'I'll be right out here if you need me.'

My chest spasming with anxiety, I slithered out of the van and into the night. Rain immediately started striking my scalp through my hair. I flinched. Demons didn't seem to see the need for umbrellas when they could travel around in Portals instead of using their feet. Fair enough—I'd probably abuse the ability if I had it.

Hyperaware that a neighbour might poke their head out a window and see me, I strode down the brick path like I was supposed to be there and briskly headed for the lattice fence that stood at one end of the verandah. Climbing this would save me blowing my limited inner reserves on a ladder.

It's weird, but right then I was grateful to Dennis and our short-lived *thing* for forcing me to learn how to sneak around school back when we were younger.

I navigated my way across the roof of the verandah, hoping I'd correctly remembered which window I was supposed to be using. Once I'd decided that the lace curtains wouldn't strangle me, I vaulted over the windowsill into Mack's room—and landed on my knees with a excruciatingly loud thump. Before I could get to my feet or create some sort of Physical weapon to defend myself, light blazed over me and burned a green blob into my retinas. Mack was sitting up in bed with a hand on the lamp beside her.

'How did you know where to find me?' she demanded.

I settled for something she might actually believe. 'I went to Dennis. Said if he gave me your address I'd do a favour for him. He was really keen to collect.'

'Though you seem to lack demonic powers, you certainly have the qualities,' Mack noted, her nose wrinkling at me. I was drenched and I suppose it must have been one of Mackenzie Roberts' Ten Commandments not to shed so much rainwater onto her shag-pile carpet.

I forced my stiff shoulders into a shrug. 'Makes sense. Turns out my father was a demon.'

No surprise on that blank face. It really wasn't much of a revelation, admittedly. I scratched the back of my neck, suddenly fearful that she was Persuading me right then and there.

'Why have you entered my home, Jennifer?' she asked.

'I'm your spy. Figured you'd want a report.'

Mack's forehead creased slightly. 'I am not ignorant of your recent movements, Jennifer. You were seen at Magic Corp—clearly in league with the demons, I might add. Most unwise. What were you doing there? I am sure that you recall you were officially suspended?'

After tearing a significant chunk off my tongue, I read out, word for word, the thoughts I was printing across my mind's eye, hoping that was the only thing she'd see. 'I left my phone charger on my desk. And it's not like I knew MC would send the Hellhounds after me while I was there. That's kind of stupid, even for them.'

'You should have known better than to endanger your friends with your presence,' Mack said, a hint of a reprimand in her tone, as if I was the only reason a horde of Hellcreatures had descended on the first floor to reap mayhem. 'There are rumours that you created a shield twenty metres in diameter and held it for longer than five minutes. Did the demons teach you to do that?'

'No, I'm just naturally that awesome,' I said, then waited for her to show some interest in my new-found skill, but her expression remained flat. 'Do you want my report or not?'

'Only if it's new information,' she said. 'I am already aware that Simon Bradley from Tech is a demon. He was seen exhibiting Persuasion at HQ earlier today.'

Something growled softly in the doorway. I shot a nervous look over there—and saw nothing. But there was a very high chance that I was sharing oxygen with yet another Hellhound. So maybe Dennis hadn't seen the damn thing because this was an indoor pet, or maybe Dennis had lied (unlikely, because I so did not peg him as a necrophiliac), or maybe Mack was strong enough to project a Persuasion field over her entire property, one that was good enough to fool even a pack of demons.

Her house could be *crawling* with Hellcreatures.

Come to think of it, I hadn't seen Mack's beloved poodles yet. I wondered if they'd ended up as someone's dinner.

I figured I didn't have time to play dumb anymore.

'Yeah, it's obvious you're not really working for MC,' I said, squaring my shoulders and trying my best not to look terrified. 'I'm not on the Kill Register. I checked. I'm earmarked for promotion, for fuck's sake.'

'Your kind should be on the Register,' Mack said through her teeth. 'You're all demons, deep down, biding your time. You will destroy everything in your path.'

I couldn't help the snort. 'Says the woman with Perception, Physical, *and* Persuasion.'

'And Portal,' she added, smiling.

'Shit, really?' I stared at her.

We were *so* screwed. Even if my companions did manage to come to my rescue, she'd just Portal out—leaving behind Hellhounds which, judging by the chorus of heavy breathing and the increasing stench, were growing in number.

Mack's left cheek twitched, a sure sign that she was losing patience. 'Yes, *really*. I will use these abilities to ensure that your kind is completely eradicated.'

'You'd have to start with yourself, since your Persuasion and Portal make you a ripe candidate for a hybrid,' I snapped. One of my temples was starting to throb and I was sure the other would soon follow suit. 'You might not remember it—see, my father Persuaded my memories into this hidden corner of my mind and I only recently—'

'No, no,' Mack interrupted. 'My parents were very human traitors who broke their contracts and were dealt with accordingly. They gave me no warning that they'd been planning anything. Very inconvenient, as I did not have time to protect myself. I would gladly forget they ever existed.'

Oh my fucking God, when was Magic Corp going to stop creating so many ticking time bombs? Merindah's dubious activities were harmless compared to this.

'Your parents weren't going to take you with them?' I gaped at Mack, hating the scratch of sympathy I felt inside my skull.

Mack shrugged, clearly unbothered. 'I would have killed them myself if they'd offered. After that, there was no point in trying to salvage my reputation. Mud sticks. So I went elsewhere. There were many interested parties, even years before we went public. My business partners and I have mutually beneficial goals.'

'So you figured betrayal wasn't as bad as breaking your own contract,' I commented.

'Oh no, I would never become a contract-breaker. No need to draw that kind of attention to myself.' Mack tsked, as though passing judgement on my reasoning skills. 'I already raised enough eyebrows when I gracefully accepted the demotion to Head of Admin; it was Magic Corp's punishment for my parents' misdeeds. But I needed access to the personnel files. Once I knew exactly who the hybrids were, we could take them to our lab and experiment on them.'

My mouth went dry. 'Experiment on them...why would you do that?'

'Magic Corp is useless against demonic incursions.' It was almost like she was delivering a lecture; her voice had dropped to a monotone and I half expected her to whip out a PowerPoint presentation, something she'd done at work when trying to drill her expectations into us.

'Surely you understand this now that you have been among the demons,' Mack went on. 'They possess abilities that can destroy us far more easily than crude normal weapons ever could. We need to fight fire with fire, meet Persuasion with Persuasion, and so on. All it takes is a harmless injection to give us the powers we need.'

'You want to experiment on full-blooded demons next,' I said as I slowly pieced it together. 'And I can give you access to them. I'm not a spy. I'm a delivery service.'

Mack's lips curled. Clearly, I'd impressed her this time. 'Yes, studying them could help us find a way to make the Persuasion injections last longer. These drugs require frequent topping up'—she gestured at bar fridge beneath her dressing table; it continued to whirr innocently, despite its (apparently) demonic contents—'but at least this way we do not have to sully ourselves by interbreeding.'

'And by "we", you mean...' I prompted.

'There is no need for Magic Corp once we start equipping our armed forces with practical powers instead of those useless apps.' There was a gleam in Mack's eyes and I had a feeling she'd been wanting to unleash her *brilliance* onto someone for a while. 'So you see, Jennifer, I am judged by what I can contribute, not by my family name. I will deliver this country from all evils, magical or otherwise.'

Oh my God. Giving our abilities to soldiers was such a monumentally bad idea—our government would have a sure path to world domination. I mean, yeah, we were freaking *Australia*, the furthest thing from a force to be reckoned with, but...shit. Imagine an army of people with all four Ps. No one could stop them, not even the other Magic Corp branches. Both normals and magic-users would be helpless.

'Don't be so dramatic,' Mackenzie snapped, clearly in reaction to my surface thoughts. 'The desire for world domination is a purely demonic trait.'

I seriously had my doubts, judging by what I'd learned in Normal History at school, but I wasn't going to argue the point. 'So what happens to the humans at Magic Corp?'

'They will resist change, which makes them a threat to us,' Mack said, flinging the sheet off her body and dropping her legs over the side of her bed. The virginal white nightgown she was wearing seemed a bit *off*, considering what she'd done—and what she said next. 'We will glean all we can from their bodies and ensure that they provide us with a reliable supply of Perception and Physical injections.'

'Fuck you,' I said. 'I don't care if you're ashamed of what your parents did. It's no excuse. This is so, so wrong.'

Mackenzie shook her head, smirking. I kind of wished she'd go back to showing no emotion at all, because this was beyond creepy. 'You are so hopelessly ignorant, Jennifer. It is a wonder you survived this long.'

'My Physical is really strong—I'm strong enough to stop even you,' I rushed out, then squinted at her in confusion. Mack had left the bed in the blink of an eye and was now standing in front of the doorway, where the snarling and growling was coming from.

I became aware of a fuzziness gathering behind my forehead. Persuasion. Oh God, had she been using it this whole time? Why hadn't I noticed before?

Mack laughed gently. 'But you just told me your powers are only a significant threat when you have WatchDog open. And oh, how odd, you seem to be without a phone.'

Did I really tell her that? I looked down at my empty, empty hand. When had I lost the phone? Oh shit.

My tongue stuck to the roof of my mouth. I was freaking out about what I might have told her without realising it, but I had to keep her talking. I had to stall so I could find some way to signal Simon without her stopping me.

'So you're not killing the hybrids?' I asked quickly. 'You're just experimenting on them?'

Mackenzie shrugged. 'Mistakes happen. Sometimes we use Hellhounds to herd the hybrids into Portals, like we attempted to do with you at the station—of course, we only know if they have that ability once they survive the journey. When we need Persuasion, we have to be a little more subtle. But if someone proves to be too much trouble to capture, we send sloshers or wingers after them.' She grimaced, as though she'd swallowed something distasteful. 'I did not expect one of my people to interfere and save you. Not to worry. She was punished.'

'But...that means...' I managed.

Mack pulled on a pink kimono-style dressing gown in one glide and threw a careless hand at the bed—the furniture and bedding immediately disintegrated, replaced by a Roaring Pool of Fire. Her exit assured, Mack turned back to me, smiling like she'd swallowed a sword and was watching me hunt around looking for it.

The pressure of her Persuasion lifted from my mind. The room blurred around me. And then I could clearly see Merindah standing beside Mack, balls of furious Physical magic swirling in her hands. I had no doubt they were meant for me.

Oh, I was so dead.

28

'I'm so sorry, Jen,' Merindah murmured.

'Yes, Merindah found herself in a spot of bother after it was discovered that she'd been falsifying her reports and possibly hiding fugitives.' Mackenzie tsked. 'I promised to help her out, to Persuade our superiors to drop her suspension and forget why they'd been investigating her in the first place. All she had to do was help me acquire hybrids for our experiments. But then how did she reward me? By running off to save you.'

'Merindah...' I wasn't sure what to say.

'I did it for them, Jen,' Merindah said, refusing to look at me. 'She said they'd be safe if I worked for her.'

My chest felt so hollow it was a wonder it didn't cave in on itself. Mack had offered Merindah a way out, a way to keep protecting the people she'd refused to kill. And I was just one person. A single life that could be traded in exchange for many more lives. Even if I was—had been—her best friend.

I wasn't sure I'd have done things any differently in her shoes.

'I get it, believe me, I so get it,' I said, linking my hands behind my back, hoping that what I was doing wasn't showing on my face or in my mind. I think I looked a bit strained—not that this was unexpected, given the situation. 'But you have to listen to me, Merindah. Mack's promises are worthless. She said she'd get me my job back if I led her to your sanctuary. You haven't told her where it is yet, have you?'

Merindah's eyes slid to Mack, but not for long. They lasered back on me.

'Merindah, I'm not lying,' I said.

I was practically screaming at her with my surface thoughts, but she knew as well as I did that I could be feeling something else entirely to the words I was deliberately thinking. Damn it, we'd been friends for years. Didn't that count for something?

'Don't waste your breath,' Mack told me. 'Merindah will do exactly what I tell her to. After her unwise decision to assist you, I located and kidnapped her mother.'

'That'll do it,' I muttered.

Mack sighed deeply. 'It's a shame you're much too dangerous to keep alive. Your apparent lack of a second P is interesting; a close study of your powers could have showed us how to remove abilities from others. Oh well.' She pointed at Merindah, then guided her finger over to me. 'Kill her. Or I'll kill your mother.'

And then Mack ran for the Portal that had replaced her bed.

But I was ready for her.

I'd spent the last couple of minutes doing something that I would have thought impossible before Simon had put the idea into my head.

That big honking Portal Mack had made? It wasn't hers anymore. When I'd focused my attention on it, the Portal had started whispering my name, making me an offer I couldn't refuse. So I'd reached out to it, thirsty for the power it could give me. And holy shit, did it ever give. Way more than the Portal in my phone ever had.

My veins were practically bulging. I felt...invincible.

I threw out my hand and Mack smacked face-first into the magical wall I'd thrown across the Portal. She glared up at me from the floor, blood leaking out of both her nostrils.

Her face—a mess.

My smugness—amplified.

Something slammed into my chest and I went down hard, wheezing. Merindah had hit me with a ball of Physical, but evidently not a spiked one because I was still alive and (mostly) breathing. Relief washed over me for a second—then I realised I was pinned in place with solid black manacles on my wrists and ankles. My best friend had just turned me into a tasty offering for the resident Hellcreatures.

'So you can't kill me yourself, but you can stand by and watch them gut me?' I demanded of Merindah.

She had the courtesy to flinch.

But she didn't let up with her powers.

The carpet in the hallway behind her was now being shredded by hungry, hungry Hellhounds. Yeah, I wasn't in the mood to become mincemeat and I didn't want Merindah tearing herself up over my death (well, I hoped that would happen—it was the least she could do), so I knew I had to do something. And fast.

I looked wildly around for Mack, to see if I couldn't give her something of value in return for my life, but she'd already buggered off through another Portal that she'd made in the corner (must have missed that when I'd hit the ground).

What a shock. Not. She'd always been good at looking out for herself. But she'd very thoughtfully given me a second Portal to play with. And it had also started singing my name, promising to add to my already considerable power. There was no way I could turn that down. No way I wanted to. I pulled *hard*.

My vision briefly went white and I screamed.

A cocoon of Physical, stronger than anything I'd ever seen let alone made, sprang out from my chest and snapped around Merindah. Her arms clamped to her sides, her mouth went wide, and then she toppled over onto the carpet.

Just as I'd hoped, she lost her concentration and, with it, her grip on her powers.

I jumped to my feet, my own hands now free, but I didn't need to funnel my power through them anymore. I'd never need them again. Not like Merindah. I'd hobbled her. I felt a ridiculous amount of pride when I saw her mouth oscillate and the cords in her neck tighten.

See? I'm more powerful than you! I thought at her.

Her panicked eyes shot to the side, towards the Hellhounds. But I'd already thrown up yet another shield in front of the creatures, a Physical curtain that filled the doorway. I would have laughed with delight at my prowess if I wasn't in so much pain.

The Hellhounds were invisible to me but the damage they inflicted wasn't—gashes formed in my construct, shallow at first but deepening by the second. I poured more energy towards that shield, as well as the cocoon keeping Merindah in place. I couldn't let her escape, not when I'd lost Mack. Merindah might have the information we needed.

And if the Hellhounds got into the room, at least she'd be safe from them for a little while longer. Until they shredded my body and my constructs died along with me, that is.

I clenched my jaw and tried to make yet another shield for myself. But with one already over a Portal and two more keeping living things in place (at least Merindah wasn't resisting as hard as the damn Hellhounds), I just couldn't. My head was pounding and my mouth was drier than the Simpson Desert.

I needed backup and I needed it *now*.

I staggered towards the window. I didn't give a shit who heard me, neighbours or police, just so long as the demons did. I was still drawing breath to shout for help when the cavalry arrived. If there really had been a Persuasion field covering the property, it had gone with Mack.

Portals roared into existence all over her bedroom, demons leaping out of them and bellowing Persuasion-fuelled commands. The Hellcreatures wasted no time in obeying. They ripped into each other with wild abandon and their black blood spewed into the air, making hypnotising patterns on the shag-pile carpet.

I only stopped staring when my chattering teeth clipped my tongue, grating over the wound I'd bitten into it earlier. The pain snapped me back to reality.

I sat heavily on the windowsill. Then I realised I probably didn't need the barricade over the Portal, because it wasn't like Mack was around to use it anymore—and I doubted the demons wanted to jump in and face the unknown dangers at the other end. And we definitely didn't need that curtain in front of the dead Hellcreatures.

So I tried to shut my shields down.

They refused my request.

I sagged. Well, that wasn't a huge problem. They would vanish when my power reserves ran out. I'd just have to sit and wait...

But then I looked at Merindah. Her face was ashen.

Oh shit. I'd forgotten to allow air through my cocoon-shaped shield. I had never needed to take this into account before—my constructs had always been weak and porous.

I yanked at my Physical again. Nothing happened. My power reserves, usually a stray thread inside me, were suddenly external and endless, spun into an unbreakable rope by the multiple Portals in the room. There were at least twenty smaller ones now and they kept on forcing more strength into my magic. Why hadn't the demons shut their Portals down yet? It hurt so freaking much!

Merindah was going to die if I didn't get that shield down.

'She can't breathe!' I said.

A Physical ball shot across the room, crashing into the construct encasing Merindah. There was only one person who could have done that and he must have climbed in through the window, because he couldn't survive the trip through a Portal.

Dennis had arrived. Thank God.

Merindah's cocoon shivered and thinned, but not enough.

'Do it again!' I screamed.

Dennis obeyed, grunting with the effort he put behind the Physical projectile he flung towards Merindah. But my shield repelled it completely this time, now a lot wiser—and a hell of a lot angrier. Dennis' construct ricocheted into the wall, gouging out a hole big enough to reveal the room on the other side. His next ball rebounded right at his head.

Dennis fell to his knees.

'Merindah!' I cried. 'I can't! I'm sorry!'

My stomach rolled as the world abruptly titled sideways. Someone grabbed my shoulders and started shaking them. I looked blearily up at Dennis, annoyed that he was touching me, but then I saw the gash in his hairline and the crimson blood smeared over his face. He was injured. Because of me.

My hip ached. I distantly realised that I must have fallen onto it. Everything hurt, actually, not just the hip. My whole body was on fire and my head felt like it was about to explode from all the power I was channelling.

Funny. I'd spent my whole childhood so sure I'd had more reserves tucked away *somewhere*, and here they were. At long last.

And my damn careers advisor wasn't even there to see it.

'Jen! Cut it out!' Dennis shouted.

'I'm trying!' I rasped in response.

My shields were growing stronger by the second, drawing more and more energy from the Portals. And I was the conduit, becoming increasingly battered and bruised the longer I was forced to hold on. Blood trickled out of one nostril and onto my lip. It tasted sweet and thick.

'Jen can't douse the shields!' Dennis snapped at the demons.

'It's the Portals,' I heard Simon say somewhere nearby. 'They're feeding her Physical and her magic won't let us close them.'

'Then stop her! She'd never forgive herself for killing her best friend.' Dennis had never sounded that angry. Ever. 'If you cared about her at all, you'd stop her!'

Barely a second later, Simon was kneeling in front of me, hands on both sides of my head. His lips, so close to mine, whispered, 'Jen, I won't do this unless you agree to it.'

I didn't need to ask him what he meant. I just knew.

And I could see no other way out of this.

'Get inside my head, Simon!' I hissed.

My scalp itched as Simon poured into my mind, sealing all the cracks that might have let me escape his Persuasion. I was trapped inside the whirling of his blue eyes.

'Release the Portals and drop the shields,' Simon ordered. 'All of them. Do it—*do it now!*'

It didn't occur to me to argue, to say that I had no idea how to comply with his command. I simply obeyed him, not to save Merindah or even myself, but because it was *him* asking. His words were gospel and I knew I had to give him everything he wanted, give it willingly, give it all. He pervaded every thought, for he had conquered the corners of my soul, and had he told me to jump off the Sydney Harbour Bridge, I'd have—

His Persuasion fled my mind.

I didn't have the strength to turn my head to see if Merindah was safe. All I could do was breathe and swallow.

'I'm here, Jen, I'm here,' Simon murmured as I shuddered, utterly spent without the Portals to prop me up.

There was no denying it now.

Portals spoke to me. And I listened.

Whether or not I'd survive travelling through one...I never wanted to be desperate enough to find out.

29

The wide berth the demons were suddenly giving me would have been comical if I wasn't so freaking tired of being the outsider, ostracised because of something beyond my control. The only demon who remained anywhere near me was Simon. He kept a firm hand on my shoulder, either to reassure me or to remind his people that I was under his protection. Both, probably.

While I'd been catching my breath, Dennis had placed himself between Merindah's crumpled form and the rest of the room. I was grateful for this, because the outright murderous scowls the demons were shooting in her direction were way worse than the looks I was getting.

'Why did you stop her, Simon?' Saul demanded, singling me out with a violent shake of his finger. 'It was the hybrid's right, to slay the human who hurt her. She is owed vengeance.'

Wait...what? He couldn't be arguing with Simon on my behalf. No way.

Simon stared up at Saul with an amount of dignity I couldn't have mustered in my entire life, let alone five seconds. 'Jen asked me to stop her with my powers. So I did. It was her right to refuse to take what was owed.'

What the hell are they talking about? I wondered. It was probably yet another demonic law (there were hundreds, apparently). Dot had admitted that they always seemed to favour anyone with demonic blood. Funny that. But the demons would have to get used to new, fairer rules if they wanted human magic-users to work with them instead of skewering them with something sharp and Physical.

'No!' Dennis yelled, a machete sprouting to life in his hand.

His Physical had never been the best in the class (at least he hadn't hidden some secret skill in *that* for years), but his objects were solid black and could last the standard two to three minutes against my thirty seconds—well, if I restricted myself to my inner power reserves, that is. It occurred to me that I had to stop thinking of my power as weak. Because it wasn't.

And it was starting to hurt people. People I cared about.

Why did Mum have to fall in love with a demon? Why did I have to end up with this weird freaky version of Portal that even spooked scary demons?

'No,' Dennis repeated more firmly, the machete held out in front of him so that it crossed his torso. 'I can see into your heads. I know what you're thinking. And you're not killing Merindah. Not while I'm alive.'

'Then we'll be sure to kill you first!' a demon hooted at him.

'What are you waiting for? Go on!' Dennis baited. I saw his eyes glaze over momentarily and he shook his head, confusion giving way to fury. He waved the machete. 'Nice try, demons! If you Persuade me again, you'll just give Jen a reason to suffocate you!'

I flinched. So did the demons.

I guess we were all afraid of little old me.

Saul, however, didn't seem to care what I could do to him, judging by that extra step he took towards me. 'You wish, human! She knows who she stands with.'

'*She* stands with whoever she wants to, thank you very much,' I muttered.

'It is good that she is on our side,' Saul went on, pointedly ignoring me and addressing the rest of the room. 'She is far too powerful to meet in battle.'

Murmurs of assent followed this. I scowled.

I'd nearly killed my best friend and they were *impressed* instead of horrified.

Simon helped me to my feet. I tried my best not to cling to him too tightly. My head was pounding and blood was rushing through my ears, making a disconcerting whoosh-whoosh sound as it went. Dennis clearly wasn't having any more fun than I was; he kept twitching at the slightest inkling of movement from the demons.

'Stop interfering with the human's mind,' Simon commanded his people. 'I'd rather not waste my power reserves defending him. Mackenzie's Persuasion field has dropped and if the neighbours call the police—'

Yeah. We did look a bit suss—most of us wearing black, hanging out in a house that definitely didn't belong to us. And this street was far too fancy and bourgeoisie for unmarked vans.

A siren started screaming on the next street over.

Everyone froze.

But within seconds it started to fade, then rapidly became more distant. The demons relaxed and laughed. Dennis and I didn't join in. And neither did Simon.

'We need to get out of here,' Simon said through clenched teeth. 'We can talk about this at my place. There's no time to argue.'

'But there is time to wonder if bringing a second human back with us will put our lives in danger!' another demon snarled. She was all dolled up and her jeans had lines of diamantes running down to the cuffs. Demons might wear a lot of black, but they still knew how to complete a look. 'Kill the human and be done with it.'

'I'll kill you first,' Dennis warned her.

'No one's killing anyone, alright?' I cried and then, I'm ashamed to admit it, I stomped my foot. Okay, time to do something less petulant and more intimating. I threw my hands towards the ceiling and more than a few demons ducked, just as I'd hoped. 'I screwed up! I let Mack get away and I didn't get enough out of her. So Merindah's the one we need to question. She'll know things.'

'What did you manage to find out?' Simon asked me.

I was so sure my voice would fail me now that my anger was ebbing, but it emerged relatively intact. 'It's bad. Really bad. It's good that we came after Mack, because she sure as hell is going to come after us. And she'll do worse than kill us.'

Us. I really was one of them now, wasn't I?

'What's she planning to do?' Dot called out.

So I told them. I told them about the experiments. I told them everything. Well, except for the fact that the bar fridge under the dressing table had a stash of powerful injections inside it. That was going to be for Simon's ears only.

If I'd thought my words would get everyone to settle down, I was so, so wrong. All I managed to do was ignite a wave of fury that would have knocked Merindah off her feet if she'd been standing. What she *was* doing was rousing, sitting up, and taking us in with venom dripping from her eyes.

I ran over to her and skidded onto my knees. 'Merindah!

Merindah, are you alright? I'm sorry, I'm so sorry, I didn't mean to, I couldn't control—'

'You done deciding whether I live or die, demons?' Merindah demanded.

I bit my tongue, trying not to feel upset that she'd ignored me.

Yeah, I totally failed.

'No, we're *not* done!' Queran, one of Simon's more vocal demons, growled at Merindah. 'You tried to kill one of us!'

'But she didn't manage it,' I interjected.

'And Jen has an excellent point,' Simon said, stepping between the two groups and giving those of us with human blood a perfect view of his rigid, immobile shoulders. 'We need Merindah alive. She'll tell us what we need to know.' He glanced over at her. 'Won't you?'

Merindah gave him an even stare. She didn't look at all surprised that Simon Bradley, software developer and The Guy Who Ditched Me at a Party One Time, was a demon, but I suppose Mack had said something. That didn't really matter right then anyway. What else Mack might have told her was of more interest to me. And I badly needed Merindah to cooperate with us. If only to save her life.

'You can't rescue your mother if you're dead,' Simon said bluntly.

'Ease up, mate!' Dennis exclaimed.

I heard the admiring comments, saw the admiring looks—the demons were pleased that their leader wasn't coddling the humans. But Simon still had to keep defending Dennis and Merindah from mental attacks; I could tell by the desperate sapphire swirls in the eyes he turned towards me. I wondered if

Dot was helping him, because her face was growing more and more drawn by the second.

'We'll rescue all of them,' I said suddenly, wildly. 'Merindah's mother and the hybrids. Mack can't be allowed to do this. We'll destroy this Operation of Evil she's got going on and make sure this shit can't happen to anyone ever again—human, demon, hybrid, whatever.'

'Mackenzie Roberts' work threatens us—and what we hope to achieve,' Simon added. Several nods echoed the small tilt of his chin that he gave his people.

'So tell us what we need to know or die!' Saul snarled.

Merindah's eyes flashed. 'Your leader'—she aimed a distrustful sneer at Simon—'is right. Mack is a threat to you. And sooner or later Magic Corp will realise you're in Sydney and come after you as well. They'll send hybrids—*trained* hybrids. With Physical and Persuasion. You won't stand a chance.'

'We need to go—bring the human,' Simon declared.

'She'll give away our position and they'll slaughter us!' Queran cried. 'No fucking way, Simon!'

I looked at Dennis. We didn't need to talk. And I didn't need to be able to read his thoughts the way he could mine. We'd defend Merindah if we had to. The demons might have treated me a fraction better than Magic Corp ever had, but Merindah was like a sister to me. She was my family, more so than the demon and contract-breaker who had left me at MC's mercy.

'I thought you wanted Simon Bradley to like you,' Merindah muttered, clearly responding to my thoughts. 'Don't throw away your chance to score over little old me.'

I wasn't sure if she was a joking, but it was something she'd say if things weren't so completely dire, if we were back at my humble studio apartment, if everything hadn't gone to shit.

She wasn't smiling. But it was a start.

'Who needs to get laid?' I muttered. 'Chicks before dicks.'

'You did not just say that,' Merindah groaned.

We both silenced when Simon held out his hand. 'Give me your phone, Merindah.' She did so. Simon pocketed the device. 'My people won't allow you to come back with us conscious. We can't let you see where we're going.'

I threw a frown at him, one that disintegrated almost immediately when I saw the shadow of regret on his face—it was barely there and I wasn't sure anyone else caught it. He didn't like pushing us around, but he had to or he would lose his people's support much faster than I'd managed to ruin my life. So, you know, a handful of minutes. Tops.

'You gonna rough me up and knock me out, are you?' Merindah asked, eyes narrow.

Simon shook his head. 'No. We're going to Persuade you to fall asleep.'

'Makes sense,' she allowed, her face going slack with relief. 'You can't trust me not to try something. Asleep's the best way to go. I'll do it.'

Dennis' fifth machete ghosted away in his hand, disappearing like all the others had before it. He cleared his throat noisily. 'So...am I fighting anyone?'

'You wouldn't last two seconds, human,' Dot told him, though not unkindly. 'Save your energy. We'll need you when we go after Magic Corp. Don't exactly see us wielding Physical weapons, do you?'

Most of the demons nodded along to this. It was a brilliant

move on Dot's part, reminding her brethren how much we needed Physical-capable humans in our midst.

Another siren screeched into life.

Dot jerked her head at the open window. 'I think we can all agree that we've spent too long here. I'll drive the Kill Squad agent back myself. And I'll put her down.'

'Good,' Saul said tightly. 'I'll ride with you, Simon. We need to discuss your *intentions*.'

Ah. Right. So Dot had anticipated this (whatever Saul was planning to say to Simon in private, it couldn't be avoided) and had stepped forward to protect Merindah in Simon's stead. I felt oddly touched by that, even if it was because—and I was almost certain it was—Dot wanted me and her brother to hook up.

'She's alright,' I told Merindah, though Dennis had a very dubious look on his face.

With one word from Simon, most of the demons began popping out of sight, presumably Portalling back inside the vans. At least I hoped that's what they were doing. They would draw way too much attention if they started appearing all over the front lawn.

I stood up and grabbed Simon's arm when he moved away, reeling him back to me. He didn't resist and immediately bent his ear to the level of my mouth.

In a low voice, I told him about the contents of the bar fridge.

Simon cursed softly. 'Do you think that's how she got so powerful—using those injections? Not just giving herself Persuasion, but a more potent version of it?'

'Wouldn't put it past her,' I muttered.

Simon blew out a breath. 'I'll deal with the fridge. Keep this between us.'

Yeah, it could be a problem if, say, someone found out that they could shoot up and smack Simon down in one of those Persuasion duels.

That *someone* being Saul. That *someone* who was currently staring intently at us.

I nodded once and made sure my expression was neutral instead of worried, so I wouldn't tip Saul off. Simon lingered behind by the dressing table as we left the room. I did my best not to look back.

Surrounded by demons who were escorting us on Simon's orders, Merindah, Dennis, and I walked out the front door and onto the garden path, all of us avoiding the grass that was so lush and green it couldn't possibly be real. I didn't dare look at the windows on the nearby houses. I was afraid that Mack's neighbours were watching and judging us. Especially me.

Yeah, totally the right thing to be worried about right then.

30

Our demonic escorts broke away from us when we hit the road, but they hung around, not immediately getting into the parked vehicles, eyes tracking Merindah like they were casing out prey. My best friend ducked inside the van that Dot pointed out to her, as if she couldn't stand to be by my side any longer. It was probably more to do with avoiding the demons, but it still hurt.

'Dot,' I said quietly, almost too quietly.

Dot must have heard me because she stopped dead, her fingers clenched on the side of the van's sliding door.

'What?' she asked with a flippant smile, but her lips barely moved. She was already acting with caution, as though she knew what I was about to ask of her.

'I want to talk to Merindah—alone,' I said, trying not to look around for any nearby ears that shouldn't be listening in. 'Please. Can you not "put her down" for a minute? Or two? I really need to do this. She's—she was, might still be—my best friend.'

The skin around Dot's eyes crinkled. 'I get it. I'll go in, pretend to do my thing, then come out and talk to my brother for a couple of minutes.'

'Just like that?' I asked, confused. 'You trust me? You trust that we won't be, uh, conspiring or anything like that?'

Her smile suddenly seemed a lot more genuine. 'I trust you. Because you care about everyone, not just the people who share

237

your powers. You're a good person, Jen. I like you. You're exactly what my brother—what *we* need.'

Then she climbed into the van, leaving me standing there, stupefied and a little embarrassed. I'd honestly believed that she only liked me because she thought I could get Simon's 'groove' back.

'You can't trust her,' Dennis told me. I nearly jumped; he'd said nothing since we'd left the house and I'd almost forgotten he was there. He frowned thoughtfully. 'But it doesn't hurt to cultivate *her* trust. It might be useful later.'

I rolled my eyes. 'I don't get close to people just because I want something out of them. That's your schtick, Mr First-Floor Lurker.'

Dennis opened his mouth, but he never got the chance to respond.

'All done!' Dot announced loudly as she exited the van and bounded away, nearly clipping my shoulder as she passed. She didn't even shut the door behind her. I guess doing that might have hinted that she had something to hide.

I entered the van in Dot's place, heart pounding, trying not to hurl.

'My throat hurts,' I said, mostly to fill the silence. I couldn't think of anything else to say, certainly not something that didn't sound like an accusation.

'Must be from all that talking you did,' Merindah said. 'When Mack had you spilling everything. Couldn't shut you up.'

I lowered my voice to an urgent whisper. 'What did I tell Mack? Did I tell her where Simon lives?'

'No, you just said you'd been to his place; you didn't elaborate,' Merindah replied flatly. As if she didn't care about what was going on, as if she didn't care about *me*. But why would she? I wasn't her mother. I was the one who'd nearly suffocated her to death—and that was after lying to her for more than a decade.

'That annoyed Mack,' Merindah noted. 'If she knew where he lived or could get the scouts to sense it, she'd have gone after him already.' Merindah's expression hardened. 'What are you doing, hanging around with demons?'

As if I'd done it on purpose. As if Mack wasn't the reason I'd had nowhere else to turn.

'What do you mean, what am I doing?' I cried. 'You're the one who started hiding fugitives! Your Big Bad Secret made it so easy for Mack to jerk your strings! Why didn't you tell me?'

'Why didn't *you* tell me anything?' she returned.

I hated this. I hated the fact that she was always one step ahead of me in everything, from our arguments to our careers. And I hated the yawning chasm I could feel growing between us, getting larger the longer we stared at each other, both of us trying not to blink.

'You wouldn't have believed me,' I muttered. 'And even if you had, and somehow convinced our careers advisor that I really don't have Perception, then Mack would have found out earlier and grabbed me back then. When I couldn't defend myself.'

'You only know this in hindsight, Jen.'

Shit. She was right.

But I wasn't going to let her heap all the blame on me. 'Why didn't you let me know about the fugitives? Don't you trust me? I might have been shocked at first, but—but I'd have understood!'

'Really.' Endless scorn and sarcasm wrapped up in one small word.

I flinched. What *would* I have done? Definitely not gone to any of our superiors and told them about it! I'd have tried to help Merindah, right? Not just tell her to stop doing it? Right?

I looked away. 'We'll never know what I would have done, will we?'

Dot chose that moment to stick her head back in, her tight expression emphasised by the shadows filling the vehicle. I was afraid those shadows were going to swallow any chance Merindah and I had of patching up this Rift of Doom.

A rift that wasn't entirely her fault. Or mine.

'You done?' Dot asked, casting a furtive look over her shoulder.

'I hope not,' I answered.

Merindah shrugged, apparently unbothered.

So that was that, I guess.

Dot watched us closely for a handful of seconds, then snorted. 'Whatever. You'd better lie down, Merindah. I don't want you to hit your head. Jen would try to kill me if I hurt you—and she'd probably succeed!'

I gritted my teeth. Why was everyone obsessed with me killing people?

Merindah nodded and lay down. I thought she was being a little dramatic, since she folded her arms over her chest like some creature of the night bedding down for dawn, but when I saw the flicker of fear in her eyes, I realised the gesture was more of a hug. She was afraid of what the Persuasion would do to her.

I quickly put my hand on her hip and squeezed. Merindah blew out a breath—a sigh of relief?—and closed her eyes.

'Sleep,' Dot told her. 'Sleep until someone tells you to wake up.'

Merindah slept.

I stared at her, wondering when her face had started to bear so many lines. Was it because she'd watched too many people die? Was it because she couldn't forgive herself for the lives she'd taken? *Why* had I never asked if she was okay, doing what she did, instead of coveting her job every time she spoke to me about it?

'Go on, I know you want to,' Dot suddenly said.

I glanced at her, startled.

'Ask me why I've got a mattress in here,' she continued, smiling a little too broadly. I had a feeling she was trying to cheer me up. I don't why she expected it to work, because it was so jarring.

A cough spasmed in my throat; it might have been an aborted laugh. 'I don't think I want to know, Dot.'

'Too bad,' she said. 'It was my girlfriend's idea—and a good one at that. It's really convenient! I'd totally let you and Simon borrow the van if he didn't have that fancy apartment of his.'

With a wink and a smirk, she popped outside again. I heard her yelling at Dennis to get his butt into the van before she left him behind for someone else to play with.

Panic bolted through me like lightning. Shit! Without a convenient Portal nearby, how could I protect Merindah? Or Dennis? Or even myself?

I held out my hand and flicked my fingers at the driver's seat, mimicking the gesture I'd seen Simon use, the same gesture my own father had shown me by gripping and swinging my wrist. Even though I was trying to form a Portal on purpose, my heart knotted painfully and my breaths came in short, sharp bursts.

I waited, my ears ringing, but nothing happened. No Portal appeared.

I was relieved. And bitterly disappointed.

'Hey, you alright?' Dennis asked as he climbed into the van.

Dot made a much more dramatic entrance, falling into the

driver's seat with a loud sigh and complaining about the fact that she had to use a key to start the engine.

'Don't you ever lose the key?' she wondered out loud. 'Isn't that annoying?'

Dennis parked himself right next to me. If I hadn't been so drained from fighting off the Hellhounds and Merindah, I'd've slapped him away. Okay, maybe just moved to a different spot. But when the van suddenly braked—Dot muttered something about humans and their obsession with creating unnecessary obstacles like traffic lights—I was very grateful that Dennis' shoulder was there to take the impact of mine.

'Am I alright?' I finally echoed when we'd passed five minutes without anyone or anything attacking us. 'I've got to somehow keep a bunch of demons from killing my best friend, I have to try to convince mortal enemies to work together to protect this country, I have a demonic power that doesn't work the way it should—and I'm not wearing a seatbelt, which should be the least of my worries, but I've seen enough action movies to know how this ends!'

'Would you rather go back to fetching coffee and losing your stapler to me every other week?' Dennis asked with a loose grin that made me remember the nights we'd sneaked out to look at the stars, our fingers tracing lines between the distant pinpricks in the sky above us.

For a moment, it felt like I was back at school, my days given to Merindah and my nights to him. We'd been naive teenagers then, with no real inkling of just how bad our futures would get.

'Hell no, I can't go back,' I said, but my words lacked any passion. I felt numb when I thought about MC and what I'd had to put up with there—maybe because it had happened in what felt like an increasingly distant past. 'I just can't.'

'Neither can I,' Dennis said, then made the critical error of reaching for my hand.

I snatched my fingers away from him. 'Nope, not happening! No way. I don't care how long you spent waiting, Dennis. And might I remind you that you didn't exactly make my life any easier? You treated me the same way that everyone else did. My life was hell.'

His hand returned to his lap and his eyes fell onto Merindah's unmoving form. 'I get it. Simon helped you when I couldn't. He got you to drop the shields.'

I clenched my fists. Maybe it was a good thing I couldn't create Portals, because I was pissed and ready to start swinging Physical. 'It's not about that, Dennis! It's about everything that happened before.'

'I think, Jen,' he murmured, still not looking at me, 'that you're a much different person than you were two days ago. I promise I'm going to be different too. I'm sorry I hurt you, but I'm here now. I'm here for you.'

And apparently he'd decided he was done, because his lips pressed into one thin line and he said nothing more.

Dot turned on the radio and cranked it up. I closed my eyes and clunked my head against the side of the van, grateful that the awkward silence was being filled by sappy sax-heavy tunes from the nineteen-eighties. Dot certainly had weird musical tastes for a demon.

When we reached Simon's apartment complex in St Leonards, I eyed the car park entrance, seriously doubting that it had enough clearance for the van. But just as I was about to mention this to

Dot, she turned back to me, concern creasing her forehead. 'Are you going to be okay if I make a Portal?'

'So long as I don't draw any power from it,' I answered, my voice embarrassingly high-pitched.

With a sharp nod, Dot flicked her fingers upwards. The entire roof—and about two feet below that—vanished into a swirl of fire, allowing the van to pass beneath the gate without touching it. Once we'd parked in a section with a much higher ceiling, she shut the Portal down with another twist of her hand and the van became whole once more. I watched the gesture carefully and saw nothing markedly different from what I had tried earlier.

'Do you think anything specific when you do that?' I asked.

Dot shrugged. 'Not really. I want it closed and it closes.'

I sighed and rubbed my temples. 'Great. Well, Dennis, if I can't close the Portals I'm sucking power from and you're the only one around, you'll just have to knock me out.'

'That's the only way he'd ever get to hold you,' Dot chortled, much to my—and I suspect Dennis'—mortification. Mercifully, her phone buzzed, giving us a much-needed change of topic. She picked it up, frowning at the screen. 'Simon's calling. Not gonna answer, since it's just meant to let me know when he's ready for us to come upstairs. I deliberately took it a little slow so we'd arrive last. You got a plan, Jen?'

Both she and Dennis looked at me expectantly. Hell, if Merindah had been awake, she'd probably have done the same thing.

I groaned and buried my head in my hands.

Going after Mackenzie Roberts and rescuing a bunch of people sounded good in theory, but actually putting it into practice? I didn't have the training for this kind of thing, since Magic Corp had never envisioned such an active future for me. I was wholly unprepared.

Oh well. It looked like Jen Cooke was finally in control of Jen Cooke's life.

I still wasn't sure if that was a good or a bad thing.

31

Dot kicked open the door to Simon's apartment and cheerily greeted the large group of demons packed into the living room. Multiple pairs of eyes (well, those that weren't glued to a late-night screening of *Die Hard*) dripped in our direction, focusing on the unconscious woman we were carrying between us—thanks to a little magical assistance from Dennis. The ropes he'd created for us were quite handy, even if he did have to keep renewing his Physical.

A gust of wind blew in through a window. The door slammed shut behind us.

Only a handful of demons remained entranced by the TV. An even more exciting source of entertainment had just arrived.

Thick, coppery liquid pooled in my mouth. I hastily swallowed the blood, trying not to graze my teeth along the section of my tongue that I'd already tortured enough for one night.

It was a miracle I managed to make any noise, let alone form coherent sentences. 'Simon! Where should I put Merindah? We're going to need to wake her up soon and ask her some questions. She'll know where Mack's keeping the hybrids.' *And her mother*, I added silently, because I was pretty sure the demons didn't give a damn about anyone's normal relatives.

'Too right,' Dennis muttered next to me, obviously catching the thought.

'Jen *is* right, we need to interrogate the human and we cannot afford to be gentle about it,' a demon noted. Clearly, she knew my name but I had no idea what hers was.

I scowled at her. Even those cute cat-shaped studs in her ears wouldn't save her from my ire.

The Physical spear I formed was lightweight in my hands, so flimsy a single sigh could have blown it away. Without a Portal to back me up I'd burn through my piddly power reserves in no time, but common sense be damned. I had to protect my family.

I strode forward (hoping Dennis' Physical was enough to keep Merindah from face-planting onto the carpet) and shoved my wispy spearhead into the face of the demon who had spoken. 'Fuck off! I'll kill anyone who hurts her.' I swung a fierce look at Simon, who'd already taken two steps in my direction. 'Even you, Simon.'

'Dot, Ness,' Simon commanded. 'Help Dennis here take Jen's friend into the spare room and then come back out. *Immediately.*'

He came towards me, resting his hand on the shaft of my weapon and tugging firmly until it was aimed at him instead. His eyes never left my face and I didn't look away from him, but I felt the air tremble slightly as his sister and the demon I'd accosted obeyed his orders.

'Jen...I wouldn't hurt her,' Simon told me softly. 'I know what she means to you. But if you can't get her to talk, that duty will fall to one of us.'

I took several deep, steadying breaths. My Physical weapon disintegrated, leaving me clutching nothing but air. I noticed Saul in the corner, a wicked smile slashed across his face as he took in the bloodthirstiness building momentum around him. These demons only understood violence and revenge. I needed them to understand my side of things. And I didn't think Simon could get them to do it—unless he wielded Persuasion on everyone, that is. But he wouldn't do that even if it was his last resort.

So I had to make sure the demons shifted torture further down on their list of priorities, in case I failed to get Merindah to talk. She might never grant me her forgiveness, but I didn't need that. I just needed to do my damn job and look after her.

I crossed my arms. 'Merindah has been through enough, okay? It wasn't her choice to leave her family—she was Persuaded to do it against her will.' I had no idea if what I'd said was actually true, but it was more than likely, given what had happened to Dennis. I swallowed, but that didn't dislodge the lump of anxiety that had made its home in my throat. 'Now picture this. You've recently found out that your mother was Persuaded to give you up. You finally have a chance to reunite with her—but then Mackenzie Freaking Roberts kidnaps her and threatens to kill her. All because you saved the life of hybrid.'

Die Hard was muted now. I took that as a good sign.

'You don't want to piss Merindah off, by the way,' I continued. 'She has her own personal stash of fugitives with Physical and Perception. And she can get them to fight Mackenzie Roberts alongside us.'

'What need have we for them when we have you?' Saul asked, chortling. 'You are our greatest weapon.'

I pinned him with what I hoped was a fierce glare, though it was tempting to look aside when the spare room's door briefly re-opened, to see if Merindah was okay. I had to trust that she was.

'I can't reliably control my powers,' I replied. 'And I want this to be our trial run. If we can't work together during a single battle, then it'd prove that my idea for us to replace Magic Corp is doomed, right? I know you want to see me fail. So here's your chance, Saul.'

Saul narrowed his eyes. I narrowed mine back at him.

'How do we know that your friend will tell us where to find Mackenzie?' Dot asked, then lifted her shoulders into a brief shrug when I moved my glare onto her. 'Sorry, Jen, but you've got to admit it's a possibility. Mack has her mother. She might lie and send us into situation where we'll get ourselves killed. We won't risk our hides on her word and nor should you risk yours. It's safer to Persuade the truth out of her.'

Nods and approving murmurs abounded.

'You will do nothing of the sort,' I snapped, fisting my hands and setting them on my hips. 'I'm going to *talk* to my best friend. I need to convince her to join us and supply us with Physical fighters. We're screwed if I don't succeed. What happens if Mack has an army with soldiers that have three or four Ps? What happens when you finally try to take out Magic Corp, only to come up against their hybrids? People who are trained to use Persuasion and Physical? Good luck with that. And we can't just sit here twiddling our thumbs. Because sooner or later, Mack will come after *us*. Don't even pretend otherwise.'

I expected someone to challenge me. Hell, I was keeping one eye on Saul in case he made a move, but he was just standing there like the rest of them, watching me without comment. Super uncomfortable, by the way.

Dennis' mouth was hanging open, which made him look so much like the demon next him—Ness, that's what Simon had called her—that for a moment he blended right in. Then Dennis grinned and brought his hands together, only to swiftly cut off his applause when he realised that no one else was joining in.

250

I swept my gaze from one demon to the next. 'You need help. You need humans and hybrids or you're never going to do more than skulk about in the shadows. So while I'm risking my own damn hide by stepping into the same room as a Kill Squad agent, and potentially messing up a friendship I can't afford to lose, you're going to sit the fuck down and think about the benefits of replacing Magic Corp with something better. Something that doesn't tear people away from their families. Something that lets you stand and fight instead of jumping into a Portal and running away.'

Head held high, I stormed into the spare bedroom.

32

The spare room had the usual dark and dreary decor I'd come to expect from Simon, though I did notice a lamp in the corner with a shade that appeared to be a patchwork of multiple panels from *The Phantom* comics. I'd seen them for sale in those novelty shops, but hadn't been able to justify wasting my money on one when I needed to pay rent—or more importantly, buy a glittery pair of sneakers that might finally win me the admiration of my peers.

God, was that what my whole life had been about before all this started? Shoes and comics? I wasn't sure whether to blame myself or Magic Corp for giving me nothing more fulfilling to focus my time and energy on.

Wait, why did Simon have the exact same lamp I'd been eyeing up last month? Hmm.

I decided to rouse Merindah. Dot, when she'd been laying on the Persuasion, hadn't stipulated that this had to be done by someone with demonic powers. So I gave it a shot.

'Wake up, Merindah,' I said.

In less than three seconds she was sitting up on the bed, arms crossed, her face as smooth as marble. I knew that look. It was the one Merindah wielded on our colleagues at parties whenever they said something wholly inappropriate and worthy of earning them a title that ended in 'phobic' or 'ist'. She never forgave people for those sorts of comments, because she believed that alcohol didn't give anyone a pass to act like an arsehole.

Apart from her slightly rumpled appearance, she didn't seem too adversely affected by her imprisonment. Well, this room didn't have an ensuite or a handy phone charger, so I guess her cell did have its problems.

I pressed my back against the door, hoping it would hold me up because my legs were shaking too badly to do the job on their own. 'Merindah, I need to ask you some things. And I'd much rather do it in here, when it's just us two, than let—than take you out there,' I finished lamely.

'That's nice of you,' Merindah remarked. 'Giving me a choice between talking to a liar or being tortured by the demons she's running with.'

Okay, maybe I deserved that. No, I *definitely* deserved that.

I realised I had my hands up between us, a defensive gesture only, but when Merindah looked at my fingers, it wasn't out of curiosity—there was fear flitting through her eyes. Fear. Because of what I could do.

My teeth took another chunk out of my poor tongue. 'Merindah. Please. Please just listen to me. I don't want anyone to hurt you—you're my best friend, damn it!—and Christ, I'll do everything I can to help rescue your mother. But you need to work with us. You're going to have to tell us everything you know.'

'*Us*,' she repeated with a bite to her tone, her gaze still on my hands.

I wondered if she was thinking about my sudden Physical prowess and if I'd been hiding that from her too.

Okay, listen, I only found out how my magic works after I hooked myself up to a Portal for the first time, I thought defiantly at her. *You*

254

think I'd have let everyone push me around all these years if I'd known I was this powerful?

'I'm a hybrid, half human and half demon—you know that, or you should, since Mack sent you after me,' I continued out loud, because I actually wanted to hear her response this time. 'Look, it'd take all night to explain. So if you peek inside my head, I'll show you everything. I'm doing what's...what seems to be the right thing.'

Oh God, let it be.

I closed my eyes and tilted my head back, trying not to twitch as I waited for her to use her Perception on me. I laid bare the past couple of days in my mind, showing her the most important moments, slipping further into my past. Suddenly, I was standing in front of my father again, begging him to let me keep his name, my mother's name, *anything*. Just one small, insignificant thing to remind me that I was loved...

I started when I felt Merindah's hands on my shoulders. Our eyes met.

And then she hugged me.

'Forgive me?' she asked.

I hiccupped into her shoulder. 'Of course I forgive you. I'd have done anything to keep Mum alive. So I get why you chose your mother over me, and I get why you didn't tell me about the fugitives. I'm sorry I didn't notice how hard your job was on you. I never even asked if you were okay.' I drew back and gave her a wobbly smile. 'I guess I'm not sorry that I've got way more power than anyone ever thought I had, but I *am* sorry I used it on you. And I'm sorry I never told you I didn't have Perception. I should have trusted you.'

Merindah's chin dipped into a nod as she accepted my apology, but she didn't manage a smile of her own. 'Do you think the demons'll have a look in my head for a Persuasion block if I ask them to? And in my mother's mind? Never seemed right, what happened. She would've wanted me over a house, right?' She hesitated. 'Maybe I don't want to know the answer to that, come to think of it.'

'She wanted you,' I said firmly. 'I bet she had to be Persuaded to give you up. Not like my parents. They didn't fight very hard to keep me.' I loosened my fists when my nails bit into the flesh of my palms. 'And my father...he never came back. Never even bothered to see if I was okay.'

'You don't know that,' Merindah told me, her voice far too gentle, as if she was trying not to spook me.

Yeah, right. I preferred to think that he hadn't bothered instead of the alternative—that he'd popped in from the other realm to spy on his daughter, seen me looking so miserable, and had done nothing about it.

Merindah was smart enough to drop that topic. She looked me up and down, then grinned. 'Jesus, Jen, I've never seen you look this confident before. I never saw you stand up for yourself, even when the younger ones got better jobs than you out of school. I'd say that demons agree with you.'

I blinked. *Simon.* 'Oh shit. I showed you way more than I meant to.'

Merindah's eyebrows rose. 'I didn't see whatever you're busily scrubbing out of your surface thoughts just now. No, I'm talking about what you were doing before you came in here. The telling-off you gave the demons. That was your most recent memory.'

I felt suddenly parched, as though I'd been standing on the sidelines of one of Merindah's weekend soccer matches, screaming at the PE teacher-cum-referee for ignoring an illegal tackle. I went over to the bed and slumped down on it, rubbing my temples. The headache was a small, prickling thing that probably had nothing to do with Merindah's Perception, but it did remind me how raw my mind still was. Would I ever recover from my father's Persuasion block? I hoped so.

'So you'll tell us what we need to know?' I asked hesitantly.

Merindah pressed her lips together. 'Don't see that I have a choice. But you better tell me why the fuck Dennis agreed to sign on. He's not a hybrid.'

'He was Persuaded away from his family,' I explained.

'Which he didn't find out until after he'd already come along for the ride.'

I clapped a hand to my mouth, belatedly smothering the groan. 'He wants to win me back. His powers are way better than anyone thought they were, but he pretended he was useless so he'd get stuck on the first floor with me. Ugh. It's still gross to think about.'

Merindah chortled. 'Idiot. As if you'd take him back after what he did. I told you to forget that dick and you'd be an idiot yourself if you didn't listen to me.'

If you'd ever told me that I'd be discussing my love life—of all things—when I should have been planning the biggest demonic incursion in Australia in years, I would have laughed myself stupid. As it was, this very thought threw me into an undignified fit of giggles. It took a couple of minutes of Merindah rolling her eyes at me and saying 'that's enough, Jen' for me to calm down.

'So,' I said. 'Do you want to help us destroy Magic Corp?'

'Shit, Jen. This is huge.'

'You can't seriously want to let MC keep getting away with this!' I cried, clenching my knees so hard that my knuckles went white. 'Magic Corp took us from our families, isolated us from the normal community, forced us into jobs we hated. They suspended you for trying to help people and—'

'Jen, breathe,' Merindah said.

I poked my tongue out at her, but I *had* been running out of air. I took a moment to breathe, then lowered my voice. 'Okay. We need the demons' help to rescue your mother and the missing hybrids. They can Persuade smaller Hellcreatures to get out of the way while we fight the other things they can't fend off. Dennis, you, and me—and those people you've squirrelled away—can handle the Physical stuff.'

Merindah rubbed the side of her face, suddenly looking very weary, and sank back into the pillows on the bed. I belatedly remembered that she might still be recovering from what I'd done to her. 'We can't work together, Jen. They're demons.'

'But we can make something better, something like MC but not as messed up and cruel,' I implored.

'Something better,' Merindah repeated. 'You think enough people will want to go for that?'

'Dennis will,' I said.

'Because you inspire change, or because you inspire his erection?' she asked wryly.

I shrugged. 'Doesn't matter. And we haven't even talked to the humans and hybrids at MC yet. I bet a lot of the people who aren't high up enough to know what's going on will want out. But here's the thing—what normal job can we possibly get with our lack of qualifications?'

'There are plenty of criminal groups who'll put their hands up for magic-users, Jen.'

'Exactly! We need to stop that happening.'

'And by "we", you mean you and Simon,' Merindah noted, watching me carefully. 'The guy who lied to everyone at work for years.'

'I trust Simon.'

'Why? Because he's unlocked the memories in your head? Because he's nice to you?' Merindah sighed. 'Jen, honestly. You thought *Dennis* was nice.'

'Well, it doesn't have to get serious or anything,' I defended, linking my hands in my lap. So we were back to discussing my love life, apparently.

'But you'll create a whole new Magic Corp with Simon by your side,' Merindah mused. 'Not serious at all. And definitely not awkward and destabilising if you two have a fight.'

'I'm not going to be the group's leader or anything like that,' I said, tossing a dismissive hand towards the door, towards the demons. 'I'll probably just go back to Admin, but I won't have to fetch tea or coffee anymore.'

'Right, you'll go quietly back to Admin after all this.' Merindah snorted. 'Sure you will.'

She knew me too well, damn it. And I wasn't sure I could condemn anyone else to the first floor—if this thing Simon and I wanted to create would even *have* a first floor. It was going to be awfully difficult to lease a building while we were on the run.

'I think we've got other problems right now,' I said.

'Worse problems,' Merindah agreed, lines spiralling across her forehead. 'Jen, how many people do you think I've got squirrelled away?'

'Um,' I said. 'Twenty?'

'Five. I've only been at this a few months. And do you think they'll want to come out of hiding when they only just went into it?'

A large and very jagged boulder seemed to have taken up residence in my throat. 'But...I told the demons you'd give us Physical fighters. We need them.'

Merindah spread her arms, as though to encompass an invisible audience, one that sat in silent judgement of me. 'It's not possible. They're not even in this state, plus it'd be bloody hard to convince them to head down to Sydney. There's no time for that. You're going to need Physical fighters a lot sooner. And you know where you'll have to get them from.'

'Oh no.' That boulder kept on growing. 'No, no, no.'

'If you're supposed to be helping your colleagues by replacing Magic Corp,' Merindah said, her stern gaze unwavering, 'you should at least ask them if they actually want things to change.'

'No way,' I rasped. 'They won't listen to me.'

'Shit, Jen, don't you see? The demons'll follow Simon. But the rest of us? We need someone. Someone to go to bat for us. Someone who'll force the demons to take us into consideration when they do manage to destroy MC.'

'Oh my God,' I said, horror sinking into my gut. 'I can't speak for that many people. I can't even speak *to* them. They completely ignore me at work!'

'I know it was easier for you when everyone ignored you, Jen.'

'Easier? I hated how they treated me!'

'You need to talk to them,' Merindah told me in a tone that invited no compromise. 'Because without them, you have no hope of taking on Mack.'

'Can't you do it?' I pleaded. 'Can't Dennis?'

Merindah shook her head. 'No, Jen. You're the one who

decided to do this. And you're the one who's made friends with the demons. It won't sound right coming from anyone else.'

'Great, thanks, throw me under a bus,' I muttered.

'Well, you threw us all under a fucking semitrailer,' she said, shuffling along the bed towards me and sliding an arm over my shoulders. 'And anyway, we won't even get to try out your crazy plan to take on Magic Corp with an alliance of demons, humans, and hybrids if we don't survive this attack on Mack's base.'

'I hate you,' I grumbled, but she was right.

Although, if things *did* go south, I'd never have to talk to any of my former colleagues ever again. I mean, I'd be dead, but...

Right. I had to remember why I wanted this attack to succeed.

'Merindah...' I stopped and drew several steadying breaths. 'What can you tell me about Mack and her base? What sort of defences are we going to find ourselves up against?'

Wow, I never thought I'd ask these kinds of questions in my life. It made me sound like Darth Vader looking for a hidden Rebel base or something. It was actually kind of cool.

Except I wasn't one of the bad guys. Obviously.

Yeah. Obviously.

33

The TV was switched off by the time Merindah and I exited the spare room and made our grand entrance—okay, we sort of slinked in, but it felt grand by the amount of attention we were receiving. I'd taken several steps forward before I realised Merindah had stopped dead, her expression completely vacant.

'Simon, call off your flunkies,' I said and eyeballed Saul, who had set himself up in a dark corner, as usual. That guy was always up to something. *Must have caused his parents a headache when they were trying to find a regular babysitter*, I thought.

Dennis snorted with laughter and I frantically shook my head at him, hoping he'd pretend that he hadn't heard that.

Simon stood from the couch and approached another demon instead, which surprised me—I'd assumed that Saul was the one responsible for Merindah turning into a statue. Yay, more demons I needed to keep an eye on. Fan-bloody-tastic.

'Enough, Queran,' Simon said firmly.

Queran muttered something indistinct, but he must have dropped the Persuasion because Merindah shook herself out and drew in line with me. It shocked me to see her so nervous and so completely out of her depth. But being at mercy of demons who can twist your mind and block your memories *is* pretty freaking terrifying.

Outwardly, Merinah remained her unflappable self. She

nodded towards Queran. 'Did you happen to see a Persuasion block in my head just then?'

After a searing look from Simon, Queran answered.

In the affirmative.

'Well shit,' Merindah said. 'That means I'm definitely not gonna go back to Magic Corp after I help you lot destroy Mackenzie's little set-up.'

'That's all it takes for you to change sides?' Ness' face wrinkled up suspiciously.

Merindah gave Ness a scornful look which she then raked across the rest of her audience. 'When you find out that someone's messed with your head, and your family's, and made sure you ended up so alone and afraid that you accepted a job which had you killing *your own people*...there's no forgiving that.'

'I realise how difficult this is for you,' Simon said. I knew he was glad that he didn't have to resort to doing what his people expected of him.

Merindah shifted on her feet and readjusted her stance, as though she was expecting someone to charge at her. 'I know you've got no reason to believe anything I'd say. So. I give you permission to Persuade me to tell the whole truth.'

'Merindah—' I started.

'No, Jen, they need to trust me,' she cut in.

'But do you trust *us*?' Simon asked.

Merindah snorted. 'You, I'm not sure about. You lied to me, Jen, Dennis, and everyone else for years. One of your minions can do it.'

The demons studied her with obvious approval, then several of them offered to Persuade her, including Queran. Dot, I noticed, didn't volunteer—and I appreciated that, given how Merindah would react to finding out that Simon's *sister* had done it in his place. In the end, it was Ness who was afforded the dubious honour and I could do nothing but watch, the back of my neck crawling as she Persuaded my best friend.

'Ugh, they already respect her more than me,' Dennis muttered as he filled the empty space to my left. 'So not fair.'

I smothered an inappropriate chuckle. 'Get used to standing in her shadow. I've done it for years.'

'Except you didn't need to,' Dennis pointed out. 'And you're not standing in it now.'

I glanced aside at Merindah, who was on my right. My fear of Magic Corp and my lack of Perception had driven me into that shadow. And finally, *finally*, I was out of it.

'I'll be the one doing the talking,' I said. 'If you could just focus on getting me the answers I need, Ness, I'd be grateful.' I stepped forward, letting everyone see that I'd shield Merindah with my own body if I had to. I turned around and looked into her eyes, disturbed by the fog that seemed to be filling them. 'Show us the building Mack's group is based in. And tell us what you know about it.'

Merindah held out her hand and a sphere of Physical burst into being above her palm, rolling and rolling, growing with each rotation. When her construct was big enough, she seized it, fingers aligned as though she was holding a cricket ball, and then she hurled it at the wall.

I was ready for this, because Merindah and I had discussed it a few minutes earlier. Everyone else? Not so much. Several demons ducked but they were too late, only managing to do so after the sphere had already slammed into the wall.

What it left behind was far more complicated than a simple

splatter. Lines of muck began to weave together, tangling and spiralling as they etched out the shape of a high-rise building.

'I've only been in the foyer,' Merindah informed us. Her voice was flat, too flat. The Persuasion made her sound like someone else entirely. 'Mack used me as a bodyguard, but she didn't want me overhearing sensitive information. She wouldn't let me go in the lift with her to the basement levels. She spent a lot of time down there. Hours. Sometimes a whole day. No one at MC ever questioned her absences, because she said she was meeting with the Minister for Magical Australians and Related Affairs.'

'She made you wait in the foyer? I hope there was a bathroom nearby!' I exclaimed. What if Merindah had needed to pee or something? Well, okay, her bladder had always been more sizeable than mine, but still.

Merindah's blank gaze remained on the wall even as her intricate artwork faded. 'Yes. I waited in the foyer. There's no reception, but there is a security guard.'

'Just one?'

Merindah nodded.

'Do you think she's got the hybrids and your mother in the basement levels?' I asked, acutely aware of our audience.

The demons were doing their best to sit and stand still, but occasionally someone would shift, their jeans rasping on the couch, their boots scratching over the carpet, their mouth whispering an apology.

Merindah answered me in that same monotone. 'Yes. No other location makes sense. The rest of the time she's either at home, Magic Corp, or dining with the Minister in a public place. I follow her around a lot. Sometimes she sends me photos of the people she wants me to collect, and I bring them back to this building. It's in Chatswood.'

Merindah created another ball of Physical and lobbed it at the wall. This time the inky lines drew streets, blocks, and train tracks. Her fingers flicked out an extra tiny speck that hit the middle of her map, forming a cross on one building.

'X marks the spot,' she said, her lips curling slightly. She was still in there, somewhere. Warm, potent relief washed over me—only to completely disintegrate when Merindah added, 'Good thing you got off at Artarmon the other day, Jen. If you'd waited until Chatswood station to bail, there would have been more Hellhounds waiting for you there. Them and a heap of innocent normals.'

I'm fairly certain my face went white.

Yeah, I'd have been toast. Well, shredded bits of Jen Cooke on toast. Because that had been before I'd started pulling on the demonic realm for power—and causing myself great pain in the process. I did notice that it was hurting less and less with each attempt. I wondered if my Portal was like a muscle, that if I used it more I wouldn't be so tired and sore afterwards.

Dennis was sporting a frown. At first I thought it was concern for me that had inspired it, but then he said, 'Who's footing the bill for that lease, though? Chatswood's cheaper than the CBD but it's not peanuts. And Mack's on a Magic Corp salary. It might be better than mine, even Merindah's, but it can't be enough to cover both her mortgage repayments and the rent in a building like that.'

All eyes were on Merindah again. She didn't talk. She didn't blink. She didn't even *breathe.*

Someone was Persuading her to suffocate herself!

34

I glanced at Simon. Sweat was gathering on his top lip and his face was twisted into a scowl. Merindah suddenly gasped for air, a hand clutching her chest.

'Merindah! Are you alright?' I cried.

She gave me a tight nod.

'Saul,' Simon said, his voice quiet and deadly. 'You will wait outside.'

'For how long?' Saul demanded.

'Until you can remember how to keep it in your pants,' Simon fired back. Evidently, he didn't mean Saul's genitals. He meant Saul's powers.

Sullen, Saul did as he was told.

'Dick,' Dennis muttered beside me. 'He wrenched control from Ness so he could toy with Merindah. I knew we couldn't trust these demons.'

'We're not all bad,' Dot assured him. 'But Saul *is* a dick.'

'Hashtag not all demons,' I said, trying to keep a straight face.

Dot snickered. I was surprised when Ness, Queran, and several other demons joined in. Simon was still looking fierce AF, but I saw his lips twitch minutely.

'I don't know anything about how Mackenzie runs her operation,' Merindah spoke up, sounding a little out of breath and more than a little pissed off. 'Where she gets her funding from is anyone's guess. I've never seen past the foyer and I don't know what defences Mack has in place, or how many people are down there for us to save. But it's a good bet her guards have more than two Ps. We could be walking into a slaughter.'

'Sounds perfect, when do we leave?' Ness asked. The sarcasm was probably warranted.

Dennis wrung his hands. 'I'll go and case out the building. I don't need to get inside, just be nearby, to read the documents on any computers they've got powered on. Payroll and rosters. That sort of thing.'

'Ooh, I had no idea Perception was that useful,' Dot said, clearly impressed.

Dennis and I exchanged glances. It wasn't my place to out him, and I had a feeling he didn't want to advertise his uniqueness to our own colleagues, much less a bunch of demons. So I didn't elaborate. I got rewarded with a big Dennis-y grin, one that was obviously fuelled by more than simple relief.

I doubted that his quirk would stay a secret for long, mind, given Simon's raised eyebrows. And I noticed Merindah looking at us oddly. Very oddly.

I did tell you he was pretending to be useless, I thought in her direction. *But let's keep this between us for now, okay? I know how it feels to have the weird, scary power quirk.*

Merindah's eyes lasered in on Dennis. After about half a minute, he reacted to whatever she was thinking by sighing and nodding. I wondered if she was renewing those old threats to rearrange his face (I'd avoided him after he'd told everyone about The Gym Crash Mat Incident, whereas Merindah had activated Aggressively Protective Friend Mode). That or she was assuring Dennis she wouldn't reveal his little secret.

I really had to stop assuming everything was about me.

I jerked my head towards Dot, then at Ness. 'Take Dennis to this building as soon as possible—Chatswood is more populated than Turramurra, so it's less likely someone will notice a suspicious black van lurking outside. Well, I hope so anyway.'

'You heard Jen,' Simon said when his sister and Ness looked at him for confirmation.

'Yeah, we all did.' Merindah cleared her throat. 'But she wasn't done.'

Oh no, I thought. *Please. Please don't make me do this.*

Dennis was already at the door but he turned back towards me, apparently as eager to listen to my awkward rambling as the demons were.

Faced with glaring silence, I had no choice but to admit that Merindah couldn't lend us any Physical fighters. No choice but to stand there, trembling, while the demons reacted pretty poorly to this information. No choice but to ask Dennis, who was the only person in the room that no one at MC suspected of being in with the demons, if he could help us get the human magic-users we needed.

'Also, we should give my first-floor colleagues a chance to choose which side they're on,' I finished, trying not to pant as my chest tightened. The temptation to run for the door and knock Dennis aside so that I could get out of this room, this suburb, this entire freaking *city*, was overwhelming.

Queran chortled. 'You want to add more disgruntled office workers to our roster?'

Dennis lifted his chin and straightened his grimace into something more defiant. 'Don't laugh, they're our best bet. They'll jump at this chance because they're all bored out of their minds on the first floor. And, uh...I've got a group chat set up for all us disgruntled office workers. I can contact them in seconds.'

'Their Physical's not going to be much use,' I pointed out, because someone had to say it. 'They're on the first floor for a reason.'

Ness tapped her chin thoughtfully. 'But can't they pool their individual powers together and make themselves stronger as a whole? It's very easy to do with Persuasion. If you gathered enough of the humans and hybrids from your "first floor" in one spot, you should have enough power for a decent shield.'

Huh. I really hadn't considered that before.

'Is that even a thing?' I asked Merindah. 'Pooling powers together?'

She shrugged. 'Might work. I've had to do it in the field sometimes. It'd be downright stupid to send one person up against a colony of sloshers or a nest of wingers when several agents can combine their Physical and make a shield strong enough to fend off all of the damn things.'

Dennis gaped at her. 'We can do that? No one told us!'

'You didn't need to know about it down there in Admin,' Merindah told him. 'It's not like you were ever going to be sent out into the field.'

Wow. Dennis looked about as angry as I felt.

'Fucking Magic Corp,' he growled.

'Wait, there's a group chat?' I asked, suddenly cottoning on to that little gem. 'Why wasn't I invited?'

'It's mostly memes and pictures of shoes,' Dennis defended weakly.

A Physical spear shot out of my clenched hand before I could stop myself. It took me a second to erase the magical construct, but my voice wasn't so easy to control. Every single syllable shook. 'You dick. This is high school all over again. You excluded me, told everyone we'd fucked, just so they would like you. And you're still excluding me, Dennis. You can't help yourself—you'd rather be liked instead of resembling anything close to a decent human being! Tell me, are there messages in that group chat making fun of Jen Cooke, AKA The Errand Girl?'

He looked at the floor. Jesus Fucking Christ.

'Yeah, he's an idiot,' I said aside to Merindah. 'You're right. You always are. As if hosting some secret group chat would help him win me back!'

Dennis visibly swallowed. 'I'll tell everyone to meet me. Us. But before I do that, Jen, I need to go check out this building and its defences. I want to make it up to you.'

'Make it up to me?' I sneered at him. 'You can't! And that's so not why you should be doing this. Get out of here before you make me hurl.'

Dennis made quick use of the door. Dot and Ness followed him.

A few seconds later, Saul returned from his exile in the corridor outside and asked what he'd missed. No one answered him, studying their laps intently instead—or, in Simon's case, glowering at the door. Saul looked decidedly put out.

Then I realised just how many people *hadn't* missed my outburst.

'Oh shit,' I breathed. 'Can we pretend that didn't happen?'

Merindah snorted. 'Nope. No take-backsies. I'm starting to see why you like demons better. Humans sure haven't done you any favours.'

'Well, one human did,' I said, smiling at her.

She squeezed me into a hug, then went over to sit on the couch where she crossed her arms and said, 'Well. Come on. I might have forgotten something or glossed over an important detail about Mack's activities. Someone want to Persuade more answers out of me? And can you remove that block on my mind while you're at it?'

Bravest woman in the room. As usual.

Simon came up beside me and leaned in close. He hesitated, as though he wasn't sure what I needed to hear. 'Jen...'

'It's alright,' I said, though I was still waiting for my erratic heartbeat to settle. 'It's fine. I'm fine. It's just...I thought all that shit from school was behind me. But it still hurts. It hurts to know I'm always going to be the odd one out.'

'You're not the odd one out, not here,' he murmured as he continued to erode my personal space. I realised I was very okay with this—mostly because it was easier to inhale that intoxicating scent of his at close range. Mmm. All the better when it was mixed in with leather, thanks to that jacket he was so fond of wearing.

I made a face at him. 'How many hybrids do you see in here?'

'I didn't mean that. I meant what you want to achieve; there are others who want the same thing. You're not alone anymore.'

'God, could you be any sexier?' I muttered.

'Should I try to be?'

I glanced down at his jeans but not for *that* reason, though his widening grin certainly made it obvious that's where his mind had gone. I'd been checking to see if he'd crammed needles into his pockets.

I rolled my eyes. 'Simon. Seriously. Did you clear out Mack's bar fridge?'

'Yes,' he answered in an undertone. 'I stepped out earlier and Portalled back to her house for a few minutes. The injections are now in *my* fridge. Behind the hummus. It's expired so hopefully no one will try to eat it.'

I snorted with laughter, then quickly masked my amusement with a cough. 'Oh my God. Behind the expired hummus. Let's hope no one gets that hungry.' I swallowed. 'Because if Saul gets his hands on these injections...he could very well overpower you.'

'I know.' Simon looked grim. 'I might need to use them myself.'

'What—why?'

'Mackenzie's artificial Persuasion is very potent. That field she threw up around her house...I've never encountered anything like it.' Simon rubbed his jaw, clearly troubled. 'I don't want to have to use the injections. But I can't afford to lose a Persuasion battle against her. My people are depending on me. And I want to protect you, Jen. I *need* to protect you. You're too important to me.'

I shivered. It wasn't just his words that affected me—it was his proximity, the bulge at the front of his jeans, and the fact that he smelled amazing. I wondered if I smelled any good to him. Thanks to my big mouth, I found out a moment later.

'You, Jen Cooke,' Simon said lowly, 'smell fucking fantastic.'

I stifled the groan, patted his shoulder like we'd had a friendly chat (not sure who was buying that, given the smirks the demons were shooting in our direction), and then ran off to find space on the couch beside Merindah.

It seemed like an eternity had passed before Dennis came back, even if it was only an hour.

Good news—the computers in Mackenzie Roberts' Chamber of Secrets were kept on overnight and had yielded the information we needed.

Thanks to Dennis' Perception quirk and my former boss'

obsession with keeping meticulous records, we knew exactly how many guards Mack had in her employ (everyone single one of them was equipped with four Ps, unfortunately), how many captives there were (they all had individual medical files), and how much the lease for six levels was (except there wasn't a whisper of who might be paying for it).

It wasn't going to be easy. But with any luck, we'd soon have some Physical-slinging humans on our side. We'd fight together, shed blood together, and maybe even die together.

If we didn't kill each other first.

35

'Well, you have to admit it,' Dot said, checking out everyone we'd assembled inside a twenty-four-hour Macca's. We were three streets away from Simon's apartment. 'This human's betrayal of you in high school did come in handy. The popularity he scored out of it resulted in all these people agreeing to meet him here, no questions asked.'

I couldn't help but look sideways at Dennis, who was sitting on my left. His face gave a violent twitch.

I was amused to see how uncomfortable the thought of impressing a demon made him. I wasn't going to poke fun at him though, because I was way more concerned about the fact that this was the kind of stuff we definitely shouldn't be discussing in a McDonald's on the Pacific Highway.

Either my colleagues really hated Magic Corp, or it was the promise of free nuggets that had dragged them out of bed at 2 AM. I wasn't even sure if knowing a demon would be in attendance would have deterred them.

Free nugs are free nugs, after all.

Dot didn't look particularly demonic. In an attempt to set 'the humans' at ease, she had swapped her usual jeans-and-shirt combo for a polka dot dress that would have looked more suitable on Minnie Mouse than on someone capable of Persuading us all to rip off our clothes and do the Chicken Dance. Well, she had promised me that unlike her brothers she hadn't inherited Persuasion powerful enough to affect several people at once. But still. It remained a possibility that at least *one* person would end up making a fool of themselves.

I just hoped it would be Dennis.

The nugget boxes were now alarmingly empty. So it wasn't a surprise when Beth Ng from HR leaned across the table and said, 'What gives, Dennis? We came out pretty late on a school night to hear some gossip about the higher-ups. So. Dish.'

'It technically isn't a "school night",' Dan Argenziano from Accounts corrected her, hands linked on the table in front of him. 'Since we've all been placed on leave for the duration of the clean-up at headquarters. They are not even deducting time from what we have owing, which I think is a costly mistake.'

Beth sighed. 'Dan hasn't taken a day off in five years—which is unfortunate for us! But it's even more unfortunate for his girlfriend, who shall remain nameless. Totally unrelated, but I think the Hunter Valley is nice this time of year.'

Beth gave Dan a pointed look. Titters ensued. Even Dan smiled, which I'd never seen him do before. That was kind of weird.

'But seriously, Dennis,' Beth continued, 'why are we here?' She tilted her head towards Dot. 'And who's that? I don't think she works at Magic Corp.'

It was obvious why Beth was the first-floor favourite. She took charge and made everyone like her in the same breath. I envied that. I still wasn't if sure any of the demons (barring Simon and Dot) liked me, especially after bringing humans into their midst. And there had been that embarrassing outburst in which I'd admitted to banging one of said humans. Ugh.

For once I was glad to be beneath my colleagues' notice. It was a lot easier to sit back and let someone else hold the reins of this craziness.

'This has gotta be related to the demon attack at HQ,' Kirsty said. She sat at the desk beside mine and was two years younger than me. 'Did you see all those people who showed up to protect us? Wild! They have powers I've never seen before.'

Dennis shoved the nearest the nugget box away from him, presumably so he could pretend that he hadn't finished all twenty of them by himself. 'They were demons.'

'Demons?' Kirsty snickered. 'They looked nothing like demons!'

'Excuse me,' Dot cut in. 'Much as I hate to say it, we demons have a lot in common with you humans. It's not our fault you look like us.'

There was a comical chorus of gasps after that. Dot grinned mercilessly, showing teeth, and several people leaned away from her. Jason (he was one of Dan's underlings in Accounts) jumped out of his chair and formed a Physical cricket bat in his hand. I guess he was trying to be intimidating, but the wild swings and terrified expression didn't really have the intended effect.

And Dennis was just *sitting there*, not bothering to defend Dot, not even trying to explain. He wasn't doing a damn thing. Just like when the other kids had made fun of me at school. It was a fair bet he still did nothing when our colleagues were making fun of me in the group chat.

God, I hated him.

Dennis flinched as though I'd struck him. I didn't apologise for my thoughts, which I could have obscured from him but hadn't, and instead I snapped, 'Jason, get rid of that bat before the normals see it!'

Jason's eyes skidded in my direction. The magical construct in his hand withered away.

'We don't have time for this,' I charged on. 'Magic Corp has been lying to all of us. And they don't intend to stop doing it. So if you want to know what the fuck is going on, sit down, shut up, and don't attack someone who actually wants to help you.'

Dot snorted. 'I'm here to help *you*, Jen. Not these humans,' she added, flicking out her tongue as though that last word had been particularly distasteful.

'Play nice, please,' I muttered.

Dot sighed dramatically, but didn't argue.

Meanwhile, Beth Ng was looking at me strangely. 'Jen—Jen Cooke?'

Look, I know I was wearing a hoodie (to avoid anyone who recognised me from those widely circulated videos), but it didn't make me *that* unrecognisable.

'Yes, I'm the one who gets your sencha tea with honey,' I griped. 'And your boyfriend there is Mr No Decaf for Me.' I pointed at Dan, then went down the line. 'Ms Can't Sacrifice Her Lunchbreak to Post Personal Mail but Thinks I Want to Sacrifice Mine. Mr Too Lazy to Walk Ten Metres to Load Paper in the Printer but Can Walk Across the Room to Tell Me Do It Instead!'

No one seemed capable of meeting my gaze, not even Dennis. He was probably thinking about the stapler he'd regularly forgotten to return to me.

Beth cleared her throat noisily. 'Why didn't you say something, Jen?'

'Why did you think it was okay to keep asking me and only me?' I demanded. 'Because I was the shy, meek Jen you pushed around at school? Because you could make fun of me in some secret group chat without any consequences?'

Yep, they were still looking at the table and its empty boxes.

Cowards.

A dark laugh snaked out of me. 'Well, guess what? Now *I* get to push you around. In return, you get the truth. You get to decide what to do with your own life. Which is far more than Magic Corp ever gave you.' I hastily filled my lungs with air before someone could butt in. 'I hate being The Errand Girl. I fucking hate it. And I bet none of you are happy about having to work on the first floor for the rest of your miserable lives.'

'Good on you, Jen,' Dot said, grinning. 'Make them feel like shit. They've earned it.'

Beth nodded slowly. 'Okay. We'll listen. Because if you're right about MC lying to us, we deserve to know.' She grimaced. 'Even if we don't deserve your forgiveness.'

And that's all it took for the rest of the table to start muttering bashful apologies.

Beth had always been so good at dealing with people. She should have known that it was demoralising for me to see younger, inexperienced workers given better positions, better pay. I hadn't said anything at the time. It wasn't a matter of simply being too afraid to stand up for myself. I knew that if I'd tried, that if I'd let my anger boil instead of simmer, they would have laughed and said things like 'did you hear? Jen Cooke finally *snapped*'.

I missed Simon. He made me feel like I wasn't snapping. That I was coming into my own. That I was now exactly who I was meant to be—who I could have been, if I'd lived my life with demons.

Dennis squeezed my hand gently, nudging me out of my reverie.

'Dennis, can you take over...?' I all but squeaked. My heart was thudding erratically inside my chest and my throat was dry. I knew that ordering more nuggets would be a mistake, though I'm not sure the fizzy drink I reached for and gulped down in exactly four goes was any better.

'There are more than two Ps,' Dennis said, sounding so much more confident than me. His hand was still covering my own and I was painfully aware that if he lifted his fingers then mine would start shaking.

'More Ps?' Kirsty asked incredulously. 'How can there be *more* of them?'

I noticed that Beth was watching Dennis with a frown fixed in place while everyone else at the table pelted him with questions.

'Yes, there's more,' Dennis answered. 'Four in total. But you can only have two out of four Ps. Humans have Perception and Physical. Demons have Persuasion and Portal. Persuasion enables you to make people do stuff...' He started explaining, but he didn't get very far.

Beth's nails tapped out an agitated rhythm on the table. 'I know. I think I have it. But I—I'm not a demon. I can't be.'

Jason from Accounts, who had only just sat down, abruptly stood up again and moved several seats away from her. Everyone else exchanged nervous glances.

Beth shifted in her seat. 'I've never had Physical. And sometimes...I find it really easy to get people to solve their disputes. Way too easy, now that I think about it. Are you saying I've been getting into their heads? Because I—I didn't mean to! I'm not a demon!'

'No Physical? How did you pass the tests, but?' one of our colleagues demanded.

Beth didn't answer. She had completely shut down. I felt sorry for her, because everyone was looking at her in the same way I'd been always afraid of them looking at *me*—with unrepentant suspicion.

'It's the apps,' I spoke up. 'Simon Bradley, Tech's senior developer, gave us apps like PercApption and WatchDog.'

'The app he gave me projected a stick out of my phone so I could hit the target in my Physical tests,' someone murmured. And it wasn't Beth.

'But you clearly have Physical, Jennifer,' Dan said. 'We all saw the videos of you fighting that Hellhound at Artarmon station. You don't have one of these extra Ps.'

Emma, who was so terrible at posting her own mail, turned wide eyes onto me. 'Except Jen keeps getting into trouble with Tom for not doing the tasks he's thinking at her, you can hear him shouting about it from halfway across the room.'

'Simon Bradley—he told the Hellcreatures at HQ to freeze and they did!' Kirsty exclaimed. 'Is that Persuasion?'

'But we're not *demons*,' Beth insisted.

'You're half demon,' Dot told her. 'Which makes you only half as awesome as me.'

I really shouldn't have grinned at the stupefied expressions on my colleagues' faces, but for some reason it did look funny from the outside. I had a feeling that this was how the demons had seen me when I'd first shown up. Naive, kept in the dark—and about to get slapped in the face with reality.

'Hybrids, that's what the higher-ups call you guys,' Jason said, then shrugged apologetically when people boggled at him. 'Sometimes you can't help overhearing things. A lot of things, actually...the higher-ups keep so much from us.'

That was my opening. But I didn't have the heart to tell them.

Luckily, Dennis did it for me. 'The higher-ups have been using people—hybrids—with Persuasion to force our families to hand us over. And then they force us to stay and sign those stupid contracts. We don't remember it, because Persuasion can make you forget things. It's so messed up.'

'Oh *shit*,' Dan said, sounding very improper and so unlike himself.

'Didn't you ever wonder why our parents gave us up so quickly?' Beth asked bitterly.

Meanwhile, Kirsty was stuck in a loop. 'They...they wouldn't...'

'Wouldn't they?' I challenged. 'They put people who quit onto a *Kill Register*. We don't get the same choices as normals, to leave when we want, to find a better job somewhere else. What makes you think MC let us choose whether or not we join in the first place? It's not fair. It's never been freaking fair.'

'It's unfathomably callous,' Dan mumbled.

Dot inspected her nails for few moments, then looked up. 'I can break any memory blocks you have. If you want. It's not gonna be pretty, but that's my offer.'

Beth eyed her. 'What does the demon expect us to give her in return?'

Dennis nodded imperceptibly in my direction, giving me the floor—er, table.

This time, I was ready to take the lead.

So I told them about Mack and what she was getting up to in Chatswood. I told them about Merindah's interstate sanctuary (she'd trusted me with its location, but I didn't dare say where it was—I didn't even *think* it). I told them about the demons coming to my rescue. I told them about everything that had been kept from them.

And then I gave them the choice. Help me and the demons—or quietly abscond to Merindah's sanctuary (Simon had promised to send along his nullifying devices, to help hide it from any magic-sensing scouts).

'...and the demons will help us protect this country from Hellcreatures and whatever else,' I concluded. 'Together, we'll replace Magic Corp with something better. And if people don't want to join up, fine. They can do whatever they want with their skills.'

'Why not go to the higher-ups and get them to deal with Mack?' Beth asked, pressing her hands flat on the table, apparently not caring that its cleanliness was highly disputed. 'Let them shut her down. And while they're busy doing that, we can start organising ourselves in secret. If we play it right, we'll have enough time to figure out how we're going to protect a whole country—with demons, of all people! We don't even have a business plan.'

I noticed that no one was bothering to argue against the concept of replacing Magic Corp.

In fact, I saw more than a few thoughtful expressions and half smiles. I wondered how many of my colleagues, if any, would actually stick around when they could go work somewhere else. They'd been just as stuck as me on the first floor—and just as restless and agitated and forgotten.

'Because, Beth,' I said before I could stop myself, 'if we say something—*anything*—to the higher-ups, then that will tip Mack off. And she might kill Merindah's mother. We can't let that happen. No, I *won't* let that happen.'

'Okay, but forget attacking about what could be an entire army!' Sandeep from HR piped up. I'd always been envious of him because he planned the work retreats for the floors above us. He even got to go along to check how things went, lucky bastard. 'How on Earth are we meant to effectively replace Magic Corp? How!? I don't know shit about using my Physical against Hellhounds! And I don't know about the rest of you, but my magic's pretty weak. We're on the first floor for a reason, Jen.'

I managed to keep my voice level. It wasn't easy, but I used Simon's quiet menace as my inspiration. 'We'll have demons with Persuasion on our side, and we'll also have the apps to back us up.' I paused, then dropped a much smaller bombshell this time. 'Plus, no one at Magic Corp ever told us this, but we can actually combine our Physical. So we might be weak by ourselves, but if we get enough people together, I reckon we can make a pretty decent shield.'

My colleagues got a faraway look in their eyes, not unlike what I'd seen in my reflection in the bathroom mirror when I wondered what else I could be doing—with my powers, with my life, you name it.

I'd planted the seeds. Now I just had to wait for my colleagues to realise that they were *allowed* to grow, that there was plenty of room for them to do it. Just not at Magic Corp.

Kirsty broke the silence by sucking noisily on the dregs of whatever was left in her cup. She coughed self-consciously. 'Yeah, Jen, this idea of yours is pretty cool and all—we can *so* make a better organisation than Magic Corp—but what I really want is for your demon friend to unblock my memories. If they are blocked, that is. Um, you can't—*see* things, can you?' she finished nervously, glancing at Dot.

Dot's eyes briefly flicked up towards the ceiling. 'No, we can't read thoughts. Your filthy secrets will remain your own.'

'Oh good,' Kirsty said, deflating with relief. 'Alright, I'm first in line for the mind scramble!'

It was funny to see how eager everyone was. And not just to have a demon rummage through their heads—no, they were looking forward to risking their lives and becoming heroes, because it was something a lot of them had secretly wished they could do. Their excitement was infectious.

But then those smiles were wiped clean with horror when Dot plunged into their minds and unblocked them.

I couldn't witness it. Not again. So I went outside into the empty play area and sat on the squishy artificial ground beside Dennis, wishing we didn't have this common, that *none* of us had this in common.

But I could still hear the crying and the cursing.

'This, this is why,' Dennis reminded me softly. 'This is why we have to do it. Why we have to work with the demons. I might not like them, but at least they got that part right. Letting people stay with their families.'

It wasn't a ringing endorsement, but it was a start.

Maybe we could pull this off after all.

'Ugh, why did I have to think that?' I muttered. 'I've totally jinxed us.'

Dennis snorted.

36

My colleagues wore downcast expressions as they drifted out of the Macca's. Some of them bought medicinal quantities of fast food on their way past the registers, not that I could blame them—and it was just past 4 AM, so it technically counted as breakfast.

I stood there, watching them go, afraid that I'd just condemned them to death for getting them to agree to attack Mackenzie Roberts' Chamber of Secrets. I was also hoping that I hadn't inspired someone to go to our superiors and report on our clandestine activities, tipping Mack off in the process.

If we were lucky, the higher-ups were still too busy to listen to any of us first-floor folk. Simon had revealed himself as a demon back at HQ and they were probably holding an emergency meeting about how he'd infiltrated them so easily.

They really ought to have noticed him slinging his Persuasion around earlier, I mused, especially since they'd had hybrids on payroll this whole time.

'It could be that Magic Corp doesn't know how to properly train them,' Beth Ng said in response to my thoughts, then took a long draw from her thickshake. 'Or maybe they didn't think the demons would try something so subtle. Simon really had the right idea.' Her lips twitched. 'I'm definitely uninstalling WatchDog when I get a spare moment.'

I snorted. Couldn't really blame her.

'For what it's worth, I'm sorry,' Beth said, turning to meet my gaze squarely. 'For how I treated you at school. And at work. I shouldn't have neglected you. I should have suggested that one of the newer graduating classes provide a bottom-rung employee to replace you. And we should not have taken advantage of your inability to fight back.'

Pinpricks darted across my eyeballs. 'Um. Just don't do it again.'

'I'll get *you* some sencha the next time we're at work,' she promised.

'Wherever we work after this, it won't be like Magic Corp,' I said. 'I don't even know what it will be like.'

Beth shrugged. 'Well, when it's time—and once I figure out what position I want—I'll join up and buy you tea. I'll even photocopy things for you if need be.'

I stared at Beth, frankly bewildered by how quickly she had accepted my crazy plan to replace Magic Corp. My other colleagues were still a little dubious, I could tell. But she was already all in. Which was a good thing, because she had the clout to convince the others to stay on. And I needed people, not mere positive thinking, if I wanted to succeed.

When Beth turned to go, something important abruptly occurred to me. 'Wait! You didn't get Dot to see if there's a block in your mind.'

'There *was* a block,' Beth answered, shadows spreading from her haunted eyes and dousing her fragile smile. 'I already found it. Years ago. Before I knew what it was, what *I* was. I got rid of it then. It was so confusing. I was sure I'd never wanted to sign that contract, but suddenly my memories were telling me I'd done it just because someone told me to. I would have needed more convincing than that! I'd always known something was wrong, even before I found the block. I think we all did, deep down, and we took comfort in things we shouldn't have, like excessive amounts of alcohol at parties we can barely remember—and those damn shoes!'

A muffled sound escaped her; not quite a laugh and not quite a sob. 'It's been lonely keeping it to myself. But I couldn't tell anyone, because I didn't know if the memories were real or if I was just...we need to stop this happening ever again.'

Smearing the back of a hand over both her cheeks, Beth briskly walked over to the second-hand Lexus belonging to Dan Argenziano (they'd come in the same car, finally confirming chronic office gossip). I noticed that she was wearing trendy Onitsuka Tigers, yellow and black ones. They didn't match or complement the purple floral dress she was wearing. At all.

I wondered if she'd rather have put something else on her feet, but had been afraid of missing out on praise from our colleagues.

I wasn't Magic Corp's only victim. There were hundreds of us.

Dennis slithered up beside me. He didn't say anything, thank God. I wasn't sure if he was giving me space or if he just didn't know what to say, but I appreciated the silence. Even if I was about to break it.

'Beth told me...' I hesitated. 'Do you think everyone on the first floor knew something was wrong? That they just...drank away their problems? Bought shiny shoes to distract themselves? And ganged up on me so they didn't feel so alone? Why couldn't we find other ways to deal with this?'

Dennis smothered a yawn. 'There was no way out, Jen. And maybe I did buy all those shoes to fill the hole left by my family.'

A grin coloured his words. 'If I hadn't been so hung up on you, those sweet kicks would probably have gotten me laid.'

I snorted. 'Well, since the Hellhounds haven't shredded the Superstars on your feet yet, you've still got a chance with one of our colleagues.'

'No one's going to be ready for anything like that right now,' Dennis pointed out. 'If they're like me, finding this shit out...it can mess with you. It's still messing with me.'

I rubbed my sternum; his words had caused an ache somewhere I'd never wanted to feel anything for him ever again. I'd been a convenient punching bag that had made people feel better about themselves when they hit it. But they weren't the root cause of all my misery; Magic Corp was.

'I know it's no excuse,' Dennis went on, grimacing. 'But what I did to you...I did it because I wanted to belong. I'm sorry, Jen. For everything.'

I reached out and took his hand. He squeezed once, then let go. I didn't know what that meant. But maybe...maybe he was finally accepting that he couldn't hold on to me anymore. That I could never be his dream version of me.

Dennis lifted his chin. 'We'll change things, Jen. For the better.'

'That's the plan,' I said. 'Although, I'm not sure everyone was sold on making a new version of Magic Corp with the demons. Dot didn't even try to ingratiate herself. I wish Simon had come with us, but Saul's causing all sorts of...'

'I'm heading off with the others,' Dennis interrupted. He jerked his head towards the cars that were preparing to form a convoy to a nearby hotel. Dot was going to fetch some nullifying field projectors for my colleagues, just in case MC wondered why so many magic-users were gathered in one spot. 'I have to practice pooling my Physical with theirs anyway, but I'll keep my Perception aimed at their phones, to make sure they don't contact Mack or anyone else.'

'You'll be up for hours,' I warned him.

'I have to do it, Jen. I have to protect you.' When I opened my mouth to argue, he sighed. 'Please. I'm still allowed to care about you. We were friends before we were ever anything else.'

'Dennis...' I blinked rapidly against the tears.

'I know, I know I fucked up,' he said and waved a hand up and down his body, as though his mistakes were written on his clothes for all to see. 'I'd do it all differently if I could. But I can't. I hate that I can't. Just let me do this, okay? For you. For the family I found when I wasn't allowed to know mine.'

Well, what could I say? 'No, don't bother, let's spend the next few hours wondering if someone's going to dob us in'? And I *did* feel bad for him. Shit, I felt bad for all of my past tormentors. That didn't sit well with me.

Did I have to forgive them? Or could I just...move past it?

Our colleagues were now hanging out of car windows and shouting at us to hurry up. They were calling both our names, as though they'd never forgotten to include me.

'Okay,' I croaked. 'Thank you. I mean it.'

'You should come with us,' Dennis said. 'We've got ages before the action tonight. Might be a good time to catch up and get to know everyone properly.'

Ugh, it sounded like torture instead of a 'good time'.

I wasn't ready to be that friendly with them—not yet, anyway.

Dot left the Macca's a few seconds later (she was the last one out), giving me an excuse to turn away from Dennis' hopeful smile. There were premature lines on Dot's face, deep ones, and I wondered if it was because she'd burned through her reserves—or because she'd had to watch so many humans and hybrids crumble before her.

'Want a ride back?' Dot asked me.

'Have you even got a licence?' Dennis demanded.

Dot fluttered her eyelashes at him, all innocence. 'What's a licence?'

'She did manage not to kill us with the van earlier,' I reminded Dennis.

He frowned. 'Jen, you don't have to spend every waking moment with the demons. You're half human, you know.'

'Don't you want Jen to make sure that we haven't done anything nasty to her best friend while she's been busy here?' Dot asked in mock horror, a hand clutching at her neck as though there was a string of pearls there. For someone who apparently didn't know what a driver's licence was, she seemed to know a lot of other human references, pearl-clutching among them.

Dennis nodded sharply. 'It wouldn't hurt to have someone there to remind the demons that they shouldn't mess with us humans. Jen might be the only one who can manage that.'

This said, Dennis turned on his heel and marched over to the waiting cars.

'Did you need to antagonise him?' I asked Dot. 'No one will hurt Merindah. God knows why, but I'm certain she's alright.'

'Of course she is!' Dot exclaimed. 'No one wants to tempt your ire, especially after seeing what you can do with your Physical. Dennis is right about you being a terrifying reminder. And,' she added when I scowled at her, 'we look after our families. You're practically part of my family already. So I've got your back—and the backs of the people you care about.'

I rubbed my temples. She was being a little heavy-handed. Next she'd be asking for a wedding invitation and I wasn't even sure what I had going on with Simon in the first place. We'd made out in a men's bathroom, avoided each other for three years, and now we were struggling to keep our hands off each other. That didn't mean we were in a serious relationship. I didn't even know what I wanted from him.

Oh God. I did know. I was just too afraid to ask for it.

'Come on,' Dot said, snagging my hand. 'Before that human attempts to get you alone again. He pants after you like one of the hounds.'

'He's not going to try anything,' I told Dot. 'Dennis knows where we stand. I think.'

Our mutual past might not be an issue anymore, but it was obvious that Dennis didn't like the idea of me spending time with demons. He still didn't trust them. And that hurt. Because it meant he couldn't trust part of *me*.

'Dot,' I began nervously. 'I was wondering...'

'Come *on*,' Dot insisted.

She yanked me towards the green Hyundai Excel. Simon had been very reluctant to let her borrow it—she was, admittedly, an even more reckless driver than he was.

After she'd buckled herself in and finished making grumpy comments about our traffic laws, I finally managed to ask her why she was being so nice to me. I mean, I was half human. Surely she had a problem with that, the way Dennis had a problem with my demonic side.

Dot gave me an incredulous look. 'So what if you have human blood? You're still one of us. And it's been really cool to watch you gain so much confidence. It suits you. I'm also really impressed that you can face the people who hurt you without exercising your lawful right to kill them. That takes serious restraint! Anyway, I'm hoping we'll become sisters when all this is over.'

'Uh.' I coughed. 'How about we just be friends?'

Dot sighed. 'I hope you don't say that to Simon.'

I had no intention of saying that to Simon—rather the opposite. And I suspected she knew it.

37

The car screeched its way down the ramp and came to a halt half a metre away from one of the pylons holding up the ceiling (and the entire apartment complex above it). I tried to surreptitiously release the breath I'd been holding. I'm not sure I succeeded because Dot smirked at me.

'I made arrangements for everyone else to sleep in the other apartments,' she said with a vague wave of her hand towards the lift. 'So it's just my brother up there. *Alone.*'

'Where's Merindah?' I asked.

'Oh, in one of the third-floor apartments—they put her out.'

She said it so casually. As though putting Merindah 'out' with Persuasion was the most normal and socially accepted thing to do to someone who was risking everything, including the life of the mother she hadn't seen in *over a decade*, to help prove that we could all work together. Merindah deserved better.

Dot frowned, obviously picking up on my disapproval (not that I'd bothered to hide it). 'It was the Kill Squad agent's idea. This way we know she won't try to escape. We trust her, Jen, because she made the offer before we could ask her to agree to it.'

I slumped down further in my seat, hating that I was envious of Merindah. She wouldn't have to spend the whole day thinking about Mack and Hellhounds and potential collateral damage. She wouldn't have to be preoccupied with her uncertain future, like I was. She was free to sleep away her problems. For now, at least.

'Chin up,' Dot said, her tone now very gentle. 'You might not die tonight. But if you *are* going to die...you don't really want to spend your last hours moping, do you?'

She held up her hands, waggled them at me, and then shoved them into the glove compartment. Her fists withdrew moments later, clutching items which had a very clear purpose.

Black silk scarves. An entire box of condoms. And a blue tube containing what I assumed was lubricant, something I'd never used, mostly because I hadn't known it was a thing when I was a teenager. At least Magic Corp had provided free condoms in the school bathrooms—babies are to be avoided, folks, at least until you sign those contracts and agree to the clause that says you have to inform MC about the existence of any offspring.

'Go get his groove back,' Dot said, winking as she tossed her stash into my lap.

I opened my mouth but couldn't find the words to fill it, so I just blushed and opened the door. Dot snickered.

I made my way over to the lift while she took the Hyundai back out, heading off to retrieve the nullifying field projectors for my colleagues. I wondered where the extra projectors were stashed if not at Simon's place. Some other hideout, I guess? The demons seemed to have an endless supply of those.

I suddenly realised that I was alone and shivering in the cool basement air. I was very tempted to sleep down there—away from complications.

Ding.

Into the lift. Up to the third floor. Knocking on the door—timidly, like I was trying not to wake the neighbours. Or maybe I was hoping he wouldn't hear anything, so he wouldn't get the chance to come out and turn me away.

Simon opened the door. He didn't smile. He didn't even say a word, just grabbed me and pulled me into a kiss that went on and on and on, my arms trapped between us. He was wearing those damn trackpants again, but I didn't really care about how daggy they were—I cared more about kicking the door shut behind me.

Oh my God. It's impossible to resist a hot, shirtless demon, especially one who's that good with his tongue.

Our kisses grew more intense as he walked backwards, guiding me past strewn pizza boxes and paper plates (clearly even demons possessed a fondness for grease and cheese). I was sure I'd meant to say something to Simon, but it was extremely difficult to remember exactly what that was.

I managed to extract my lips from his when we got to his bedroom door. 'Simon...I don't like that I have to rely on you to stop me using my powers when there's a Portal nearby. It's dangerous. What if you're not there with me next time? What if—what if it *kills* me?'

Simon's palm grazed my cheek. 'You haven't had much practice. It's possible you won't always need me around to control your powers.' His other hand was underneath my shirt, resting against my back, radiating warmth. 'But I don't think we have the time for you to learn how to do it yourself. You'd need rest if we tried anything now.'

'It's hurting me less and less to draw on the Portals and it doesn't tire me out that much anymore, I swear,' I protested—but not very hard. This might have had something to do with the kiss he planted on my neck. I tilted my head back and gave him more access, shuddering as my skin tingled beneath his ministrations.

Good God, he really knew what he was doing. And he knew exactly how to deal with me.

'If you turn up at that building tonight, Jen, too exhausted to defend yourself, let alone help us...' Simon trailed off, his breath ghosting past my ear. '*That's* dangerous. I'd be tempted to make you stay behind.'

I reared back to glare at him. 'You wouldn't dare. Because that's the kind of thing that would piss Dennis off and you really don't want me siding with him.'

Simon smiled. 'No, I wouldn't, and right now I'm more interested in doing something else he'd disapprove of.'

A pleasant, incessant throb began between my legs. I was about to coyly ask what he had in mind when his eyes fell to my arms. And what was in them. I'd completely forgotten about the supplies his sister had given me.

'*Dot*,' Simon growled.

'Well, we did need the condoms.' I shook out the scarves, hoping I didn't look as nervous as I felt. 'And we did talk about tying you down. To make sure you're, you know, not in control or anything.'

He bit into his bottom lip and made a distinctly primal sound.

'And, Simon? I don't want to make *you* stay behind tonight because you can't concentrate or because you're too, uh, tense.' My face heated up immediately after I used the double entendre. I nearly apologised, but when he looked at me again, his eyes completely dark, I knew it didn't matter if what I'd said sounded stupid to me. It didn't sound stupid to him.

In fact, nothing I said ever seemed stupid to him. He always listened. And he was willing to risk everything for me and my deluded dream of human/hybrid/demon unity. I had no idea why he was going along with—with *any of it*.

I think I tried to say something to this effect. I must have succeeded.

'Because I believe in you, because I trust you,' Simon said in a low voice, pressing in and letting me feel just how much he wanted me. 'And I know that with you at my side, I will be able to destroy Magic Corp once and for all.'

'I...I better...' I fumbled.

'You better regain control of the situation.' He smirked. 'And of me.'

'Take off your pants,' someone ordered breathlessly and I was startled when I realised it was me.

Simon obeyed and stood there for my inspection, completely naked, completely male, and completely mine for the taking.

I thought I would lose my nerve. I didn't. I led him into his bedroom and he dutifully lay on the bed, stretching his arms out and keeping still while I tied his wrists to the barred headboard with trembling fingers.

I'd never been on top before and I was so sure I would mess it up. But then I took a moment to look down at him, at what he was offering me, and abruptly forgot why I'd been so worried. I trailed my hands all over him, finding sensitive areas that made him squirm, delighting in the power he'd given me, and enjoying the strained noises he made when I applied my lips to where my fingers had been.

The last—and first—time I'd had sex, it had been a frenzied, clumsy coupling in a school gymnasium, and over all too soon because we'd been afraid of getting caught. This was different. Slower. More sensual.

'Please, I want to see you,' Simon whispered.

Oh, right. I still had my clothes on. Well, I *had* been kind of distracted.

I arched an eyebrow at Simon. 'Who's in control here?'

Air hissed between his gritted teeth. 'You are.'

The heady rush I got from that, from him agreeing to submit to me, was disorientating and I had to force myself to remember to breathe. Once my vision had stopped sparking, I shuffled over to the side of the bed and peeled off my clothes, grinning over my shoulder at Simon.

The hunger in his gaze was a lure and I was immediately drawn back to him, his obvious desire emboldening me. I straddled his chest, watching his eyes coast lower, and lower still.

'Like the view?' I asked. Embarrassment was a distant memory.

'I'm sure I'll like the taste even better,' he baited. 'If you'll allow me to find out.'

Maybe it was because my arousal was stronger than my fear. Or maybe it was the extremely hot suggestion he'd made and how he'd said it. But I did it. I sat on his face, knees braced either side of him, a hand clenched in his hair as he pleasured me, his tongue darting over my most sensitive nerves and delving deep inside me.

I'd never known it could feel like *this*.

My whispered pleas swiftly grew into wordless whimpers. Fuck. I wasn't going to last long and we hadn't even—

Panting, I scuttled off him. When he looked at me questioningly, I said in a voice that sounded far too confident to be mine, 'That's enough. You've had your fun.'

He smirked, his lips coated with—*me*, I realised. I leaned forward and kissed him, licking, biting, tasting my desire in his mouth.

'Mine,' I whispered.

'Yours,' he agreed and I rewarded him by moving my kisses back down his body.

He was hard. Very hard. When I ran my tongue up the length of him, slicking his warm, salty skin, he cried out, begging me to keep teasing him. I realised he was enjoying this, enjoying being at my mercy. So I indulged him, delighted by how desperately he writhed beneath me. I could have kept toying with him for hours—if I hadn't accidentally pressed my damp folds against his thigh. I couldn't restrain the moan at *how fucking good* it felt.

I tore into the box of condoms. Belatedly, I remembered to slow down and spent a deliciously long minute rolling the condom along each and every inch of him, grinning when he gasped and thrust up against me.

I reached for the lube next. I wasn't sure how much I was supposed to use and I squirted out a generous amount of the stuff, recalling how dry and awkward my first time had been. I'd been impatient that night, so impatient that I hadn't cared if I wasn't quite ready—well, I'd certainly cared afterwards, when I'd had to sneak back to my dormitory, wincing all the while.

I tightened my fingers around Simon's pulsing member as I hovered over him, looking into his beautiful blue eyes.

'Are you okay?' he asked quietly. 'We can stop, if you want.'

Even now he was worried he'd hurt me, worried he was pressuring me into something that I'd regret. God, it was probably his most attractive feature. And it didn't exactly inspire me to stop. I nudged my entrance over the tip of him, waited until his breathing hitched—and then slid right down his shaft.

He groaned, long and loud. I would have savoured his reaction had the wide girth of him not suddenly swelled and *pressed* until I was arching my back and crying out in surprise. The hot, exquisite burst between my legs had arrived a lot sooner than I'd expected it to. I mean, I'd only just got onto him! This was way too fast!

'I—I'm sorry,' I gasped. 'I didn't—I didn't mean to—'

'I liked feeling you squeeze around me,' Simon said breathlessly. 'I want to feel you do it again. And again.' He licked his lips. 'And again.'

'Unh, who's in control here?' I rasped.

Simon laughed. 'Neither of us!'

I wasn't really sure what to do next, but when I looked down at his heaving chest and the cords tightening in his neck, my body told me that it could take over. So I let it. My hips rolled and soon I was orgasming again, this time with enough force to send me toppling down onto his chest. His skin was slick with sweat and he smelled even more amazing than usual, if that was possible.

His desperate kiss sent a shock racing down through my body, straight to my aching folds. He shuddered and sucked in a deep breath. I knew he was close. I clenched hard, tensing myself around him, preparing to follow him over the edge. He hit his peak and moaned my name, causing one last bolt of pleasure to slam into me.

I rode it out until I became too sensitive, then flopped onto the bed beside him. I lay there for several long moments, my ear on his chest, listening to his steadying heartbeat while I waited for my own to stop racing.

Eventually, Simon admitted that he was losing sensation in his fingers so I untied him. He kissed my forehead on his way over to the ensuite.

I jumped up and waddled after him. 'God, I really need to pee!'

Simon graciously stepped aside and allowed me to get ahead of him. So there I was, sitting naked on his toilet while he dropped the condom into the nearby bin. He flashed a satisfied smile at me and I felt oddly at ease despite the fact that I was peeing in front of him. Once I'd dealt with that and washed my hands, I returned to the bed to wait for him to join me. I didn't have to wait long. I curled up on my side, smiling as his scruffy hair became even more chaotic when he leaned against a pillow.

'I see you managed to stay in your head the whole time,' I teased.

'I knew that I had no excuses, that you trusted—and expected—me not to lose control. And it...' Simon drew a breath. 'It hasn't been that good in a while. I was able to let go.'

Very loath to move, I lazed, basking in the post-coital glow and enjoying the knowledge that I'd been the one responsible for getting his groove back. But when his eyes started to close, I knew I had to get in quick if I wanted to finish our earlier conversation. 'Simon, if you need to get into my head tonight to stop me, to save my life or someone else's, then don't hesitate. Just do it. I trust you.'

'Jen, I don't want to assume...' he murmured.

'Then don't. Because I'm telling you it's okay.'

Simon's hand found the dip of my waist and squeezed gently. 'I must ask something of you in return. I'm going to carry one of those Persuasion injections we got from Mack's place with me tonight. If I use it, and it causes me to lose control of my powers, you'll need to find a way to stop me. Incapacitate me. Get Saul to take me down. Whatever it takes.'

'I'll do what I can,' I promised him, then hesitated. 'Right, um, I don't want to make an assumption of my own so...so...' This was hard. But I had to say it. I had to know. 'Are we going out now?'

Yeah, it was like I was back at high school all over again. But I'd never checked with Dennis and I was wondering how different my life would be if I had, if I'd known that he'd wanted a serious relationship, not just a one-night stand. If I'd asked Dennis that question, and if he'd given me his answer, would he have said anything to his friends the next day?

I was done with keeping quiet. I was done with not asking for what I wanted and regretting it year after agonising year. Done with fearing the consequences.

I was trembling. Shit.

Simon leaned over and pressed his lips to my shoulder. 'Where do you suggest we go for our first date?'

'Well...' I said, unable to kill the grin that was starting to hurt my cheeks. 'There's this building in Chatswood, with a whole bunch of super powerful people inside—including my old boss. I hear it's going to be a fun time.'

Simon laughed. 'Jen, after all this is done, I'm going to take you on a real date, where no one's lives are in danger and I can spend all evening making sure you know how wonderful and amazing you are.'

That...sounded wonderful and amazing itself.

I grinned even harder.

'But right now?' he said, his eyes no longer lined with exhaustion. 'I'm going to show you just how much control I have over my powers.'

And then he rolled me underneath him and pried his name from my lips.

38

We all piled out onto the pavement—human, demon, and in-between—and mobilised in front of our target. Some of us had our feet planted in more expensive sneakers than others, but almost everyone seemed to be wearing jeans. Well, Beth Ng was clad in a pair of R2-D2 leggings, which she'd insisted were pants instead of tights. No one had dared to tell her otherwise.

I had to laugh at our attempts to park on the crowded street, especially since one space was between a chunky Toyota and an honest-to-God Maserati (it got more than a few admiring looks, touches, and comments—I'd been hoping we'd be united by more than a mutual appreciation for car bodies, but oh well, baby steps). Dot tried to squeeze her van into the spot twice, but the Maserati freaked her out too much and she chose to park further down the block, closer to Chatswood station.

My eyes quit following her progress and instead roved up to the tall buildings standing on either side of the station. Covered in darkened glass (there were a handful of lights still on inside, but not many), they made me think of the towers from *The Lord of the Rings* movies (absolute classics!) and I wondered if maybe that was some sort of omen.

'You okay, Jen?' Merindah asked me when I shuddered.

She'd been awake for barely half an hour, but that had been enough time for me to lay out our entire plan to her. A plan which wasn't complicated or particularly great. It relied on us encountering the night-time skeleton staff and hopefully only as many demonic pets as we could handle.

Like I said, not particularly great.

Mack's so-called Research Division took up three basement levels, where you'd expect to find cars instead of people with magical powers. We knew otherwise, thanks to Dennis using his Perception to pull up a handy, but hardly detailed, floor plan the previous night while casing out the joint with Dot and Ness.

'Set up the nullifying field,' Simon instructed the demons.

Clearly, they were already using some Persuasion, because the normals walking past (did Chatswood really have to be this damn busy on a weeknight?) didn't seem to notice us skulking about. That or they'd seen dodgier groups. I doubted it.

The nullifying field projectors were meant to conceal the fact that forty-something magic-users were congregating in a spot where there definitely shouldn't have been anything of note. I wasn't sure if the magic-sensing scouts would notice anyway, since they hadn't exactly found Mack's base of operations before then. She'd probably been Persuading everyone at work to ignore Chatswood. Or maybe she had a Persuasion field on the building during work hours, when more scouts were clocked on? There certainly wasn't one on it now. It might have been too big for her to hide all the time.

But yeah, better to be safe than sorry.

The projectors were so small they could have been dash cams—hell, they even had suction-cup mounts and actually looked like they belonged there, stuck to the side of the building. That was a relief, because everyone's Persuasion was going to be needed inside, not out here deflecting curious gazes and awkward questions.

Time for Simon's next order. 'Those of you who are starting further up in the building—go. *Now*.'

I watched the Portals sprout up all over the pavement and steeled myself against the tantalising pull of the Fiery Vortexes That Could Very Well Kill Me. My chest stopped tightening when the Portals vanished, taking ten bodies with them. A little more than half the demons remained.

Simon touched my shoulder. 'Are you alright?'

'Yeah,' I breathed. 'It's just...hard to resist the Portals. Now that I have taste for the power they can give me.'

'What else have you got a taste for?' he asked, smirking.

That was so lame, I nearly said, but then I decided I could do something far more pleasant with my lips. I grabbed the collar of that leather jacket of his and pulled his mouth down in line with mine.

'Jen...' Simon hesitated, his eyes darting to our audience.

Oh God. Did he not want them to know about us yet? Why hadn't I asked—

'Fuck it,' he muttered. 'There might not be a later.'

His kiss was gentle at first but he quickly deepened it, pulling me flush against him and practically devouring me. My colleagues whistled and told us to get a room; the remaining demons were decidedly more vocal and whooped enthusiastically. I was surprised my cheeks didn't heat up.

Well, I did have other things on my mind.

'Did you bring it?' I asked quietly when Simon released me.

He nodded, a hand on the noticeably bulging pocket of his jeans. It was not a comforting thought, knowing he had one of those injections on him, but this was 'just in case'. Just in case we met too many people with too much Persuasion. Just in case Mack knocked him onto his butt. Just in case he was using too much of his natural power on something else and he needed to get inside my head to stop me drawing on Portals.

'I won't have to stop you,' Simon said. He didn't need Perception to know what I was thinking and it was honestly kind of frightening that he already knew me so well.

'Simon...' I hesitated.

'You reach for the Portals because you want to, because you like how it feels,' Simon told me, his eyes shadowed and serious. 'You like being powerful. I think subconsciously you don't want to stop feeling that way. So this time...don't hold on. Let the Portals go.'

'Oh, I see,' I said, unable to stifle my growing smile. 'It's that easy, huh? You think you know more about me and my powers than I do?'

He brushed his fingers over my jaw. 'It's easier when someone trusts you and refuses to accept your excuses. I'll stop you if have to. Just as I know you'll stop me.'

'Okay, *fine*, I'll give it a go,' I said with a long, drawn-out sigh. 'So long as we can still have that date you promised me. If we can manage to fit it in around replacing Magic Corp, that is.'

Simon leaned in again, his breath ghosting over my lips. 'I look forward to doing both of these things with you.'

We broke apart when a nearby demon pointedly cleared their throat. Making out and engaging in witty banter would have to wait. We were about to storm the castle.

Well, storm the high-rise building. Whatever.

***

As per Simon's orders, ten demons were somewhere above us in the building, having already popped out of their Personal Fiery Vortexes. I hadn't witnessed their arrival, but it was hard not to imagine the Portals flaring into existence, potentially alerting firefighters and/or police (would the Portals set off the sprinklers? I had no idea—I couldn't remember them being activated during the attack at Magic Corp) to the fact that we were crashing a party we definitely weren't invited to.

That part of our attack force was starting on level four because it belonged to some sort of cancer charity (and it was right above the floors Mack had leased). We figured Hellhounds weren't allowed up there—it would mean risking discovery, something Mack wanted to avoid. Those demons were supposed to ensure that nothing came down to take us out from behind.

Meanwhile, I was shuffling into the foyer like I was up to no good, flanked by Simon and Merindah—and followed by a sizeable group of people who could fill most of a tour bus headed for the Blue Mountains.

A security guard marched forward, one hand held out in front of him and another hooked onto his belt. I didn't see any buds in his ears, so he hadn't been listening to podcasts or music to pass the time. He was pretty trim, actually. He probably thought he could chase any trespassers down; it was a fair bet he didn't know there were creatures in the building that could chase *him* down.

'Sorry, folks,' he said pleasantly, sending a nod in Merindah's direction. 'No further without passes, you know the rules.'

Merindah was likely the only one in the party that he recognised, from all her lengthy stays in the foyer. The security guards stationed there had been hired by the building's owner and weren't on Mack's payroll, but that didn't make Mr Stickler for Rules any less of an obstacle.

I could see Merindah tensing as though she was preparing a shoulder tackle, something she'd been known to do to normals who happened to stand between her and the last packet of toilet paper at the supermarket. No one stayed in her way for long. Merindah had a mean shoulder, the type that had made her the bane of everyone's existence on the soccer field back at school.

'Are there any levels accessible without passes?' Simon asked, hopefully forestalling any rash action my best friend might have taken.

'Listen,' Mr Stickler for Rules said, clearly suspicious. 'I'm giving you folks ten seconds to turn around—'

'Answer me!' Simon barked.

The guard's eyes glazed over. 'No. There are no levels accessible without passes.'

'Have you got a pass for levels B1 through B3?'

'No.'

'Can they be reached via the stairs?' Simon tried.

'Those doors are locked at night. Told them not to, especially since I don't have a key. It's a fire hazard.'

Simon patted Mr Stickler for Rules on the shoulder. 'Thanks. Now go home and stay out of trouble.'

The guard lumbered off, his expression vacant. No one dared to argue with Simon's decision to save the normal, mostly because he'd threatened to stop protecting the mind of any demon who questioned him in the middle of our attack. Simon could be kind of scary sometimes.

Merindah extended her hand and shook it. A Physical crowbar appeared in her grip.

'Yeah, nah,' Jason from Accounts said with a wink in Simon's direction. 'Stand back, Merindah. This one's ours.'

Since it had been widely known on the first floor that he'd had something of a crush on Simon, I wondered if he was trying to impress him. Which was kind of hilarious, given how badly Jason had reacted to finding out that he worked with hybrids just hours beforehand.

A handful of MCers bunched together, nervous and clearly trying not to show it. They took deep breaths, nodded at each other, and began to pool their Physical. This wasn't a skill they'd known existed half a day ago, but they'd been busy since I'd last seen them. I wondered how long they had spent trying to get it to work.

And fancy that, it *did* work.

Their chosen weapon was an oversized battering ram; it must have been heavy because they grunted when they hefted it in their hands. The construct was thick and completely black, as solid as the foundations of the building around us.

'Let's do this!' one of my esteemed colleagues crowed.

They barged their way in through a fire door that probably wouldn't have given much resistance to a crowbar, much less a freaking battering ram, and nearly toppled down the stairs because of the momentum they'd carried with them. Laughing far too loudly, they let the construct mist away and started high-fiving each other. It was hard not to smile at that.

The journey down the concrete steps was cramped, but at least we didn't have to suffer the eau de piss scent I'd encountered in practically every other stairwell in my life. Merindah took the lead. She created a shield that curved into a prominent point and marched it forward, like she was intending to use it as a cowcatcher—well, Hellcreature-catcher.

Dennis kept one step behind her, funnelling his own Physical into her shield, shoring it up and making it that much stronger. Merindah's construct had looked pretty damn solid to begin with, but she had told me beforehand that she wasn't going to refuse backup—even from someone like Dennis.

'There's a lot Hellcreatures down here,' Beth whispered beside me, my only companion at the rear of the pack. I was there because I was being held in reserve. As for Beth, I'd suggested this position for her because while my non-amped Physical wasn't that great, hers was non-existent. And okay, I liked her. She was still the only one, apart from Dennis, who had apologised to my face.

'Wait, how many is "a lot"?' I demanded of Beth.

'Hard to tell—I'm sensing a giant blob,' she answered.

'And this blob contains what, exactly?'

'I don't know. They're big. Bigger than Hellhounds.'

Our group reached the door to B1 and went no further. We'd planned to start there.

Dennis hadn't been able to tell us much about what might be on each level, so we weren't taking any chances that we'd miss something. Saul had pointed out, in that dour voice of his, that it was more likely we'd run into the first layer of protection on B1 instead of anything important. I'd told him that we would be stupid not to ensure a creature-free escape route and he had muttered something that might have been 'the hybrid has a point'. So I guess I won that round?

Merindah and Dennis stood aside, allowing our most eager colleagues to start hitting the door with a newly-formed battering ram. Those humans and hybrids who were less gung-ho hung back, discussing in hushed voices which Physical objects they should create for the imminent fight.

Simon's phone abruptly rang.

My heart did its best to escape my ribcage.

Holding up a hand to forestall any questions, Simon answered his phone and thumbed the call off moments later. He turned back to us. 'There are hounds on the above-ground levels. My people will be able to overpower them with Persuasion, but it will take time.'

They were relying on PercApption to figure out where the Hellthings were, so I couldn't blame them for being a little slow.

'At least there's no trolls up there,' Simon added.

'So we get the big things,' Dennis said. 'That's probably for the best, right?'

Yeah. Great. We get the big things.

39

'Almost got it!' Kirsty cried from her position at the front of the battering ram—and with one final, reverberating bang, the door to level B1 was open.

'Oh shit!' That was Jason, his eyes wide and his man bun in disarray.

Merindah and Dennis instantly moved forward and blocked the exposed doorway with a shield. Their construct very nearly shattered half a second later when something slammed into it; a giant crack now ran from top to bottom.

'We need more power!' Merindah snapped.

A separate batch of my colleagues scurried forward to strengthen the shield.

'That sounds like a troll,' Dot said. No one corrected her.

'Can't you combine your powers and Persuade the Helltroll?' I demanded of the nearest demons.

'Trolls, *plural*,' Ness answered, her lips twisting. 'But we'll try.'

She and Dot trotted down the stairs to join Simon at the doorway, the other demons hot on their heels. Veins swelled and bulged in their necks and their faces were soon slick with sweat. The hammering on the shield paused—only to start back up again moments later, even more fierce than before.

'You only stopped three of them!' Merindah roared.

Another crack appeared in the shield.

So not good.

And then our situation got even worse. My colleagues' eyes began travelling up towards me—no, not at me. Behind me. Above me. Whatever it was, I was standing between it and our attack force, along with Physical-less Beth Ng.

'Something's coming down the stairs!' Beth cried.

The concrete steps beneath us shook violently. Something *was* coming. And we were bottlenecked in the stairwell, with enemies ahead of and behind us. If the creatures from B1 got out, it'd be like being caught between two trains barrelling towards each other on the same track. Except our corpses weren't likely to derail the creatures.

Simon raced upstairs, ignoring his people as they cursed at him for withdrawing from the Persuasion field they'd woven together, and threw his hand forward in a frantic wave. His Portal exploded out of his grip, hitting the wall opposite me. Hanging there, still expanding, it blew a blast of scalding air into my face and began whispering my name with increasing ferocity. Beth gasped and took a giant step back.

'Go big,' Simon told me. 'I've got you.'

I knew he did. And that made it dangerously easy to do it.

Distantly noting that my fingers were stretched towards the Portal as if trying to touch it, I steeled myself, drew a breath—and yanked with every fibre of my being.

Blazingly hot power slammed into my palm, so hard and fast I was convinced it was going to snap my wrist. Gasping, my other hand braced on the railing, I forgot my fear and *welcomed* the surge. Thick strands of Physical burst free from my chest and wound together, spooling into a shield that smothered the stairwell above us. It occurred to me that this construct was sturdier and darker than anything my colleagues could ever create, even if they combined their powers.

'There's so many of them,' Beth moaned, hands over her face.

I didn't see the Hellcreatures. I never would. But they were nothing—*nothing*—compared to me.

I blasted my shield upwards, obliterating everything in the stairwell, all the way up to where the rest of our attack force was. Something twinged inside my head, not exactly painful but definitely a little *off*. I had to stop using the Portal. Except that was the hard part. Because Simon was right—I loved this. I loved being powerful.

'Drop it,' he murmured. 'Let me know if you need help.'

Merindah and her mother. My colleagues. The demons. *Simon.*

They needed me a lot more than I needed this power trip.

With a strangled yell, I sliced clean through the cord of power connecting me to the demonic realm. The Portal vanished in an instant and I half fell against Simon, ridiculously pleased with myself. He didn't congratulate me—hell, he was already dragging me down the stairs.

'How soon can you do it again?' he asked.

'Not soon enough!' I warned. I was already recovering, so much faster than ever before. But I felt...*bruised.*

Happily, Merindah didn't seem to need me or my frankly awesome abilities. She'd already split my colleagues into two groups—defenders and attackers. The defensive line hung back from the door, the shield across it strengthened by their combined efforts.

Screaming like some ancient horde, the rest of my colleagues burst through the magical barrier and stampeded into the room.

They used Physical axes and blades to hack into a Helltroll (I'm assuming it was a Helltroll, considering the amount of gunk that exploded out of it) that was being kept in place by the demons, then moved onto another. And another.

Not to be outdone, the defensive group dropped the shield and hurtled forward, also getting in on the action. Black blood flew, splattering both skin and concrete.

Once enough space had been cleared, our whole group filed out into the first basement level. It had the expected car park aesthetics—there even faded yellow lines beneath our feet—but instead of vehicles, there was a mass of snarling and roaring Hellthings in there. And not all of them were under someone's control.

'Look out!' Bethany said, pointing. I assumed a creature was headed right for us, especially when she added in a tremulous voice, 'Stop! Or slow down! Or something!'

She'd never deliberately used her Persuasion before. That was obvious.

'I—I can't stop it—!' she cried, thick crimson droplets dripping out of her left nostril.

I hefted a ghostly grey stick, sourced from the minimal power reserves I always carried inside me, then made it grow into a pike, like the one I'd used on the Helltroll back at the Royal Botanic Garden. I had no idea what sort of creature I was up against, but what the hell. I wasn't alone for once. I had backup.

'I need more power over here!' I snapped.

Without waiting for a response, I threw myself in front of Beth and shoved my construct into the air.

It definitely connected with something—blood slapped across my face and torso. I kept my mouth shut, but the gunk still went everywhere. I'd totally skewered my foe. Whoa. Nice. My weapon was solid and black in my hands, thanks to whichever colleague had thrown me their power.

But the Hellthing didn't stop moving. It writhed and jerked and snorted fetid breaths at me. A line of ichor began to creep down my Physical construct, alerting me to the fact that the creature was now inching its way towards me. Fuck. I grunted and thrust forward again, but that only pushed the creature back half a foot—at *best*. I was stuck. And I had no idea how long my weapon was going to last.

'Over here!' Simon called.

He'd made a Portal nearby and was Persuading the beast towards it, even making beckoning motions with his hands. The Hellthing resisted him, snorting and stamping the floor in annoyance. I rammed with all my might; this time Whatever It Was moved a full metre away.

Not good enough. Nowhere *near* good enough.

But then Beth got beside me, fastened her hands over my weapon, and threw her weight behind each jab. Together, we nudged the creature over to the Portal, metre by agonising metre—until we finally managed to give it one last healthy shove. My pike lost its shape at the last second and we stumbled out of range as the Portal closed in on itself.

'What was *that*?' I gasped.

'Hellhorse—it even had fire coming out of its nostrils,' Beth said grimly.

I blinked. 'Really? Wow. "Ghost Riders in the Sky" much?'

She stared at me; clearly, she had no idea what I was talking about. Dot's laugh more than made up for her silence—I guess her taste in music was a little broader than the nineteen-eighties.

Everyone else seemed to be taking a breather, so I assumed we'd dealt with the immediate problem and had time to prepare for the level beneath us.

'Mack should find room in the budget to pay the Hellcreatures,' I noted. 'They're worth ten security guards each.'

Dennis threw me a wry grin. His face was streaked with ichor. 'That would have been helpful, if they'd been on payroll. Would've known what we were heading into.'

'If these were the first line of defence,' Merindah said, striding over to us, 'makes you wonder what we'll find next.'

I shook my head in disbelief. 'No fair. You hardly got any Hellstuff on you.'

Totally vain of her to have shielded herself from splatters. But okay, maybe I was only grumpy because I hadn't thought to do the same. And I was *smothered*. Yuck, yuck, yuck. Although, the stench of Hellcreature blood wasn't as bad as some of my colleagues were making it out to be. I guess it's not surprising that the hybrids and demons among us had a more indifferent reaction. We were probably a little more inclined towards it—the creatures were the main food source in the other realm, after all.

'Hellstuff,' Merindah repeated. 'Jen, it's called blood.'

Dennis grimaced as he pulled something out of his hair. '"Stuff" might be the best word for it. This definitely isn't blood. Brain, maybe.'

I noticed that everyone's eyes kept darting back to the stairwell. We needed to keep moving. And yet...I didn't feel like this time was being wasted. We were all grinning and cracking jokes, even the demons. A few of them teased Dennis about his obvious discomfort with being covered in Hellstuff. He snarked back that they'd probably freak out if they got bits of *him* all over them.

'Point made,' Ness said with a snort. 'Gross.'

'Obviously not gross to some of us,' Dot remarked, 'otherwise hybrids like Jen and her friends wouldn't exist.'

Ness shuddered. 'Not something I needed to think about, Dot!'

Simon didn't involve himself in the increasing chatter. Instead, he headed towards a pair of doors set into a giant concrete box in the middle of the room. Several other members of our group also went over to have a look.

'I'm not sensing any Hellcreatures behind those doors,' Beth piped up.

His mouth set into a grim line, Simon kicked said doors open and then stood aside, letting everyone see that there was nothing inside the box. Well, nothing alive anyway. Bars, chains, harnesses, and all sorts of restraining equipment greeted us. My guess was that the Hellthings were usually kept in there, so that they could be experimented on. The machines and cameras crammed into every crevice seemed to confirm my suspicions.

'Well, Mack and her friends had to start somewhere,' I murmured.

Merindah's eyes were blade thin. 'These Hellcreatures were let out recently. I felt a sensation of sudden freedom off them just before we busted our way in.'

No one said anything, but I'm sure we were all thinking it.

Mack had guessed that we'd go after her. And she was ready for us.

'Merindah, your mother...' I trailed off.

'No, it's alright,' Merindah interrupted me. 'Mackenzie won't hurt my mother until I'm there to see it, to cause the most damage.'

'You know, I'm glad we brought you along,' Queran piped up.

Merindah glared at the demon. 'Because you'd already be dead without my Physical?'

'There is that,' Queran agreed. 'But this way we can make sure that you're the one who deals the killing blow to Mackenzie Roberts.'

'Why would you do that for me?' Merindah asked suspiciously.

'Because it's your right to take her out,' Queran said, his face solemn. 'She's the one who hurt you and took your mother. You are owed vengeance. Any punishment is yours to give. So it has always been in our realm.'

Merindah pressed her lips together, then nodded. 'Thank you.'

I was surprised—and thrilled—when no one in the group argued that this 'right' was restricted to demons only. Saul didn't even make a comment. I hoped this meant that the demons were beginning to see humans as equals.

Or at least, something close to it.

We piled out into the stairwell again. Some of my colleagues wanted me to take the lead, but I think my panic was obvious because they started apologising, which was weird. I guess they were feeling guilty about how they'd treated me all those years.

'No,' Simon spoke up on my behalf. 'We need to keep Jen in reserve. She's powerful, but it hurts and weakens her to amp up her Physical like that. She has to remain at full strength for as long as possible.'

I swallowed. Great. He was making it sound like they were all relying on me, like I was the vital piece in some game. We were so freaking—

No. We were not screwed. Because you know what? I was pretty awesome, now that I knew what I could do. I breathed out a sigh of—not relief, but acceptance, maybe? Then I realised everyone was staring at me, waiting for me to say something.

So I did.

'Let's level up,' I said, then frowned. That wasn't quite right. 'Um. Level down. I meant level down.'

Surprisingly, everyone laughed.

Well. Who knew. All it took was a life-or-death situation for my colleagues to finally laugh at one of my jokes.

40

The door leading to level B2 was rattling around in its frame by the time we reached it. The growls had started too, low pitched and filled with danger and intent. My breath caught.

What if the damn things had figured out how to use doorknobs and were about to burst into the stairwell? Clearly, some of my colleagues were thinking the same thing, because they threw themselves at the door, bracing their weight against it. But the knob stayed still. Their combined sighs of relief practically blew the hair off my face.

'I sense Hellhounds,' Beth piped up beside me. We were both hanging back again. 'Just ten of them. Easy as pie.'

'Pie isn't easy, you humans only make it look easy,' Dot muttered, looking for a moment like she was lost in the memory of some baking fiasco. I nodded in sympathy. My attempts to bake were always thwarted—I liked to think it was the oven in my rental letting me down, not my actual cooking abilities.

'I'm not sensing that many Hellcreatures down on B3 either,' Dan Argenziano noted, impatiently slapping his hands on his razor-sharp pants (didn't he ever get creases!?). I'd never seen him with his blood up before—I suspected Beth hadn't either. He seemed to be enjoying himself.

'Alright,' Simon said, cautiously surveying the steps below us, as though they had turned into a cascade of lava. 'We can split up then. We need some humans and hybrids—make sure it's enough of you—to deal with this level. The rest of you—follow us down. My people upstairs should be along shortly. They can help mop up if things go south.'

Dennis was already shaking his head. 'No, there's people behind this door, at least fifteen of them, and they have orders to herd us and pin us down at the next level. I'm—' He broke off and I knew why. I was the only one he'd willingly told about his Perception quirk; Merindah had needed to pluck it out of his thoughts. I knew Simon had been suspicious earlier, but he hadn't confronted Dennis.

'How the hell can you know that, Dennis?' Kirsty demanded. 'I'm only reading Hellhounds and nothing else.'

Dennis flung a desperate look in my direction, as if he wanted me to reveal his secret for him, to make it sound better than it probably did in his head. He'd hidden a part of himself from the people who trusted him. For years. I understood his hesitation.

'Please, Jen, tell them,' Dennis mouthed at me.

Weird. I'd never had to act as someone's voice before. I'd always been too busy looking around for someone else to speak for me.

'Okay, Dennis' Perception is a little different,' I began and his face smoothed out with relief. 'It lets him read emails and text messages from a considerable distance, which I'm assuming is how he saw those orders he's talking about.' I paused, watching the wide eyes spread faster than any contagion could. 'It's a weird quirk, but it's pretty damn useful. Especially now.'

Just like my Portal quirk, I thought.

Finally, heads started nodding and expressions became thoughtful instead of accusatory. I wondered how many of my colleagues were suddenly preoccupied with their own hidden quirks.

'Yeah, but there's no *intelligent* minds behind this door,' Kirsty insisted.

'Some minds are harder to read,' Merindah said. 'Especially if they're shielded by Persuasion.'

Dennis stared unseeingly at the door. 'I can tell you how many digital copies of the orders are in there. Assuming that's how many phones they've got...I guess that equals how many people we're up against. Like I said, at least fifteen. I could be wrong.'

I felt my gut clench. 'So that's fifteen people who might have Persuasion...'

'Then the whole group needs to go in,' Simon said.

'Is that all you have to say?' Saul fired back. His hands crashed down onto the stairwell's railing, making it shake. 'Where is your plan? Do you even have one? You aren't giving us specific enough orders!'

'He's not wrong,' Merindah commented and I shot her a betrayed glance. She rolled her eyes at me. 'Jen, we can't keep throwing ourselves into the fray and hoping it works. We're not a disorganised rabble, and we can't be rabble if we want to successfully replace Magic Corp with something else.'

Ugh. She did not just side with Saul.

'Fine,' Simon said, releasing a breath that sounded like disjointed static. 'My people can stall the humans while you MCers get the hounds. But you will need to turn your Physical onto the humans next. We might not be able to hold them for long.'

'Are we killing the people too?' Jason asked. He was actually *smiling*. As if he couldn't wait to add notches to his—well, wherever it was my colleagues notched things. Their desks, maybe? They'd never had the opportunity to make those notches before.

'We can't kill everyone who gets in our way,' I argued. 'That makes us no better than them!'

Funny how 'them' no longer meant demons.

'Try to incapacitate the humans,' Simon ordered, nodding at me. 'If they fight back, do what you must to protect yourselves. But try to remember what we'll be doing when all this is over: defending normals, not killing them.'

'Lofty words!' Saul sneered, but left it at that.

This settled, Merindah stepped forward and created a new shield. She shook out her shoulders and adjusted her posture into something looser while she waited for those who had Physical (barring me, of course) to add to her construct, to help make it into something bigger and better.

But not bigger and better than what I could do.

'Save it,' Simon told me in an undertone, a hand on the pocket of his jeans.

'Yeah, let's not run out of power-ups before we hit the boss level,' I muttered.

Below us, the shield kept growing, fed by the combined powers of my colleagues. And I found myself wondering. I really did wonder. Could I pass on the energy I yanked through Portals to our Physical fighters—or even someone who didn't have the same powers as me? Since no one was going to be able to teach me the ins and outs of my unique Portal quirk, I was just going to have to experiment.

But this is so not the time for that, I told myself. *Focus.*

Dennis reached for the doorknob with a trembling hand. It

turned easily—far too easily. It wasn't locked. He swallowed, nudged the door open, and then flung himself away from it. Half a second later, the Hellhounds spilled out of B2, their teeth tearing into the tasty Physical construct in their way. My colleagues resisted the creatures and managed to take two steps forward, all the while doing some gnawing of their own—on their lips, making blood bead and fall.

With one last heave, they forced the shield inside the vast room beyond. Our offensive Physical people followed them in, jabbing spears and other pointy objects out through the construct. Black slime smothered their shield and formed an inky curtain that obstructed the view of the room beyond.

Yeah. I was pretty freaking glad my colleagues were on our side.

'Can't see what we're aiming at!' Kirsty complained.

I nearly laughed. For once she was getting a taste of what it was like to be me.

The demons flooded into the room after my colleagues, presumably laying down enough Persuasion to protect everyone's minds from the injected humans within. With a sound that could only be described as a shriek (though it was probably meant to be a bit more fearsome), Beth threw herself into the doorway ahead of me. Smiling, I started to follow her in.

But then my steps suddenly faltered.

There was something else on the stairs, something below me. I didn't know what it was. The hair on the back of my neck rose rapidly.

I couldn't turn my head. I couldn't move. They didn't *want* me to move.

Someone with Persuasion! They've got me pinned! I thought loudly—was that even possible?—in the direction of the doorway.

'Jen needs help!' That was Merindah's voice, full of strain.
She'd heard me and had spoken for me. Just like she always had.
But she couldn't save me.
Not this time.

41

Someone came up behind me and kicked the door. It closed with a bang that echoed throughout the stairwell. I used my peripheral vision to case out my new companion and found myself profusely glad it was a stranger and not Mack. I'm not sure why, since this situation was bad enough.

I gritted my teeth. 'Go on, then. Kill me.'

'Roberts wants you alive,' my attacker informed me. 'Turn around.'

'Jesus Christ, you look more like a cosplayer than a guard,' I managed to say after my feet had obeyed her command. She wore a red satin sash over her navy uniform, which was stylish and had a flattering cut, as though a certain Mackenzie Roberts had had a say about its design. 'Flunked out of the police force, did you?'

'I left on my own—they only have those useless apps and I'd much rather have the injections,' the guard said with a snort. Then her eyes hardened and her Persuasion pressed firmly on my mind. 'Walk downstairs. Roberts wants you. Now.'

'What does she want with me?' I grated out as my knees bent and straightened, taking me away from the door. Shit, had no one heard Merindah? Could *no one* break away from the attack and come after me?

Merindah! Dennis! Beth! Anyone! I thought frantically.

'Well, it's obvious, isn't it?' the guard chortled, walking ahead of me.

The door to B3 was so close. Wide open. Not even guarded. Well, not by anything that ordinary old Jen Cooke could see.

Ordinary. The hell I was.

'My ability to pull more power through Portals,' I murmured.

'Is that how it works?' She actually sounded interested. 'I'll let Roberts know later. But for now, you'll make a good hostage, one we'll Persuade to—'

'Jen!' Simon called. The door to B2 boomed shut again.

'Stop right there!' my captor roared and my feet immediately stilled.

She swung around to face the incoming threat—and since she didn't stipulate that I couldn't do the same, I copied her. I noticed that I could move my hands again, which was a bonus. The guard had allowed herself to become distracted and her magic had weakened.

But my mounting hope plummeted faster than my stomach did.

Simon was twenty stairs above us, one hand clenched on the railing, the other curled into rigid claws beside his thigh. He was frozen, at the mercy of a human. Panic made my heart start to work double time. Mack had her guards hopped up on those portent injections and powerful though Simon was, he couldn't fight my captor off.

His blue eyes filled with cold fury.

'Roberts, the plan worked,' the guard reported into a phone she'd plucked from her pocket. 'Targeting Cooke lured the demon leader away from the others. He followed me down. Yes, *of course*, I stopped him. He's not that dangerous.'

I saw Simon's cheek twitch. He obviously didn't like being reduced to 'not that dangerous'.

Shit, can no one come out and help us? I was thinking. *Or are the guards up there too much for them handle?*

Mack's voice squawked something.

The guard shrugged. 'Sure. I'll deal with him. Thought you wanted some demon subjects, but I guess now's not a good time.'

The phone disappeared back into her pocket and her hand went for the gun on her belt. Well, how about that. She was just going to shoot Simon. So human.

I held out my palm and called on my Physical. My feet remained immobile, as though they were encased in hardened concrete, but I wasn't worried. I didn't need to move my feet to help Simon.

When her gun rose, her finger on the trigger, I lobbed a spiked ball at the guard's head. Happily, it connected. Unhappily, my ordinary Physical was just as weak and pale as ever. But it was solid enough to provide a distraction.

'Wha—' she choked out.

I wasn't even watching her—I was watching Simon. And I saw the guard's Persuasion drop for those crucial few seconds. His hand dived into his jeans and extracted his 'just in case'. It wasn't a syringe, more like an EpiPen, but I still had to tear my eyes away as he jabbed it into his arm.

I didn't know how long it would take for the extra power to kick in so I threw a second ball, then another. My third attempt was barely visible, but it still hit its mark.

'Stop that!' she snapped at me.

But Simon was already inside my head. I could feel him. He was a dark stain spreading throughout my synapses and stealing back every iota of control from the guard. He was powerful. Really, really powerful.

'No, *you* stop that,' I told the guard.

Her jaw and arms went slack as Simon came down the stairs, his blue eyes whirling hypnotically.

'Run at the wall and knock yourself out,' Simon growled.

My would-be captor complied. When at first it didn't work, she tried again. And again, and again—until she fell onto her back, her face blank, her chest barely moving.

I bent down, pinched her gun between two fingers, and held it out to Simon.

He shook his head, breathing raggedly. 'Jen, I don't...I don't need it and neither do you. Let's end this now. We don't need the others. I just have to make you a Portal and we—we'll be unstoppable.'

I tossed the gun away from the guard. Yeah, there was no way I was going to hold onto that. Simon was right. We didn't need it. Plus, I was pretty sure neither of us knew how to use the damn thing, so we'd probably end up putting a hole in one of our friends instead of an actual enemy.

Simon's presence was strong, so strong that I wavered, afraid. 'Simon, what are you doing? Are you making me...?'

'No,' he said with a hefty amount of vehemence. 'I'm only in there to shield you. It's so easy. And I can do so much more. I can Persuade everyone inside this building.'

'Yeah, until you run out of juice and collapse,' I told him. 'We don't know how long these injections last.'

But I had to admit, I was awfully tempted to storm through the open door and smack down everyone in sight, with Simon at my side.

'Don't get carried away,' I warned Simon. 'You know how much trouble I get into when I let my powers overwhelm me. You could kill yourself going solo. And I don't know if anyone can stop you.'

Simon nodded and pressed his forehead against mine. I gasped. His presence had settled into my head, which I found strangely comforting—but I was taken back by the feelings he flooded through me. They ran so much deeper than I'd realised.

'Jen, I need to tell you—' Simon began.

'Shit!' someone screamed nearby.

Simon and I sprang apart. I had enough common sense left to shut the B3 door and brace myself against it. It'd be embarrassing if something snuck through there and sucker-punched us.

'What is it, Ness?' Simon demanded, peering up the stairwell.

'Oh, just...' A pause, followed by heavy panting. 'Just ran into our people from upstairs.'

Dot's voice drifted down to us. 'Some of the humans nearly stabbed them.'

'We've cleared out all the Hellcreatures!' Jason called. 'And we're done with the humans on B2 as well. We're good to go.'

Done with the humans. God.

'How many—how many are dead?' I asked, swallowing hard.

'All of them,' Dot said, coming into view. She caught my frown and threw me an agitated sigh in response. 'They had guns. They were trigger-happy. And our Persuasion couldn't put them down—they were way too strong for that.'

I looked at Dennis, Merindah, and the rest of my colleagues. They were covered in crimson splatters. They wore the blood of humans. The blood of the normals I had sworn to protect when I'd signed my contract with Magic Corp three years ago—and

I still wanted to protect those people. Okay, maybe when they weren't literally gunning for me, that is.

'Kill or be killed,' Dennis said, but his voice was flat and his eyes were on his feet. Even though he had to have noticed the blood coating his white Adidas Superstars, there was no disgust or annoyance on his face. He just looked...empty.

'There'll be time to talk about it later,' Merindah said roughly. She was the only one of my colleagues who wasn't pale and visibly shaken. With a jolt, I remembered that she'd killed people before.

I really wished I had been able to understand and be there for her when she'd been in the Kill Squad. I couldn't undo that, but I could make up for it and be there for her now. Actually, everyone was going to have to be there for each other when this was all over. If it ever was. Or maybe we should make sure we hired or trained up some psychologists. Because damn, we needed them.

'I see you dealt with Jen's problem,' Dot said, indicating the body on the floor.

Saul sneered. 'You left the human alive.'

Simon's cheeks went taut. I could see—and *feel*, because he was still in my head—that he was struggling to keep his power surge coiled up inside him instead of unleashing it on Saul.

'Simon made the guard run at the wall until she passed out,' I piped up. 'Not something he tended to do when he was whipping your butt in your little Persuasion duels. Baby steps, Saul. You can't expect Simon to degrade himself to your level in one night.'

Saul surprised me by laughing—it was more of a brief, sarcastic hoot than anything else. Judging by the stares he got from the other demons, this was a bit out of character for him. I wasn't sure whether I should feel honoured or worried.

'Okay, this is it,' I said and slapped the door behind me. 'We've hit the bottom level. It won't be easy. We could be facing hell itself in there. So what's our game plan? Suggestions, anyone?'

Suggestions were made. Discussion was kept brief.

Then we were ready. Sort of.

42

The door to level B3 opened into an antechamber that was suspiciously empty. We charged in anyway, shield raised and totally prepared to meet the blips that our Perception people could sense. But then one by one we slowed, determination withering into confusion.

We milled around for a bit, studiously avoiding the door at the other end of the room and waiting to see if we'd failed to notice any Hellhounds and/or Hellhumans (hey, they deserved that label more than any demon I'd met). This sudden lull in the fighting was probably some ploy of Mack's to make us nervous and twitchy. And it worked; tempers boiled over and people started daring each other to open the door ahead of us. My colleagues even let the shield drop while they argued.

Simon, I noticed, stayed silent. His eyes were briefly vacant, but then they landed on me and he gave me a smile, albeit one that was so forced and so tight it caused his teeth to peek out from between his lips.

'If you don't say something and take control now,' I warned him, 'then Saul probably will.'

Simon nodded sharply and raised his voice. 'Be on your guard, everyone. The threats that our Perception people picked up on will be behind *this* door.'

'Yeah, this is the last part visible on the floor plan,' Dennis added. 'Whatever's in the next room was left off for a reason.'

'Mack's prisoners are probably—' Merindah began, but that's as far as she got. Because the door we'd been eyeing up banged open and Mack's next lot of guards poured into the antechamber.

Their combined Persuasion hit us like a wave, so intense it was almost Physical, and I staggered back a pace as my feet nearly went out from under me. I wasn't the only one who'd lost my balance; Beth would have hit the floor if Simon hadn't caught her. He was shouting at her, trying to coach her, but I knew it wasn't going to help. She had no idea how to use her Persuasion properly.

Luckily for us, there were those among our number who *did* know what to do. And they wasted no time in pushing back.

It must have taken a lot out of the demons, because some of them screamed as they used their magic. The effect was pretty much instant—my thoughts cleared so fast I nearly swooned. I felt dizzy and light-headed, like I'd stood up too quickly.

My colleagues recovered just in time to erect a new Physical shield for a fresh wave of Hellhounds to start ripping into. The Hellhumans stayed back, resisting the Persuasion being sent their way, and unholstered their guns. Which pretty much sealed their fate.

But I couldn't do it. I couldn't do what everyone else was currently doing. I couldn't use my powers to kill.

'Knock 'em down if you can't out-Persuade them!' Ness howled, sitting astride one of the guards and smacking them repeatedly in the face with their own gun.

Beth threw herself onto the man creeping up behind Ness, performing a rugby tackle that would have made our old PE teacher proud. All around her and Ness, there were humans and

342

hybrids coming to the rescue of demons. Some of them had drained their magical cores completely, but they still had fists and far more enthusiasm than experience. The scene would have been almost comical if this wasn't a matter of life and death. And the guards were quite willing to inflict the latter.

Simon was panting heavily and leaning against the wall. I had no idea how many people or Hellcreatures he was trying to Persuade, but he had yelled 'freeze!' several times and my colleagues didn't seem to be having any real difficulty going up against the non-human threats in the room. The same could not be said for the demons.

'Fuck!' Queran cried, his arm oozing inky blood as he backed away from the invisible menace that had clawed into him.

Merindah swooped by and rapidly sliced her Physical weapons through the air. I assumed she cut the Hellhound accosting Queran down to size because there was an explosion of sticky tar, like a grisly mini-fireworks display.

We were making progress, so that was good. We were getting closer and closer to the door.

I wouldn't have to use my powers at all!

A Hellcreature decided to annihilate my precious few moments of hope by violently colliding with me. I staggered sideways and called on my inner reserves, desperately trying to create something fast enough—and hopefully strong enough—so that I could fight back against whatever had hit me. Breathing was hard enough; forget trying to defend myself.

Dennis flew over and took out the creature, but I was still headed for the floor.

Someone grabbed my shoulders, rightened me, and shouted into my face, 'You need a Portal, hybrid, don't you?'

It was Saul.

I jerked my head up and down in response.

'I'll make you one,' he told me. 'Your human friends tell me a very large creature is on the other side of the door!'

Saul tossed his hand at the space next to me, calling forth a Portal.

I didn't get to ask him what manner of nightmarish creature he thought the newcomer might be, because the entrance at the end of the antechamber only stayed rectangular in shape for about two seconds. Its frame splintered and flew across the room, smacking into a guard and a demon who were grappling with each other—I wasn't sure if they'd both drained their reserves while trying to Persuade each other, or if flesh hitting flesh was more satisfying for them, but so long as the person from our side was winning, it didn't really matter.

What mattered was the wall completely disintegrating as something elephant-sized burst into the room. That specific animal metaphor occurred to me due in no small part to the trumpeting sound it made, so loud that the floor shook beneath our feet. The spasms of pain on everyone's faces revealed that no one had thought to cover their ears.

'Hellephant?' I gasped.

Saul shot me an aggravated look.

Okay, maybe I'd guessed wrong.

'Stop coming up with stupid names and do your job, hybrid!' Saul snapped. 'We need you!'

He suddenly got a very sour look on his face and looked away. Yeah, I'd never expected to hear those last three words out of his mouth either.

I sucked in a breath. And then I sucked a serious amount of energy out of Saul's Portal.

Oh wow, that hurt. My temples tightened, my gums ached, and my back hit the door to the stairwell as it kept coming, an astonishing blast of power that threatened to rip me in two. I ignored the screams of panic, the acrid scent of black blood, the copper twang of red blood—and let my magic give birth to the biggest construct I'd ever seen.

My Physical spread over the bare wall behind me like an insidious waterfall of black paint, becoming as high as the ceiling and as wide as the room itself. I tilted my head back to watch it—stunned, savouring, smiling in awe. I kept feeding my construct with more and more power, even though my veins knotted beneath my skin, even though my ribs constricted around my lungs, even though my lips cracked and bled.

Then, at last, it was ready. And it had a mind of its own.

Saul stepped away, mouth gaping open, but he couldn't escape it. No one could.

My Physical curtain swept harmlessly past the demons and my colleagues, seeking other targets. I didn't want to kill the guards. I swear I didn't. But I lost control of my construct the moment it left the wall and they were thrown off their feet, hurtling several metres backwards until their heads slammed into the concrete floor.

Loud, awful snaps heralded their deaths.

The Not-Hellephant brayed in terror half a second before the Curtain of Doom reached it. Multiple crunches, multiple pops—and then the creature exploded. Ichor hit me in the chest with enough force that I lost all the breath from my lungs. I was freaking glad I'd shut my mouth and eyes at the last second.

The Portal whispered sweet nothings. But I was done with letting anyone or any*thing* control me. I stomped down hard on the connection between us. The Portal stopped roaring at me and went silent.

Gingerly, I opened my eyes.

Everyone was smothered in black blood. Absolutely smothered.

'Nice one, Jen,' Merindah acknowledged, giving me a quick once-over. Then she looked down at her ruined clothes, a furtive grin making an appearance. 'A little warning next time might be nice.'

'Serves you right for being so vain,' I shot back.

Dennis scuffed the bottom of his stained shoes through the alarmingly large puddle that the creature had left behind. 'I've never seen one of those before.'

'A Hellephant?' I asked giddily.

He shook his head. 'No, Jen. Just no.'

'Simon, back me up here!' I called.

It freaked me out a little that he had to visibly pull himself together before he stalked over. Simon flashed me a smile, though it was sharper than I'd have liked. 'It wasn't an elephant. We don't have those in the demonic realm. Are you okay, Jen?'

'Yeah. I cut the connection after ten seconds.'

Simon's eyebrows rose. 'You're getting faster.'

'I need to get way faster,' I said. 'That nearly flattened me.'

My heart faltered when I remembered the snaps. Oh God, the snaps. I'd broken necks and killed humans.

Shit, shit, *shit*—

Simon abruptly wound an arm around my waist and swung me into his chest. He knew I needed the hug. He didn't have

346

Perception and I sure as hell didn't have Persuasion, but he was…inside me. A constant burring at the back of my skull, more familiar than distracting.

I found I didn't mind him being in there. Hell, I *loved* it.

I saw the dark vomit on the floor, almost indistinguishable from the ichor, and fought the inappropriate urge to laugh. We'd all have to remember to keep our mouths shut in future. Not something I'd ever thought would be a problem back when I was sitting at my desk and dreaming of going out into the field.

Apart from the ickiness of it all, I liked the field. And I intended to stay there.

Now that I'd caught my breath, I noticed that the opposite wall's new gaping entrance, courtesy of the Not-Hellephant, had revealed a maze built out of concrete instead of hedges. And while my Perception-gifted colleagues reported that they could still sense Hellthings (Dennis also let us know that the numerous phones up ahead hadn't gone away either), it's a little hard to figure out what's where when you can't see very far ahead.

'We can Portal to the other side of the maze,' Ness suggested, her mouth collapsing into a firm line as she looked at Simon. 'Those of us who still can.'

'You don't know what you'll find there!' I exclaimed. 'You might need some Physical backup.'

Ness' eyes flicked to me. I stared defiantly back at her.

But before she could either nod in agreement or start an argument, a voice boomed out of the speakers set into the ceiling (they seemed to have escaped most of the Not-Hellephant's death throes because they weren't *too* muffled).

That voice belonged to Mackenzie Roberts.

And she didn't sound at all worried about us being there.

'You should listen to the filthy hybrid, demons,' she said, sounding a bit nasal (I wondered if her nose was doing okay after its encounter with my Physical barrier back at her house—hopefully *not*). 'But by all means, Portal to end of the maze. Those of you who don't perish will soon wish you had.'

'She means to experiment on you,' I reminded the demons in a low voice. They shifted in agitation. 'We can't give her that opportunity.'

'Jennifer Cooke...' Mack's tone gained a vicious snap that I'd never heard from her before, including that time someone put cling wrap over the toilets at work. 'You might think you're powerful, but magic isn't the only power that exists in this realm. Once those demons abandon you, you'll be reduced to nothing once more. Because that's all you've ever been, Jennifer. Nothing. As for the rest of you—come after me and you'll be sorry. Especially you, Merindah. Surely you care about your mother's well-being.'

Merindah gave no response. In her place, I'd have said something stupid and rash. But she just stood there, stoic and as still as a statue.

'Wow, monologue much?' I mused, trying to lighten things up a bit.

'She's worried,' Merindah commented. I couldn't imagine what she was hiding under that steely exterior right then. 'There can't be many guards left.'

Dennis frowned. 'How can you be sure? I can't see anything in her surface thoughts, she's too good at hiding them—but there are phones, lots and *lots* of phones.'

Merindah threw Dennis a pointed look. 'She's been spying on

us ever since we entered the building. She knows what you can do now.'

'And Merindah's been under Mack's thumb for months,' I added, receiving a grateful nod from my best friend. It was comforting to know that, despite what had gone on between us, we could still communicate using that wavelength reserved for best friends. No Perception required. 'She'll have seen and heard Mack nervous, right?'

'Yes, but only once,' Merindah confirmed. 'When one of the guards received an injection that made him more powerful than her. She ordered me to—I made him redundant.'

'You killed him,' Dennis accused.

'She didn't want to!' I said.

Merindah laughed darkly. 'No? How do you know that, Jen? Well, I'll tell you who I'm going to kill next. And that's you, Mackenzie!' she finished in a roar.

'That would be an improvement on your spotty performance, Kill Squad agent,' was all Mack said before we heard a decisive click. She'd turned her microphone off.

Dot pulled a hair elastic out of her pocket. It took her more than two goes to gather her short hair into a stubby ponytail. She looked rattled. 'This Mackenzie's dangerous—even more dangerous than our enemies back home.'

'I'll deal with her, don't worry,' Simon said.

Saul snorted.

'*I'll deal with her*,' Simon repeated in a growl, sweat streaking down the sides of his face.

'You've never felt like this before,' Saul observed, new-found respect pressing down on his already creased brow. 'Such raw power. More than anything Jon ever had. None could defy you.'

'Not right now,' Simon agreed. And despite the strain, despite his earlier reluctance to use the injection, I saw not a single trace of uncertainty in him.

He was completely confident.

That scared me. Well, it also caused another reaction that I wasn't going to admit to out loud. But damn. He was sexy as hell.

Simon slowly smirked. Yeah, he was inside my head and I knew he'd caught the gist of my thoughts, if not the words. I busied myself with looking anywhere but at him.

'So long as we have you and Jen on our side,' Saul said, striding towards the maze, 'we will not encounter defeat.'

I nearly choked. He'd used my *name*.

'What happened to "hybrid"?' I called after him.

'Keep proving your worth and I will not need to revert to it!' he tossed back at me.

Was it just me or was Saul getting weirder by the minute?

43

When I hit yet another dead end in Mack's Labyrinth, I had to stop myself kicking the smooth grey wall in frustration. Still, I guess it was better than running into a Persuasion-gifted human with a gun and/or a vicious Hellthing. I closed my eyes and mentally broadcast my failure, hoping my nearest colleagues would pick it up and know not to come this way. It was strange 'talking' to them like this, after so many years of keeping myself closed off from them.

Beth, who'd assigned herself as my maze buddy, sighed and gave me the run-down on how everyone else was going. 'Fifteen dead ends—sixteen. No, seventeen. Surely there must be a way through. Or are we just wasting our time?'

A scream answered her.

Beth and I exchanged glances, then broke into a synchronised sprint. We skidded around three corners before we found the problem. Two demons—both of them bore weeping claw marks on their arms—were facing off against an invisible menace in a passageway that surprisingly didn't have a dead end. In fact, these walls were as straight as an arrow and led all the way to the door at the opposite side of the room.

Before I could do anything more useful than standing and staring, Merindah leapt off the top of a nearby maze wall with hooked Physical blades shooting out of her hands, the magical constructs midnight black and ready to cut.

She sliced and diced the Hellthing to pieces within seconds. Dark splatters went everywhere. Problem solved, right?

Except we had other, bigger problems to deal with.

Beth was staring at the ceiling, horror-struck. I also looked up and immediately regretted it. There were numerous cages hanging from the ceiling and I suspected they weren't as empty as they seemed. As if triggered by our watching them, the floors of the cages swung open, one by one, dropping their apparently demonic contents all over the labyrinth.

'Are you ready for the next wave?' Mack's voice asked from the speakers suspended above us. She didn't laugh maniacally the way a cartoon villain would have, but she did add, 'Impress me.'

What the hell. Had she used this maze as some twisted method of execution? Had she forced hybrids to perform here, to show off their abilities and quirks? Had she sent her own guards into this maze to make sure the injections had held?

'Yes, to all of the above,' Merindah said, answering my thoughts. She fell into step beside me and Beth as we hurried down the corridor. 'She records everything that happens here. I watched the videos on her phone when I was with her. But some of them were filmed in places that didn't have mazes like this, so I don't think this is the only facility she has.'

Lots of shouting and swearing abounded in the labyrinth now. I heard Simon's voice delivering the usual 'freeze!' nearby, which meant he was okay—for now. I was worried about what would happen when he ran out of power. We had no idea how long this artificial boost would last.

Merindah threw out an arm which I caught in the

chest. Winded, I did my best not to double over, hyperaware that we were about to get rushed by something clawed and snarly. I might have started to panic. But then a knot tightened inside my head and I could have sworn I heard Simon—oh. Never mind. False alarm.

'What's she doing?' Beth whispered. 'It's only Dennis.'

Merindah crouched, as if preparing to fight. Weird. The obstacle blocking our path was Dennis. Not a creature, not invisible, and definitely not our enemy.

Dennis howled a challenge and produced a Physical machete. He was reacting as though he was seeing a demonic creature when he looked at Merindah. And it was clear that Merindah saw the same in him. They were going to kill each other.

'NO! Beth, help them see!' I shouted and threw myself forward, hands extended and encased in wispy grey gloves.

'See!' Beth cried desperately. But she was no good at this—it was a miracle her untrained Persuasion had protected her in the first place—

Somehow, I was faster than Merindah. Somehow, I got between her and Dennis.

I screamed at them and waved my Physical-clad hands, demanding they listen, demanding they stop. They kept on coming. I sucked in an unsteady breath, preparing to meet my end—but I didn't die. I was able to rush that breath right back out of my lungs and over my lips.

Dennis and Merindah were practically sandwiching me. They'd faltered just as their weapons had kissed the thin Physical film covering the flesh of my palms. My construct only lasted an extra couple of seconds.

'Thank God,' I said and my legs gave out.

My friends caught me and kept me upright, their hands braced under my armpits while I hung there, emotionally exhausted and my core drained of the reserves I carried around inside me. My head was banging, but I just *knew* I could conduct more power from the demonic realm if I had to. Whether or not it would kill me, I still didn't know.

'That was a nasty trick,' Dennis growled.

'Mack can cast a pretty big Persuasion field,' Merindah said as she and Dennis walked me back towards where everyone else was gathering. 'And she's more powerful than any of her guards. Are you sure Simon can match her?'

'Of course he can!' I winced, realising those words had sounded more indignant than confident. That injection he'd stuck himself with had to work. It had to. 'Mack must be running out of steam if she only has enough power to mind-whammy some of us. Simon will have no trouble.'

Merindah pressed her lips together, doing that silent and steely thing.

Yeah, she wasn't buying it. I'm not sure I was either.

When we regrouped, we tallied up our wounds—some of those were own goals, so to speak. Demons seemed to be better off in general, because of their ability to resist a mental attack, but they weren't unscathed. The fury blazing in their eyes echoed what I was feeling.

And then I saw how bad things really were.

Simon knelt down beside a woman whose arm was flung out across the concrete floor. A metre from her fingers, but obviously having been thrown from her grip, was a phone, the same model as the ones the guards were carrying. Except she wasn't a guard. She wasn't wearing a uniform, or a gun, or anything that could have protected her. She was in hospital scrubs. And she bore the face of someone I knew.

She'd been branded a contract-breaker. The gossip had lasted for an entire month—or at least that's how long the people clustered around the water cooler had discussed it. Everyone had asked each other the same question: who breaks their contract after a sudden promotion and a big honking pay rise?

'It's Speth Newton,' Dennis murmured next to me. 'A hybrid, if her file was accurate.'

Well, yeah, it was obvious *now* what had happened to her.

'Is she dead?' I asked quietly.

Simon raised his glistening eyes. His grief filled me until I felt like I was drowning, so I dropped my hand onto his shoulder, trying to jar him out of it. His fingers grasped mine. The overwhelming sadness we shared in my mind slowly receded.

'Yes, but the others are alive.' Simon swallowed. 'Just.'

My gut clenched. Dan kept moaning that he hadn't seen her, he really hadn't, he'd seen *a Hellhound, damn it!* He had been so tough a few minutes ago, so full of confidence after years of being trapped behind a desk.

And now...he was broken. The fight had gone right out of him.

'If that's all Mack's got to throw at us,' I said roughly, pushing past Merindah and stalking my way down the unguarded passageway, 'then she must be running out of guards and creatures to do her bidding. I'm coming for you, Mack! And I bet you're afraid of me now. You've seen what I can do.'

There was an insistent tug inside my head from Simon.

I stopped and swung around, startled to see the stream of people heading my way, Merindah and Simon in the lead. They were following—*me*.

It was Simon's turn to touch my shoulder this time, a reminder to slow down and not let Mack get the better of me. 'Jen, wait. We need to evacuate the hybrids who attacked us. Some of them are badly injured.' He glanced at Dennis. 'How many guards are left?'

'No idea,' Dennis said tersely. 'There's a lot of phones behind that door, but Mack knows what I can do. There might be fewer guards than that—there might be more.'

Simon nodded, then turned to his sister. 'Start getting the hybrids out of here.'

Dot's eyes flashed. 'Simon! Don't you dare send me away—I do not need protecting, I am not some *child*—'

'You're the only one in our clan who I trust to do this,' Simon told her.

She glowered for several moments before finally relenting. Then she fixed her gaze on me. 'Jen. Make sure he doesn't do something stupid. You're all he's got now.'

'He's got a lot more than me,' I said, tipping my chin at our combined forces.

Everyone gave me jerky nods in return. Soft curses came from our Physical-gifted people as they formed a new shield, and tension sharpened the shoulders of those drawing on their Persuasion. The threat we faced was stronger than any one of us, but not as strong as all of us combined. It was an awesomely unifying moment.

Dot headed back towards the exit, flanked by the people she'd singled out with a sharp fingernail. I noticed she had chosen the least impressive members of our group to go with her. Beth looked immensely relieved to be assigned to this group; Perception and Persuasion was probably the worst combination anyone could have in this situation. Plus, I figured she wanted to look after Dan—he kind of resembled a zombie.

'We can't last much longer,' Saul griped, his shirt stained with sweat and blood.

I knew he was strong. Not quite in the same league as Simon, especially right then, but strong enough that this admission scared the crap out of me. And we'd just lost seven demons to the group who were evacuating the hybrids—seven demons who could have made all the difference, no matter how weak they might be in Dot's estimation.

Once Simon gave the order, we began filing towards the door like kids heading for some perverse school assembly. Except there were no demerit points or detentions here.

No, here was almost certain death.

'Don't be so dramatic, Jen,' Merindah said in reaction to my thoughts. Several of my colleagues murmured in agreement, as though afraid to speak any louder lest our old school principal tell them to keep it down.

'I can't help it,' I grumbled. 'I so don't have the energy to keep my surface thoughts clear around you guys at the moment. And I only did that when I didn't like any of you. So I guess I might like some of you now. Oh God.'

Dennis snorted.

I realised I was shaking and told my body to quit it. Yeah, that worked. Not.

But then Simon darted an arm around my waist and pulled me in close, letting me feel the heat of him—he was running *way* too hot. And the presence inside my mind was starting to writhe. So not good.

We clustered around the door. After some quick discussion,

it was Simon who reached for the doorknob, Merindah at his side. They would be going after Mack as a team; he would distract—hopefully immobilise—Mack with Persuasion and Merindah would take her out of action. The rest of us would be dealing with threats of the non-Mack variety.

'Don't die,' I told everyone.

'I don't intend to die before you do, Jen,' Saul muttered beside me. 'I would not degrade myself by allowing a hybrid to outlive me, after all.'

I was still giggling hysterically when the door swung open and admitted us into darkness.

44

It wasn't complete darkness.

Glowing monitors that should have been in real hospitals, not this laboratory of horrors, lit the scene before us. Instead of the reek of antiseptic, there was a scent of decay; it lodged at the back of my throat and grew thicker with each swallow. Clinical beeps stood in for heartbeats. The only natural sounds were the deep, modulated breaths of people whose bodies had been turned into prisons.

Among those lying there, supine and lifeless, was one normal. Merindah's mother. I was impressed by my best friend's restraint in not dashing forward immediately.

Mack's guards might have had something to do with that.

Most of them had formed a straight line—there were about twelve of them—but one diverged from the pack to hold a gun on Merindah's mother. They could have been mistaken for robots, because their faces didn't show any misgivings about working for their untoward employer, or the fact that they would soon be ordered to open fire on fellow human beings. Er, fellow beings.

Mack stood out in front of her guards, right in the middle, arms folded and head held high. She was wearing a navy Karen Millen dress, which would have looked entirely out of place in this situation if she wasn't, well, Mackenzie Roberts. Even the bandage taped over her smooshed nose didn't erode any of her style.

'I see you found us—*eventually*,' Mack said, scorn slathering its way over her words like oil. A tick started up in her forehead as she studied us; it noticeably worsened into outright spasms when her gaze landed on Simon.

Yep. She'd noticed that Simon's power levels had shot up into the stratosphere.

But even if she did feel threatened by him, it wouldn't stop her ordering her guard to kill Merindah's mother.

'Don't worry, we're on it,' Dennis murmured. 'Merindah trusts us to protect her.'

Well, great, yet another mental conversation I wasn't privy to. But they couldn't exactly keep me in the loop when I had no way of hearing them.

'Do any of you wish to surrender?' Mack asked. 'You could serve this country and live a little long in the process.' She shook her head when no one answered her, as if disappointed in us. 'Very well. Kill them. Kill them all.'

She took a giant step back as her guards advanced, firmly putting them between her and us.

Our semispherical shield, which the Physical-powered members of our cohort had brought into the room, was promisingly solid—but then it met bullets and went almost translucent. Everyone's magical cores had to be rapidly approaching empty by now. And that included the demons.

Dennis and two of my colleagues detached themselves from the group maintaining our defences and threw their hands forward in unison. A barrage of balls—far more spiky than anything I could ever remember them making before—shot through the shield and rammed into the man standing over Merindah's mother. He went flying and hit the concrete floor, neck bent awkwardly. None of his fellow guards bothered to check on him. It was pretty obvious he was gone.

The demons kept up their side of the fight, their Persuasion pooled and synchronised. They hissed, ground their teeth together, and bent their fingers into claws. The guns opposite us wavered, their barrels tilting towards the ground, but the hands holding the weapons refused to drop them.

Sharp and pointy Physical constructs were being raised along our line, sluggish and slow instead of whipping right up. Dennis and his companions, who had reacted quickly to start with, were now moving at a glacial rate. Even their grimaces took an eternity to spread across their faces.

Both sides did their best to hinder each other, with magical constructs and sheer willpower, but the stalemate couldn't possibly last. Just as I thought this, Queran cried out and crumpled to the floor, scratching at his scalp and writhing so hard he nearly knocked himself out on a nearby bed. The demon beside him crouched down low and dragged Queran, moaning and twitching, back into the empty labyrinth behind us.

Shit. Our Persuasion-powered people were dropping like flies.

I was hoping the guards would start dropping next. Surely they had to. Right? At least the Big Bad was Simon and Merindah's responsibility, though that wasn't much comfort considering just how *big* and *bad* Mack actually was.

Could they take her out?

Or were we completely and utterly doomed?

Merindah had gone for that cowcatcher shield again. She and Simon strode forward, cutting a path through the guards like they were passing through curtains, and homed in on Mack. My former boss flinched and took several steps back, but there was no escape. A charcoal sphere shot up around the three of them, generated by Merindah's power and kept there by her unstoppable will.

No one attempted to get inside that ball of magic. It was an unspoken agreement between the guards and us: *this is not our fight.*

Outside the sphere, there was pandemonium. Most bullets shattered against our shrinking shield; others made it through and struck the walls, gouging chunks out of the concrete. Magical projectiles—daggers, spears, and what looked like the wonky silhouettes of retro flying saucers—flew back in response, often wild and unaimed.

Anything that hit Merindah's construct failed to leave a dent on it. I wasn't sure how long that would last, since the sphere had now lost its opaque qualities, giving us an unrestricted view of what was happening inside.

Merindah, clearly struggling against the Persuasion being unleashed by Mack (Simon was doing his best to protect both their minds, but he could only do so much), was now hunched down low beside Simon, wisps of unsteady Physical curling out of her palms. Mack's hands were bare for the moment, which was a relief. We just had to hope that Simon could keep her from deploying her Physical.

But hope alone wasn't going to do us much good. Merindah and Simon were in serious trouble—and it looked like everyone else was heading that way too.

And I just stood there, behind a line of swaying bodies, tearing holes into my pockets and trying not to reach for my powers. I was meant to be held in reserve. But when is backup supposed to swing in and save the day? When? When is too early and when is too late? Should I spring into action before all those deadly projectiles started hitting the bodies in the beds? Or should I wait?

How was I supposed to know!?

A body hit the floor beside me—Dennis. He was on his knees, gasping for air with his hands clutched to his stomach. I frantically looked him over, but I couldn't find gunshot wounds or any other alarming holes. I would have been relieved had his eyes not been rolling disturbingly around in their sockets.

'We can't keep this up,' Dennis wheezed. 'We've burned through our power reserves, Jen. We need you.'

I nearly whooped in relief. Someone had made the decision for me! Thank Christ.

I bent down and briefly hugged Dennis. He was as bony as ever and hadn't gained a single centimetre of height since high school. I found myself overwhelmed by the need to protect him and everyone else I'd grown up with. For better or worse, they were my family.

'What should I do?' I asked, flexing my fingers.

'I don't know! Just—something!' Dennis cried.

But what *something* did he expect from me?

I looked around at my colleagues. Some were leaning against the wall; others were on their knees. The shield protecting them and the first two rows of beds was an impressive size, but it was thinning at an alarming rate.

But even if I bolstered the construct with my own Physical—and oh yeah, that relied on me being able to get my hands on a Portal in the middle of this chaos—that wouldn't fix things because it would collapse the moment I did. Power is great and all, but if conducting too much of it knocks you out? Yikes.

I had to provide something more drastic than simple defence.

I looked around for help and ended up grabbing the shoulder of the nearest demon. Ness. She was wearing the same mask of exhaustion that was slapped onto every other face around me.

'Can you make me a Portal?' I shouted. It seemed appropriate to shout, like they do in action movies, because there was a lot of action going on. And it was *noisy*.

'I can't!' Ness snapped. 'My reserves are tied up in my Persuasion!'

Alrighty, then. A small Portal would have to do. My hand went to my pocket but came up empty. I nearly screamed at myself for not remembering to replace the phone I'd lost at Mack's place.

Stupid, stupid, stupid—

I spun to Dennis. 'Do you have WatchDog?'

He wasn't supposed to have it. But there were a lot of things he wasn't supposed to have. Like personnel files on a USB stick. And a creepy years-in-the-making plan to get back with me. I needed his shadiness to come in handy once again.

Dennis grinned, gave me two thumbs up, and threw his phone at me. I caught it one-handed, beyond relieved that he'd already tapped in his passcode so I didn't have to see that photo of me he was apparently using as his lock screen. I drew a breath, stabbed the app with my thumb, and let rip.

I didn't immediately fall flat onto my face. Score!

As for the pain? Hold, please.

Actually, the energy the app gave me was pretty laughable. I guess I'd started relying on the massive bursts that the bigger

Portals hurled my way. Whoops. But the source of my reserves didn't matter when I had to use them to hurt people.

Oh God. But I have to.

I stormed into No Man's Land (I was hoping it looked impressive, a la Wonder Woman, but I seriously doubt I pulled it off) with Dennis trailing behind me by about a pace. Bullets pinged away from the small shield I'd erected around the two of us, reliably solid so long as I kept one hand wrapped around the phone in my pocket. My other hand was busily creating a Physical spear that lengthened into a vicious point.

I was keenly aware of the power requirements that both the shield and the weapon needed in order to remain solid. It reminded me of the time Dennis had described playing the piano to me—he'd said that because you're using two hands to play two different sequences of notes, you need to slice your brain in half.

Now I understood what he'd meant.

'So we reach the guards—and then what?' Dennis breathed in my ear.

I gnawed on my lip, considering our options. 'Do you have enough power to make a skipping rope? Like the ones we used in that Helicopter Helicopter game at school? You know, where someone stands in the middle and swings the rope round and round and everyone else has to jump out of the way or they'll get "out"?'

Dennis stared at me.

'Are you *serious?*' he asked, voice cracking.

'Serious as a heart attack.' Come to think of it, that wasn't the best thing to say right then—overusing one's powers without taking enough of a rest can actually result in cardiac arrest for magic-users—but this so wasn't the time to update my banter lexicon. 'Dennis, I want you to make the rope as thick and painful as possible. Maybe put some spikes on it? I'm hoping these guys won't jump out of the way.'

Dennis gave an abortive laugh.

'Fuck,' I muttered. 'I didn't really think this through, did I.'

'Better than anything I could have thought of,' Dennis assured me.

'You're just being nice.'

'Jen, we can't afford to be nice right now. Unless we want to get ourselves killed.'

The rope that appeared in Dennis' hands was bloated and distended, as though it was a snake that had just swallowed a crocodile—something that had definitely happened at least once up north. I'd seen the pics online. Except this 'snake' also grew gleaming armour and wickedly curved spikes, transforming into a truly impressive weapon.

'Ouch,' I said.

Dennis' words were as sharp and jagged as his construct. 'Don't forget to jump.'

You better believe I jumped.

While Dennis started swinging his Physical rope around at a dizzying rate (I didn't envy him; I remembered how disoriented I used to get when I was the one stuck in the middle for Helicopter Helicopter), I kept moving towards the guards. My shield followed me, splitting so that a small bubble remained behind to cover Dennis. My body ached all over and my scalp squeezed my skull, but this seemed strangely unimportant, a distant nuisance. Nothing could stop me.

It was just. So. Fucking. Easy.

I took a running leap as the rope came past again. It hit the ankles of the nearest guard and she went down, a comical expression of surprise splashed across her features. She recovered quickly—but not quickly enough to avoid the spear that smashed through her shoulder. I wanted to leave it at that, let her live, let her escape.

Her hand retrieved the gun from her lap.

I killed her before she killed me.

They say you're not a murderer if you kill someone in self-defence. Hah. It's hard to believe that when your hands are dripping with someone else's blood.

45

There was no time to grieve for my enemy. I had to hastily hop to avoid Dennis' Rope of Doom. It whispered along the soles of my Nikes, hitting and toppling the guard closest to my left. I looked back and saw my colleagues following my lead, jumping when they had to and running full tilt at the guards when they could.

The demons got their second wind once a few more uniformed bodies hit the floor. Now facing less resistance, they were able to get the rest of our attackers to lie down and go to sleep. I hesitated as my companions approached, fearful of what they might do to the incapacitated bad guys.

Dennis touched my arm, his voice gentle. 'We can't risk them waking up—they won't stop trying to kill us, Jen. They're afraid of failing to carry out their orders. It colours every thought inside their heads. The consequences are *bad*.'

'Sure, have fun with that killing-in-cold-blood thing,' I said, flashing him a toothy grin. I must have looked terrifying because Dennis actually took one step back.

Blinking away the tears, I put the carnage behind me and raced over to Merindah's sphere, which was one of two Physical objects left in the room. The only other construct was the spear in my hand.

Simon and Mack were still locked in silent conflict, faces creased in concentration, an incredible tension binding them together. The muscles in their necks contorted with the immense effort of trying to shred each other's minds. Merindah was back on her feet, but she was struggling against whatever Persuasion-fuelled commands Simon hadn't managed to deflect. It was obvious that he needed another boost of some kind.

'What do we do?' That was Saul.

Who are you talking to? I wondered as I ripped my hand off Dennis' phone.

My spear vanished. I was surprised at how easily I'd shut the Portal down—and grateful that I'd managed it because drawing energy from the demonic realm fucking *hurt*. Even adrenaline has its limits as a painkiller.

When my companions failed to say anything, I rolled my eyes and took charge.

'Add your powers to his!' I snapped at Saul. 'All of you.'

'My reserves are bone dry,' a nearby demon said.

'I have some left,' Saul said, pinning me with a dark stare. 'What are *you* going to do, Jen?'

'Get Simon to stop holding back,' I muttered.

Saul nodded, apparently accepting that, and went to the edge of Merindah's sphere, joining the only other demons who had some juice left—so yeah, Simon had Saul and two other people to boost him. That was it. Their grimaces synchronised as they aimed their swirling eyes and powers at Mack.

'What about us?' one of my colleagues asked. 'We can't just stand here!'

Couldn't they do any thinking for themselves?

Holding in the frustrated growl, I jerked my hand at the beds around us. 'Get these people out of here and regroup with the others outside. Now!'

I had a very, very bad feeling about this mental battle. Things could easily get Physical if Mack managed to shrug off Simon's Persuasion—she might even bring the whole place down around our ears. I wouldn't put it past her to do something like that, especially if she felt like she had no other option. Simon let me know he agreed with my assessment of the situation.

I was a little pissed off that he'd wasted some of his power just so he could communicate that to me. And he was wasting more of it by the second—I could feel him burrowing further and further into my mind until I was sure he'd get stuck in there.

I moved closer and pressed my hands against Merindah's sphere. It wasn't warm or cold to the touch—in fact, it felt like my palms had gone completely numb, as if there was nothing in front of me at all. But when I tried to push the construct, an uncomfortable static-y sensation spread up my arms and into my chest.

I latched onto that remnant of Simon inside me.

You can't win, I told him.

A shot of indignation, mixed in with a bucket full of denial, bounced back at me.

I frowned until my face throbbed. *No, Simon. You can't. Because you've kept a part of yourself in my head and you should be using that to fight Mack.*

I can't remove it, he said, sounding strained.

I'm pretty sure my mouth dropped open in an entirely unattractive fashion. Had I heard actual *words* from him? How? Just—how!? We'd been able to trade vague feelings up until that point, but this was something else.

Wait, why couldn't he get out of my head? What was wrong?

He answered my unspoken questions. *If I don't anchor myself in you, if I don't have you to keep me in check, I might—I'm afraid I'll lose control and destroy her.*

Agony shadowed his features and tightened his cheeks until it looked as though the fight was sucking the life right out of him. Merindah had her hands pulled down tight over her head and I realised it was *hailing* inside the sphere—well, it wasn't actual hail, but there were little black pellets flying out from Mack's hands. They continuously struck my best friend's arms and cheeks, drawing blood. Simon was also taking some damage but I'm not sure if he noticed.

Merindah's fingers stabbed upwards, forming an umbrella-shaped shield. Her construct lasted all of five seconds before it disintegrated, but she tried again. And again. She wasn't going to quit. That wasn't her style.

'Merindah, take down the sphere!' Dennis yelled at her. 'We've got your back!'

The Physical sphere died. This time, Merindah's umbrella held.

Enough of that bullshit, Simon. I wet my lips, hoping no one else knew just how close he was to collapsing onto the floor and losing this battle. *We both know you can control yourself—you've proven it time and time again. Seriously. You have to get out of my head.*

I want this too much, he admitted, his mind-voice weakening.

What? Being inside my mind?

Yes.

I swallowed twice in quick succession, but my tongue failed to unstick from the roof of my mouth. *I don't mind you being in there. Honest. But right now, you need all the power you can get. I will find a way stop you if you go off the deep end, I swear, but I don't think I'll have to. Simon? Get the fuck out of my head!*

He didn't dick around this time. He just went.

A keen sense of emptiness filled me in the wake of his departure. I gasped and spent a solid minute reeling while the fight in front of me intensified. I was fervently glad that Mack didn't take advantage of the sphere's absence to throw something at the rest of us—mind you, she was too busy shunting every iota of willpower into countering the wave of strength that Simon was suddenly exhibiting.

I lost my battle with gravity and abruptly pitched forward. I managed not to faceplant on the floor, but it was a near thing. My ensuing crouch was anything but steady; my ankles wobbled underneath me.

Unable to stand or provide any meaningful assistance, I simply—*watched*.

Simon's lips were curled into a grim smile as he took one step forward, then another. Mack's mouth opened and emitted a high-pitched burbling sound that stopped just shy of a scream. She dropped to her knees, defeated by his superior skill and power.

Now unburdened by Mack's Persuasion, Merindah stalked past Simon. I expected her to use Physical blades on my former boss, to do something so sickening that it would feature in my nightmares forever. Part of me *wanted* to see that, to see Mack pay for her crimes in blood.

But Merindah looked down at Mack with detached disdain, her hands bare of magic. 'I'm done killing. But I'm not squeamish about turning you over to the demons—or maybe I'll leave you for your so-called business partners deal with.'

'Just kill me now! It's kinder!' Mack roared at her. 'Do it, Merindah!'

Saul's feet halted beside me on the floor. 'Best to kill her now.

Your human police won't do anything to her if your government is involved.'

'Well, Mack never outright said it was the government, just that we'd be giving powers to our country's armed forces...' I trailed off. He did have a point. Unfortunately. I called over to Simon, 'Get her to tell us who's involved. It'll make things really freaking complicated if it's someone in public office, but we need to know.'

Mack shook her head vigorously as Simon knelt in front of her. The demons around me leaned forward, eagerly waiting for him to rip Mack's mind apart.

Oh God. He was going to do it. I couldn't feel him anymore and I can't explain how or why I knew, but I did.

He wasn't going to stop at Persuading the truth from her.

He was going to destroy her.

'Simon, no!' I grabbed Saul's belt and hauled myself to my feet. When I wavered unsteadily, Saul slapped his hands onto my shoulders, keeping me upright.

Simon glanced at me. His blue eyes stopped swirling and his expression cleared.

'You won't get anything out of me, you filthy demons!' Mack snarled.

A Physical shaft appeared in her hands, capped by a serrated spearhead. I flinched. My magical core was drained and I had no Portal to draw on.

But Mack wasn't aiming for us.

The spearhead drove into her gut and blood sprayed over her laughing lips. The shaft of her weapon slid out of her body, then punched back in, again and again, until finally it slowed—and disintegrated. It was all over in a matter of seconds.

Reduced to a mass of torn flesh, Mackenzie flopped backwards.

Her head made a perversely satisfying thud when it struck the ground.

Not so satisfying was the fact that she'd ended it before anyone with a beef could.

'You shouldn't have distracted him, hybrid!' one of the demons hissed—not Saul though, since he now seemed to be Team Jen Cooke.

'I'm *never* going to be like that, like Jon,' Simon said hoarsely, glaring at the circle his remaining people had formed around him. 'And if any of you want me to be him, then you're following the wrong man and the wrong cause.'

Saul quickly jumped in. 'Jen was ensuring that Simon's beliefs were upheld. You have no right to challenge her, Leezi. Or do you want to earn yourself an execution?'

Yikes. Demons and their freaking rules. I had no idea which one Saul was referring to.

Simon walked over and positioned himself beside me. This simple gesture was apparently enough to make Leezi back off. The rest of the demons bowed their heads. Okay, weird. But I took this as a good sign. That and the fact that no one tried to argue with Simon or attack us.

Simon leaned into me, murmuring, 'Thank you. For stopping me. I'm never using one of these injections ever again.' A shudder passed through him. 'The drug's still not out of my system. But at least I won't need to rely on it anymore.'

I squeezed his hand, then turned to face everyone. 'We won! It's over.'

'No. It's not.' That was Merindah. She had a spark in her eyes, one I didn't recognise. This was the part of her I didn't know, the part that had defied Magic Corp long before I'd been forced into a position to do it myself. 'She wasn't protecting her business partners, whoever they are, out of loyalty. They scared the shit out of her. She didn't want to report back to them with her failure. And this'—Merindah delivered a kick to the cooling corpse on the concrete floor—'was her way out. Coward. We won't be taking the easy way out when they come for us.'

Dennis looked as shaken as I felt after Merindah's speech. Well, he'd had that stunned-mullet expression the whole night, but still. It looked *much* worse now.

'Let's get out of here,' Dennis said.

'No disagreement there, human,' Saul replied and I was amused to see him help Dennis, who was now limping, over to the door.

Simon ordered the demons to assist my colleagues, who were still in the midst of unhooking Mack's victims from the machines beside their beds. Some of the kidnapped hybrids woke but remained groggy, confused about where they were and why they had trouble walking. Others remained comatose which wasn't promising, but there weren't so many that we couldn't carry them.

'Merindah, aren't you going to talk to—?' I cut myself off, gesturing at her mother who was being guided out of the room.

Merindah shook her head. 'She might not even recognise me until the demons remove the block in her mind, if there is one. I hope there is.' Grief passed over her face like a shadow. It made her ensuing grin seem very forced. 'But not long now until we can have a chat, hey? I've waited over a decade. I can wait a few more hours.'

I watched everyone dripping out through the door, my anger warring with acute despair. I had no idea how to help the people we'd rescued or how to pay for any medical services they might need—and oh yeah, Mack's mysterious friends were going to come after us. It was only a matter of time.

As a bonus, I was *definitely* on the Kill Register for real after all the shit I'd been getting up to.

'Merindah's right,' Simon said when he and I were the last two people left in the room. The bodies on the floor were being valiantly ignored by the both of us. 'This isn't over. As long as we're hunted, we can't set up our own version of Magic Corp and start defending your country. We'll also need your government's backing at some point—so long as they aren't Mack's secret business partners.'

I groaned and buried my face in his chest. 'Just give me this one victory.'

He chuckled. 'Alright, I can't deny you that. I couldn't deny you anything, Jen Cooke.'

'You're laying it on a little thick, Simon Bradley,' I told him, grinning.

'Come on,' he said, giving my hand a tug. 'Let's get out of here so I can take you on that date—and tell you what my real name is.'

Merindah coughed loudly and stepped back into the room, telling us to hurry up or we'd get left behind.

I sighed. It had been nice to pause and think about all the things Simon and I could do once we had more than a minute to ourselves, but there was the fact that we'd done some serious breaking and entering—a hell of a lot of breaking, now that I thought about it.

Of course, breaking and entering had been the fun part.

Leaving wasn't going to be quite so easy.

Just as Simon and I headed towards the door, metres and metres of empty floor in front of us, the exit became somewhat unavailable.

Thanks to the freaking Portal that cut us off from it.

46

The car-sized Portal sent out a blast of air so violent it caused Merindah to fly back about five paces. She staggered onto her feet, gripping the doorframe in her attempt to keep upright, but I knew she wouldn't make it back into the room.

This Portal was about to get bigger, *much* bigger—I could tell, because the voice it used to call my name was steadily growing from a whisper to an all-out roar.

'Holy shit!' I cried.

'Get out of here!' Simon yelled at Merindah just before we lost all sight of her.

The edges of the Portal exploded outwards, until it ran from ceiling to floor—not unlike a giant stage curtain that had been coated with gasoline and set alight. I blinked furiously, trying to force moisture into my eyes, but that only made them feel even grittier. God, it was hot. And bright. Did I mention it was hot?

'The bigger it is, the longer it takes,' Simon told me.

'The longer it takes for what?' I demanded, trying not to freak out.

His face was ashen. 'To form. To transport. Jen, this is bad.'

And then I saw just how bad.

Five. Ten. Fifteen—*twenty* people burst out of the Portal and landed perfectly on their booted feet. They weren't wearing the snazzy uniforms that had bedecked Mack's guards. They wore standard fatigues and had such stony disdain on their faces that I knew they'd swat me like an insect and immediately forget I'd existed. As for the lack of firearms? Well, they didn't need them. They had Physical weapons in their hands—all very solid, all midnight black, all of them jagged and mean.

Seconds later, I found myself on my knees, hands behind my head, fog evaporating from my thoughts. Weird, I couldn't remember—ah, shit. Persuasion.

I rubbed my temples. Simon had slid into my skull again; that was the only reason sense had returned me. He was still standing, but he had a hand braced on my shoulder to steady himself and the pressure from his grip was intensifying.

I'm okay, I told him silently. *Help me up.*

Simon hauled me to my feet. His presence inside my mind felt like a pane of glass on the verge of shattering. So not good. And yet Simon was holding his own against twenty opponents (obviously, they weren't as amped up as Mack had been or we'd have been toast). Holy shit, if his brother had been *better* than him and as ruthless as Dot had made him sound...it was a good thing Jon 'Bradley' had never got his hands on these injections.

'So you can protect two whole minds,' one of the newcomers sneered. 'Good for you, demon—but you won't last!'

Our attackers adjusted their stances, weapons angled towards us. There was no further discussion. They weren't going to offer us an olive branch; they were going straight for the kill.

'Don't stop me,' I said, a tremor in my voice.

'Don't stop me either,' Simon breathed.

And then I yanked hard at the Giant Honking Portal.

Someone screamed. Probably me. I'd never seen a Portal quite this big before and I'd never pulled so much power from one either. Yeah, this wasn't the smartest thing I'd ever done. It felt equal parts awesome and terrifying. My skin tingled all over and my veins were *buzzing*. I had to get this energy out of me. And fast. Preferably before it burnt me up.

I screamed again, this time in defiance. Dark cords whipped out from the centre of my chest, dragging me several paces forward until Simon hooked his arms around my midsection. The Portal was singing my name with increasing volume. It wanted me. And now Simon could feel it too.

'Is it always like that?' I heard him cry.

I might have answered him. I'm not sure. My psyche was taking a hit, a massive one, because even though these reserves came from somewhere else, I was still the fragile bag of bones that had to conduct that immense, searing power.

Our opponents collapsed into piles of flesh and fabric. Their arms and weapons were held down by coiled Physical ropes, but we weren't out of danger. I'd only put a small dent in their concentration and they weren't dropping their mental attacks. I could feel Simon's arms trembling as he held me against him.

How much time did we have until Simon's artificial boost gave out?

His hands, fastened over mine and keeping them trapped against my abdomen, tightened until I thought the bones in my fingers might break. His voice was an agonised croak. 'Jen, I can't keep this up. I've never...never fought so many minds before. And the drug's wearing off.'

Okay, the situation wasn't great, but my Physical had them pinned! We still had a chance to get out of this. Right?

That was when the Portal spat out another classroom-sized group of attackers.

'Fuck!' I exclaimed. 'That's so not fair!'

'It's probably a compliment,' Simon rasped, a smile threading its way through his words. 'They think you're dangerous.'

'I *am* dangerous!' I snarled and straightened out of his grip.

'Then show them,' he baited me.

I hesitated, reluctant to source more juice from the High-Definition Portal than I already was. There were two reasons: conducting that much power could destroy me—and I knew that using it would result in fresh blood on my hands. When would it stop? When would I stop *killing* people?

Simon's lips touched my ear. 'They'll kill us. And we won't be able to stop them going after our people. We can't let them do that and I—I don't want to lose you, Jen.'

His presence inside my skull became a spasming knot of fear and grief and longing for more, so much more—

So I did it.

Not just for him, but for everyone else these people might yet hurt.

My back arched and though my throat was far too raw for any more screaming it still tried, making me wheeze. The Portal offered me *so much* power. I did not refuse it.

I generated a Physical wall, as tall and wide as the ones enclosing us, and hurled it with all my might. But it drew up short, an immense black slab caught inside a net of thick sludge erected by our new friends. My construct struggled and fought, shimmering and warping with strain, but there were just too many people shoring up the obstacle in its way.

They had a handy exit at their backs. We had a concrete wall at ours. It was a dead end, quite literally.

The moment Simon weakened, even slightly, we were done for.

And I was stretched to breaking point; I couldn't keep funnelling this much foreign power forever. Sooner or later my wall would disintegrate and those pointy weapons would turn us into pincushions. But while I was still standing...

I let the Portal seize control of me, let it get its hooks into my soul, and met its demands with one of my own. Something that should have been impossible.

You never know unless you ask, right? And oh yeah, the Portal agreed to do it.

Not so impossible, after all.

'Jen, what are you...?' Simon trailed off, confused.

'I'm going to bring this building down on our heads,' I grated out. 'I'm going to crush them and whatever equipment they might be keeping in here. They can't be allowed to hurt anyone else, Simon! I'm smashing this fucker to pieces.'

Simon grinned tiredly at me. 'I wish we'd managed to go on that date.'

I twisted my lips into a grin of my own. 'We're not dead yet. And also, the Portal says I can funnel power into your Persuasion, even though it's not one of my Ps. Neat, huh? Do you need a boost?'

He frowned. Because of our connection, he understood that it might not work, that I had no idea if I was about to kill us both.

But hell, what other option did we have?

'How long will it take for you to build up enough power to take out the building?' Simon asked.

'Five minutes.' Maybe. If I knew what I was doing, which I totally didn't.

'Then yes,' he said. 'I need a boost.'

I sucked in a giant breath, then let it bleed out over my chapped lips. 'Okay, what's our exit strategy? I'd like to do the escaping thing, if possible. Are you able to make us a Portal? Or can we use theirs?'

'We don't know where that Portal leads,' Simon answered grimly. 'If I leave my Persuasion running, it will be hard for me to form a Portal. Even harder if I have to maintain it.'

'Hell, Simon,' I said. 'I'm not even sure I'll survive the trip. Just give it a shot, okay?'

He laughed and nodded.

This sorted, I surrendered to the Portal and filled myself to the brim. Mindful that the wall I was maintaining wasn't being much use and might only serve as a distraction, I killed it. Then I sent millions, billions, *trillions* of feelers into the building around me, into the foundations, into its very heart. I was poised to shatter everything from the roof down, but first I had to throw some of the Portal's energy into the man beside me. So I pushed in his direction and kept pushing.

Simon grunted but he held on. His resolve strengthened my own.

'Shit,' he said in amazement. 'Can you send me any more?'

'Apparently,' I replied after trying.

'No, no, not too much, it'll burn me up,' he protested weakly.

Veins stood out on his temples and his chest was rapidly rising and falling. That scared me, because I knew I had to be running out of time myself. But our enemies were dutifully dropping to floor, just as Simon had commanded them to do.

I was beginning to think we might actually make it out of this alive.

Yeah, I probably jinxed it.

I opened my mouth to ask Simon if he could get started on a

Portal, but I didn't get the chance—he swiftly seized me into a kiss that burned all the way down. It was hot, desperate, and hard, like he knew this kiss was the last one he would ever give me.

He tore himself away from me and tossed a frantic gesture at the space behind us. His much smaller Portal spluttered into life, but it only lasted a handful of seconds before cutting out. Simon cursed. I knew he'd keep trying, but I wasn't sure if he was going to succeed.

Frankly, I had my own success to worry about.

I drove my fist into my palm, envisioning a giant version of my hand on top of the building, smashing down with the force of a hundred Not-Hellephants. I didn't need to repeat the gesture—the foundations were already compromised. This was going to be way more impressive than what I'd done to the Hellhounds at The Rocks.

I was blind to everything in the room. All I could see was the building standing above us.

And it was about to fall.

'Come on, Jen,' Simon said, grabbing my arm.

I couldn't move. The destruction was taking everything I had.

'Jen, come with me *now*,' he all but snarled.

His potent, amped-up Persuasion clawed into me and forced my feet to turn and start moving.

'You got a Portal working?' I gasped out as I wobbled after him.

Simon's voice was tight with tension. 'No. This one just opened up so I don't know whose it is, but it's got to be better than that other one.'

'And if it's not any better!?' I cried.

'It doesn't matter—*keep going!*' he urged, still Persuading me to approach the Portal that may or may not deposit us in the middle of yet another soul-crushing fight.

Blood was roaring in my ears. My legs were distant appendages belonging to someone else. It was only a matter of time before I stumbled.

And stumble I did.

My chest hit the ground and for several seconds I was winded and useless. When my muscles finally loosened, I sucked gulp after gulp of air into my lungs, knowing I had to get up, get to the Portal, get out of Dodge. But Simon was gone, he was gone—I couldn't feel his presence!

I flung my eyes around, panicked, and then I saw him sprawled beside me, unmoving and slack. He was unconscious.

Yeah, not exactly the best news.

Gritting my teeth, knowing it would hurt, I wrenched a smidgen of extra power from the smaller Portal that we'd been running for, hoping to keep it open for as long as possible. Somehow I got onto my knees and slid my arms around Simon's midsection.

I couldn't lift him. Shit.

Dust continued to rain steadily over my face. Level B3 was about to get awfully small in a minute or two. On the other side of the room, our attackers were slowly rousing—the person responsible for putting them down was now out cold himself.

'Shit, shit, *shit*,' I articulated, furious with myself. Simon had used the last skerrick of his energy on getting me to move and had paid the price. *All my fault!*

God, I was so close to the Portal. I could easily jump in.

But that would mean leaving Simon behind.

'Fuck you, Simon!' I shouted at him. 'I'm not going into that Fiery Puddle of Doom alone—you owe me a date!'

I didn't expect to hear a canine bark of agreement.

I blinked—there was a shape growing inside the Portal, something four-legged and shaggy and missing bits and pieces of his solidifying form. Jesus Christ, he was like some sort of dog ex machina.

'Fido!?' I cried.

My magical pet yipped in confirmation. Fido then leapt over to us, grabbed a mouthful of Simon's jacket, and started dragging him back towards the Portal. I had to jog to keep up with Fido and in doing so almost tripped on a chunk of concrete that had fallen from the ceiling. More chunks were rocketing into the floor around me. I was so sure we were going to bite the big one.

Fido growled at me. I dutifully put on a burst of speed, only to draw up short when I reached the Portal. The very thing that might kill me.

Scalding wind scoured my face, drying my eyes in an instant—not an unusual thing to happen around these Eyes of Sauron, but I dug in my heels, afraid. Fido entered the Portal without hesitation and vanished, taking Simon along with him. And I just stood there, relieved that Simon was safe and panicked about my own predicament.

I waited for Fido to come back. To take the horrible choice away from me.

He was a no-show.

'Jen, you're dead either way, just do it,' I told myself.

I jumped into the Fiery Vortex That Could Rip Me to Pieces.

A cocoon of swirling fire encased my body and began to squeeze, getting tighter by the second. Flames enthusiastically licked at my face, so frightfully close I could have licked them back if I'd wanted to.

Oh my God, I thought. *I'm going to die.*

After ten torturous seconds, the Portal tired of this game and rudely spat me out. The surface I landed on was made up of rock, grit, and blood—my blood. I'd skinned my knees and the palms of my hands. But I was alive. *I was alive!*

My mind violently rejected my connection to the Portal and it snapped shut behind me. I concentrated on breathing for a few moments, bile dripping its way over my lips. My personal reserves were non-existent and my ability to conduct any more external power had been thrown out the window.

And I was annoyed—*ropeable*—that I'd obviously survived a trip through a Portal. I'd really like to have known I could do this back when my dad had left me to fend for myself. But if he'd taken me with him, would I have met Simon?

'Simon—Simon!' I realised out loud and started fumbling around. The demonic realm looked uncomfortably similar to Mars, albeit with breathable air (thank God). Most of the terrain seemed to be covered in red dust, though great swathes of rock had been baked black by flames. Some patches of ground were even *steaming*.

I found Simon facedown nearby, a tangle of limbs, completely out. Beside him stood Fido, missing ear and all. I hastily navigated the uneven slope, preparing to fall on my magical pet in delight, but drew up short when Fido started whimpering.

Not a good sign.

Then I heard the roar, felt the blast of heat upon my face—and looked up. And up. And up.

A trail of fire slashed its way across the darkened sky (was it night-time or was the demonic realm always this apocalyptic!?), lighting up the piles and piles of gold coins lying between me and the edge of the crater the Portal had thrown us into.

An awful suspicion occurred to me.

Only really big Hellcreatures could make Portals. But not all of them hoarded gold and snorted fire.

When the next line of flames started heading in my direction, I didn't scream, didn't even move. Wasn't even sure I could run far enough in time.

Helldragon. Had to be.

I was so freaking screwed.

Jen Cooke will return in

Bound to the Demon

ABOUT THE AUTHOR

Alyce Caswell lives in Sydney, Australia with one husband, one son, two wallabies, four kookaburras, and countless bush turkeys.

When she isn't drinking her way through a giant pot of tea, Alyce is either buried in a Scottish romance novel, watching a Christmas movie, rocking out to New Wave music, or realising she accidentally wrote a novel that's an allegory of her autism spectrum disorder. With demons and powers and stuff.

You can contact her via email (alycecaswell@outlook.com) or on Twitter (@alycecaswell).

www.ingramcontent.com/pod-product-compliance
Lightning Source LLC
Chambersburg PA
CBHW020249120726
47904CB00001B/137